FIRE WITCHES OF SALEM

COLLECTION TWO

THE MAYHEM AND EMBER TRILOGY

CARRIE PULKINEN

Fire Witches of Salem Collection Two
Mayhem and Ember
Mending Mayhem
Mastering Mayhem

ISBN: 978-1-957253-25-1

MAYHEM AND EMBER

FIRE WITCHES OF SALEM
BOOK FOUR

CARRIE PULKINEN

CHAPTER 1
EMBER

Six months ago, if you'd told me I'd get a haircut from an imp, I'd have called you crazy. If you would've said I'd lose my sword in a twenty-foot-deep crevice beneath the biggest church in town, I'd have laughed. And the mere mention that my baby sister would be getting it on with a demon prince in the room down the hall would've had me in stitches.

Yet here we were...and the haircut wasn't even a good one.

I rummaged through my mom's sewing kit and grabbed her sharpest pair of fabric scissors before returning it to the shelf and padding across the living room in my socks. My door was the first on the left. Beyond that, Patrice slept in Cinder's bed, and at the end of the hall, Miles and Shade shared my parents' space. In between, Ash lay in her bedroom, snuggled up with Chaos, Prince of Hell.

I shook my head. That wasn't even the craziest thing that had happened over the past few weeks.

After flipping on the light, I strode through my room and stepped into the bathroom. I could hardly bear my reflection. I'd showered and even put on a bit of makeup this morning, so I didn't look terrible—aside from my hair—but the tightness of my eyes and the set of my jaw told the story of a woman who'd had the crushing weight of the entire world thrust onto her back in one fell swoop.

And she wasn't sure how much longer she could carry it.

"One thing at a time, Em," I said to the woman I barely recognized. "Focus on the things you can control. Complete one task, and then you can worry about the next." Otherwise, I might curl into a ball on the floor and cease to exist.

Up first, fixing my hideous hair.

I glared at the side the imp had chopped off with a pair of garden shears. Granted, the slimy little sucker was going for my neck, so I should've been glad he only took off ten inches of hair. But it would take me at least two years to grow it back to the length I liked.

Switching my focus to the long purple locks on the other side of my head, I sighed. This was a thing I could control. A problem I could solve, even if the solution wasn't appealing in the slightest.

I gathered a fistful in my hand and closed the scissors around it. I tried to, at least, but my hair was too thick. Working the blades open and closed, I sawed off a clump, leaving jagged edges and lament in its wake.

"Oh, honey. Let me help you." Ash's voice startled me, and I jumped, dropping the scissors into the sink.

"I didn't hear you come in." I picked them up and grabbed another fistful of hair.

"Give them to me." She held out her hand, so I placed the handles in her palm. "That little bugger did a number on you, didn't he?" She grabbed some clips and pinned up the top layer of my hair.

"It's driving me bonkers. One side is too short to pull back, and the other gets in my way if I don't." I rested my hands on the edge of the sink and focused on the coolness of the porcelain seeping into my skin and the scent of citrus emanating from the plug-in air freshener next to the mirror. "Where's your demon?"

"In the shower." She began snipping, ten-inch-long strands of purple falling around my feet. "What's our next move?"

I ground my teeth even harder. "I want my sword."

She paused, pursing her lips before continuing my haircut. "You don't need it to fight. You could stop a monster with a spell and your bare hands if you had to."

"I want it," I said, my bottom teeth never losing contact with my top. "It's as much a part of me as my hideous hair."

"It won't be hideous much longer." She unpinned a section and snipped some more. "I'm sure the church is closed. The foundation can't support it after what Mayhem and Chrys did to it, and I doubt they'll let us in."

I lowered my gaze at the mention of our once-friend, Chrys. Her body still lay under enchantment in our basement. Hopefully, her mother would claim it soon.

Snapping my eyes to the mirror, I looked at my sister. "So what if it's closed? That's never stopped us before."

"You could get a new one." She cut the last section and began evening it out.

I turned my head to see her. "Why would I do that when I can retrieve my old one?"

With her fingers on my scalp, she turned me toward the mirror. "We still have to summon Mayhem, find Cinder and then our parents, all the while battling the bigger and badder beasties that are slipping through the veil. The less conflict we put upon ourselves the better." She shrugged. "It would be easier to get a new one."

"There's a six-month waiting list to have one forged, and anyway..." I picked up a piece of hair from the sink and slid my fingers over the smooth strands. "Mom gave it to me for my twenty-second birthday. It's special."

Ash's expression softened. "I hear you. All right. Step one: retrieve your sword. Step two: re-summon Mayhem the right way. Step three: break the curse and save the world."

"You make it sound so simple." I dropped the hair and returned my hands to the edge of the sink.

"We both know it's not." She ran her fingers through my locks, shaking them out. "There you go. I think the length suits you."

I turned my head from side to side, examining her work. Slightly longer than chin length, my hair felt lighter and looked thicker and healthier. "Not bad, sis. Is there anything you aren't good at?"

She laughed and said, "Be right back," before slipping out of the bathroom and returning with a broom and dustpan.

As we cleaned up the hair and dropped it into the trash can, I eyed the demonic sigil on my sister's arm. The thing that linked her to Chaos. She swore she was in love with the demon, but I had to wonder if the magical tattoo she'd given herself wasn't responsible for fabricating the emotions.

"Aren't you going to remove that?" I followed her out of the room and into the kitchen.

"Chaos says it's safer if I keep it. Mayhem is royally pissed, and as long as I bear Chaos's mark, he won't hurt me." She filled the coffee machine with grounds.

"Is that what he says?" I crossed my arms, unconvinced. Demons were liars, or so I'd been taught. I'd actually never had a conversation with one until Chaos came into our lives, but I had a feeling his brother was as pissed at him as he was at us. A tattoo wouldn't keep anyone safe, no matter how much vim she'd put into it.

Ash sighed and turned to face me. "I know it's hard to comprehend, but I promise you... Whether I have this tattoo or not, I am in love with Chaos and he loves me. I'm not asking you to understand it, but I do need you to accept it."

It made no sense, a light witch and a demon from the Underworld fitting so well together, but they did. While I hated to admit it, they seemed almost perfect for each other...in an opposites-attract, forbidden-love kind of way.

Oh, for Hecate's sake. I didn't even read romance novels, but Ash had talked so much about them and her favorite tropes, I felt like I'd read dozens. "You're right. What do I know about love?"

As if on cue, the demon emerged from the hallway and strode across the room to sweep Ash into his arms. "Good morning, little witch."

He planted a kiss on her lips, and her energy shifted, exuding calmness. Pulling away, he winked at her before turning to me. "Ember," he said with a nod.

I didn't have to understand, only accept. "Where's Mayhem's skull?"

"In a drawer in Ash's room, where it will stay until we're ready to summon him." He opened the pantry and pulled out three boxes of cereal.

"I put a ward on it." Ash took six mugs from the cabinet. "Just in case."

"Good." I set a gallon of milk on the counter next to the bowls Ash had lined up.

"When you summon my brother, I suggest you combine the power of all five witches to create the containment circle." Chaos poured a bowl of the sugariest cereal we had, cramming a handful into his mouth before adding the milk. "He's a force when he isn't angry. I'm afraid he'll be a hurricane after what we've done."

I shook my head. "You're talking a step ahead. We have to focus on one thing at a time."

"And first on the to-do list is returning to the church to get her sword." Ash poured three cups of coffee and handed them to us before sinking onto a stool at the counter.

"Can't you get a new sword?" Shade strode into the kitchen

and poured himself a bowl of Raisin Bran. "I replace my knives all the time."

My teeth clicked. How I despised redundant conversations.

"It was a gift from our mother," Ash answered for me. "And there's a six-month waiting list for forging enchanted silver."

"Is it safe to go down there?" Patrice emerged from the hallway, followed by Miles. "The building shook and groaned against the crevices. It might not even be standing this morning."

"All the more reason to get this done now. Eat up." I popped a protein bar into my mouth, put on my boots, and headed downstairs to the storage room, grimacing as I passed Chrys's body. We had cleaned her up and laid her on a table before casting a preservation spell and covering her with a sheet. That had been difficult enough. Calling her mother with the news, well... Ash had volunteered for that job, and I'd been happy to hand over the reins.

I let my gaze wander over her outline beneath the sheet, my chest tightening with emotions I couldn't name. I still couldn't comprehend the betrayal. Her last words were *I had no choice.* But there was always a choice, and hers was obvious. Why she chose the dark side, I had no idea. Nothing about what happened with her made sense.

But I couldn't think about that now. I had a coven to run, a world to save, and no clue how to do either.

Thirty feet of enchanted nylon rope hung on the wall next to a shelving unit filled with supplies for our shop. We hadn't been open to the public in weeks. We relied on the income to pay the taxes and utilities for the building, but at the rate we were going, we'd be sitting in the dark before long. I hadn't been to work in weeks either. Honestly, I was surprised they hadn't fired me yet.

I grabbed the magically strengthened rope, slung it over my shoulder, and did my best to ignore the body in the basement as I made my way upstairs.

Chaos and Ash stood at the sink, washing dishes, which was weird as all get-out. My little sister had domesticated a demon. Go figure.

My phone chimed as I lay the rope on the counter, and I fished it out of my pocket to find a message from Chief Higgins. "Well, shit."

"What?" Miles asked.

I rolled my neck, stretching out the tension. "Another rift opened last night inside the monster museum. Chief called them oversized mosquitoes, so I assume it's a swarm of fae."

"We can take care of it," Miles said. "Go get your sword, and we'll rendezvous here in an hour."

A sinking sensation formed in my gut, but I pursed my lips and ignored it. I hated splitting up the team—strength in numbers and all—but we were running out of time. "Do we have any bottled shadow spells left?"

Ash grabbed her bag from a hook on the wall and peered inside. "Three."

"Give them to Miles." I turned to him. "Can you and Patrice handle it? I don't know how long this will take, so I need Shade with me to keep us cloaked."

He cut his gaze to his friend before nodding. "We've got this, right, Patrice?"

"Freeze them, shove them through, and seal the rift. Easy-peasy." She took the bottled mending spell Ash offered.

"Good." I slung the rope over my shoulder. "Let's head out."

Shade rode shotgun while Ash and Chaos took the back seat in the van, and we made our way to the scene of the crime. Thankfully, the drive was an uneventful one. No dark witch minions tried to stop us this time, though I wouldn't have minded a little scuffle. Fighting I was good at. Hecate knew I sucked at being High Priestess.

"We need to be on alert for Boston witches." I rolled to a stop two blocks from the church and killed the engine.

"You don't think they ran off to lick their wounds?" Shade adjusted the straps of his knife harness. "Without their leader, they're probably trying to act like nothing happened so they don't get banished."

"Or they could be organizing again." Ash looped her satchel over her head to wear it cross-body. "Who knows how dark witches think?"

"Either way, be on high alert. Cloak us, Shade." I waited for our shadow witch to do his thing. Once the fog rolled around us, turning the outside world grayscale, I hopped out of the van and opened the side door before lifting the hatch out of habit.

My shoulders slumped at the empty space where my sword should have lain. The daggers strapped to my thighs and ankles would have to do if we ran into trouble. And honestly...I hoped we would. Fighting was in my blood. Being locked in battle was the one time I could clear my head, shut off my thoughts, and let my instincts take over. Whatever daunting task that lay six steps ahead didn't matter in that moment. All I had to do was kick butt, no name-taking required.

"We'll get it back." Ash rested a hand on my back, and I straightened, grabbing an extra knife to hide my emotional display.

The coven thinking I was a weak crybaby was the last thing I needed. I shut the door and turned to Chaos, who carried the rope. "That's not fireproof, so put it down if you're going to light yourself ablaze."

He raised his brows. "Are you expecting a battle?"

"I'm always ready for a fight." I jerked my head toward the church, and, invisible to the rest of the world, we strode two blocks toward the entrance.

Caution tape looped through a makeshift chain-link fence surrounded the property, and a stout man in a hardhat held an iPad toward a woman in a tailored suit. I raised my hand, telling my team to stop and listen to their conversation.

"I don't know how an earthquake could have only affected this small area," the man said. "Are you sure it wasn't an act of God? Is the congregation worshipping false idols or something?" He guffawed at his own bad joke.

The woman flashed an indignant look and crossed her arms. "Can the foundation be repaired?"

"It'll cost a pretty penny, but we can do it." He swiped his finger on the iPad, and I motioned for the others to follow.

Ash hurried to walk beside me. "At least they can fix it. I wonder how they'll get the money though."

"I'm sure the congregation will pay for it." I stopped beside a piece of fence that wasn't fastened to the next section and moved it forward, creating enough space for us to pass through.

My mood darkened as we approached the entrance, and when I grabbed the door handle, Ash let out a muffled sound of disapproval. I hadn't let her check for magic before I touched it.

I motioned to the door. "Humans are in control here. Nobody put up a ward on a church that could collapse at any minute. It is locked, though."

"We still have to use caution. Confess, expose, my magic sleuth. I call on you to reveal your truth." She cast her magic-revealing spell, finding nothing, as I expected, before tugging a lock-picking kit from her satchel and going to work. "Better safe than sorry."

"Sometimes, too careful can get you killed," I said.

"There's no such thing as too careful these days." She smiled triumphantly and opened the door.

I strode inside, heading straight to the passage that led to the underground. The building groaned as we made our way through the dark, twisting halls and descended stair after stair. Scents of decay and dust clung to the air particles, making my nostrils feel like sandpaper with each inhale, and a humming sound vibrated through the basement as we approached the entrance to the room where it all went down. I stopped, turning and giving my team a questioning look.

"I sense a rift." Chaos rested a hand on Ash's lower back and closed his eyes. "Lower-level demons and something... other."

Shade took two knives from his harness, gripping them tightly. "Of course this couldn't be easy."

"Where's the fun in easy?" I nodded to Ash's bag. "Get the freezing and mending spells ready. Chaos, you handle the demons. The rest of us will take care of the 'other.'"

Without a word, he brushed past me and entered the room. I followed on his heels, and Ash and Shade took up the rear of our hunting crew.

Inside, we found total chaos, and I don't mean my sister's boyfriend.

A swarm of lesser fae, with their brown wings and razor teeth, swooped this way and that, dive-bombing a group of imps. Hadn't we dealt with these little shits enough?

The imps fought back, throwing books, religious artifacts, scraps of wood...anything they could get their slimy little hands on, and I cracked my knuckles. I hated imps more than I hated fae.

Chaos shouted, "Stop," and even though the fae kept attacking, the imps obeyed the Prince of Hell's command and skittered toward him like good little puppies.

"Standing tall or on your knees, in the name of the goddess, I force you to freeze," Ash cast the spell, and the oversized mosquitoes stopped midair.

My chest swelled with pride. My little sis had grown so much over the past few weeks, finally coming into her power. Power strong enough to take out the entire coven if the curse came to fruition...

I could not let that happen.

Chaos ordered the imps through the rift before helping Ash and Shade shove the fae through. I paced to the massive crevice

Chrys and Mayhem had opened in an attempt to kill us and peered over the edge.

Darkness engulfed the bottom of the pit, but my sword lay down there somewhere. I grabbed the rope Chaos had dropped and looped it around one thigh and then the other, making a harness so they could lower me.

A sinister growl that sounded more alien than animal reverberated in the shadows to my right. I swiveled my head toward it, and out stepped one of the ugliest creatures I'd ever seen.

CHAPTER 2
EMBER

He stood five and a half feet tall, with stark white—was it hair or fur?—atop his almost-human head. Two insect-like antennae jutted up from his scalp, bending forward like an ant, and enormous black eyes locked onto me as his thin lips—for lack of a better word—peeled back to reveal pointy, dagger-like teeth.

He took a step toward me, and his massive, brown cockroach wings fluttered, the sound reminding me of the nasty insects that dive-bombed me when I visited Texas one summer. A shiver spiraled down my spine before lurching into my stomach and making it turn.

What was it about humidity and bugs? Ick.

I grabbed a dagger from my thigh holster and widened my stance. "Chaos, are you going to take care of this guy or do I get to vanquish him?" I snapped my head toward my team and found Ash sealing the rift.

"Wait! We missed one." But I was too late. The fabric of reality stitched together before my eyes, and I jerked my gaze back to the beastie in question.

The giant roach-man sprung, half-running, half-flying toward me and screaming like a swarm of cicadas. I swung a dagger, hitting a wing, and let me tell you, those friggin' things were like armor. The moment the blade made impact, it snapped, the force reverberating up my arm and into my jaw, making my teeth ache.

He lashed out a clawed hand and ripped my shirt. I jabbed the knife at his chest, but the second blade broke as easily as the first. What the hell was this thing made of? Titanium?

With an ear-splitting screech, he slammed into me, grasping my shoulders in his claws and tackling me. My back smacked the ground, and all the air left my lungs in a *whoosh*. I gasped, which was a huge mistake. Roachman sneered, and a glob of gooey saliva landed right in my mouth.

It tasted like salty snot and regret.

I spit it back at him and gagged as I struggled beneath his weight. Someone...it could have been Ash or Chaos...threw a fireball at him, and it bounced off his roach armor, not singeing it a bit.

He growled, and another bit of gooey mess hung from the corner of his lip, threatening to hit my face. I kept my mouth closed this time and grabbed a dagger from my holster. What good it would do, I had no clue, but I refused to become breakfast for a cockroach.

He reared his head back, ready to chomp my face, and I caught a glimpse of a chink in his armor. I jabbed the dagger into the soft spot just below his ear hole, and praise the goddess, it didn't break. Roachman squealed and rolled off me, and I scrambled to my feet.

Ash threw the binding spell at him, but he flapped his blade-proof wings and jetted to the ceiling before it reached him, hanging on like he had suction cups in his hands and feet.

"What the hell, Chaos?" I hocked up the biggest loogie I could and spit the rest of the roach goo from my mouth. "Make your demon friend behave."

"He's not a demon." Ash grabbed my arm and dragged me out from under the creature from not-Hell. "He's a fae."

"What?" I fumbled with the rope still tied around me like a harness. "How did he get so big?"

"He's midlevel," Chaos said. "Most likely a scout for the greater fae horde."

"Fabulous." I got one knot untied when the flitting of roach wings assaulted the air and the sucker swooped to the ground, grabbing the rope that was still tied to one leg and jutting upward to the ceiling once more.

My feet left the floor with a jerk of his arm, and he hauled me halfway up, leaving me dangling upside down like a witchy chandelier in the middle of the room.

Blood rushed to my head, but I swung myself upright and grabbed the rope. "How do I kill him?"

"Beheading is the fastest way," Chaos said. "Unless you can find an opening in his exoskeleton to stab his heart."

I freed my other leg from the harness and glared up at Roachman. He yanked my dagger from his neck and hurled it to the ground, heaving a giant breath against the pain. As his chest expanded, so did his armor, revealing an opening right beneath his heart. Or...where I assumed his heart would be.

Lifting my leg, I snatched a knife from my ankle holster and silently prayed to the goddess it would be long enough to reach the prize. Clutching the metal handle between my teeth, I hauled myself up the rope, which was a lot harder than I remembered from gym class. When all this was over, I needed to hit the weights.

I peered down at Ash, who rummaged through her spell kit, no doubt trying to concoct something to weaken his armor. Chaos kneeled beside her, taking the ingredient bottles as she handed them to him, and Shade...

Was he on his phone?

"Bastard," I mumbled around the steel between my teeth. Returning my attention to Roachman, I hauled myself up a little farther, but my vision wavered and my lips suddenly didn't feel the coolness of the handle pressed against them. My whole mouth went numb.

Nausea churned in my gut, and I gagged. The knife fell to the ground, and I tried to move my jaw, to speak, to scream, to...anything.

But I couldn't feel my face.

"Don't let him bite you, Ember," Shade called and held up his phone. "According to the witchy web, these guys are venomous."

Fan-friggin'-tastic. That explained the numbness spreading down my neck.

I hurried a few feet down the rope and let go. My knees

buckled when I hit the ground, and I rolled before jutting to my feet again.

"Heh..." was the only sound I could muster, so I pointed to my mouth and pressed my hands against my cheeks and my head.

Ash's face pinched with concern. "He already got you?"

I nodded.

"If you can bring him down, I've got a softening spell that might weaken him enough to get a knife through." She held up a steaming copper bowl.

If I'd had my sword, I would've lobbed his head clean off by now.

"Hey, ugly." Shade hurled a knife, but it bounced off Roachman's armor and tumbled into the crevice where my sword lay, out of reach. He tried again, this time hitting an impenetrable wing.

If my mouth worked, I could have told them about the two soft spots I'd found, but my tongue had swollen to the size of a lemon. I couldn't close my lips, much less make sound pass from them. Hell, it was a miracle I could even breathe.

"Are you sure that spell won't reach the ceiling?" Shade asked. "Or what about hellfire?"

Chaos flexed his fingers, gathering fire in his palms before shooting it toward our foe. The Roachman screeched and wrapped his wings around his body, shielding himself from the flames. As the demon called his fire back, smoke billowed from the creature's form.

Cracks spread across his rigid wings, the surface peeling

from the heat of Hell, but Roachman hung on, hissing and fluttering, raining charred bits of wing onto us.

"You'll have to go hotter." Ash poured the powdered potion into her hand and closed her fingers around it.

"I hit it with everything I have. I will try again." He gathered more hellfire, and I turned to the mess the imps had made of the basement. Surely there was something here I could throw at the beastie. My last knife attached to my ankle had a blade only three inches long. Even if I could get it beneath the armor, it wouldn't pierce the heart.

While Chaos worked on barbecued roach fae, Ash and Shade whipped up another potion. I threw boards aside, rummaging through artifacts and tools the church stored in their basement. Sadly, no razor-sharp swords lay in the clutter, but a pair of hatchets caught my eye.

I stumbled over a prayer bench, twisting my ankle as I stepped on the edge of a two-by-four. The numbness from the fae venom spread into my shoulders and down my chest, squeezing my heart and lungs until it felt like I was breathing through a straw.

I managed to grab the hatchets, but as I rose, I tipped backward, crashing into the shelving unit attached to the wall. My vision tunneled, my pulse slowing until I could barely stay conscious.

"Hold on, Em!" Ash kneeled next to me, her blue hair barely registering in my pin-prick-sized field of vision. She poured a potion into my mouth. At least, I assumed that was what she did. I'd lost feeling everywhere except my legs.

"Here's the second one." Shade handed something to her,

and my vision dimmed into darkness, my breaths slowing, ceasing.

A tickle formed in my throat, spreading into my chest and down my arms. I gasped, and the breath I raked in filled my lungs fully, making them burn. My lids flew open, my blurry vision swimming back into focus, and I sat upright, gasping again before coughing like a teenager the first time they took a hit of a blunt.

"He has…soft spots," I said between coughs.

They helped me to my feet, and we crawled over the mess to stand next to Chaos. He breathed heavily, sweat beading on his brow as he blasted another heatwave at the fae.

"That's enough." Ash clutched his arm. "You might be immortal, but you can still get vanquished. Save your strength. Ember has a plan."

I peered up at Roachman clinging to the ceiling. His back faced us, but his charred wings had retracted, leaving his head exposed.

"His exoskeleton lies in layers over his chest, like fish scales," I said. "We can stab him beneath one if you've got a long enough knife."

"If we can get him down." Shade held up a weapon. "It's my last one."

Clutching the hatchets in one hand, I retrieved my three-inch knife and traded him for the long one. "He's also soft beneath his ear holes. Aim for that, and make it count."

He nodded once and threw the blade. It rotated through the air and hit home, right in the fae's neck. The beastie let out a pained screech, losing his grip on the ceiling and hanging on by one clawed hand.

I hurled the first hatchet at his wrist, but he swung, shielding himself with a burned wing. He reached his other hand to the ceiling, and I threw, the hatchet tumbling head over handle and slicing into my target.

Roachman fell, his amputated claw still clinging to the ceiling as his back smacked the ground. Ash hit him with a freezing spell, and I stood over him, a nine-inch dagger clutched in my hand.

"Don't *ever* try to come between a woman and her sword." Lifting an armor plate, I jabbed the dagger into his flesh and twisted before yanking it out and thrusting it in again. "And never try to swap spit without consent."

The fae raked in a breath and wheezed, "Our...world...now." His head lolled to the side, and he stilled, his lifeforce returning to the ether.

"Since when can fae talk?" I wiped my hands on my pants and straightened.

"His level and higher always could." Chaos jostled the corpse with his boot. It didn't move.

"In English?" I picked up the rope and made another harness, wrapping it around my thighs and tying it at my waist.

"They learn quickly, as do demons." He helped Ash return the supplies to her bag. "Did you think English was my first language?"

"I never gave it much thought. Here..." I tossed the end of the rope toward him. "Make use of your brute strength and lower me into the pit. I want my sword, and then I want a scorching hot shower. I hate roaches almost as much as I hate rats."

He gripped the rope and slowly lowered me into the crevice. With my feet against the dirt wall, I rappelled twenty feet and hit bottom. "Don't let go," I shouted and turned on my phone's flashlight.

The hole was massive, somehow growing wider at the bottom than it was at the top, and I had to wonder how much of this was Chrys's doing versus Mayhem's. Chrys was a powerful witch; she'd shown us that plenty of times before she summoned the demon into her head.

But was she this strong? Sadly, we would never know.

I shined the light around the dirt and caught a glimmer of enchanted silver. "There's my baby."

I grabbed her handle and swung her in two perfectly balanced figure eights before gripping her with both hands and sending fire licking up the blade. *Ahhh...That's more like it.*

After extinguishing the flames, I holstered the sword in my back scabbard, picked up Shade's dagger, and shouted, "Bring me up."

Chaos pulled me out of the crevice, and I untied the rope, freeing myself from the harness. I shot a flame at the fae's body, trying to cremate the beastie, but his armor protected him from the fire, even in death. I barely singed him. "It's like these suckers were made to be a fire witch's sworn enemy."

"All three of us together?' Ash asked.

"It's worth a shot." I sent out another flame, giving it all the heat I had, and Chaos and my sister did the same. The exoskeleton burned a bit, flaking like the wings had done when Chaos hit them earlier, but it would take us an hour to turn the giant cockroach to ash.

Sweat beaded on my forehead, and my breaths became labored. Fire was my inborn gift, so it didn't tax my vim, but this much exertion took a physical toll on my body.

And that pissed me off royally.

"Burn you overgrown insect." My anger sparked more flames inside me, and I pushed out another heatwave. Dead or alive, this sucker would not get the best of me.

"You're wearing yourselves out," Shade said. "And I can't keep us cloaked forever. Let's push him into the crevice and be done."

"Works for me." Ash extinguished her fire like she'd had control of it her entire life, and Chaos followed suit.

My nostrils flared on an irritated exhale, but he was right. We had too much shit to do to waste our energy on a dead fae. "All right, but I get the honors."

I stomped toward the roach and rolled him to the crevice. With my boot against his shoulder, I shoved him over the edge. He hit the ground with a satisfying *thud*, and I wiped my hands on my jeans.

"Let's go summon a demon prince." The words barely had time to cross my lips before my phone buzzed. I swiped open the screen and groaned. "There's *another* rift."

CHAPTER 3
MAYHEM

All I saw was darkness. All I heard was silence.

All I felt was pure primal rage.

I was finally free of my prison, my spirit possessing a witch of such immense power I could move earth, making it swallow my enemies whole. Burning through her body and claiming it as my own would have allowed me to keep her magic, adding it to mine and becoming more powerful than Chaos and Discord combined. I could have rivaled Lucifer himself.

But the blue-haired witch...the one they called Ash...ruined it all. My host's body was no match for the binding spells she'd cast on us. If my vessel had given up control when I demanded it, I could have broken free. But my insolent human receptacle had refused.

She was a witch after all, and witches were the vilest creatures to ever walk the earth. I would be freed from this dark prison sooner or later, and when I was, I would find a way to their side of the veil and kill them all for what they'd done.

And my brother...

I imagined my hands curling into fists at the thought of the traitorous bastard, my talons digging into my wrists, the phantom pain the only thing reminding me I still existed in this realm of sensory deprivation.

Chaos would pay for his betrayal. Whether he'd willingly gone along with their subterfuge or he'd been bound under a spell didn't matter. I would take revenge, and I would start by killing the one he claimed to love.

CHAPTER 4
EMBER

"It's a good thing the rift happened in a witch's backyard." Ash set black candles around the circle of salt she'd poured while I eyed the skull.

It looked like a regular human, yet the energy it exuded felt like pinpricks running through my muscles when I touched it. "Right? Monkeys can only escape from the zoo so many times before the humans get suspicious."

Police Chief Higgins, one of the few mundane in Salem who knew real magic existed, had explained away an imp attack in a hardware store by calling them monkeys. Today, a trio of the buggers had made it through a tiny rift in Inga's yard, and thankfully, she'd messaged me before getting anyone else involved.

Dragging my gaze away from Mayhem's severed head, I admired the near-perfect ring Ash had poured. We'd decided to perform the summoning in her studio, away from the windows of the storefront—and the prying eyes of passersby—and far from the irreplaceable grimoires in the library.

Her tattoo equipment sat on a counter against the wall, and a wooden storage unit stood in the corner. LED track lighting hung from the ceiling, casting the room in artificial brightness, but we'd be dimming those soon. Magic worked better in candlelight...especially for fire witches.

Clutching the salt in both hands, my sister bounced her gaze from the floor to me three times before she finally held eye contact. "At the rate the veil is thinning, we'll need to bring in more of the coven to help keep the beasties at bay. You know that, right?"

I clenched my jaw. She was right. I knew she was, but it didn't make it any easier to admit. "If we tell them every-thing..." I blew out a hard breath. "They're going to blame me. I'm responsible for this coven, and everything is going to shit."

"No one will blame you."

Yes, they would, and they should. "If Mom and Cinder were here, they'd know exactly what to do. They don't make mistakes like I do."

Ash gave me a WTF look, lifting one hand and dropping it at her side. "All of this is happening *because* of Mom and Cinder's mistakes. Mom messed with the wrong demon. Cinder acted alone when we could have helped her. They screwed up too."

I fought to keep my lower lip from pouting. Why did my little sister always make such good points?

"And we won't have to tell them everything." She shook her head, drumming her fingers on the canister. "It's almost Halloween, so some thinning is natural. We'll say the rest is Chrys's fault. That she summoned a demon to take over the coven, but you stopped her."

I laughed dryly. "You mean *you* stopped her. You performed the exorcism and the vanquishing."

"Which I couldn't have done without you. I don't need any of the credit." She caught her bottom lip between her teeth. "You might have to stop me soon if we can't get to Cinder and Discord before I..."

"Hey. Stop that." I clutched her shoulders, dipping my head to catch her gaze. "We're going to break the curse."

"Or die trying." She smiled sadly and shrugged out of my grasp. "I don't know, Em. Some of the thoughts I have aren't very light-witch-like. Here." She handed me the salt and tugged her phone from her pocket.

I looked at the canister, the little girl with her umbrella and yellow dress taunting me, and put it next to the skull. These witches were my responsibility. Mom and Cinder might have started the trouble, but *I* was to blame for the ones who had died. "We won't lose anyone else."

"Not if we can help it." She handed the phone to me and offered a piece of chalk. "Draw Mayhem's sigil in the center of the circle, and we'll be ready to activate the containment when the others get back."

"Me?" I held the phone and chalk toward her. "You're the artist. This is your wheelhouse."

She raised her hands, refusing to accept them. "It doesn't feel right for me to do it. He's not my demon."

"Well, he's not mine either. I'd rather not have anything to do with him." I set the items next to the skull and crossed my arms. "And you better get whatever romance novel trope you're thinking of out of your head. Just because you like getting it on with a demon doesn't mean I want to."

She laughed. "I'm not trying to set you up with Chaos's brother, but one Prince of Hell is all I can handle. Mayhem will owe whoever draws his sigil a favor, and I would rather it not be me."

"But you're good at handling demons."

"I'm good with *my* demon. It's someone else's turn, and that someone is you."

I glared at Ash and picked up the chalk. "Fine. But don't even think about putting his mark anywhere on my skin. The faster we break the curse and send the demons back to hell, the better."

A shadow crossed her features, her gaze drifting to the floor as she drew her shoulders upward. She straightened, looking at me as if my third eye were suddenly visible, and shook her head. "Do you even hear yourself when you speak?"

"What kind of a question is that?" I squinted at the sigil on the phone and kneeled at the edge of the ring.

"Guess not." She bumped her fist onto the salt canister, closing the little metal spout. "Tell me what you said."

I sighed and sat back on my heels, searching my brain for whatever wrong thing I might have uttered. "I told you I don't want his mark on my skin."

She crossed her arms. "After that."

The tension in my neck increased, causing an ache at the base of my skull. You'd think, after unlocking her full power and getting her brains banged out nightly by the supposed love of her life, she'd be less emotional... Oh.

Well, feck. "I'm sorry, Ash. I didn't mean—"

"You didn't mean the sooner I lost my soulmate the better?"

"No, I didn't." I glanced at the sigil again and pressed the chalk to the wooden floor, dragging it downward before looping back up. "I wasn't thinking about that part of our predicament."

"You never do," she mumbled under her breath.

I pretended not to hear. Goddess knew I wasn't the best when it came to peopling. Tiptoeing around emotions and sugar-coating words had never been my strong suit; that was no secret. It wasn't often I thought to ask a ghoul how its day was before lobbing off its head.

"It goes left." Ash squatted next to me and pointed at the design.

I compared what I'd drawn to the image on the screen. "Damn, you're right. Do I need to start over?"

She handed me a damp rag. "Erase it with intention, and it should be fine."

"I'd rather not take chances." I dragged the cloth over the sigil, scrubbing off the chalk until the circle was clean. "This is why you should be doing this."

"You'll get it this time." She offered a smile, and I returned the gesture. One good thing about my little sis… She never stayed mad at me long.

I laid the phone in the circle and tried again. Ash nodded at each swoop and angle, and I paused at the bottom loop before bringing it left and completing the design.

"Perfect." She used my shoulder to push herself upright.

I stood, taking the phone and chalk with me and setting them on the table by the skull. The back door opened, and four sets of footfalls plodded toward us…my team, filing into the room. Chaos slid an arm around Ash's waist, and she rested her hand on his chest.

I really did feel bad for wishing her man away. Maybe someday I'd learn how to express things like that in words, but today was not that day. Instead, I turned to Shade. "That was fast."

"We're getting good at battling imps." He took off his knife holster and laid it on the table.

"It helps when you've got a demon they obey," Patrice said. "We convinced Inga that Chaos used a spell to control them, but now she wants the recipe."

"Luis and Madeline were there too." Shade curled his lip at the skull. "A few others showed up before we left, and they all but demanded you call a meeting."

"Maybe we should tell everyone what's going on." Miles peered at the sigil in the middle of the floor. "One demon we can hide, but two?"

"Absolutely not." I paced around the circle, turning at the top and retracing my path. "I will call a meeting to enlist their help, but *no one* is to know about the demons or the curse. Understood?"

Shade gave a mock salute, and the others nodded.

My phone chimed, and I closed my eyes, letting out a long exhale and steeling myself for whatever beastie had busted through this time. I swiped open the screen to find a message from Chrys's mom. "Crap. Ivy's here with the funeral home. Ash, come with me. The rest of you, stay here and keep the doors closed."

Ash followed me through the library and out the back door, where a pair of men in suits were pulling a stretcher out of a van. Ivy wore dark glasses, and her jet-black hair was piled on top of her head in a messy, curly bun.

She stepped onto the porch, and Ash hugged her. "I'm so sorry this happened."

Ivy sniffled. "Thank you for keeping her here. I don't... I don't know what got into her."

A demon got into her. She already knew that. I held the door open for the stretcher and slipped past them to lead the way toward the storage room. Ash and I stepped inside, standing against the wall to make room for the men, and Ivy hesitated in the doorway.

She removed her glasses, revealing red-rimmed eyes with puffy, dark circles, and she shuffled into the room. Gasping, she covered her mouth before a sob rolled up from somewhere deep in her soul.

Her legs wobbled as she stumbled toward her daughter's body. We'd covered Chrys with a dark blue sheet, which Ivy gingerly grasped and pulled down. Another sob ripped from her chest, her pain palpable, making Ash tear up.

Pressure built in the back of my eyes as Ivy kissed her daughter's forehead and covered her again. Her entire body trembled on a deep inhale, her hands curling into tight fists with her exhale. I couldn't begin to imagine how she must've felt.

"How could you let this happen?" She whirled toward me, her expression livid and pained. "You're in charge of this coven. Her blood is on your hands."

My brows shot toward my hairline, and I straightened my spine. Guess I didn't have to imagine. "We did everything we could to save her."

She stepped toward me, pointing her finger accusingly. "You should have stopped her before any of this happened. She never should have had access to dark magic, let alone instructions for summoning a demon."

"Whoa." I raised my hands, palms toward her. "She didn't learn it from us."

"We should step outside so they can move her." Ash placed a hand on Ivy's shoulder.

She shrugged off her touch and moved toward me. "This is your fault, you incompetent, wannabe priestess. Your mother and Cinder never would have let this happen."

I ground my teeth, Ash's words echoing in my mind. *This is happening because of Mom and Cinder.* But I couldn't say that out loud.

Ivy shook her finger at me. "I don't know what killed them,

but whatever it was, it should have happened to you." She pointed at Ash. "To both of you."

"That was uncalled for." Ash moved between us and gestured to the door. "Let's wait outside."

Ivy took one step toward the exit before spinning around. "You should have paid more attention to what was happening in your coven."

I crossed my arms, my jaw ticking, my patience thinner than single-ply toilet paper. "She's your daughter. Maybe you're the one who should have paid more attention."

She gasped, fury sparking in her eyes, and I thanked the goddess our basement had a concrete floor because I had no doubt she'd have summoned the roots from every tree in Salem to tear me to shreds. "You..."

I should have shut my mouth right then, but my temper flared, rendering me unable to stop the words from flowing. "Don't *you* come into our house and accuse us. Chrys brought dark magic into this coven. *Your daughter* tortured and killed one of us for goddess knows what reason. She lied, she hid things from us, and she used us. I...we...had nothing to do with her decisions, but her upbringing sure as hell did."

Another gasp, and she pressed her hand to her chest. If she'd worn pearls, she would have clutched them.

"Ivy, please." One of the men from the funeral home, who had been silently watching the exchange, gently grasped her elbow and led her out of the room before she could piss me off anymore.

Ash closed her eyes for a long blink, shaking her head.

"What?" I snapped.

"She's a grieving mother, and you blamed her for her daughter's death."

"She accused me of teaching Chrys dark magic and then wished us both dead." I jerked my hand toward the doorway she'd left through, doing my best to keep my middle finger from jutting up. "I had to say something."

She sighed. "Of course you did."

I could tell from the tone of her voice she didn't approve of the way I'd said it, but I didn't want to argue. Should I have shifted the blame onto Ivy's shoulders? Probably not, but I also didn't have to stand there and let her accuse me of everything.

Yes, I should have been paying more attention. Yes, I might have noticed something off about Chrys's behavior if I'd thought about it. Yes, I had screwed up royally every chance I'd gotten through this entire ordeal.

That didn't mean I was responsible for the decisions Chrys made.

The man returned to the room. "She's waiting in the car. If you'll excuse us, we'll get out of your hair."

"Be my guest." I stepped into the hall with Ash and waited for them to load the body onto the stretcher. They wheeled her out the back door, and I locked it behind them.

"I told you everyone would blame me," I said as we made our way toward the studio.

Ash stopped outside the door and clutched my shoulders. "No one will blame you for the thinning veil, but they will blame you for what happens next if we don't give them a heads up so they can protect themselves."

I sucked in a massive breath and blew it out hard. "You're

right. We need to call the meeting." I shoved the door open and stepped inside.

"How did it go?" Patrice clasped her hands over her chest.

"Don't ask." I picked up the skull and dropped it into a bag before handing it to Ash. "Shade, Miles, set up the emergency meeting. Mayhem will have to wait."

A low growl rumbled from Chaos's chest. "The longer he waits, the angrier he will become. Postponing this will only serve to make him harder to control."

I put my hands on my hips. "We managed you just fine, didn't we?"

CHAPTER 5
EMBER

"Her plan, it seems, was to take over both the Boston Society of Magic and Salem." I stood at the podium in the hotel meeting room, facing twenty-plus members of our coven and trying not to sweat. "She summoned the demon, attempting to harness his power to make it happen."

They sat silently, filling five rows of chairs beneath a small chandelier, as I explained everything that was going on.

Okay, not *everything*, obviously. If they knew Ash hadn't ended the curse, but instead *was* the curse, all hell would have broken loose...and we were dealing with enough of the Underworld already, thank you very much. Besides, my sister was fine so far, and she had a demon who could calm her instantly if she decided to go nuts.

As long as he didn't go nuts with her.

Honestly, of the three Holland sisters, Ash was the best one of us to bear this curse. I'd have already brought it to fruition. Not on purpose, of course, but I tended to act before I thought, and Ash was the opposite.

I stared over their heads at the plain beige wall behind them while they processed what I'd said. The carpet beneath their cushioned chairs, dark blue with a gray, swirly pattern, held flecks of glitter from some goddess-knew-what event that had happened earlier in the week.

Or hell…it could have happened six months ago. Glitter was the herpes of the craft world. You could never get rid of it.

"I don't understand why she would do this," Inga finally said from the second row.

"None of us do." I paced across the raised platform, turning on my heel and returning to the podium. "But the damage has been done, and we need your help to keep the beasties at bay and the humans in the dark until we can mend the veil."

"How are we supposed to mend it when the rifts are happening so fast?" Luis asked. "Why haven't you done it already?"

My jaw tightened, and I cut my gaze to Ash, who nodded her encouragement. I didn't need encouraging. I needed her to get up here and answer these questions before I said something I shouldn't.

Why hadn't we mended it already? Gee, why hadn't we just gone ahead and done it? "Don't you think we would have if we could? It's a complicated situation."

"It doesn't sound complicated." He crossed his arms. "Chrys thinned it by summoning the demon. She's dead, and the demon was vanquished. Unless there's more you aren't telling us…"

"There's nothing more." My nostrils flared as I ground my teeth. "We're working on it." Heat rose up my neck to climb across my cheeks, my other set of cheeks clenching so tightly I could have cracked a pecan.

"We have to find Cinder first." Ash stood and joined me behind the podium. "I've researched the phenomenon, and we need the power of three elemental witches to mend it properly."

Luis sat up straighter. "Isn't your boyfriend a fire witch?"

Ash looked at me, the poster child for the deer in the headlights expression.

"Three witches of the same bloodline," I said. "Same element, same blood, powerful spell that will drain our vim to the point of near death. It's complicated." And not entirely true, but whatever.

"Oh." He relaxed his accusing posture, and I let my glutes return to their normal, unclenched state. "How do you know she's alive? She went missing months ago."

"We have reason to believe she is," Ash said.

"Reason which we can't divulge," I added before he could ask what.

We'd told so many lies since this started happening, both by omission and bald-faced, I couldn't keep up with them anymore. "While we're working on finding Cinder, we need you to be vigilant about the rifts. Binding and sealing potions are your friends, shadow spells when you can get them, distractions when you can't, and when in doubt, stab them through the heart."

I jumped off the platform and strode through the door before they could ask any more questions I couldn't answer honestly. Ten minutes later, my team filed out and met me at the van.

"Thanks for leaving us to handle the rest of the interrogation." Ash yanked the side door open and climbed inside. I slid into the driver's seat while Chaos, Shade, Miles, and Patrice filled the rest of the seats.

"It's all good." Shade lowered the visor to check his hair in the mirror, sliding his hand over his blond locks and smoothing them back toward his manbun. "I handled it. Next time, I can run the whole meeting if you need me to."

I caught Ash's eyeroll in the rearview mirror before I put the van in gear and headed home. I would never let Shade run a meeting, no matter how much his ego wanted to. Ash, on the other hand, would be much better at keeping the peace. Maybe next time.

Actually, I hoped to Hecate there wouldn't be a next time.

"They all seem to have bought the story that Chrys is to blame for everything," Patrice said as I pulled into the lot behind our building.

"And I don't plan to give them any more reasons to think otherwise." I put it in park and opened the door. "No more side quests. It's time for the next part of our plan."

We entered through the back door, passed through the library, and gathered in Ash's sigil studio. I motioned for Chaos to join me in front of the two grimoires I'd laid open on the table. "This is the one Ash used to contain Mayhem at the church." I pointed to the book we'd confiscated from Chrys. "And this is the one I used to contain you after we got you out of Ash's head." I pointed to our book. "Which do you recommend?"

He chuckled and closed the second book. "You did not contain me in that circle. I complied for Ash's sake."

I reopened it and flipped to the page in question. "It says it's for holding demons."

He shrugged. "Lower-level fiends, of course. Possibly some mid-level. There isn't much that can contain a Prince of Hell, but Chrys's spell can. It worked on me...several times, I'm ashamed to admit."

"Well, isn't that peachy?" I drummed my fingertips together, silently berating myself for choosing a weak spell when I was supposed to be saving Ash. Things could have gone *very* differently if Chaos hadn't already been enamored of my sister when we exorcized him.

As much as I'd hated their budding relationship in the beginning, we'd have been screwed hard and fast without it... and not in a fun way. But it didn't matter now. What was done was done and all that jazz.

"Let's do this thing." I shot flames from my fingertips to each of the candles on the floor.

Ash lit the ones on the tables and turned off the overhead lights. "It's a short incantation. Can everyone memorize it?"

I scanned the Latin on the page, committing it to memory before stepping out of the way so the others could do the same.

Shade glanced at it quickly and nodded. "I still remember it from last time."

"Before we do this..." Patrice wrung her hands. "I don't understand why we can't summon them both at once. Get all three of them together so they can end the curse and we can mend the veil right now."

"Discord will not be easy to summon." Chaos took Ash's hand and moved toward the circle. "Cinder freed him from the dark prison, so he owed his debt to her and no one else. He must be enticed to cross the veil again, and you will need Mayhem on your side to convince him to comply."

"And Mayhem is already the unhappiest camper I've ever met," Ash said. "You were busy with Chrys when we exorcized him, but let me tell you... He was pissed."

I stood on the opposite side of Chaos and grabbed his hand. "They're right. The longer we leave Mayhem in prison, the pissier he's going to be. Chaos needs to reason with him, make him understand the plan. Then we can convince Discord to bring Cinder and our parents back."

"Whatever it takes to set things straight so we can have some peace in Salem." Shade slapped his palm into mine, and Miles joined hands with Ash, both, once again, taking no issue with sharing a demon's power.

Patrice, ever the reluctant one, splayed her fingers before clenching her fists and splaying them again. "I should save my vim in case someone needs healing. You've all been using his magic more than any witch should."

My teeth click audibly, my grip on the guys' hands tightening with my frustration. I should have known better than to bring a healer on board and ask her to do anything but heal. Yes, we were light witches and consorting with demons went against our very nature, but sometimes even those closest to the goddess had to work in the gray areas to get things done.

"It's for the greater good," I said, my teeth still clenched tightly.

She inclined her chin. "It isn't right, and Hecate would agree."

I exhaled and yanked my hands free to press my fingers to my temples. I'd already brought her into the fold. She knew as much about the problem as the rest of us, and we would need her healing eventually. I couldn't send her packing like I wanted to, so I made a face at Ash that hopefully said *help me out here.*

My sister opened her mouth to speak, but Chaos beat her to it. "Hecate spends a great deal of time in the Underworld. Your goddess wouldn't be as opposed to my help as you might imagine."

Patrice jerked her head back as if she'd been slapped. "Don't speak ill of our goddess."

"I'm not speaking ill." Chaos held his hand toward me. "I'm simply stating a fact. Hecate exists in the gray areas. Dark witches worship her too."

"We need you, Patrice," Ash said. "I'll temper the demon magic. You'll hardly feel it."

I grabbed the guys' hands again. "If you don't help, he might break free and kill people. Do you want that on your conscience?"

Ash cut me a look, but Patrice gave her head a tiny shake

and slipped her hand into Miles's. "This is the last time," she whispered.

I didn't mention the fact that we had another demon to summon after this. One step at a time. "Give it everything you've got. Mayhem has no loyalty to us, and he doesn't listen to reason from Chaos. No doubt he won't want to listen to us either, so we'll have to make him."

We recited the containment spell three times, and I hoped to Hecate we pronounced the Latin correctly. The air around us buzzed with magic, building with each recitation until the atmosphere thickened like pudding.

With one final push, we sent the magic into the circle, the candles flickering in response to our spell. The vibration in the room lifted, returning to normal, and we released our hands.

Patrice rubbed her palms on her pants. "I still felt it."

I fought an eye roll and turned to Chaos. "Test it."

He arched a brow, holding my gaze until I really did roll my eyes. "Test it, please?"

He reached toward the containment circle, his palm pressing against the invisible magic. "It will hold him. For how long, I can't be certain." He rested his other hand against the circle and shoved before nodding his approval.

I turned to the summoning spell and scanned the page. "I never thought I'd see the day when I willingly summoned a demon."

Shade clutched a dagger in each hand. "We're here for you."

But should they be? As acting High Priestess, it was my job to keep my coven safe. If something happened...if the circle didn't hold...Mayhem could kill us all. And then what? Salem would have two Princes of Hell on the loose and not a soul who knew what was happening.

Ash seemed convinced he wouldn't harm her as long as she bore Chaos's mark, but I had my doubts. If I had been imprisoned for centuries, rational thought would be tough to grasp.

I set the book next to the skull. "I want the three of you to wait upstairs during the summoning."

Shade laughed incredulously. "Not a chance."

I eyed the skull before pinning him with a steely glare. "I mean it. Take Miles and Patrice upstairs. Actually, you should all leave the building. Go have lunch or something."

"You can't be serious." Miles sheathed his daggers, concern etching lines on his forehead. "If he breaks free..."

"That's exactly why I want you out. This curse is on my family. It has nothing to do with you, and I won't risk your lives by exposing you to the hurricane we're about to unleash."

"Ember makes a good point," Chaos said. "When Mayhem materializes and sees five witches with their weapons drawn, he will assume you are threatening him, and he will act accordingly."

"They're right, guys." Ash nodded. "We have to reason with a livid demon. The fewer distractions, the better."

Shade glared at Ash and then at me. "Okay. We'll wait upstairs, but we'll be down at the first sign of struggle."

"I would expect nothing less." The tension in my shoulders eased a tiny bit. "Since you're staying upstairs, Patrice, can you bottle freezing and mending spells for the coven?"

"Of course." She nodded and hurried up the steps, no doubt relieved her presence wasn't required for the summoning.

"They'll need shadow magic too," I said. "Bottle as many as you can without overtaxing your vim.

Shade's jaw ticked, and Miles grasped his shoulder. "Come on. I'll help you."

The guys headed to the stairs, and Shade paused on the bottom step. "If you need help down here…"

"We'll let you know." I held my breath as their footsteps receded, and when the kitchen door opened, I exhaled hard. "Thanks for backing me up."

"It's the right thing to do." Ash picked up the skull and offered it to me.

Pinpricks gathered in my palms, spiraling up my arms the moment my skin touched bone. A shiver swirled through my body, making my arm hairs stand on end as I set it in the circle, centered over Mayhem's sigil.

Rubbing my hands together to dissipate the sensation, I returned to the table and grabbed the grimoire. "Let's invite a little Mayhem into our lives."

CHAPTER 6

MAYHEM

Time was meaningless in my dark prison. Each minute that passed could have been hours. Each day could have been a century. Every second of excruciating silence added fuel to the flames of my rage.

I ignored the faint tickle at the base of my head. Deprived of all my senses, my mind often fabricated sensations that could not be. I'd had no corporeal form since Isabel trapped me, taking my skull and vanquishing me to this fate worse than extinction.

My fury flared at the thought of the treacherous witch, the idea that Chaos now did another witch's bidding twisting the knife of betrayal.

The tickle intensified, spreading over my scalp and turning to pinpricks. It crawled through my essence like fingers jutting into my soul, threatening to shred the very fibers of my being.

In this fluid form, I did not breathe, yet my perceived lungs seized, collapsing on themselves, a crushing weight snapping ribs that did not exist. Words in an ancient tongue echoed in my mind, calling to me, coaxing me toward the veil.

My prison fought back, tightening around me like a boa squeezing the life from its prey. But the witches calling me were stronger than the one who imprisoned me. The magic holding me unraveled, and the new power sucked my spirit form through a tunnel of blinding light.

The veil, normally an iron wall, impassable for a creature of my level, tore open like a sheet of thin parchment. In the form of purple smoke, I poured through the rift.

My skull lay in the center of a summoning circle, atop my mark, which was perfectly drawn. Anticipation caused my energy to flash and spark, and I heard a faint gasp somewhere in the room. I paid the sound no mind as I billowed around my skull. Finally, after Hades knew how long, I would be reborn.

My energy intensified, and I spiraled like a funnel cloud, drawing my skull upward into my essence. Lightning cracked within the circle, my magic building, vibrating, creating flesh and bone.

My feet hit the floor, and a triumphant roar ripped from my lungs. My gaze locked on the blue-haired witch, and I lunged, slamming into an invisible, magical wall. I roared again, this time lowering my head and ramming my horns against the circle.

The magic held.

"Release me." I glared at my brother. "Let me go, and I will spare her life."

"You and I both know that's a lie." Chaos crossed his arms.

"But if you even attempt to harm my witch, the dark prison will feel like a vacation in paradise when I'm finished with you."

I would like to see him try. "Why did you summon me?"

"We need your help," Ash said.

I glanced at her, dragging my gaze down her form. I saw nothing special about the woman who had entranced my brother. Aside from the color of her hair, her features were unremarkable. "Did you not learn from our previous encounter with a witch who needed our help?"

"These women are not Isabel. They won't betray us like she did." He slid his arm behind her waist, pulling her to his side to drive his traitorous point home.

My hands curled into the tightest fists my talons would allow. "Release me."

"We will when you learn how to behave," the purple-haired witch said, and I focused on her for the first time.

Titling my head, I studied the woman. She wore tight black pants over her long, slender legs, and a matching shirt clung to her curves, reminding me of how long it had been since I'd felt a woman's touch.

I tore my gaze away, lest I become entranced like my idiot brother. "How long was I imprisoned?"

"Nearly four centuries," he said.

It had felt like an eternity. "And you?"

"The same. I've only been free for a few weeks, and we are running out of time."

I scoffed. "Time is irrelevant to an immortal."

"The veil is thinning," Ash said. "In a few more weeks, there'll be nothing left to separate this world from yours."

"A problem not of my concern." I slammed my shoulder against the circle, and the magic pushed back, vibrating through my muscles and making my skin crawl. "Who created this ring?"

"We all did," the purple-haired witch said, "and if you don't learn how to be a good little demon, you'll never get out of it."

"Ember..." Ash said, warning drawing out her words.

They *all* did. I pressed my palms against the invisible wall. Perhaps these women weren't as powerful as I once suspected. Allowing the magic to seep into my skin, I sorted through the essence of each witch who cast it. Three lesser vibrations consorted with three more of immense power. I disregarded the lesser and focused on the latter.

When the magic registered in my psyche, I jerked away, fuming at what I'd discovered. "Traitor," I growled and jabbed my talons into the circle, hoping to tear it apart. The energy pulsed but did not give.

"You aided *five* witches to entrap me?" I thrust my horns against the wall, punched, and kicked. Still it held strong. "You will pay for what you've done, brother. Lucifer *will* hear of this."

Ember had the audacity to laugh. "So basically..." she chortled. "You're threatening to run home and tell your demon daddy that your brother hurt your feelings."

"Insolent witch!" I roared and pounded against the circle. How dare a mortal ridicule Mayhem. "I will kill you all."

She shook her head, crossing her arms over her chest as she took two overconfident steps toward me. "We've already exorcized and vanquished you once. You think we won't do it again?"

"Seriously, Em." Ash grabbed her arm. "Can we *not* provoke just one demon?" She looked at me. "The sooner you calm down and listen, the sooner you'll be free. We're on the same side, believe it or not."

"I will never be on a witch's side." I roared again, the sound building in my gut and belting out at a decibel loud enough to shatter their eardrums. The witches clutched the sides of their heads, their knees buckling beneath them as I continued my auditory assault.

"Mayhem, stop," Chaos demanded.

I roared even louder.

CHAPTER 7

EMBER

The walls and floor shook with Mayhem's scream. The sound brought Ash and me to our knees, and covering my ears did nothing to relieve the sensation of daggers stabbing my brain. I stumbled to my feet and lunged toward the table to grab Ash's satchel. Yanking it down by the strap, I returned to the floor, where Chaos kneeled beside her, shouting at his brother to stop.

"Tell me you have a silencing spell in there." I slid the bag toward her.

"What?" she shouted.

I stuck my fingers in my ears and mouthed *silencing spell* before gesturing to the offending demon. She nodded and rummaged through the bag, pulling out a small pink bottle triumphantly.

I uncorked it, grabbed her hand to give her as much vim as

she needed, and hurled the contents into Mayhem's face. "Sound offending, words unending, we call on the goddess to make the noise cease," we said in unison. As the particles gathered around his throat, the magic cut off his roar, casting the room into glorious silence.

Well, silence except for the ringing in my ears and the sound of footsteps pounding down the stairs.

"What the hell was that?" Shade shouted as he and Miles raced into the studio.

"Shh..." I covered my ears, wincing at the sound. "Give us a minute."

My head pounded with the high-pitched tone assaulting both my ears, but I rose to my feet and turned toward the culpable demon as Chaos helped Ash stand.

Mayhem stood nearly eight feet tall, with more muscles rippling beneath his dark purplish-gray skin than I ever thought possible. Thick horns with a spiral texture jutted outward from the sides of his head before arching up like a bull's, and a set of what I could only call tusks protruded from both his upper and lower jaws.

Aside from his bad attitude and unnecessary volume, he was a magnificent sight to see. Thighs, thicker than my waist, led down to cloven hooves, and upward...

I squeezed my eyes shut and turned to Shade. No way would I allow myself to find that *thing* attractive. He was a monster. A creature from Hell, for Hecate's sake.

"That was Mayhem feeling powerless and yelling like weak men tend to do when no one wants to listen to them." I glanced at the demon again, and he pounded his chest, no doubt shouting at the top of his lungs for us to set him free.

"Damn." Miles looked Mayhem up and down. "He's big."

Ash shrugged. "No bigger than Chaos. Will you go up and ask Patrice for some headache powder and something to stop the ringing in our ears? I'd rather not waste my vim on another spell right now."

"Sure." He bounded upstairs while Shade eyed Mayhem.

"I guess he doesn't want to cooperate?" He moved closer to the containment circle, and the demon slammed his shoulder against the magic, making it pulse. Shade flinched.

"Nope." I rubbed my temples to counter the pressure in my skull. "If he would just listen, he'd understand how we can help each other."

Shade tilted his head. "Doesn't he owe you a favor since you freed him?"

"Indeed he does." Chaos tugged Ash to his chest and rubbed her head tenderly. "And that favor should be to break Ash's curse."

"But we need Discord for that, so for now, we have to figure out how to tame the savage beast." I pressed my thumb between my eyes, but it didn't ease the pain.

Miles finally came down and handed Ash and me each a steaming mug. "She put both powders into one drink and said you need to take it all at once."

I hadn't planned to sip the stuff. Tipping my head back, I chugged the bitter, nearly boiling-hot potion. It burned all the way down to my stomach, and if fire wasn't my element, I'd have been scorched. Instead, a coolness spread through my body, quieting the ring and easing the splitting pain in my head to a dull, manageable ache.

"I guess Patrice is still afraid of a couple of hellions?" I set the mug on the table and wiped my mouth with the back of my hand.

Miles shrugged and gave a tiny nod. "How long will the silencing spell last on him?"

I eyed the demon, my gaze dropping to his unmentionables three times before I managed to hold his gaze. In my defense, I wasn't the only one having trouble not looking at his junk. Miles, Shade, and even Ash's gaze bounced up and down his nakedness.

With a package that impressive, it was hard not to look.

I took a deep breath and blew it out hard, a wave of fatigue washing over me, though I'd had plenty of time to recharge after this morning's battle. If I wanted to be introspective, I could have admitted it was mental and emotional fatigue. But I was the fighter, the warrior. My brain didn't get tired because I used my body more.

"We just want to have a civilized chat." I parked my hands on my hips. "I think we've demonstrated our power enough, and we have Chaos on our side. If you want out of this circle, you need to listen to what we have to say."

His nostrils flared and the tendons in his neck tightened, but at least he kept his mouth shut.

"We will remove the silencing spell if you promise not to try busting our eardrums again. Can you use your big boy words and talk like a grownup?"

"That's not helpful, Em," Ash muttered. "Don't patronize him."

"He deserves a lot worse." I arched a brow at him, and he narrowed his deep-purple, soul-penetrating eyes.

"It's the only way to gain your freedom," Chaos said.

Mayhem's gaze bounced from his brother to each of us before he settled on me and spread his hands as if conceding.

"Now we're getting somewhere." My sword lay on the table, and I caressed the skull pommel before running my fingers over the rosewood handle. "Ash will undo the silencing spell, but if you try anything at all, I will lob off your head and vanquish you back to your prison for another four hundred years."

My sister made a disapproving sound with her throat, but I ignored her. I'd dealt with plenty of men like Mayhem at Spellbound Axe. Maybe they weren't demonic, but eighty percent of our clientele consisted of testosterone-laden Neanderthals who thought drinking beer, throwing sharp objects, and proclaiming themselves alpha males would make them so. In reality, they were just insecure assholes, and the best way to put them in their place was to exert your own dominance.

Mayhem was no different.

Ash looked from me to Chaos, who nodded, and she recited the undoing spell. "What I've done is now undone. As I will it, so mote it be."

The moment the silencing spell lifted, a growl rumbled in Mayhem's chest, his lips pulling up into a sneer.

"Ah-ah." I held up a finger. "We're in control of this situation."

"We'll see for how long." He arched a challenging brow.

I picked up my sword and spun it at my side before clutching it in both hands. "Okay. Back to prison you go."

"Ember!" Ash scolded, but I lifted it, ready to swing.

"Wait." Mayhem held up his hands in surrender. "Perhaps we can make a deal."

"No deals. Demons lie." I adjusted my grip. "Bind him, Shade."

"Gladly." He picked up a freezing spell and popped the cork.

"Brother…" Disbelief widened Mayhem's eyes.

Chaos crossed his arms. "These witches aren't to be trifled with. I've never met another who possessed such power."

He backed away from the circle's edge, his eyes calculating. "I will hear what you have to say."

"Good choice." Shade recapped the potion. "I would not want to be on Ember's bad side. The woman's got a temper."

I smirked. "Only because you love to piss me off."

Mayhem stretched his neck, his vertebrae popping and cracking like industrial-strength bubble wrap. "Tell me, witch. What spell have you used to entrance and enslave my brother?"

I returned my sword to the table and leaned against the edge, crossing my legs at the ankles. "She didn't use a spell. It's all L-O-V-E love."

He let out a scoff of disbelief and shook his head at Chaos. "Is this true?"

"It's fate." Chaos rested his hand on Ash's back.

A growl rumbled in Mayhem's chest. "Doubtful."

"She summoned me accidentally, not knowing my mark

was demonic." He pressed his lips to the side of her head. "What else could it be?"

Mayhem scoffed. "Accidents do not mean fate."

"She summoned me without my skull."

Surprise lifted his dark brow. "Impossible."

"Yet here I stand. Ash is the victim of Isabel's curse..." He dropped his hand and stepped toward the circle.

"These are Holland witches?" Mayhem asked, his deep, rumbly voice tinged with disbelief.

Chaos nodded. "Ash is the third born, the bearer of the hex, and only we have the power to break it."

Mayhem narrowed his eyes at Ash, his gaze flicking between my sister and her demon. "It's impossible without Discord."

"Our sister is already taking care of that." I pushed from the table and stepped toward him. "She summoned him, and he took her to Hell to find our parents. The gears are already in motion, and you were the final cog in our wheel."

"What makes you believe I will comply?"

I lifted a shoulder dismissively, and his gaze followed the movement. "You don't have a choice. If you refuse to help us, I'll send you back to prison. We've already vanquished you, a shedim, a horde of imps, and a chicken snake. It won't be difficult."

He stepped toward me. "A chicken snake?"

"A basilisk," Ash said. "And don't forget the fae scout."

My muscles crawled beneath my skin at the memory. "An overgrown cockroach with nearly impenetrable armor. Ever met one? They're nasty."

He curled his lip. "I despise the fae."

"Don't we all?" I matched his expression. Well, I curled my lip anyway. Without the tusks and protruding brow, I couldn't mimic him identically.

Chaos tapped a finger against his thigh, as if formulating a plan. "With the veil this thin, there could be an uprising brewing. If we don't mend it, and they take over this world, ours will be next."

A look passed between the demons that I didn't dare try to decipher. Could there be an uprising brewing? Why else would they send a scout across the veil if not to check out our realm?

Hecate have mercy, we did not have time for side quests.

"A war with the fae..." Mayhem's dark eyes brightened. "You should have led with that. I'm always willing to kill those maddening creatures. When do we begin?"

"Hold that thought." I raised a finger. "I need a word with my team."

I jerked my head toward the door, and Ash, Miles, and Shade slipped through. "You too, Chaos."

We joined the others in the library, and I pulled the door shut. "Do you really think the fae are planning an attack, or were you just blowing smoke?"

"Both," Chaos said. "Mayhem's favorite pastime is killing the fae that attempt to enter our world. If he believes he'll get to battle them here, he is more likely to conform to our strategy."

I paced in front of Ash's desk. "But you think they might really have a plan to attack?"

Ash wrinkled her nose. "The scout did say 'our world now.' I doubt he meant he was going home."

I dragged a hand down my face. "Goddess, help us."

"Hopefully we can find Cinder and Discord and fix the veil before that happens," Miles said.

Ash lowered her gaze. "Hopefully." The sadness in her voice made my heart ache, but it had to be done.

"One thing at a time." I continued pacing. "If acting like we're about to go to war with the fae will make Mayhem join our side, then that's what we'll do."

"Is it safe to come down?" Patrice called from the top of the stairs.

"Not quite." She would shit a cinder block if she saw Mayhem in his demon form. Chaos scared her enough. "We need him to transform. Where are you keeping Chaos's clothes?"

"I'll go up and get him something." Ash ascended the steps, and the rest of us returned to the studio.

The moment I opened the door, Mayhem slammed his meaty shoulder against the circle, making it pulse. A glimmer of opal crawled across the invisible wall, the first sign of the magic weakening. I cocked my head, lifting a brow in warning, and he narrowed his eyes, a growl rumbling in his chest.

"What did I say about trying to break free?" I picked up my sword and tested its weight, spinning it from side to side. "We have to be able to trust you. To trust each other."

He exhaled a humorless laugh. "I will never trust a witch."

"You can trust I'll lob your head clean off the second I sense your betrayal."

He crossed his arms, making his biceps bulge. "You talk in circles, witch. I tire of your repetition."

I opened my mouth for a comeback, but the beastie had a point. I could only threaten him so many times before I either acted on it or the threat became hollow. "First rule of existing in this realm: You have to be in human form, so go ahead and make that happen."

He scowled. "I was summoned to this realm long before you existed. I know the rules of your world."

"A lot has changed since then," Chaos said.

"Humans fear witches as much as demons." He rested his hands on his hips, drawing my gaze to his donkey-sized ding dong and reminding me just how long it had been since I'd... Well, you know.

I turned to put my sword on the table to stop myself from staring. "Most humans don't know witches are real. Not ones like us with actual powers. The ones that do also know we are the people who keep Salem safe from your kind."

"It's your kind who summons mine. If they knew who the real threat was..."

I closed my eyes and pressed my lips into a thin line. I wasn't the only one keeping this conversation on the merry-go-round. "Will you please transform into the least menacing version of yourself so we can go kick some fae ass?"

"We could use your insight," Shade said. "Their scout nearly took out our best fighter."

I snapped my head toward him, ready to berate him. I handled Roachman just fine, thank you very much.

"My insight in exchange for my freedom. I accept those terms."

"Nope." I raised my hands. "I drew your sigil. The debt you owe is to me, and I want you to break my sister's curse."

"As do I, brother," Chaos said.

Mayhem cut his gaze between the three of us, his eyes calculating. "Agreed."

He said the word, but something about his expression told me freeing him wouldn't make our lives any easier. Curling his hands into fists, he strained, tightening his jaw as purple smoke billowed around him, filling the containment circle until the beast inside was no longer visible.

Something cracked—maybe his neck?—and the thick cloud swirled around him before vanishing as quickly as it had formed.

Miles gasped, Shade swallowed hard, and me...? My ovaries might have exploded at the sight.

He stood maybe an inch or two shorter than Chaos, which put him at around six-foot-three. He had black hair, wavy on top and short on the sides, with a matching goatee and piercing, deep-set, otherworldly blueish-lavender eyes.

I could have bounced a crystal off his pecs if not for the dark hair sprinkled across his flawless skin. A trail of it led downward, over defined abs cut into an eight-pack. Or was it ten? I didn't have time to count because my gaze dipped lower, against my will, and locked on his package.

Good goddess. Why did I have a sudden craving for sausage?

Muscular thighs completed his statue-perfect appearance, and I finally tore my gaze away from his lower half to meet his eyes. He smirked, the expression both amused and menacing at the same time.

He spread his hands. "Not what you expected?"

Looks-wise, I wasn't surprised in the least. He was hot as hellfire, like his brother; part of his arsenal to prey on the weak, as demons liked to do.

What I did not expect was the visceral reaction my body had at the sight of him. Parts of me clenched while other parts tingled; warmth spread through my abdomen, though a chill cascaded down my spine, all of it coming together in a *wowzers I need some of that.*

I *so* did not need any of that, but damn. I knew who I'd be dreaming about tonight.

"Got the clothes." Ash slipped through the door and laughed. "And he's got you all entranced."

I blinked and shook my head, chasing away the naughty thoughts that had taken up residence in my brain. One Holland sister getting down with a demon was enough. Mayhem was a means to an end. Nothing more.

Ash handed me the clothes, dark jeans and a t-shirt. No underwear. Did Chaos go commando? I shook my head again and chunked the garments at Mayhem's head. He caught them before they reached their target...demon reflexes and whatnot.

"Put those on, and I'll break the circle." My eyes finally obeyed the command from my brain, and my gaze remained on his face as he bent down to step into the jeans. When he pulled on the shirt, the tension in my jaw loosened, but it would take a cold shower to rid myself of the unwanted hormones coursing through my veins.

I eyed the salt ring surrounding him and glanced at Chaos, who nodded. Ash rested a hand on my shoulder and said, "It's time."

My stomach tightened, my insides tying into nauseating knots. Once he'd gotten his hissy fit out of the way, he'd become compliant with all my requests. I had to hold up my end of the bargain.

Locking my gaze on his eyes, I stepped toward the circle. "Do not make me regret this."

CHAPTER 8

MAYHEM

The moment the witch swiped her boot through the salt circle, my senses came alive. The high vibrations of their light magic raised the hairs on my skin, and the scents of herbs and chemicals assaulted my nostrils. My nose twitched at the stench.

My brother kept a protective arm wrapped around his witch, but the one they called Ember and the two males stood tense, ready to draw their weapons at the first sign of my malice. I held in a laugh.

If Chaos weren't here, I could take the four of them out before they had a chance to call on their magic or swing a sword. Instead, I would bide my time, make them believe they could command me like they did my brother, and when his guard was down...then I would strike with a force they couldn't begin to imagine.

I stepped out of the circle and inhaled deeply, my face

contorting as the pungent odor burned my nasal passages and throat. "What is that sharp, offending stench?"

Ash and Ember looked at each other, the former shaking her head before the latter said, "What stench?"

"I believe he means the smells of bleach and the other products you use in your home," Chaos said. "The scent is one that didn't exist when we last visited this realm."

Ember made an uncouth snorting sound through her nose. "You're offended by the smell of clean? Why doesn't that surprise me?"

Her boldness of speech and coarse mannerisms would have caused her imprisonment when last I was here, yet something about her brashness intrigued me. She seemed wild, untamed, and I wondered how many men had tried to put her in her place and failed.

I raked my gaze down her form, taking in her slender curves, imagining the feel of her skin beneath my fingertips. If she were any being other than a witch, she would be mine by the end of the day. Taming this shrew would be easier than teaching Cerberus to sit. She would do my bidding whenever and wherever I chose.

But witches were the vilest of creatures, and the mere thought of bedding one made my stomach turn. I would never make that mistake again.

"My eyes are up here, sweetheart," she said, and I flicked my gaze to hers.

"I haven't seen a woman's bosom in centuries. It's unfortunate my first had to be yours." I started toward the door, but

Chaos blocked my exit. The male witches flanked him as if they stood a chance of keeping me from my destination.

"First of all…" Ember's voice drew my attention, and I turned to her as she continued, "Nobody says bosom anymore. You need to watch a few hours of television to get up to speed on modern vernacular."

I had no clue what she was talking about, but I didn't dare admit my ignorance to a witch. Instead, I simply crossed my arms. "Noted."

Her nostrils expanded, and she angled her head while clenching her jaw until the tendons in her neck protruded. Fisting her hands, she tipped her head toward the ceiling and paced a short distance before returning and pacing again.

"And second?" I asked.

She stilled and faced me. "What second?"

"Generally, when someone precedes a statement with the phrase 'first of all,' there is something else they intend to say."

She scoffed. "Are you kidding me right now?"

I arched a brow, happy to goad her, though I couldn't fathom why she questioned my seriousness. "Not in the slightest."

She splayed her fingers, her gaze cutting to the sword lying on the table next to her. "Chaos…" she said through clenched teeth. "Get a handle on your brother before I do something I shouldn't. I need some air." She grasped her sword and marched past me, her shoulder purposely hitting my arm on her way to the door.

"Give us a minute." My brother pressed his lips to Ash's

forehead, and she nodded before gesturing for the males to join her outside.

When the door closed, I turned a livid gaze to Chaos. "I should stab you through the heart and ask Lucifer to smother you in the tarpits for what you've done."

He shook his head, his expression one of pity. "I would vanquish you before you lifted a talon. Brother, you need to understand…"

"I understand enough. You've fallen victim to yet another witch's wiles, and when she's done with you, she'll send you back to the dark prison without a second thought."

He exhaled hard, closing his eyes much longer than a blink. "Who's the one talking in circles now?"

I opened my mouth to argue, but my words would be useless. The conviction in his voice said he believed in this fantasy with every fiber of his being. For the first time since my fury flared over his involvement, I felt something else.

Pity. The great and powerful Chaos had been enticed… tricked…once again. Perhaps he wasn't as intelligent as he claimed to be.

He spread his hands to his sides. "You know as well as I do what would happen if the veil collapsed. It's our duty as Princes of the Underworld to maintain the balance between realms."

"You speak of duty, yet you play house with a witch."

"This development surprised me as much as it enrages you, but who am I to question fate?" He leaned against the table, crossing his arms. "You'll be happy to hear that the only way we can mend the veil is by returning to Hell. With Discord's help, we'll repair it on our side while the Holland sisters take care of theirs. We'll be home soon, and you'll never see these witches again."

His eyes tightened as if the mere thought of leaving this world pained him, and I shifted my gaze to the sigil so carefully drawn on the floor. "Tell me more about the fae invading this realm."

"Swarms of lesser fae have been breaking through for weeks. This morning, we encountered and killed a scout, which makes me believe the greater fae are planning to invade. They will decimate the human population if we allow it to happen. Do you want the fae to control two realms?"

"Perhaps we should slaughter the humans first and claim this realm for demonkind."

"Lucifer would never allow it. You know he relies on the souls of the damned to fuel Hell. Our only choice is to help this coven protect their world...and to end Isabel's curse."

My lip curled at the mention of the wicked woman's name.

"Think of what she did to us," Chaos said. "Do you want to allow the curse to come to fruition when she never paid the price?"

I waved a hand, dismissing his question. "We will find her descendants and make them pay. Once Discord joins us, they'll be easy to identify."

"On that we can agree. The price will be paid for her betrayal, but our contract with her is null. I have no intention of letting her win. Do you?"

"You make a good point, brother. I will help you end the curse, but know that it is out of spite, not for your little witch."

And once the curse was broken, then I would get my revenge.

CHAPTER 9

EMBER

"It's too quiet in there." I leaned toward the closed door, straining to hear the demons. "I think they left through the storefront."

"No, they didn't." Ash grabbed my wrist before I could turn the knob. "Chaos wouldn't let Mayhem roam free, trust me."

"He better not." Fighting the urge to bust in and check, I strode to her desk and sat on the edge. "What is it with him, anyway? It's like he's singled me out to be the one he hates when I didn't do a damn thing to him. In fact, I'm the one who drew his sigil. He should be thanking me, not pissing me off."

Ash pressed her lips together. "You haven't exactly been nice to him either."

"Why would I? He's…" I started to say *a demon* but thought better of it. See? I could learn. "He's insufferable. Infuriating."

"He's been in prison for four hundred years," Miles said. "Maybe cut him some slack."

"Maybe I'll cut off his balls."

Ash laid a heavy hand on my shoulder. "Let's put Mayhem's castration on the back burner for now and focus on our next steps. We can't do this without him."

"Ash is right," Shade said. "I don't trust the guy, but we have to at least pretend to get along if we're going to save Salem."

"I will never get used to you two agreeing." The door opened, and I shot to my feet. Chaos crossed the threshold first, striding to Ash and clutching her hand as if he had to remind his brother of their connection.

Mayhem entered the library next, his posture cocky as hell, his expression... Honestly, I couldn't read it all, but his calculating eyes raking up and down my body made my blood run cold everywhere except my nether region.

Damn demons and their damn sexy human forms.

"I need shoes and a few hours with your television so I can acclimate myself to the current century."

I almost told him people in Hell need ice water, but that idiom didn't seem appropriate, seeing as how he *was* from Hell. Instead, I held my tongue, glanced at his feet, and tugged my wallet from my back pocket. "Miles, can you buy him a pair of size twelves?" I handed him my credit card.

"How do you know that size will fit?" Mayhem curled his lip. "Don't witches have to cast spells for everything they do?"

I stiffened, scrambling for a good comeback, but Ash answered for me, "She worked at a shoe store for five years. If she says you're a twelve, you're a twelve."

Miles slipped my card into his pocket. "Got it. Anything else?"

"Undergarments," Mayhem said. "The seam of these trousers chafes my—"

"Get them a pack of undies." I tried to stop the image of the demon's junk from playing in my mind, but it was no use. He had some really nice junk.

"On it." Miles headed for the back door.

"Shade, go with him," I said.

His chest inflated as he cut his gaze between the demons. "I'm not an errand boy."

Good goddess, I did not have the patience for his ego. "Are you not a team player, either?" I cocked my head. "We don't go anywhere alone until this fiasco is sorted."

Mayhem laughed. "Consider yourself a babysitter, if it makes you feel better."

Shade's mouth tightened, and he inclined his chin, giving me the stink eye before turning on his heel and following Miles out the back. I would've loved to say my tension eased when the ego left the building, but the bare-foot, undie-less demon standing next to me exuded enough to make Shade seem like a shy puppy.

I pinched the bridge of my nose. "How can today not be over yet?"

"A few more hours, and it will be." Ash headed for the stairs. "Let's go up, and I'll order us dinner."

The demons walked behind Ash, and I took up the rear to make sure Mayhem didn't turn and bolt. Patrice stood in the kitchen, and the moment we walked through the door, her eyes widened, the bottle she held slipping from her hands and shattering on the floor.

"Oh! Umm." She kneeled, her gaze never straying from the guys as she picked up a shard of glass. "Ow! Dammit."

Blood pooled on her fingertip, and she hurried to the sink to rinse it. She had turned our kitchen into a healer's workshop, with dried herbs hanging in the window, bottles of spells lined up against the backsplash, and bowls and utensils spread across the countertop.

"I'll clean that up. Where are Miles and Shade?" She applied a styptic powder to her wound before wrapping it in a bandage.

"I've got it." Ash grabbed the broom and dustpan from the pantry and swept up the mess. "They're buying shoes and clothes for Mayhem."

"Okay." Her gaze bounced between the demons.

"He's not going to hurt you." I cast Mayhem a challenging glare.

He arched a brow in return. "Not tonight anyway."

"I know." She wiped the counter with a rag, pink flushing her cheeks. "I set up a ward on the stairs. Well...more like an alarm for anyone with ill intent. I've mixed so many potions, my vim is a little taxed."

"Ember and I will set up more before we go to bed." Ash returned the broom to the pantry and swiped open her phone. "How do tacos sound?"

My stomach growled at the mere mention of nature's most perfect food. "Throw in a twelve-pack of Corona, and I'm sold."

"On it." Ash sank into the middle cushion on the sofa. "I'll ask the guys to pick it up on their way back.

Chaos gestured for her to slide over, and he took the middle seat before motioning for Mayhem to join them. "I found reality shows to be the best way to learn the current culture." He turned on the TV, and I climbed onto a stool at the counter.

"I'm meeting Inga outside to give her the spells." Patrice loaded a canvas bag with bottled magic. "I'd like to spend the night with her if that's okay. It'll free up a bed for..." Her gaze flicked to Mayhem.

I couldn't say I blamed her. I'd rather not sit here with an untamed demon in the house either, but I didn't have the option to leave. "No problem. I'll text you in the morning to touch base."

"Good luck sleeping." She flashed a hesitant smile before turning to the sink and washing the dishes she'd used.

I wouldn't need any luck at all to sleep tonight. Chaos seemed to have a handle on his brother, I had enough vim to set up some good alarms, and my reflexes when I first woke up were fast enough to behead Prince Pissy Pants in a heartbeat if he set them off. Plus, I was so damn tired I had no doubt I'd pass out the second my head hit the pillow.

Patrice left to meet Inga, and twenty minutes later, the guys returned with shopping bags, two dozen foil-wrapped tacos, and the beer.

"At last." Mayhem ripped open the pack of underwear and dropped his drawers in the middle of the living room.

I tried to look away. I really did, but damn. "Lesson one, dude. We don't show the world our naughty bits. From now on, change in the bathroom."

"You've already seen my 'naughty bits,' so what's the problem?" He pulled on the undies and stepped into his jeans.

"Just..." I squeezed my eyes shut. "Keep watching TV so you can learn."

Miles handed out the food, and Shade set the twelve-pack on the coffee table. We all grabbed a beer, and Ash ate on the couch with the demons while Mayhem absorbed an episode of *Big Brother*.

Miles and Shade joined me at the table, and I popped the cap off my beer, taking a long pull and sinking deeper into my chair. The crisp, effervescent liquid tickled on its way to my stomach, and I let out a massive sigh.

Sadly, it was not a contented one. At the rate we were going, I might never experience that sensation again.

I took a bite of taco number one and closed my eyes, focusing on the flavor explosion of *al pastor*, cilantro, and chopped onions. The second bite of spicy, seasoned pork tasted better than the first, and before I knew it, I'd downed three tacos and moved on to my second beer.

"I guess Patrice is done playing with monsters?" Shade wiped his mouth with a paper towel.

"She's helping Inga," Ash said around a mouthful of pork.

"Nobody gets to bow out until this is through." I stood and tossed my wrappers into the trash. "Which is why we need to summon Discord ASAP. Hopefully we can fix this before any more overgrown insects break through and make the situation worse."

"Can we create a strong enough containment circle without Patrice?" Miles asked.

"I don't think she contributed much." Ash joined us at the table, leaving the demons with the TV. "I withheld as much of Chaos's magic from her as I could, and she didn't share much with us. She's truly afraid of them."

"Can you blame her?" Miles grabbed a second beer and popped the top. "She's a healer. We can't turn her into a fighter."

"We'll make it work." I tossed my empty bottle into the recycle bin. "Right now, we need to set up wards on the hall and bedroom doors. Nothing with ill intent gets into our rooms."

"What about out?" Shade leaned toward me, lowering his voice. "You're not afraid he'll take off while we sleep?"

"I'll stay up with him," Chaos said from the living room. "Recharge your vim in peace."

"Works for me." Yes, it went against my very nature to trust a demon, but Chaos had proved his loyalty to Ash a thousand times over. He might not have given a flying flip about me, but he wanted to save my sister as much as I did.

I grabbed a handful of crystals from the drawer, and Ash helped me set up the wards. Of course, I knew now that the ones I used against Chaos wouldn't have stopped him if he really wanted through, but I made sure to cast ones with alarms so I'd have a second to wake up if things went south.

With our protections in place, I headed for the shower, and just like I suspected, I was dead to the world as soon as my head hit the pillow. I could have slept a full twelve hours if not for the woman's agonizing wail ripping through the morning fog.

CHAPTER 10
MAYHEM

A tormented screech of pain sliced through the quiet morning, and I tilted my head toward the sound. "I haven't heard a scream like that since Lucifer tried to keep a banshee as a pet. Is it a normal occurrence here?"

"Not at all." Chaos shot to his feet and darted down the hallway, no doubt running to his witch's side to protect her.

I pulled on the size twelve boots Ember was certain would fit, nodding my approval when they did. Her talent would be useless most of the time, but it had come in handy today. Rising, I prepared to make my escape when Ember stormed into the living room.

She wore baggy pants, which, from my six hours with the television, I had learned were called sweats. A cropped t-shirt left her midsection exposed, and she tucked her disheveled purple hair behind her ear before stepping into the combat-style boots she'd left by the door.

"What happened out there?" she asked.

"How would I know? I've been inside the entire time."

"Ever heard of a window?" She yanked a cord, raising the blinds and filling the room with pale morning light. "Shit. And Patrice is twenty minutes away. Ash, guys, let's go."

The others filed out of the hall, stumbling as they put on shoes and strapped weapons to their bodies. "What's going on?" Shade asked as he tied his blond hair back in a band.

"Someone is bleeding out on the street." Ember pointed at me. "You stay here."

I laughed. "Not a chance."

She made a face at my brother, her mouth tight, her eyes strained.

"I will watch him." Chaos motioned toward the door.

Her mouth twitched as she blew out a hard breath. "Cloak us the second we step outside, Shade. Sound too. Ash, grab a couple bottles of shadow in case we have to split up."

Her sister did as she was told, and we hurried down the stairs and out the back door, my heart pumping with an excitement I hadn't felt in centuries.

Natural fog blanketed the ground outside, but as I stepped onto the sidewalk, another mist gathered around us, turning the already-desaturated world into shades of gray. Fire, healing, shadow magic... What did Miles bring to the team, I wondered. With his stormy gray eyes and jet-black hair, I would guess he could control some type of energy. Lightning, perhaps?

We exited the alley behind the witches' home and followed the path toward the one responsible for the scream. A crowd had gathered around the woman, making it difficult to see her injuries.

The witches paced the perimeter in search of the culprit while Ash attempted to peer through the crowd. "Do you sense anything demonic?" she asked my brother.

He inhaled deeply, searching the area for the telltale low vibration, and I did the same. "Nothing," he said before looking at me.

"I agree. It's probably a case of human-on-human violence. They rarely need much coaxing from our kind."

Sirens wailed in the distance, and the other witches returned to the scene. "Shade, uncloak me so I can elbow my way through the crowd," Ember said.

There was no need for that. I called on my mind power, bringing it to the surface after four hundred years of inactivity. The base of my skull buzzed with power...what people in this century called electricity...and I sent my magic toward the two men standing closest to us.

The one in blue turned to the one in brown and landed a punch to his jaw. Brown fought back, slamming his fist into Blue's stomach, and the crowd backed away, giving the men room to brawl and the witches ample space to examine the victim.

"Chaos!" Ember snapped, her jaw tightening.

He raised his hands in a show of innocence before pointing at me. "I cause confusion. He causes violence."

She glared at me, a mesmerizing fire sparking in her eyes. "Stop it right now. This is not how we operate."

I pulled my magic away from the men and focused it on a woman. She slapped the man standing next to her. Ash and Miles kneeled by the bloody victim on the ground, finally having room to reach her, thanks to me.

Ember drew her sword, clutching it in both hands, her teeth never parting as she spoke. "Turn it off now."

I arched a brow. "Make me."

The witch had the audacity to swing. Her actions caught me off-guard, and I didn't step out of the way in time. The razor-sharp edge nicked my arm, making blood pool in the shallow wound.

Astonishment and irritation mixed with a strange feeling of admiration. I could have forced her to turn on her friends in that instant, yet she straightened her spine and held her head high as if she actually thought she could vanquish me.

"Is that all you've got?" I teased.

"Enough." Chaos laid a hand on my shoulder. "Save it for the fae."

I wiped the blood from my arm and flicked a drop toward her before reeling in my magic.

"After swallowing roach goo, I'm not afraid of a little demon blood." She stood at the ready, her muscles flexed, her stance wide.

"You should be." I crossed my arms, the wound already healing. "It can drive people insane."

She flicked her gaze to Chaos, who said, "It's true."

"Fabulous." She rolled her eyes and shifted her attention to the body.

The woman had been disemboweled. A jagged, vertical cut from her neck to her pubic bone allowed her intestines to spill onto the pavement. Her lifeless eyes stared into the cloudy sky, and her mouth was frozen in a soundless scream.

"Anyone sense a rift?" Ember rose and glanced at me before focusing on my brother.

"I do not," he said.

"Neither do I. Not in the vicinity, anyway." I paused, an unmistakable energy registering in my psyche. The vibration pulled me north, and I strode toward it, my gaze bouncing over the scene, though vision would do no good for battling this vile creature.

"Where do you think you're going?" Ember shouted after me.

I turned around to find the witches backing away while several human workers examined the body. "To find the one responsible and end him."

"Not without us." Ember gestured for the others to follow, and she jogged to catch up. "What do you sense? Is it a demon after all?"

"It is not." I continued my trek, following the energy down an alley. A translucent mosaic pattern rippled in the air ahead of me, and I stopped, opening my senses even more and inhaling the rancid stench of fae.

"Is that what I think it is?" Chaos stopped beside me.

"Indeed it is." I cracked my knuckles, a smile lifting my lips. "A worthy adversary straight out of the gate. I believe I'm going to like it here."

The ripple shifted, and high-pitched chittering rang in my ears.

"Would you like to fill us in?" Ember stood on my other side, unafraid, though if she knew what lay in the alley ahead, she would have run and hidden.

"It's a fae foot soldier," Chaos said. "One rung above scouts."

"Where?" Shade asked.

"Look for the ripples in the air." Chaos pointed, and the fae moved across the alley. "They have cloaking powers, as do the upper fae horde."

"Fabulous. Now we're in the middle of a *Predator* movie." Ember held her hand toward Ash, who poured a blue substance into her palm. She hurled the granules at the fae, and they bounced off its body.

"Well, frack. That didn't work."

"It's part of their biology, not their magic." I gathered hellfire in my palm. "You can't counter it with a spell."

I hurled a fireball at the fae, and it screeched, scurrying up the wall. Its shroud failed for less than a second as it recovered, revealing two sets of human-like arms with taloned hands, large, faceted eyes, translucent wings, and pinchers protruding from each side of its mouth.

Ember sucked in a breath. "Oh, for Hecate's sake. Why do they all have to look like bugs?" Gripping her sword in both hands, she activated her fire magic, flames licking up the blade.

The fae's shroud returned, and it lunged, knocking Shade to the ground. His shadow magic rolled into him, bringing the world into full color, and he shot to his feet, clutching a wounded arm. "The asshole bit me."

Blood oozed from two puncture wounds on his biceps. "Are these venomous too?"

"From scouts up, they all are," Chaos said. "And they become more toxic the greater the fae."

"Guess we better mix a ton of antidotes when we get home." Ash pulled a bottle from her bag. "Hide from sight our magical plight. With the power of Shade, my intent is conveyed."

The world turned to grayscale again, and she clutched his good arm, dragging him to the alley entrance. He stiffened, the poison paralyzing him in seconds, and he collapsed to the ground.

Miles gathered energy between his palms. His efforts resulted in a baseball-sized sphere of electricity, and he threw it at the mosaic ripple. The fae darted out of the way before shimmying up the wall and leaping onto his chest, knocking him onto the pavement.

Ember swung her fiery blade, hitting the fae, and it leaped onto the wall, uninjured. She helped Miles stand and dashed toward her sister, returning with a plastic bottle. The fae rippled to her left, and she spun, hurling a fine white powder into the air. What spell she cast, I did not know. The fae dashed away before the powder reached it.

"What was that magic supposed to accomplish?" I asked.

"It's not magic; it's baby powder, and it clings to everything. If I could see the bastard, I could kill it." She searched the alley, squinting as if narrowing her vision would bring the pest into focus. "Why are you here? What do you want?"

"This is our world now," a gravelly, seemingly disembodied voice replied.

"The hell it is." She threw another mist of powder in the direction of the voice, but it missed its mark.

"Hell is next," he said.

Ember flew backward, slamming into a brick wall. She grunted and squeezed the bottle, coating the fae's head and torso in white powder.

Its pinchers opened and closed two inches from her face. "Witches will submit or die."

"I'll take option C." She reached down, retrieving a knife from a thigh holster, but the fae had armored exoskeletons. She was about to learn how useless her blades would be when my brother barreled into the pest, dragging it to the ground and punching it in the face.

Its pinchers caught his wrist, and as he pulled free, they sliced into his skin, leaving a deep, jagged cut on his arm. Chaos stood, stumbling backward, the venom already taking hold. Ash and Miles grabbed his arms, leading him to the alley exit and lowering him next to Shade.

Ember threw a dagger, lodging it in the fae's neck. It screeched, spinning and flailing as it grasped the handle and pulled it out.

"Demon blood should not affect me." It spit and wiped Chaos's blood from its pinchers. "How?"

"These aren't just any demons." Ember thrust her flame-licked sword beneath an armored plate, slicing into the fae. "They're Princes of Hell."

It coughed, its bug eyes moving in different directions, and green fae blood oozed from its mouth. Ember removed her sword, and with an elegant, ethereal spin, she swung, chopping off the creature's head.

I stood there, stunned, my mouth agape as the beast collapsed to the ground. She brushed past me, rushing to the others and checking their wounds. She offered Chaos a bandage before helping Shade to his feet, and a feeling of both admiration and awe warmed my chest.

Ember was no ordinary witch. She was a warrior. A leader.

A goddess to rival Athena herself.

"We need one more shadow spell so we can get rid of the body," she said.

Shade nodded. "I think I'm okay now."

"No." She touched his shoulder. "You need to recharge. I'll cast the bottled one."

Ash tossed her a glass container, and she removed the cork, reciting the same words her sister had used.

The world around us returned to gray. I had been so enamored watching her fight, I hadn't noticed when our surroundings shifted to color.

My brother and the women approached the body while the men returned their supplies to the bag Ash had carried. Chaos shot a stream of hellfire at the fae's severed head, turning it to ash.

"I can cut him into pieces if we need to," Ember said. "His exoskeleton looks as strong as the scout's."

"I believe the four of us can penetrate his armor." Chaos looked at me, and the witches followed his gaze.

Ember scoffed. "You mean the big, bad demon prince, whose favorite pastime is supposedly killing fae, is actually going to help now?"

Her goading broke me from my stupor. "I rather enjoyed watching you struggle. Perhaps I've found a new favorite pastime." In truth, it was not the struggle I enjoyed. It was her ingenuity, the way she commanded the situation...how stunning she looked while battling a foe who could kill a normal witch before they had the chance to utter a single spell.

Her jaw ticked. "Let's get this over with before the cloak wears off."

Ember lifted her hands, palms toward the dead fae, and released a stream of flames. Chaos and Ash followed suit, the exoskeleton flaking beneath their heat. I joined them, and the four of us worked together to burn through the overgrown insect's armor.

Slowly, slowly, the fae began to crumble. Five minutes passed. Six. Seven, and finally, the creature turned into a pile of ashes.

Ember heaved a breath and leaned against the wall, wiping her forehead with the back of her hand. "That was fun."

I couldn't tell if she used sarcasm, but I had to agree. Watching her fight a worthy adversary had been thrilling.

Miles approached with Shade and handed the bag to Ash. "I guess we know what happened to the woman."

"Maybe." Ember retrieved her knife from the ground and

sheathed her sword. "But humans are capable of much more violence than that, so we can't rule anything out."

"Did anyone get a close enough look at the body to see if all her organs were in place?" I asked.

"It'll take an autopsy to figure that out," Ash said. "Why?"

"If the woman is missing her liver," I said, "the fae was responsible for her demise."

Ember dragged a hand down her face. "Giant bugs who eat liver. My worst effing nightmare."

The fact this witch had entranced me with her battle skills was mine…

CHAPTER 11

EMBER

"You have to let us do this, or the entire coven will know what you are." I fisted my hand around the powdered potion Ash had mixed. After we'd cremated the fae soldier, we'd returned home and taken a moment to brush our teeth and change. Shade and Miles had stopped to get clean clothes, and the rest of us gathered in the kitchen.

"It's painless." Chaos sat on the stool next to Mayhem and rested his forearms on the counter. "You won't feel any different."

Mayhem scoffed. "I'm not afraid of pain, but I will not allow you to destroy my demonic nature. I *am* a demon. You can't change that."

I closed my eyes and tried not to grind my teeth. If I ever got the chance to see a dentist again, he'd probably pass out when he saw the nubs I had left. "We aren't trying to change you, though Hecate knows if we could take that ego down a notch or two, we would."

Mayhem narrowed his eyes. "You speak as though you aren't afraid of me in the slightest."

I held his gaze. "I think we've established that I'm not."

His expression shifted, one brow lifting, drawing up the corner of his mouth. "You should be. I could do things to you that you've never dared imagine."

A warm shiver formed at the base of my neck before heat spread through my body. I could imagine...*had* imagined plenty since my eyes first locked on his unwrapped package.

But nope. I was not going there. No way.

I lifted one shoulder dismissively. "Doubtful."

"Try me." His gaze smoldered, so I rolled my eyes and looked at his brother before my panties got wet.

Chaos drummed his fingers on the counter. "Cast the spell on me so he can see it's harmless. Surely the one you placed on me weeks ago has lost its potency."

"That's a good idea." Ash took my free hand. "We're used to him now, so it could be wearing off without us noticing."

I shook my head. "Do you remember how much vim it took to cast it last time? I'm not sure we can do it twice in a row."

"Last time we did it, Chrys's suppression spell was active on the house," Ash said. "We're operating at full power now."

"A High Priestess who isn't strong enough to cast a spell twice." Mayhem chuckled. "Why am I not surprised?"

Whatever heat had built in my body from his smolder turned to ice. "Let's do it, and then I want the biggest, fattest breakfast burrito we can find."

Ash opened her vim to me, her magic flowing from her hand and into mine. I did the same, letting our powers mix and meld, bringing it all to the surface. "Aura strong, magic deep, we hide your essence from all who seek," we said in unison before blowing the fine pink powder toward Chaos.

"As we will it, so mote it be." My breath came out in a rush, and I tugged from my sister's grasp, splaying my fingers and fisting my hands three times while the fire magic coursing through my veins cooled to a simmer. Ash was right. With Chrys's stupid hex lifted from the house, I'd have no problem casting the spell again.

"I feel no different." Chaos held up his hand and ignited a ball of hellfire in his palm. "My powers are intact."

"Hmm…" Mayhem eyed his brother and shrugged.

"If you ever want to leave this house again, you need to demon up and let us do this." I tossed two bay leaves into a copper bowl. "Or are you afraid?"

His gaze snapped to mine, the intensity in his eyes almost making me regret goading him before his lips twitched as if he were suppressing amusement.

Ash crushed the lady's mantle, marjoram, and wolfsbane and dropped it into the bowl along with the liquid mix she'd concocted. I added the final ingredient—a single drop of cinnamon oil—and the potion sizzled and popped before turning to powder.

With the mixture complete, Mayhem inclined his chin. "Very well. I will play along with your game for now."

I glanced at my sword hanging on the wall. "It's your only choice, buddy."

He chuckled, this time not bothering to hide it, but at least he didn't argue.

Ash took my hand, and we recited the incantation again, blowing the powder into Mayhem's face this time.

He stiffened, his brow furrowing in confusion. "Are you certain it worked?"

"It worked." I returned the herbs to the cabinet while Ash washed the dishes. The second time we cast the spell, I did feel the tax on my vim, though it wasn't nearly bad enough to warrant the three-hour nap I'd have liked to take.

Mayhem summoned hellfire into his palm, turning his hand over and letting the ball of burning light roll across the back of his hand before he extinguished it. Seemingly satisfied his powers remained intact, he nodded and looked at me. "Tell me about these breakfast burritos."

"They're divine. Let's go."

After walking three uneventful blocks—thank you, Hecate—we chowed down on chorizo and egg burritos, drank way too much coffee, and returned to Ash's studio, where Shade and Miles were waiting.

She poured the salt circle and lit the candles at each point of the pentagram before taking a piece of chalk from a drawer and holding it up. "Who wants to do Discord's sigil?"

"I will." I grabbed the chalk from her hand before one of the guys volunteered. Not that I didn't have faith in their artistic abilities, especially Miles's. He was a great artist, but Ash felt like it was cheating or something for her to draw another demon's mark. Chaos was *Ash's demon*. I had to make damn sure Mayhem didn't become mine.

"Hold on. You need to see this." Miles gestured for us to watch a video on his phone.

Chief Higgins stood behind a podium, the Salem police emblem, four feet in diameter, hanging on the wall behind him. An American flag hung from a pole to his right, and four microphones of different shapes sat on the stand in front of him.

"The woman who was murdered this morning is believed to be the third victim." His expression was somber, but a spark of anger tightened his eyes. "The manner of death is identical with all three, and they happened within the span of two days."

"Shit. Turn it up." This was bad. Very, very bad.

"If anyone has information, we encourage you to contact the police department non-emergency line as quickly as possible. Until the culprits have been captured, we will be enforcing an eight PM to sunrise curfew within the city limits. Stay vigilant, folks, and lock your doors."

I stretched my neck. "So the disgusting flyman killed three people before we took him out."

"Or there's more than one," Ash said. "We never found the rift he got through."

Miles returned his phone to his pocket. "Or there's a serial killer on the loose. We need to know if their livers were missing."

"On it." I dialed Higgins's cell and put it on speaker.

He picked up on the second ring. "Don't tell me..."

"Had their livers been taken?" I asked.

He missed a beat before he replied. "Yes. What kind of monster are we dealing with?"

"It's a fae from across the veil," Shade said. "We killed it this morning."

"You could have told me that before I called a press conference." Annoyance dripped from his voice, as usual. "Now I have my men on the hunt for a serial killer."

"You could have called me when you found the first victim." I matched his tone.

"It looked mundane." He blew out a hard breath. "I hate to say this, but has anyone in your coven considered joining the force? You could be a paid consultant."

Now there was an idea... "Maybe when all this is through. Keep your team on the hunt and call me if anyone else gets killed."

"I thought you said you took the perp out," he said.

"We did, but there could be more soon. A lot more."

"Great." He hung up the phone, and I shoved mine into my back pocket.

I made a grabby motion to Ash, and she handed me her phone with Discord's sigil on the screen. Dropping to my knees, I laid it in the circle and pressed the chalk to the floor.

"He'll owe you nothing," Mayhem said.

I glanced over my shoulder to find him staring at my butt. Typical. "That's why you're here. Convince him like Chaos did you."

I returned to my canvas, dragging the chalk downward before looping up and creating a sharp ninety-degree angle. The phone pinged, and a message from Patrice slid across the screen. I finished the sigil and rose, handing it to Ash. "It's Patrice asking if we've summoned Discord yet."

Ash typed on her screen. A moment later, it pinged again. "She says she's not comfortable being in the house with the demons." She shrugged and laid her phone on the table.

"As long as she keeps her mouth shut about the source of this fiasco, I don't care. We'll go to her if we need healing." I held out my hands, and Shade and Chaos took them. Ash stood between her demon and Miles. "Everyone remember the incantation?"

Mayhem strolled toward Miles, reaching for his hand.

"Not you." I pinned the unruly demon with a hard glare. "Just stand in the corner like a good boy."

He arched a brow. "You allow Chaos to participate. Why not me?"

"I trust him." I couldn't believe I uttered those words aloud, but there I was, admitting I trusted a demon. He might have been a pain in my ass at times, but with the way he treated my sister, I couldn't deny it. This Prince of Hell had no ill intent toward us. And he loved Ash beyond belief.

Mayhem crossed his arms. "Are you sure that's a wise decision? A witch trusting a demon?"

"It is what it is. Now hush so we can finish this."

Ash swallowed hard and nodded, and pain tightened my chest. How awful it must have been knowing her relationship with the love of her life had an expiration date and she…we… were helping to bring it on sooner.

Chaos opened himself, letting his magic run from his hand into mine. It tingled, filling me with a power that could be addictive if I wasn't careful. I let it flow into Shade, and he gasped before letting out a slow, satisfied breath.

Very addictive.

We recited the words like demon-summoning pros—which it looked like we were becoming—our magic mixing and melding, the energy in the room thickening like boiling water with flour. The weight of Mayhem's gaze on me was palpable, but I didn't dare look at him. Latin was tricky. If I pronounced one syllable wrong, the entire spell could explode. On the final word, we focused our energy on the salt circle, activating the containment ring.

"Not bad," Mayhem said, though he didn't sound the slightest bit impressed. "But my former host could have created one just as strong on her own."

My mouth tightened, and I did my best not to grind my teeth. He was baiting me. I knew he was, but I couldn't help myself. "Your former host..."

My mind blanked. I'd hoped for a barbed, snarky comeback, but he was right. Chrys could make a circle just as strong. She *had* on several occasions. Could I have made one strong enough to hold a demon prince? According to Chaos, not with the spell I'd used before. But this one was different. It wasn't dark magic, but it hovered in the gray area, for sure.

And I certainly wasn't going to take chances by going solo just to impress this infuriating asshat.

He smirked. "Are you planning to finish that sentence this decade?"

"No. No, I'm not." I strode to the table and opened the

grimoire to the summoning spell before scanning the words. "Let's bring in Discord and finish this."

"What are you offering him?" Mayhem walked toward me with a cocky gait and glanced at the summoning spell.

"A chance to right a wrong." I turned the grimoire toward Shade, and he and Miles studied the spell.

Mayhem laughed. "If the curse on your bloodline is the wrong to which you're referring, you will be sorely disappointed. Isabel is the one who wronged you. We simply did as she requested in exchange for her soul."

I crossed my arms. "Which you never got to claim because she outsmarted you."

Ash touched her fingers to my elbow, her silent reminder to cool my jets. We had more important things to do than to waste time one-upping an arrogant hellion.

"Everyone ready?" I closed the book.

"Good luck convincing him to pass through without an offering," he said. "We came easily because you released us from prison. Discord is already free."

"What did Isabel offer when she summoned you?" Ash asked Chaos.

"Her soul," Shade answered for him. "He already said that."

"We will entice Discord with the chance to claim our prize." Chaos moved next to his brother, laying a palm on his shoulder. "For Isabel's debt finally to be paid."

"Revenge." Mayhem nodded. "It might work."

"It's worth a shot. Shall we?" Ash held out her hand, and Chaos took it. "Someone hold on to Mayhem. If Discord senses his brothers here, he's more likely to come through."

"And bring Cinder with him?" Miles took Ash's other hand.

"If she is alive," Mayhem said.

"She is. Come on." I grabbed Mayhem's hand, and pinpricks spiraled up my arm to lodge in my chest. I grasped Chaos with my other hand, but he didn't affect me like Mayhem. He never had.

And those pinpricks coming from the latest addition to our demon collection...? Not *un*pleasant in the slightest. He felt like raw power, and my body wanted more.

Shade strolled around the circle to take Mayhem's free hand, and I watched him for a sign that the pinpricks registered in his psyche like they did mine. He didn't react, but I had no doubt once the demon shared his energy with us, then Shade would feel it. How could he not?

"Ready, set, go." I let my magic run down my arms and into the demons on either side of me. Okay, yes... I did send a smidge more power into Mayhem, just to remind him I wasn't some dainty little kitchen witch. He might've been a hurricane, but I was no light afternoon rain.

He cut his gaze toward me, one corner of his mouth lifting either in amusement or appreciation. I didn't dare ask which.

Chaos opened to me first, the familiar tingles of Underworld magic seeping into my palm and filling my body with power. I allowed it to flow into Mayhem, and he chuckled.

"Are you holding back, brother?"

Chaos's fingers twitched. "As should you. Witches are mortal beings."

Shade gasped and swallowed hard, and Mayhem laughed again. The pinpricks buzzing through my body intensified before a tidal wave of untamed magic blasted through my psyche, setting my nerves ablaze.

I did my best not to react, but damn. This demon made every part of my body tingle.

Every. Part.

I cleared my throat to stop my voice from coming out as a squeak. "All of us together."

We recited the summoning spell in unison. Nothing happened.

I squeezed the guys' hands. "Again, and this time give it everything you've got."

The demon magic running through me intensified, and we spoke the words three more times. Still nothing.

"I told you that you needed an offering." Mayhem tried to pull from my grasp, but I tightened my grip. "Share more of your power. We need to make damn sure Discord knows his brothers are here."

A raging river of strong, feral electricity flowed into me, spiraling through my body and making my toes curl in my boots. I fought a gasp, again not daring to let him know how he affected me. I refused to give him the satisfaction.

We performed the summoning a fifth time, a sixth, and light flickered inside the circle. A stream of dark green smoke poured into the ring, the impression of a featureless face forming in the fog, reminding me of the scene in *The Mummy* when Imhotep's face formed in the sandstorm...creepy AF. It moved around the perimeter, pausing first on Chaos and then Mayhem.

"Have you the amulet?" Discord's voice echoed, sounding a million miles away.

"We have the means to avenge our imprisonment," Chaos said. "Join us in the mortal realm so we can identify Isabel's descendants and claim our prize."

"I owed a debt to the witch who freed me, and no one else." Something about the way he said it raised the hairs on the back of my neck... Past tense. Whatever Cinder had asked for, he'd already done it.

And she hadn't come back.

"That's our sister, Cinder," Ash said. "She needs you to find our parents and bring them all here to break my family's curse."

His distant, ominous laugh sounded like it came from the deepest depths of Hell...which it did. "That was not the debt she asked I pay."

Mayhem dropped my hand and stepped toward the circle. "Join us, brother. We have fae to battle."

"Find my amulet, and I will consider it." In a flash of light and a thunderous boom, the smoke dissipated, taking the demon to his own side of the veil.

"What the actual eff?" Ash looked at me with a furrowed brow. "In the journal, that's exactly what she said she would ask for."

I swallowed hard, the blood draining from my head to my feet as the realization sank in. "It was..."

"Too much to ask," Mayhem said matter-of-factly.

"Too many requests," Chaos added. At least he had the peopling skills to sound worried for us.

"But she freed him from four hundred years of imprisonment." Ash's mouth hung open as she looked from me to the demons. "How is that too much to ask?"

I ticked the list off on my fingers. "Take her to Hell, find our parents, save them from the demon who took them, bring all three of them back to this realm, break the family curse...and not kill any of us along the way."

Ash covered her mouth, shaking her head before lifting her hand and dropping it at her side. "All she asked for in return for his release was a ticket to Hell."

I nodded. "Because she thought she could do all the rest by herself." Which was typical of Cinder. Our eldest sister excelled at everything...except asking for help.

Ash extinguished the candles and carried them to the storage cabinet. "We need a new plan."

"We need to go to Hell ourselves and bring her back." I swiped my foot through the salt to break the containment circle. Really, I just wanted to kick something, but whatever.

Chaos's expression was so grim, I didn't need an interpretation. "I'm afraid that isn't possible. Your sister is lost."

CHAPTER 12

MAYHEM

"This doesn't make sense. Why can't we go to Hell and get her?" Ember paced the length of the library before turning on her heel and returning to the desk where her sister sat.

Ash's fingers flew across the keys of her computer...a device they swore contained no magic, yet it had the power to access the knowledge of this realm as if tapping into the Akashic Records.

"And he won't bring her back because we don't have some necklace he lost eons ago?" Ember waved her hands in the air, clearly having a fit of hysterics.

I leaned toward Chaos. "Are you affecting her brain?"

"He wouldn't dare," Ash said, her eyes never straying from the screen.

I looked to my brother for confirmation, and he shook his

head. He had been tamed...whipped...by a witch. How pathetic. Although...

I let my gaze wander over Ember's form. I wouldn't mind her attempts to tame me if it meant I could ravish her every night as she tried. Perhaps I should challenge her to a wrestling match so she could work out her hysteria...naked, of course.

"What does this artifact even do? Why does he want it so bad? We were this close." She held her thumb and forefinger half an inch apart before turning and pacing again.

I moved to block her path, taking her shoulders in my hands. "Calm down, woman. Sit, and I will answer your questions."

"Oh, boy," Ash said under her breath, and my brother chuckled.

A vein pulsed in Ember's neck, and her lips flattened, a wildness I hadn't yet seen swirling in her eyes. Her jaw moved from side to side as she held my gaze, silently challenging me, a Prince of Hell. She was either unafraid or unaware of the fact I could snap her neck with a twist of my wrist.

Slowly, she lowered her gaze to my right hand on her shoulder. Flicking back to my eyes, she arched a brow, still not saying a word. Her fingers curled into fists at her sides, and she cocked her head. "Get. Your. Hands. Off me."

As if by instinct, I jerked from her shoulders, releasing her. How odd. My normal reaction to a demand like that would have been to grip her tighter.

She brushed past me and returned to the desk. "I guess you didn't think to have *that* conversation with him while you binged reality TV?"

"I did not." Chaos lowered his eyes before looking at me. "Telling a woman of this century to calm down will have the opposite effect of what you hope to achieve. It's a lesson I learned the hard way." He gently squeezed his witch's shoulders.

She patted his hand. "Lucky for him, he's a fast learner."

"To answer your first question, Ember…" Chaos sat on the edge of the desk. "We cannot take you both to Hell because if four beings of such power as ours were to pass through the veil at the same time, it would collapse."

"You don't know that for sure." She crossed her arms, jutting out one hip and tapping her foot. "I say we try it and see."

"I agree," I said. "It's the only way to know for certain." And the idea of watching her do battle in my realm made my dick twitch.

"Hold on." Ash held a palm toward us. "Let's explore your leap-first look-later method."

Ember rolled her eyes. "Then it becomes a plan."

"Which is my specialty." Ash smirked. "Say we do make it across without collapsing the veil. How would we return without someone to summon us?"

"What are we? Incompetent slugs? We'll bring you back." Shade's voice drew my attention to the two men in the corner. I had forgotten they played a role in this game.

Ember gestured to them grandly. "Problem solved."

"Not quite." Ash swiveled her chair toward us and folded her hands in her lap. "Think about it. The biggest issues with the veil started when Cinder summoned Discord, right?"

"Obviously." She continued pacing.

"So the main damage occurred when Discord came through, and then they both crossed over." She opened a large book and traced her finger down the page containing our marks before tapping it. "Read this." She turned the volume toward her sister.

Ember stopped and examined the page. "'Discord, Chaos, and Mayhem are the original Princes of Hell, created by the Lord of the Underworld himself. Their strength and power are unmatched, and all of demonkind obey them.' What is this? An ego-stroking session? They're demon royalty. We know."

"Not that. Read the section titled 'Warnings.'"

She sniffed and looked at the passage again. "'Summoning an entity of this power will weaken the veil between worlds. You must keep the demon contained for a period of one week before sending him back to his realm. Doing so too soon may cause...irreparable damage.' Well, damn."

She inhaled, opening her mouth to say more, but my brother cut her off. "With my summoning, the veil only weakened marginally."

Ash nodded. "It's worse since I brought Chaos over, but the damage didn't double. Same with Mayhem."

Ember crossed her arms, drumming her fingers against her biceps. "When Chrys brought him over, you vanquished him right away. That didn't cause irreparable damage."

"Because he didn't have a corporeal form," Shade said. "Now he does."

"I haven't sensed a rift today, and we have been out in the city twice. Let's keep it that way." Chaos rose to his feet. "*If* someone is to cross over to the Underworld, we must wait at least a week."

"Waiting is not my thing. I need to battle another beastie ASAP." She rested a hand on her hip, drawing my gaze to the curve of her waist. How could a warrior of her magnitude possess such delicate features?

"What's the amulet he wants?" Miles asked. "Maybe if we can find it, no one will have to go to the Underworld."

"It was a gift from Lucifer." My lip curled. Discord was the first Prince of Hell and had always been the King's favorite. Lucifer allowed him into the most private parts of the palace, making him privy to the inner workings and plans of our realm. He was the Lord of the Underworld's pet.

Chaos chuckled. "It wasn't a gift. Discord won it in a bet."

I frowned. "He told me it was a gift."

"Because the bet was about whether or not you could beat Cerberus in a wrestling match when they were a puppy." He laughed again. "They were half your size, and they took you down in sixty seconds, sitting on your stomach and nibbling on your pants with all three of their mouths while you bellowed about it not being a fair fight."

"Oof." Ash scrunched her face, and Ember rolled her lips inward, holding back a laugh.

Cold flashed in my chest before hellfire rose from my gut, spreading through my body and making my ears burn. It *hadn't* been a fair fight, and Chaos knew it. Yet there he was, ridiculing me in front of this coven.

I should not have cared. I was the third Prince, the afterthought. My brothers having fun at my expense was nothing new, but the fact that these four witches…that Ember… now knew of their mockery made my stomach roil and my skin crawl.

Unable to meet her gaze, I turned toward the bookshelves and examined the mess they called a library. Ancient grimoires lay haphazardly on the floor, and dust coated the empty spaces on the shelves where the books should have been.

"What does the amulet do?" Ember asked, her hysteria under control, but I couldn't answer.

My blood began to boil, anger flushing out the shame my brother had caused. How dare he attempt to humiliate me, to say to these witches that I was less than his equal. That I couldn't best a *puppy*. It was time to prove what Mayhem could do.

I focused on Shade, sending my mind magic into his psyche. His eyes widened. Then they narrowed. He glared at my brother, cracking his knuckles before taking a blade from his holster. With a guttural roar, he charged toward Chaos, plunging the knife into my brother's neck.

Chaos turned, swinging his arm and knocking the witch backward. Shade careened into the wall, cracking the sheetrock, but my magic was stronger than any injury he might have sustained. The witch lunged again. Chaos caught him by the throat and lifted him from the ground.

"Brother…" He said, his tone scolding.

I focused on Miles, sending him the same pulse of magic I had given Shade. He fisted his hands and blew out a hard breath like a bull ready to charge.

I felt the tip of the blade on my chest before I noticed Ember had drawn her sword. She stood in front of me, her eyes narrowed, her head slightly cocked. "What did I tell you about being a good boy?"

"Boy?" I growled low in my throat. "I am more man than you could handle."

She pressed her blade harder against my chest. "Release them. Now."

Miles gathered energy between his palms as he glared at my brother. With his free hand, Chaos removed the knife from his neck. Shade, who had been thrashing in his grip, now hung limp.

"Please, Mayhem." Ash moved next to her sister. "We can't do this without you. We need to work together."

I cut my gaze from her to Miles. He lifted his hands, preparing to throw his magic.

"Alright then. Back to Hell you go." Ember gripped her sword with both hands. Had the blade not been precisely over my heart, I would have let her stab me.

But I had no intention of returning to Hell now. Not when I had havoc to spread through Salem.

I released my hold on the men. Miles gasped, looking at the energy in his hands as if he couldn't recall summoning it. He made fists, extinguishing the power, and Chaos dropped Shade on the floor.

The witch coughed before sucking in a large breath and rubbing his neck. "What the hell was that?"

"That was Mayhem attempting to prove a point." Chaos rubbed the puncture on his neck, his fingers bloody from the wound.

"Which he won't do again. You are not to mess with any coven member's mind. Ever." Ember twisted the blade, reminding me she would take no issue in vanquishing me should I not behave to her standards.

How far would I have to go for her to act on her word? Perhaps I would find out before this was through.

"Your powers are different. Chaos causes confusion and panic that sometimes turns into fights." She sheathed her sword. "You go straight to violence."

"We are not the same, if that's what you're implying," I said. "Much like you are the brawn while Ash has the brains."

She nodded her head, shrugging one shoulder at my insult. "That's fair."

"She's smarter than you think," Ash said, defending her sister's intelligence. I doubted Ember needed defense from anyone, though. I'd never met a woman so fierce.

Shade rose to his feet. "Do that again, and I'll suck the life out of you so slowly, you'll beg me to vanquish you."

I lit a small ball of fire and let it roll over and under each of my fingers before I extinguished it in my palm. "I would like to see you try, shadow witch. I won't be tamed like my brother."

Shade puffed out his chest, but Miles rested a hand on his shoulder, calming him.

Ember crossed her arms. "Check your egos, boys. We're on the same team."

I arched a brow. "Are we?"

Her mouth tightened. "We're pretending like we are. Now, what does the amulet do, and why won't Discord accept our summons without it?"

CHAPTER 13

EMBER

"There's nothing in the book about it, and I couldn't find anything on the witchy web." Ash turned to the index of the stolen volume and searched again, but if she couldn't find it the first time, it wasn't there. Ash was a research master.

"It would have no documentation." Mayhem strolled toward the staircase and headed up without another word.

Silence hung over us for a beat or two before Ash hit Chaos's arm with the back of her hand. "You embarrassed him. Go apologize."

The demon shrugged. "I spoke the truth. It was time he knew."

"He's embarrassed," Ash said again.

"Embarrassment and shame are two emotions my brother is incapable of feeling." He took a tissue from Ash's desk and cleaned the blood from his fingers and neck. The wound was already healing.

"I'm siding with Chaos on this one. He's pissed for sure, but embarrassed? That guy?" I laughed. "Come on. Let's head up."

I ascended the stairs and found Mayhem in the kitchen, shoveling chocolate chips into his mouth. What was it with demons and sugar?

He swallowed and filled his hand with more. "The amulet increases power. Whatever magic the being possesses will multiply when they wear it."

I tilted my head, an idea wriggling in the back of my mind as the others joined us. "What else?"

He shoved the handful of chocolate into his mouth. "It's the only reason Discord is the most powerful of princes. Without it, he's no stronger than Chaos or me."

"Isabel must have taken it before she imprisoned him." Chaos held out his hand, and Mayhem begrudgingly filled it with chocolate. "Lucifer made him swear never to take it off, especially in this realm. It's too powerful for a mortal to bear."

"And he won't come back to earth unless he can be stronger than his brothers?" Shade sank onto a stool. "He sounds like a pompous prick."

"Takes one to know one," Ash said with a grin.

"Ha ha." Shade rolled his eyes and laughed.

I would never get used to their new dynamic. A month ago, they'd be close to strangling each other by now. A month ago, everything was different. Everything...

The wriggling idea burrowed deep in my brain, dissolving

all traces of doubt. "I know where the amulet is." Of course I did. It made so much sense, any other explanation sounded ridiculous.

"Care to share?" Ash grabbed a box of crackers from the pantry and sat next to Shade.

"Isn't it obvious?" I met each of their expectant gazes, but no one had a clue. "Chrys had it. How else could she have gotten so strong so quickly?"

Ash stopped chewing, her brow furrowing as the gears turned in her mind. "But...how did she find it? If Isabel had it, wouldn't it have been hidden...? And how would Chrys even know it existed?"

"She must be Isabel's descendant." Miles took a beer from the fridge and sat at the table.

"That makes sense." Shade joined him. "She said she had no choice. When Cinder confided in her about her plans to summon Discord, Chrys did as Isabel had instructed and tried to free the others so she could beg for forgiveness."

I grabbed a beer and paced the length of the kitchen. "And the whole Boston ordeal was her trying to claim what was hers by birthright. Isabel was the High Priestess of Boston in her time."

"Wait." Miles picked at the label on his bottle. "If Isabel was High Priestess, isn't their current leader a descendant?"

"No," Ash said around a mouthful of crackers before she swallowed. "Their leadership changed families around three hundred years ago. I couldn't find the reason in my research, but her descendants haven't been in charge for centuries."

Mayhem dropped the empty chocolate chip bag on the counter and wiped the corners of his mouth with his fingers.

"The trash can is over there." Ash pointed, giving him *the look,* as if she could command him the way she did Chaos.

He ignored her. "Chrys is not Isabel's descendant."

Ash's eye twitched, so I grabbed the bag and threw it away. "How do you know that? Chaos said it would take all three of you together to identify her bloodline."

He took a beer from the fridge and drank a long, slow pull. "You forget I spent time inside her, melding with her power. I am certain she is not a descendant."

"She could be." I took a swig, the icy bubbles cooling me on their way down. "She's so many generations removed, her blood was diluted with other families' magic. Maybe you missed it."

"I missed nothing but the chance to burn through her vessel and take her power as my own." He arched a brow accusingly, as if I would ever allow that to happen on my watch.

"I believe him," Chaos said. "When I was inside Ash, I recognized her bloodline as soon as she told me who she was."

"Did Chrys tell you who she was?" I sat on a stool by Ash.

"She told me nothing." He set his empty bottle on the counter.

"Recycle bin is blue." Ash cleared her throat, but he ignored her again. "Most likely, she's not a descendant, but we won't rule it out entirely. How she found the amulet...how she knew it existed...doesn't matter at this point. *Something* helped her gain all that power, and we need to find it."

"Guys!" I slapped my hand on the counter, making Ash

jump. "You both said Chrys helped you grow your power. Did she use an artifact of any kind? Did you notice a different necklace or anything?"

Miles and Shade looked at each other, both scrunching their faces in concentration before Shade shook his head. "She didn't give me anything while we practiced except the knowledge of how to tap into power I already had. She was always wearing different jewelry. I don't pay attention to stuff like that."

He lifted his hands in an *I don't know* gesture. "I wasn't even aware she was training Miles or Ginger. She kept us separated and swore each of us to secrecy."

My shoulders slumped. "Miles?"

He shook his head. "If she had the amulet, she kept it hidden."

"Well, frack." My elbows thudded on the counter. "It wasn't on her when she died. I checked her pockets too."

"It could have fallen off in all the commotion," Ash said.

"If it's in the church basement, we'll never find it." I rested my chin on my fists. "That place looks like a tornado blew through it."

"I didn't sense its power while I resided inside her," Mayhem said. "If it were on her person, I would have felt it, and if she knew where the amulet came from...that it belonged to my brother...she would have hidden it before she summoned me if she were wise."

"So you don't have to be wearing it for it to increase your magic." Miles peeled off the label, closing his fist around it when Ash gave him the side eye.

"Perhaps not," Chaos said. "Discord, Lucifer, and Hecate know its full power. We know only what he told us."

"Hecate?" I straightened.

Mayhem nodded. "She and Lucifer forged it together, sharing their magic to create it."

"Well, then. Let's ask her where it is." I rose and went to the herb cabinet to gather supplies for our ritual. If they had led with that bit of information, we wouldn't have wasted the last half hour discussing theories. "Ash, get the candles and sage ready."

"On it." She opened the smudge drawer and gathered the dried herb, laying it on the counter before unrolling a length of twine.

Shade joined us in the kitchen. "Don't tell me you throw away your smudge sticks every time you use them."

Ash opened another drawer and gestured to the four bundles inside. "Of course we reuse them, but we're asking a goddess for help. She gets a new one. We'll use it to cleanse our space and make it ready for us to receive her guidance, and then we'll leave it as an offering."

He leaned a hip against the counter and crossed his arms. "You're not worried about forcing your demons out of the house?"

"Sage alone cannot physically repel us," Chaos said.

"But the odor is pungent enough to make us voluntarily leave." Mayhem wrinkled his nose and rose to his feet.

"Sit down. You're not going anywhere." I dropped crushed mugwort, a dash of wormwood, and some yarrow and mandrake into a copper bowl. "You two are as much a part of the family curse as we are. Hecate needs to see us working together."

I took the bowl to the living room and set it on the coffee table. Ash put black candles on either side, and I added two dog figurines to the altar.

"How can we help?" Miles asked.

"Oh, shit." Shade stared at his phone. "*Boston Live* released a story about a serial killer who has disemboweled his third victim in the city. Three there. Three here. That makes six total. It can't be the same fae we killed this morning."

"Livers removed?" I dragged the table away from the sofa so we could sit on the floor around it.

"It doesn't say." Miles gazed at Shade's phone over his shoulder. "Should we tell them what's going on?"

"No." I rubbed my forehead to chase away the headache threatening to form. "We got lucky when the Boston Magic Society blamed Chrys for the library incident. The less contact we have with them, the better."

Miles flashed an incredulous look. "But people are dying. If they knew about the fae, they could help."

Ash laughed dryly. "I doubt a bunch of dark witches will care about humans getting murdered. Let Boston deal with Boston."

"But they will care about a fae invasion and the potential collapse of the veil if it happens." Shade returned his phone to his pocket.

I tapped my finger against my lips as an idea formed in my mind. "Miles, do you still have the number of the woman you seduced? What was her name?"

He cringed. "Wendy. But I didn't seduce her."

"You just led her on and promised her a dinner date if she let you into the BMS library." I arranged the pillows on the couch, making our space more inviting for the goddess. "Totally not seductive. Do you have her number?"

His shoulders inched toward his ears. "Yeah..."

"Call her. Make good on your promise and arrange a dinner date. You'll find out what Boston knows and gently feed her information that she can report back."

"How diabolical." Mayhem grinned. "I like it."

Miles sighed. "I'll text her after the ritual."

I shook my head. "Do it now, and then you and Shade go patrol. The curse is a family affair. I don't want anyone else's energy clouding our intent."

Shade's brow slammed down. "It's our intent too. We all want to end this."

"Your Priestess is right," Mayhem said. "Hecate can be tricky. Her mystery eludes comprehension, but she is more likely to respond if the request comes only from those directly involved."

Shade let out a dry laugh. "You speak like you've actually met her."

Mayhem shrugged. "I have."

"As have I," Chaos added.

"Hmpf." Shade jerked his head toward the door. "C'mon, Miles. Let's go kick some fae ass without them."

Miles followed him downstairs, and I gathered fire in my fingertip to light the sage.

Ash opened the window, and I smudged the room, fanning

extra smoke into the four corners. "Negativity be gone. Only love and light may remain."

Yes, I might have fanned some in Mayhem's direction, but in my defense, he had a helluva negative attitude that grated on my last nerve. He coughed hard, narrowing his eyes at me. Chaos wrinkled his nose, his lips peeling back in disgust.

Neither of them moved from their seats, and I had to admit I was a little disappointed. It would have been fun to watch them get sucked out the window like the vampires in *True Blood* when Sookie rescinded their invitation.

Ash let out a tiny cough before closing the pane. "That's strong. I forgot how potent a new smudge stick can be."

I held her gaze, trying to keep my expression neutral. The smell wasn't strong at all.

"Let's do this thing." She plopped onto the floor, sitting cross-legged at the coffee table, and I extinguished the smudge stick before setting it by the bowl.

Chaos joined Ash on the floor, sitting next to her, which meant I had to sit by Mayhem. Ash smirked as we settled on the floor across from them, and I pursed my lips. My little sis read so many romance novels, I could only imagine what tropes she was applying to our situation. Forced proximity? Enemies to lovers? Thank the goddess we had more than one bed.

I laid my arm on the table, and Ash rested her hand in mine. The guys did the same, and I reluctantly...*very* reluctantly... slipped my other hand into Mayhem's. The same, not unpleasant, pin-pricking sensation danced across my palm before spiraling up my arm. He wasn't actively sharing his power, but something magical permeated his skin, spreading through my body and waking up nerves I never knew existed.

"Hecate prefers to call our king Hades, so it's best if that's how you refer to him during the ritual." Chaos's voice drew my attention away from the sensations in my body and back to the issue at hand.

I said a silent thank you to my sister's demon before tugging from Ash's grasp and lighting the candles. Staring at a flame, I allowed my vision to blur until everything in my periphery bled into nothingness. The fire flickered in response to our magic, stilling as we all cleared our minds and focused on our goddess.

"Everyone ready?" Ash asked.

We all murmured our agreement, and she lit the bowl of herbs ablaze before placing her palm in mine once more. "We call on the goddess Hecate," she said. "Please accept our offering and show us a sign of your presence."

I opened my senses, searching the ether for a signal that the goddess had heard our request. All I felt was the low, prickling vibration of the demon sitting next to me. Funny... I couldn't recall feeling Chaos's energy this strongly, even when he'd held my hand.

"Hecate, please hear our words," I said. "We are desperate for your assistance."

"Do you feel her?" Ash asked.

"I don't." I looked at her, my vision swimming back into focus.

"She either didn't hear your plea, or she chose to ignore it." Mayhem kept a tight grip on my hand.

"Shoot." Ash tugged from my grasp and stood. "We forgot the crystals."

She padded to the shelf and grabbed a piece of black tourmaline and labradorite before setting them by the candles.

"Good choice." I laid my arm on the table and took her hand again.

"What do the crystals do?" Chaos asked.

"Black tourmaline is for protection and grounding," Ash said. "We need the grounding properties now, but we used its protection to get through the electrified doorway at the BMS library."

"I remember." He smiled, flashing her an endearing look.

"Labradorite enhances intuition and psychic abilities," I said. "It will help us sense her in the ether."

"Apparently, you don't perform this ritual often or you would not have forgotten such an essential part," Mayhem said, goading me yet again.

"Excuse me for having a lot on my already-overflowing plate. At least I didn't lose a wrestling match with a puppy." I fought the urge to stick out my tongue.

His teeth clicked. "Chaos slipped marrow from hellcat bones into my pocket before the match. Had I known, it would have ended differently."

I pressed my lips together. If I wasn't hyper-focused on connecting with Hecate, I'd have laughed. "Let's try again while the offering is still burning."

I stared at a flame again, allowing my vision to blur, opening myself to the ether once more. "We call on the goddess

Hecate. Please accept our offering and show us a sign of your presence."

We waited, searching, focusing... Nothing.

"Chaos, you try," Ash said.

He recited the same words. Ash said them after him, but still I felt nothing.

"Your turn." I squeezed Mayhem's hand.

"If she ignored the three of you, I doubt she'll heed my call."

"Try," Ash and I said in unison.

He cleared his throat. "Hecate, please cast all animosity aside and hear the witches' plea."

Animosity? What history did he have with the goddess of witchcraft? I made a mental note to ask him later.

"Make your request," Chaos said. "She could be listening but prefers to keep her presence shrouded."

"It's worth a shot." I straightened my spine. "Goddess, as you must know, these demons cursed our bloodline centuries ago. They have agreed to help us break it and to restore the veil to its rightful state, but we need your help."

"You forged an amulet with Hades," Ash said. "One that Discord won in a bet. It's here, in our realm, and we need to find it. Please guide us on our quest. As we will it, so mote it be."

I stilled, focusing on nothing but the ether, seeing nothing but the flame, hearing nothing but my pulse in my ears. My body swayed, going deeper and deeper into the trance. I stayed there, waiting, feeling, listening.

Nothing. No answers. Not even a tiny clue.

With a deep inhale, I brought my senses back to the present

and tugged from Ash's and Mayhem's grasps. "Well, that was a waste of time."

Ash's brow furrowed. "She's never ignored us before. Could it be because the guys are with us?"

Chaos stood. "We'll wait downstairs while you try it again."

Mayhem rose to his feet, and I gave him a pointed look. "Do not leave the building."

"I wouldn't dare." Amusement danced in his eyes as he lied.

When the demons left the room, I dumped the offering and refilled the bowl with fresh herbs before smudging the living room again. Ash sneezed four times before closing the window.

"I think I'm developing an allergy," she said.

"Maybe so." Or maybe her connection to Chaos was making her react to the herbs. Or worse...the curse was trying to take hold. Ash...the third-born Holland witch...would wipe out the entire coven if it came to fruition. Something inside her would have to fundamentally change for her to purposely hurt people. She was the kindest person I knew, but her reaction to the sage didn't bode well.

I lit the herbs as she sat across from me, and we made the offering again, pleading with the goddess to hear us, to help us.

"Anything?" I asked.

"Nothing," Ash replied.

"Damn." Fatigue washed over me, but it wasn't my body that was tired. It was my soul. If our goddess had abandoned us, how could we ever complete our quest and set things right?

I stood and returned the crystals and figurines to the shelf. "We could scry for it."

Ash took the bowl and candles to the kitchen. "We could, but I don't think I have enough vim left."

I rolled my neck. "I don't either, honestly. Not after how much we've used today."

She rinsed the bowl and dried it with a dishcloth. "We could also think rationally and look for it in the one place it most likely is."

"Good idea. And we can grab some lunch while we're out. I'm starving."

CHAPTER 14
EMBER

We stood on the sidewalk in front of Chrys's building, a two-story, brown brick structure with green shutters. Clouds blanketed the sky, the sun's warm rays unable to penetrate the thick layer, and chilly October air whipped through my hair, blowing it into my face. I pulled it back and tugged a band from my wrist with my teeth, but when I tried to tie it into a low ponytail, it slipped through my fingers. It was too short to pull back.

"Dammit." I put the band back on my wrist and tucked my purple locks behind my ears.

Mayhem gave me a quizzical look. "Is there a problem with your hair?"

"An imp gave me a bad haircut." I started toward the steps and paused. "Ash, are there any wards?"

My sister stepped forward and did her thing, sending golden sparkles toward the building. The front walk was clear, but thank the goddess I asked, because Ash's magic clung to the door and windows, revealing a nasty spell.

My lip curled. "I'm beginning to hate earth witches. Can we neutralize it, or do I get to unravel it the fun way...with my sword?"

"What makes you think an earth witch cast this spell?" Mayhem stepped toward the front porch, but Chaos stopped him with a hand on his forearm. "Was Chrys the only magical being residing here?"

"I don't think. I know." I pointed to Ash's magic-revealing sparkles, trailing my finger to the flowerbed beneath a window. "Follow the glitter. The ward is rooted in the ground."

"Fascinating," he said. I didn't detect sarcasm in his voice, but I doubted he found witch magic the slightest bit interesting.

"It's fresh too." Ash examined the hex, her eyes calculating. "Like yesterday fresh. And if my gut is right, it's to keep out witches. The human residents won't feel a thing when they pass through it."

"Her mom did it." My shoulders slumped. "She probably cleared out the apartment already."

"Maybe not." Ash rummaged through her Mary Poppins bag and handed a bowl to Chaos before dumping a few herbs into it. "Grief has a way of paralyzing people. Going through a deceased loved one's belongings is difficult at best. It can also be devastating."

"She put the ward up to keep you away from her possessions until she found the strength to go inside." Chaos held the bowl steady as Ash added three drops of oil, making the potion pop and sizzle.

My sister nodded. "I couldn't bring myself to go inside Cinder's room when we thought she was dead."

"Knowing Discord, she most likely *is* dead." Mayhem started up the steps.

"Whoa. Hold your horses." I grabbed his arm, and prickly tingles shimmied up to my elbow before I let go. "Ash has to deactivate the ward first."

He rubbed his arm where I had touched him, his brow furrowing as if he felt the electric sensation too. "The ward is to keep out witches, which I am not." He opened the door and strode right on in like he owned the place.

"You don't know which apartment is hers," I shouted from the sidewalk.

"Then I will try them all." The door clicked shut behind him.

"Mother effer." I cast my gaze to the left and then the right, making sure no humans were around before I drew my sword. Clutching it in both hands, I raised it above my head, sucking in a breath and steeling myself for the blast of magic I was about to feel.

"Ember, wait." Ash poured a potion on the ground where the spell was rooted. "It'll take a few minutes to dissolve."

"We don't have a few minutes with Mayhem on the loose." I barely heard Chaos say, "I can..." before I brought my blade down, slicing through the hex.

The moment the enchanted silver hit magic, a sharp, vibrating pain shot up my arms and rattled my teeth. The spell popped, creating a flash of blinding light and making my ears ring so loudly I couldn't hear anything else.

Pushing through the pain, I opened the door and strode inside. It took a minute for my eyes to adjust to the dim hallway. I blinked, willing the world back into focus, and when my vision cleared, I found the first door on the left ajar, the jamb busted where the lock had been engaged.

"Are you kidding me? Mayhem!" I whisper shouted.

He strolled into the hall, carrying a bag of candy, his mouth full of chocolate. "That is a human's apartment," he mumbled around the stolen treat.

"That..." I gestured to the busted door. "Is called breaking and entering." I snatched the bag from his hands and shook it. "And this is theft. It's not how we operate."

"Oh my goddess." Ash entered the building, followed by Chaos. "Please tell me no one was home."

"The only lifeform I sensed was a feline, who darted under the sofa the moment I entered." He tried to take the bag from me, so I yanked it away and marched into the apartment.

I set the candy on the counter and returned to the hall, closing the broken door as best I could before glaring at the demon. "You can't just bust into places. There are rules and laws we have to follow, not to mention how dangerous it is to pass through a ward that could have hidden, deadly magic woven through it."

Ash laughed dryly. "Hello, Ms. Pot. Have you met Mr. Kettle?"

She brushed past me, heading to apartment 1E. "We're

lucky that ward didn't have an alarm. You both need to chill the eff out and think before you act."

My sister sent her magic-revealing sparkles toward Chrys's door, but they dissipated, a few clinging here and there while the rest dissolved. "There's evidence of an old ward, but it's not active." She pulled out her lock-picking equipment and did her thing.

"A witch of her power wouldn't need one." Mayhem closed his eyes, his lips curving up slightly at the memory before he rested a steely gaze on Ash's back.

Chaos moved to stand behind her, blocking her from Mayhem's view.

"We're in." Ash rose and pushed the door open before stepping inside.

"Is this not breaking and entering?" Mayhem crossed his arms. "Don't you have laws you must obey?" This time I definitely detected sarcasm.

"It's just entering. No breaking involved." I gestured to the door Ash and Chaos had disappeared through. "Go."

He looked down his nose at me. "Ladies first."

I lifted my chin. "Age before beauty, your royal pain in my assness. I'm not letting you out of my sight."

He fought his grin, and I didn't miss the amusement dancing in his eyes before he stepped inside Chrys's apartment. I followed, gently closing the door behind me.

The air hung stagnant, like the doors and windows hadn't been opened for weeks, and dust motes floated in the living room, glinting in the long rays of afternoon sun filtering through the blinds. A book lay open on the coffee table, and

Ash peered at the pages, bringing her fingers to her lips on a quick intake of breath.

"Those are the sigils Chrys used to control Shade and Miles." She sank onto the sofa. "Where did she find a grimoire with this kind of power in it?"

I stood next to her and looked at the pages. It felt wrong to have a seat in the living room of our nemesis, so I crouched, leaning my elbows on my thighs. "You're right. We should take this home. It could give us clues about her involvement in this ordeal."

I hovered my hands over the book and recoiled when the sticky funk of dark magic washed over my palms. "It's thick. We need to cleanse it before we handle it."

"Cleanse it of what? It's not dirty." Mayhem slammed the grimoire shut and lifted it up and down as if testing its weight. "It's not thick either. Just a few hundred pages."

I straightened. "Thick with dark magic, smartass."

"If light witches aren't careful, it can seep into our psyches and make us sick." Ash stood and strode toward the kitchen. "But since it doesn't seem to bother you, feel free to carry it home for us."

He dropped it onto the counter. "I'm here for the amulet, not to be your pack mule."

"I'll carry it." Chaos grabbed the book and tucked it under his arm. "Ash, can you locate the artifact?"

Mayhem yanked out a drawer and dumped it on the counter. "We'll find it if we have to tear the place apart."

He pulled on the next drawer, and I popped my hip against it, slamming it shut. "We don't have to tear anything apart. If it's here, Ash will find it. Now, be quiet and let her search."

"'Magical amulet' is so vague. It would help if I knew exactly what I was looking for." She took a deep breath and closed her eyes. "There are so many artifacts in here, it's hard to differentiate them."

"Don't start doubting yourself now." I rubbed her back. "You've got this."

She nodded and stilled, her energy pulling inward as she opened herself to whatever it was she felt when she used this power. Mayhem arched a skeptical brow, his eyes... Honestly, his eyes had been calculating since the moment we brought him into our world.

Without a word, Ash paced across the kitchen toward Chrys's bedroom, and a smile spread across my face. I elbowed Chaos. "Look at her go. I'm so proud of her."

"As am I." He followed her, flipping the light switch on his way into the room.

Mayhem turned to the cabinets, opening each one until he found Chrys's stash of snacks. He stuck his hand into the Twinkie box, ready to steal yet another treat, so I slapped the door hard, bouncing it off his arm.

"Can't you go five minutes without shoving sugar into your mouth?"

In half a nanosecond, his expression morphed from mildly amused to downright scary. His brow slammed down over his eyes, the purple in his irises glowing, his lip pulling into a sneer.

The change in his demeanor barely had time to register in

my mind before he moved, his arm jutting out, his thick fingers wrapping around my throat. I gasped, and he squeezed, lifting me from the ground as a sinister growl rumbled in his chest.

His grip tightened, leaving me mere seconds before he crushed my windpipe. The rhythm of my pulse whooshing in my ears quickened, and I prayed to the goddess I could maintain control over my bladder.

"You push me too far, witch." His voice turned gravelly, underworldly. "I am a Prince of Hell, and you will…"

Before he could finish his tirade, I lifted my knee, snatched a dagger from my thigh holster, and shoved the blade two inches into his chest. His eyes widened in shock, and his grip loosened enough for me to drag in a breath as he lowered me to the ground.

"I could snap your neck," he growled.

"Not before I could pierce your heart." I pushed it in a smidge farther.

His eyes locked with mine, and the purple glow faded to a gentle pulse. We stood there, frozen in a draw for what felt like an eternity. His gaze dipped down to my mouth, his eyes tightening as they met mine. I couldn't tell if he wanted to kill me, eat me, or bang my brains out right there in the kitchen. Maybe it was all three.

"Hey, Em?" Ash called. "I found something."

I pulled my blade out an inch. "Truce?"

He loosened his grip, resting his hand at the base of my throat. "For now."

I stepped backward, out of his grasp, and ran the tip of my

dagger under the faucet to rinse off his poisonous blood. "Sorry about your shirt."

He glided his finger over the slit I'd made with my blade and shrugged.

"Ember?" Ash called again.

"Coming." I gestured for him to go first, and he conceded, striding into the bedroom like our little standoff hadn't just happened.

I took a step, and my knees nearly buckled. I caught myself on the counter and inhaled a deep, hopefully calming breath while my stomach roiled. There had been nothing little about that standoff at all. He'd gone from being a thorn in my side to giving me a near-death experience in a blink.

Maybe I had pushed him too far.

After two more breaths, I tested my legs. Thankfully, they held, and I put one foot in front of the other, willing my hands to stop trembling as I joined the others in the bedroom.

Or rather...the bathroom.

Chaos and Ash stood on either side of the toilet, peering into the tank. Mayhem loomed toward it, but Chaos put a hand on his chest.

"That's not..." He leaned forward, and Chaos pushed him back, freeing enough space for me to slide in.

An unassuming red stone rested at the bottom of the tank. Twisted wire created a cage around it, with a long black cord laced through to make it wearable. "Is that it?"

"It's a piece of it," Ash said.

I dunked my hand into the tank to scoop it up, but Ash

grabbed my arm. "Don't touch it. Look what it did to Chrys. It drove her mad."

"That's only one theory." I tugged from her grasp. "How else are we going to get it home if we don't touch it? Bring the whole toilet with us?"

"I will carry the amulet," Mayhem said.

"No." Chaos widened his stance, blocking his path to the commode.

"What's the matter, brother? Afraid to be the least powerful prince?"

Chaos let out an irritated sigh. "It's a broken shard, and we don't know which aspects of the magic reside in this piece. Until it's complete, no one touches it."

"We need to contain it." Ash slipped her bag off her shoulder, laying it on the counter before removing the lid from a clear plastic container and dumping out a wad of cotton balls. "We can scoop it up with this and put a ward on it to keep the magic from seeping out."

"How are you going to keep the toilet juice from spilling? It doesn't look watertight. Hold on." I slipped past the demons and returned to the kitchen, rummaging through the drawers until I found what I was looking for.

I returned to the bathroom and clicked a set of tongs triumphantly. Because everyone knew before you used tongs, you had to click them. I didn't make the rules.

"Ready?" I clicked them again.

Ash held up the container. "Do it fast before the magic travels up the tongs."

I grabbed the offending artifact and dropped it into the box.

Ash set it on the counter, resting the lid on top before taking out her mixing bowl and three jars of herbs.

"Crappity crap. I'm out of garlic." She held up an empty jar.

"I'm sure there's some in the kitchen. Do you have enough marjoram and patchouli?"

"Plenty." She dumped them into the bowl and crushed them with the back of a spoon.

I paced to the kitchen yet again and located a bottle of garlic powder. When I returned, I found the guys in Chrys's bedroom, going through her drawers. "What are you doing?"

Chaos opened a jewelry box. "Looking for clues."

Mayhem scoffed. "My brother's little witch ordered us out of the room, and he obeys her like a hellhound on a leash."

He slammed the box shut. "She asked us to look for clues."

"Why do I have to keep reminding people we're on the same team?" I strode past them and joined Ash in the bathroom.

She mixed the spell and used a makeup brush to apply the powder to the box before holding her hand toward me. "Cast it together?"

"Of course." I took her hand and focused on the container. "Vessel tight, vim bright, hold the magic until the end of our plight," we said in unison. "As we will it, so mote it be." We sent our energy into the spell, and the powder glowed dark green before flashing once and dissipating.

Ash tapped the plastic, yanking her finger away the moment it made contact. "I think it's good." She tentatively tapped it three more times before picking it up. "It's contained."

Chaos appeared in the doorway with the dark grimoire tucked under his arm. "Would you like me to carry that too?"

Mayhem stood behind him, that same calculating look in his eyes, so I took the container from her. "I'll hold on to this one." No way was he getting his hands on it.

"Will it be enough to convince Discord to cross over?" Ash asked.

"Absolutely not," Mayhem said. "It was his most cherished possession."

I eyed the stone shard. "Fabulous. How do we find the rest of it?"

CHAPTER 15
MAYHEM

Our initial search for the remaining piece of the amulet proved fruitless. After Ember and Ash had neutralized the dark magic coating the stolen grimoire, they had scoured the pages in search of a clue as to where it might be. They'd found nothing, and though they possessed the ability to scry for it, Ember had insisted they slumber before trying. It seemed witches became less powerful the more magic they used, and the sisters, no matter their lineage, were no exception.

My body, in this mortal realm, also required rest, so I had lain in their sister's room. When I awoke three hours later, I went to the living room to watch the television.

Now, I stood outside Ember's doorway, watching her sleep. Silver light from the moon swept across her face like silk, her expression one of serenity. It was an expression I doubted her features could hold if she were awake.

She carried the weight of an entire coven on her shoulders. The tension in her jaw and the tightness of her eyes were the result of being thrust into a position of authority she did not want. And she had assumed the role of High Priestess because of a series of events that began to unfold when the vile Isabel summoned us...used us...with no intention of ever upholding her side of the bargain.

My lip curled at the thought. Isabel had used her wiles to trick us, offering her body to us whenever and wherever we chose. The strength of her magic when I'd lain with her had been intoxicating, but I knew now that it was a ruse. She'd sworn I felt it because we were meant to be. That fate had brought us together, and that she belonged to the three of us. That she would happily sacrifice her soul and that of her firstborn if it meant spending eternity with my brothers and me.

How could we have been so stupid?

Looking back now, I could see the warning signs. The lack of good signs. Though my anger with these witches for not allowing me to burn through their adversary and claim her magic still simmered in my soul, I had noticed the way Ash looked at my brother. The admiration in her eyes and the trust in him she exuded were unlike any I had ever witnessed. Not from anyone...especially Isabel.

The same was true about the way Chaos looked at Ash, how he interacted with her. His enamor with her ran deeper than the physical, but to say fate brought us here to be with these witches, that all of this had been set up four hundred years ago...

The idea was not only preposterous, it could be detrimental to my exacting of revenge.

A snort drew my attention back to Ember's bed. She stirred, wiping the drool from her cheek with the back of her hand and rolling to her side to face me, still fast asleep.

She had nearly vanquished me today. To be fair, I had nearly broken her neck, but the fact I'd let my guard down enough to allow her the opportunity was more than alarming. Still...when her knife had entered my chest, mere inches of muscle separating my heart from the would-be blade of my demise, I hadn't felt fear, panic, or even the anticipation of returning home.

No, what I had felt was even more alarming than the fact she could have done it. Admiration and respect had tightened my chest along with the other sensations warming my groin and making my dick harden. She was a formidable opponent, and if her performance in the bedroom was half as skilled as the way she fought, she could be an extraordinary partner.

It was a shame I had to kill her.

I would wait, however. They had enticed me to stay with the promises of fighting fae and making Isabel's descendants pay for her crimes, but the real prize existed in pieces in this realm and these witches had the power to find them all.

The magic of Discord's amulet would be mine, even if I had to absorb it broken shard by broken shard. And my first dose of power lay on the nightstand next to Ember's bed.

Her wards blocked entry to anyone with ill intent. I possessed none toward her at this moment in time, so I crossed the threshold without hesitation.

The second I stepped into her room, a blast of vibration shot into the space. She moved so quickly, had I not been a demon, I would have missed her attack. Reaching under her pillow, she retrieved a nine-inch dagger, which she hurled toward me while simultaneously shooting to her feet. I dodged the blade, and the point stuck in the doorjamb where I had stood.

She exhaled a curse and grabbed a knife from something attached to her bedside table, pointing the blade at me. "Take a step closer, and you can go to Hell."

I raised my hands in a show of innocence. "I mean you no harm."

"No?" She crept around the bed, putting it between us. "Then why are you in my room? And don't you dare say you wanted a little naughty time because I am not interested."

I had to laugh. "As much as I would enjoy ravishing you and making you beg for more, that is not why I'm here."

Her sword hung on the wall above her bed, and she laid the knife on the mattress to retrieve her favorite weapon. "You're the one who'd be begging, mister cocky with a capital C. I'd make you scream my name."

"Don't make promises you can't keep. Nothing gives a demon more pleasure than torturing those who don't hold up their end of a bargain." Though I would love to watch her try, especially with her current state of undress.

Her hair, disheveled from sleep, hung in tangled waves around her face, framing her delicate features. The tightness around her dark brown eyes had returned, and she licked her lips, drawing my attention to her mouth.

My gaze dipped lower, admiring the outline of her nipples through her thin t-shirt, and then sliding down her form to the simple black panties covering the spot I had the sudden urge to lick.

Snapping out of my stupor, I gestured to the enchanted box on her nightstand. "I'm here for the amulet."

"You can't have it." She leaped onto the mattress and grabbed the container before dropping to the floor in front of me. "We're giving it to Discord, so he'll bring our sister and parents back."

I pulled the dagger from the wall behind me and tossed it pommel over tip, catching the handle on its descent. "You feel a sense of loyalty to your family."

"Of course I do." She eyed the blade, clutching her sword in both hands. "Don't you?"

"Not the way you do." I turned the dagger handle toward her and set it on the nightstand before raising my hands once more and backing toward the wall. "Your sister can find things with her mind. What is your special power?"

She took the blade and returned it to the bed, beneath her pillow. "Aside from controlling fire, which we all can do, I don't have one. That's why I learned to fight."

"Are you not envious of Ash? Would you not give anything to possess more magic?"

She relaxed her posture, lowering her arm so the sword pointed at the ground. "I could never be jealous of her. That power belongs to her. She inherited it from our father, and it suits her just like the feeling of a weapon in my hands suits me."

I nodded, regarding her. "Perhaps your ability in battle is your magical gift."

She laughed. "Doubtful."

"Are you sure?"

She opened her mouth to respond, but the words escaped her. She shook her head, her posture relaxing more. "Aside from my fire, I have to work at everything I do, and apparently, spellcasting needs to be at the top of my list." She waved a hand at the door. "I can't even set up a ward to keep out ill intent."

"I had no ill intent toward you. I simply came to claim what should be mine." I took a step toward her. When she didn't stiffen, I took another. "I passed through your ward with no issue, yet your alarm still activated. Why?"

"The alarm was for anything demonic. I'm going to put this down. Don't make me pick it up again."

"I have no intention to." Though I couldn't shake the temptation of taking the amulet shard she still clutched in one hand.

"Good." She returned her sword to the rack above her bed and stepped toward her dresser, where she put the box into a drawer before taking out a pair of sweats and pulling them on. "Why do you think the amulet should be yours? Discord made the bet and won."

My jaw tightened at the reminder. "Why should he hold more power than me? Than Chaos? We should be the same, equals."

She tilted her head, studying me. "Equal doesn't always mean same."

"How could it not?" I held her mesmerizing gaze. The

common dark brown of her irises should have been unremark-able, but as I looked into them, I felt a pull in the core of my being. An invisible tether attempting to form, threatening to drown me in her eyes.

"My sisters and I are equals, but we're very different from each other." She sank onto the edge of the mattress, folding one leg beneath her. "We all have our own strengths and weak-nesses, but when we come together, there's no stopping us."

"Does one of you not possess more abilities than the others? Surely your differences, your weaknesses, aren't equal in their detriment." I leaned against the wall, crossing my arms.

Ember sighed, casting her gaze to the ceiling and tilting her head side to side as she thought. "If I had to pick one, now it would be Ash. Our mother had bound her fire magic to try and keep the curse from coming to fruition. Now that the ties have been broken, she's the most powerful witch I've ever met."

"And it doesn't bother you, being magically weaker than your sister?" I couldn't fathom how it could not.

She shrugged. "Not really. She lacks self-confidence, and she's careful to a fault, but she also keeps the coven running and provides protection to my team. We couldn't keep the beasties at bay without her."

"I see."

She arched a brow. "Do you?"

"No."

"I guess that's the difference between light witches and demons. We love our families, and we're loyal to our covens." She picked up her phone and swiped the screen, letting out a relieved sigh before setting it on her nightstand.

"Discord bet against me and won a token that gives unnatural power to its bearer. Chaos allied himself with witches and allowed you to vanquish me back to my prison, denying me of the magic I should have received through my summoning. Whatever love or loyalty I could have felt for my brothers died with their betrayal. They don't want my power to grow."

"Maybe because they're afraid of what you might do with it. Or maybe it's not even about you." She stretched her arms over her head, her cropped shirt lifting above her abdomen, revealing the delicate skin beneath her breasts.

Heat pooled in my groin, and I looked away, contemplating her words. "Do you fear Ash since she came into her power?"

"Not Ash herself." She rose and strode to the dresser again, taking out her standard black clothes and laying them on the surface. "But I do fear the curse and what it could make her do."

"Are you willing to stop her, should we not locate the rest of the amulet in time?"

Her head snapped toward me, her eyes narrowing in warning. "We're going to find it, and you are going to end her curse. Now, it's almost dawn. I'm going to take a shower, and then we'll discuss our next steps. Close the door on your way out and get ready to move."

"Are you not taking a weapon into the bathroom? What if I decide to take you up on your offer to make me scream your name?"

She smiled slyly. "I have more weapons hidden in this house than you can begin to imagine, and next time, I won't hesitate to go all the way to your heart."

My stomach tightened, my heart pounding out a rhythm that said she already had.

CHAPTER 16
EMBER

"That was weird, wasn't it?" I stood in the bathroom towel-drying my hair and talking to my reflection like a crazy person. After the heart-to-heart I'd just had with a *demon prince* and the way I'd warmed to him, I might be certifiable.

Since the moment we'd brought Mayhem into this realm, he and I had communicated by taking jabs and mocking each other. Hell, we'd almost killed each other less than twenty-four hours ago. This was the first real conversation we'd had, and dammit if he didn't show a bit of humanity during it.

I hung the towel on a rack and pulled on my underwear, pausing before I grabbed my pants. I hadn't missed his reaction to seeing me braless and in my skivvies, and dammit again if I hadn't found a smidge of pleasure in his heated gaze.

After shoving my legs into my pants, I grabbed my shirt,

pulling it on as I walked back to the bathroom. "Damn sexy demon, and his damn insecurities."

He felt inferior to his brothers. That much was obvious, but I didn't get why. Ash's struggle with self-esteem made sense. Her fire magic had been bound her entire life, and though we'd all tried to make sure she didn't feel less-than, she always did.

As far as I'd seen with Mayhem, he was just as strong as Chaos, though maybe a little rougher around the edges. His mind magic was nothing less than deadly, so if demons really were as evil and human-hating as we thought, it seemed to me that Mayhem was *more* powerful in the brain games department.

I turned on the blow dryer and blasted my hair, running a brush through it as I went. Humanity. Insecurities. Mayhem had shown me a vulnerability I'd have thought he'd keep to himself. I wished he'd kept it to himself, but here I was feeling an inkling of...something...for a demon.

Was it fondness? Nah, I wouldn't go that far. I still wouldn't hesitate to lob off his head and stab him through the heart, and the lobbing might be why I didn't push my blade all the way in yesterday. That *was* why. He'd had me by the throat, and while I could have vanquished him, his skull would've gone with him and he'd be free from prison and the debt he owed me.

Maybe he wasn't the wicked, selfish son-of-a-bitch hell-bent on making our lives as hard as possible that I first thought, but he was still a friggin' demon and he couldn't be trusted.

My hair dried in half the time it used to, and after running my fingers through it, I put on my boots and headed to the living room. A few pale rays of early morning sun provided the only illumination in the space. I flipped the light switch on and paced past the couch and into the kitchen.

Shade had stayed the night with Miles at his house, so I only brewed half a pot of coffee. As it percolated, I stared at the *drip, drip, drip* of liquid falling into the pot and contemplated everything that had been put on hold while we tried to end the family curse.

Shade's house had burned to the ground days...maybe weeks ago. I couldn't tell you how much time had passed since Ash found Cinder's journal and possessed herself with Chaos. The days had bled together into one fuzzy, chaotic mess of mayhem and discord.

Their names sure were appropriate.

I grabbed four mugs from the cabinet and set them on the counter when my phone's ringtone blasted from my pocket, making me jump. I'd forgotten to change it back to silent mode when I woke up.

Spellbound Axe lit up the screen, and I closed my eyes, pinching the bridge of my nose before answering the call. "Hey..." Wariness stretched out the word. "I'm sorry I haven't called you back. I've—"

"Six voicemails, Ember. I've left you six voicemails and sent five texts, and you couldn't be bothered to return one of them." To say my boss sounded beyond pissed would be an understatement. "What could you possibly have going on in your life that you couldn't check in and let me know if you ever planned to come back?"

Battling demons. Solving murders. Trying to stop the fae from taking over Salem. My jaw clenched. "Does it matter?"

"No. You're fired." The vibration on my phone told me she'd ended the call.

"That's what I thought." I shoved it into my pocket, poured myself a cup of socially acceptable chemical dependency, and leaned against the counter.

Ash's laughter drifted into the room, followed by the sound of drawers opening and closing. I was halfway done with my coffee by the time the lovebirds joined me, and Ash gave me a quizzical look as she stepped into the kitchen.

"Where's Mayhem?"

"In Cinder's room. He woke me up before dawn, trying to take the amulet shard from me. I sent him to get ready to move."

Ash flicked her gaze to Chaos before widening her eyes at me. "He's not in there. Chaos checked before we came out."

"He—" I slammed down my mug, sloshing coffee onto the counter. "Are you sure?" Without waiting for an answer, I paced across the room and went into the hall.

"Mayhem!" I shouted, not trying to hide the irritation in my voice. I stomped into Cinder's room. The bedsheets lay in a tangle, and a wet towel had been carelessly dropped on the hardwood. "You slimy, effing snake."

My boots thudded in the hall as I marched into my parents' room, checking the bathroom for good measure on my way out. "That demon is dead."

I strapped on my weapons and sheathed my sword in my

back scabbard before returning to the front to find Ash and Chaos waiting by the door.

I barreled down the stairs and yanked my phone from my pocket to call for backup. "I'm going to kill him. I'm going to cut off his effing balls and wear them as earrings."

"There's an image I'll never be able to unsee." Ash locked the upstairs door, and she and Chaos followed me through the library and out the back.

I pressed the phone to my ear, and Shade answered on the second ring. "There's a demon on the loose. I'm sharing my location. Find us."

"We'll be out the door in five."

I pressed End and activated location sharing, which we should have kept on for all of us, all the time. I made a mental note to tell everyone later as I stomped through the parking lot and fumed.

Humanity and vulnerability, my ass. Mayhem had known exactly what he was doing, triggering the alarm on my door and the exits in a fake attempt to take the amulet. I'd been tired last night when I set them, and I'd connected them all to the same spell to use less vim. Setting off my room deactivated the others, and he'd played on my emotions to make me lower my guard.

"Where is he?" I stopped abruptly and whirled to face them, making Ash flinch. "I'm sending him back to prison."

She held up her hands. "Let's take a breath and think before we storm through the entire town and make testicular jewelry. Did he get the amulet?"

My hands balled into fists. "Of course not."

"Okay, that's good." She lowered her arms. "Did he mention something he wanted to do? Somewhere he wanted to go?"

"No. No, we just talked. He's jealous of his brothers and wants to gain more power so they can be equal." Or so he said. He probably made it up so I'd feel sorry for him, the bastard.

Chaos closed his eyes, going utterly still for a second, two, three, four. "He's close. This way." He turned and strode onto the sidewalk.

"Do we need to drive?" I asked as we followed after him.

He stopped, closing his eyes again and taking a deep breath. "Approximately two miles to the north, I sense his energy."

"You can feel him that far away?" Ash asked.

"We are connected, no matter how unruly he may be."

"We're driving. Load up." I put my sword in the floorboard compartment and started the engine while my sister and her demon climbed in.

Trying my best not to peel out of the alley, I hung a left and followed Chaos's directions to a sheep farm north of town. "Can you cloak us, Ash?" I slid out of my seat and opened the hidey hole to retrieve my sword.

She rummaged through her satchel and shook her head. "We're out."

"Oh well." I slammed the door.

"If anyone sees something they shouldn't, I can make them forget." Chaos walked on my right side, and Ash took up my left.

I wanted to tell him *absolutely not*, but at this point, we might need his mind-melting power. "No one but Mayhem gets hurt."

He chuckled. "I will do my best."

We crept past the farmer's house, clinging close to the wall before darting across to the barn. Two men worked inside, cleaning out stalls and refilling water troughs, so we tiptoed around to the side, my heart hammering in my chest as I devised my plan to vanquish a demon prince.

I would take his head, though after our first imp attack, I knew that wouldn't kill him. He'd run his mouth while I held him by his lush, dark hair. But then, I'd silence him with a dagger to his heart, and his corporeal form would disintegrate before getting sucked through the veil.

I know, I know. I said I'd wear his balls as earrings but come on. That's just gross.

"Is he in the barn?" I whispered.

"No. He's this way." Chaos strode toward the pasture like he owned the place, and there was nothing we could do but follow.

We found Mayhem crouching next to a blob of white and red. More splotches of the same shape and color dotted the field, and I shielded my eyes against the sun rising on the horizon.

"What the actual eff?" I marched toward the demon but stopped short when my gaze landed on the ball of fur. No, not fur...wool. Every sheep in the pasture had been gutted.

A spark of anger tinged with disgust lit in my belly, the flames rising to my chest. I grabbed Mayhem's shoulder and shoved, but he could have been a boulder sitting amongst the death and destruction.

"You slaughtered a herd of sheep?" I side-kicked him in the back, and he rose, his hands covered in blood. "You disgusting, lying snake."

"I did not kill these animals," he said.

"Bullshit." I unsheathed my sword. "Ash, freeze him."

Her shoulders crept toward her ears. "Yeah, that spell won't work on him. We'd have to use a containment circle."

"Oh, for Hecate's sake." I reared back, gripping my sword like a baseball bat.

"Mayhem speaks the truth." Chaos wiped his hands on a rag Ash handed him. "Their livers are gone. This was the work of the fae."

"That's okay." I rocked on my feet, tensing for attack. "He still left the house unescorted. It's reason enough for me to vanquish him."

"Hold on." Ash laid a hand on my shoulder. "If you send him back to hell now, we'll never know why he left or what brought him here."

"I don't give a shit." My muscles coiled, the tension in my arms and shoulders ready to swing with all my might.

I moved the sword half an inch when Chaos grabbed my wrist in one hand, yanking the sword from my grasp with the other. The nerve of this guy! If my sister wasn't in love with him, I'd vanquish them both.

I grabbed a dagger and lunged at Mayhem. Chaos caught me around the waist and dragged me back, holding me tightly against his chest. "Ash, get your demon under control."

Her face scrunched. "He's not the one who's out of it."

"Are you kidding me right now?" I struggled against Chaos's hold, but it was no use. I might as well have been trapped beneath a collapsed building. "He broke the rules and left the house. He betrayed our trust."

Mayhem had the audacity to laugh. "You made no such stipulation last night."

"It was implied," I said through clenched teeth, struggling again against the demon's strength.

"Implications aren't rules, and you never trusted me. There was nothing to betray." He lifted one shoulder dismissively.

"You lied to me. You told me stories to make me feel compassion for you so you could get out the door without setting off the alarm."

His brow furrowed. "Demons are known to lie, but everything I said to you was truth." He turned to Ash and held up his bloody hands. "Do you have another rag?"

She took one from her bag and gave it to him. "Whether or not you had permission to leave aside, what brought you here?"

"I sensed a rift while the rest of you were indisposed, so I came to investigate." He gestured to an invisible spot ten yards away. "It's rather large, and based on the number of dead sheep, I'd say at least five fae soldiers came through. I would seal it if I were you."

Ash tugged two bottles from her bag and cast a magic-location spell to make the rift visible. A horizontal tear in the veil stretched at least six feet wide and three feet tall. "Whoa. That's huge. I'm going to need help with this one."

Chaos released his hold, and I pointed at Mayhem. "Don't move," I said before taking my sister's hand.

She blew the mending powder onto the rift and opened to me, allowing her energy to flow out of her hand and into mine before we recited the spell in unison. The edges of the rift stitched themselves back together, leaving a three-by-two hole in the fabric of reality.

"Again," Ash said as she took another bottle from her bag and blew the powder toward the tear.

A surge of power filled my psyche, making me gasp. Chaos had taken Ash's other hand, sharing his magic with us.

"It feels good, doesn't it?" Mayhem stood next to me and wiggled his brows. "But you're getting filtered magic. Imagine getting it right from the source." He held his hand toward me, and for half a second, I was tempted to take it.

What little he'd shared with me during the summoning had been intoxicating enough, so instead, I shoved my hand into my pocket and focused on the rift. Chaos's and Ash's magic spun in my chest, hers calm and serene, his...well, it was chaotic. There was no other way to describe it.

I let it meld with my power, and we recited the incantation two more times, giving it all we had. The tear slammed shut, the fibers of the veil weaving together, blocking any more giant bugs from getting through.

I tugged from my sister's grip, breaking the connection, and heaved in a breath. "That was a doozy."

My head spun, but I couldn't tell if it was because of the rush of demonic magic dissipating in my system or the effort it had taken to seal the rift.

"What the hell?" a gruff voice said from behind us. The sound of a shotgun cocking followed, and I spun to find the men from the barn glaring at us. The one in brown coveralls lowered the barrel, pointing it directly at me.

"Now might be a good time for some mind magic," I said under my breath as I held up my hands, my fire power building, rolling from my chest to my arms. "Chaos, Ash, do your thing."

The guy in a blue t-shirt turned on his buddy, landing a punch square on his jaw. Coveralls stumbled, losing his grip on the gun and dropping it. He picked it up again and slammed the stock into Blue Shirt's stomach.

"Run," Ash said, grabbing me by the arm, but I rooted myself to the ground, refusing to budge.

If Chaos and Ash had been doing *their* thing together, they would have made Coveralls hand over the gun before Chaos scrambled both their minds, making them forget the last ten minutes.

But no, this wasn't their thing. This was Mayhem's work.

"Turn it off." I reached for my sword, but the demon caught me by the wrist and twisted my arm behind my back with so much force, my bones nearly snapped.

"Focus your violence on the ones causing trouble. I'll help you." Mayhem shoved me toward the men, and Blue Shirt clocked me in the eye.

Pain exploded across my cheek, and I stumbled, pressing my hands to my face to make sure nothing was broken.

"We don't hit women, asshole." Coveralls leveled the gun at Blue Shirt.

Normally, if a man laid a finger on me, I'd be the one

breaking arms. And that gun? I'd have ripped it from his hands and slammed the butt into his temple, sending him to Sleepyville, whether Mayhem had control of his mind or not.

Instead, a sense of calm washed over me. I took two steps back and raised my hands in a show of innocence. "Hey guys, let's talk this out. There's no need for violence."

"The hell there isn't." Coveralls fired, the sound nearly busting my eardrums as Blue Shirt flew backward, landing on the ground with a thud.

"Release them, brother." Chaos grabbed Mayhem by the throat and lifted him...all two-hundred-plus pounds of him... two inches from the ground. "Or I will help Ember vanquish you."

"Nobody needs to get vanquished." I patted Chaos on the shoulder. "I'm sure we can all come to an agreement if we talk it out."

Chaos cut his gaze to me, narrowing his eyes before turning a steely glare on his brother. "Release *her*."

Her? Was another human here that I hadn't seen?

"As you wish, *brother*." He spat out the last word.

My head spun, and I blinked rapidly as Chaos lowered him to the ground.

"Jonah!" Coveralls shouted and tossed the gun aside. He raced to the man he'd shot, dropping to his knees and sobbing. "I'm so sorry. I don't... I don't know what happened. Someone call an ambulance."

"Ash, call Patrice." I squeezed my eyes shut, shaking my head and attempting to clear my mind. What the hell had just happened? I was about to grab my sword and force Mayhem to let them go, but then...

All I'd wanted was for everyone to stop fighting.

Had Ash cast a calming spell on me? She'd done it before when I'd gotten unruly, but it had been ages. Believe it or not, I had my temper under control way more now than I did five years ago.

I scratched the back of my head. "Ash, did you...?"

"Patrice is five minutes away." She opened her satchel, dropping to her knees beside the wounded man, and all I could do was watch in confusion. "Ember, come put pressure on the wound."

"Yeah. Okay." I joined her on the ground, and Coveralls sat back on his heels.

"I couldn't have done that. I would never." He blinked at me, his eyes dazed. I knew the feeling. "Who shot him?"

"You did." I pressed a towel to the top part of the wound while Ash used tweezers to pick the buckshot out of the lower half. "Guns are dangerous."

"So are humans who meddle in magical affairs." Mayhem crossed his arms, and Chaos closed his eyes for a long, irritated blink.

Anger boiled in my gut at the audacity of the demon. How many times would I have to tell him before he finally got it through his thick skull? "You shouldn't have done that."

He inclined his chin. "He would have killed you otherwise."

"No, he wouldn't have."

He scoffed. "You think you can outrun a shotgun blast?"

Clink, clink, clink. The tiny pieces of metal landed in Ash's bowl.

Footsteps, muffled by the grass, grew closer, and I lifted my gaze to find Shade and Miles *finally* arriving.

"Holy shit. What happened?" Shade asked.

"Mayhem happened." My voice sounded more like a growl. "Can you cloak this area in case any more farmhands decide to check on the sheep?"

"How big...?" He scanned the field, taking in the carnage of the lambs. "Whoa. Mayhem did all that?"

"I did not decimate the livestock." Mayhem straightened his spine, dropping his arms to his sides but keeping his muscles flexed. "I located the rift where the fae are getting through, and I believe some thanks are in order."

"You—" I clamped my mouth shut. There was no use arguing with a sociopath. His twisted perception of reality kept him from thinking like a normal person...and by normal, I meant people without murderous tendencies.

Gray fog rolled around us as Shade did his thing, and I moved the towel to a different part of the wound so Ash could pick out more shrapnel. Coveralls hauled himself off the ground and stumbled toward his discarded shotgun.

"Miles, can you take over?" I motioned for him and lifted my hands so he could apply pressure. Jumping to my feet, I darted around them just as Coveralls picked up his weapon.

"Who shot Jonah?" Bleary-eyed and snotty-nosed, he swung the barrel toward me, but this time my brain actually worked.

I grabbed the gun and wrenched it from his hands before

twisting his arm behind his back the same way Mayhem had held me before my thoughts went haywire. "Shade, grab a binding spell so I can neutralize this guy. He's caused enough trouble."

"On it." He dug through Ash's bag and tossed me the bottled spell.

"Standing tall or on your knees, in the name of the goddess, I force your ass to freeze." I dumped the powder onto Coveralls' head. His muscles seized, and a squeak emitted from his throat before he fell face first into the dirt.

I rolled him over so he wouldn't suffocate and dusted off my pants before whirling toward the demons. "Would either of you care to tell me what the hell just happened?"

CHAPTER 17
MAYHEM

The healer approached with another witch and stopped to peer at her phone. "The map shows they're right in front of us, but this is an empty field. Shade, is that your doing?"

The shadow witch took a deep breath and lifted a hand toward the women. His fog rolled outward, grass that once appeared gray turning green as the cloak extended and engulfed the witches.

"Oh... Oh!" Patrice ran toward the injured man and opened her healer bag. "How much blood has he lost?"

Ash and Miles stood, giving her room to perform her duties. "Not much," she said. "Thankfully, the gunman isn't a good shot." She sanitized her hands with another chemical possessing an offensive stench and offered the bottle to Miles, who did the same.

"Whoa. That's..." The other witch stared at the field of mutilated animals before blinking up at me. "Who are you?"

"My name is—"

"That's just Dave." Ember walked toward me, her tone dismissive. "He's Mark's brother. You met Mark, right? Ash's boyfriend."

"Yes. Hi, I'm Inga." She offered a timid wave.

"Dave?" I furrowed my brow.

"Just go with it," Chaos said under his breath.

Ember cleared her throat. "He prefers David, but whatever. At least we don't call him Dick. That would be more appropriate."

I was about to respond that I in no way resembled a phallic appendage when Inga asked, "Where are you from?"

"The deepest depths of Hell."

A maniacal laugh escaped Ember's throat. "Texas. He means Texas. Have you ever been? It gets so hot, you feel like you're in Hell. Humid too."

Chaos moved closer and said, "She can't know who we are. I'll explain later."

I regarded him before cutting my gaze to Ember. She mouthed the word *please*, and I suppressed a smile. I could go along with their ruse...since she begged.

"I'd say it's a pleasure to meet you, Inga, but under the circumstances..." I gestured to the man and then the field.

"What happened?" Patrice asked.

"Well, see..." Ember's expression revealed she scrambled for an answer, so I assisted her.

"A large rift formed, and several fae got through, slaughtering the sheep in their wake. This gentleman…" I motioned to the frozen gunman. "He accused the victim of disemboweling his flock and decided an eye for an eye was the best course of action. Sadly, we couldn't stop him from firing, but Ash and Ember tended to his wounds while awaiting your arrival."

The sisters blinked at me three times before Ember recovered. "Sad story, isn't it? Will he survive?"

"He'll be fine." She removed a pair of gloves and rose to her feet, eyeing me suspiciously as she picked up her bag. "I left a few marks from the buckshot, so it'll look like he barely grazed the skin."

She cut her gaze to Chaos, then Ash, and back to Ember. "I hope you froze him fast enough that he won't remember."

Ember ushered Inga toward Patrice. "Thanks so much for your help."

"A hospital could have done the same thing. Is there anything else…?" She glanced at Chaos and me.

"I know, and we're sorry to have bothered you." She lowered her voice. "Shade dropped the cloak too soon and got a little spell-happy, freezing them both. We were afraid he'd die before the binding wore off if we waited to call an ambulance."

"I…" He stiffened, his lips forming a thin line, and I held in another laugh. "Do you have any idea the amount of effort it takes to shadow an entire field like this?"

"You're doing a great job." Ember flashed a tight-lipped smile, her message less than subtle, before turning to Patrice. Any news from your end? More murders or beasties getting through?"

"You haven't heard?" She reached into her bag and pulled

out a smaller one. "A couple who'd been living beneath an overpass were found hidden in some nearby brush. It happened overnight between Salem and Boston."

"They're organizing," I said. "We must find the ones who did this."

"Here." Patrice offered the smaller bag to Ash. "I bottled some pain powders and healing creams. I need to get back to my workshop to make more. It sounds like we'll need them."

"Thanks, Patrice. Keep me posted." Ember lifted a hand as they walked away, and as they exited the cloaked area, she spun toward me. "I want answers. What makes you say they're organizing? If they're hoping to take over this realm, don't they already have a plan?" She lifted a finger, counting each question. "How do we find invisible predators? Why did they kill these sheep? What the hell were you thinking turning these men on each other, and which one of you messed with my mind?"

I attempted to suppress my smile, but the fire in her eyes and the emotion in her words made a strange flitting sensation rise from my stomach to my chest like a swarm of moths attempting to escape, attracted to the flames of Ember.

She put her hands on her hips. "Is this funny to you?"

"Not in the slightest."

"I can't hold this shadow much longer," Shade said.

Ember paced four steps in one direction before returning to her starting point. "Let's go. I need food before I can think clearly. Chaos..." She jabbed a finger toward me. "Not you. Chaos, can you *gently* make them forget we were ever here?"

"Of course," he said.

"Ash, stay with him and make sure he behaves. We'll meet you at the van." She jerked her head toward the front of the farm. "Demons first."

"Are you sure? I rather enjoy watching you walk away."

She faltered. If only for a fraction of a second, she lost her steely composure, showing that my words affected her as I intended. "Move it."

For some Hades-knew-why reason, I did as she commanded and returned to the van, climbing into the front passenger seat to await the others. Ember paced outside the vehicle, talking to herself in a voice too quiet for me to make out her words.

Apparently, Shade had given her a portable shadow spell because, while he stayed behind with my brother, the world outside our bubble remained grayscale. I didn't see the others approach. One second, we were alone, and the next, Chaos, Ash, Shade, and Miles stood outside the van.

It was no wonder shadow magic was a highly coveted power for demons to possess. Imagine the hysteria we could cause—in this realm and ours—if we could remain undetected. I had met many witches in my eternal existence, but the concentration of power in this small coven made them the greatest I had ever witnessed.

And Ember... It seemed I couldn't get enough of her.

We parked in the lot behind their home and walked three blocks to a restaurant. Shade returned to Miles's home under Ember's order to bottle more shadow magic. He had protested, as he tended to do when he wasn't involved in the coven planning.

I understood the frustration of being left out. I was always the last to learn of Lucifer's plans, *if* I learned of them at all. But Shade held no position of authority in the coven. He was not of the ruling bloodline, so he had no valid argument. I was a Prince of Hell. I belonged to the royal bloodline. Lucifer and my brothers had no acceptable reason for leaving *me* out, yet they did it all the time.

I refused to dwell on it. Once I obtained the amulet, I would show them power. Let them cast me out if they chose. I could build my own army, be king of my own realm.

And I could take Ember as my queen.

We stepped inside the restaurant, and a plethora of savory aromas tickled my senses, making my stomach growl. A young woman with blonde hair and jewelry in her nose greeted us at the door. Her nametag read Stacey.

"Welcome to the Twisted Thistle. Table for four?" she asked. "How about this one by the window?"

Ember shook her head. "That one in the back corner, please."

Stacey giggled. "You must be locals then. I've only lived here a couple of months. Come on." She picked up four menus and led the way to the table Ember had requested.

Long and rectangular, it had cushioned benches on either side rather than chairs. Ash slid across one, and Chaos sat next to her. I waited for Ember to do the same, but she cocked her head at me instead.

"I'd rather not be pinned in." I gestured for her to sit.

"Neither would I." She crossed her arms, so I did the same.

"Would you prefer a table?" Stacey asked. "There's an open one in the middle over there."

"Sit, brother," Chaos said. "I tire of your stubbornness."

"And I tire of your arrogance." I glared at him before lowering onto the bench and making room for Ember.

She sat next to me, and as she adjusted her position, her thigh rested against mine. The moths, having gone dormant on the way here, flitted back to life in my chest. What a strange effect this witch had on me.

"Can you move over? Half my ass is hanging off the seat." Ember wiggled, her left hip rubbing against mine.

My stomach tightened, and though I enjoyed the sensation, I moved away, breaking the physical contact between us lest I lift her over my shoulder and carry her to the Underworld.

How I had gone from despising all witches to desiring this one in a matter of days, I had no clue. She was nothing like any woman I had ever met, and perhaps that reason alone had enamored me. She certainly didn't use her wiles to try and seduce me, yet a seductress she was, nevertheless.

Maybe it was her element that called to me. She commanded fire as if she were born in Hell, her power more potent than any mortal's I could recall...aside from her sister. Ash could be the strongest of them all, yet Ember expressed no envy.

She must have kept it buried deep in her soul.

Once the amulet belonged to me, I could make her more powerful than every witch in her coven combined. Together, we could rule this world and the Underworld.

"Hello?" Ember's voice and her two snaps directly in front

of my face drew me from my thoughts. "Earth to Dave. What do you want to drink?"

"The blood of my enemies." I cast my gaze to Stacey, who stood at the table holding a pen and a notepad.

She giggled. "You're a funny one. I always wanted a man who could make me laugh."

"You can have him," Ember said. "And he'll have iced tea like the rest of us."

"You got it." She wrote on her pad before smiling at us. "Y'all make a cute couple."

Ember laughed dryly. "We most definitely are *not* a couple."

"Oh, I'm sorry." Her smile faded, but I couldn't suppress mine.

A cute couple... Cute wasn't the word I would have used, but Stacey's words stirred the moths in my soul.

She turned but hesitated, swiveling back toward us. "Is there anything I need to do to prepare for Halloween? I hear this town gets crazy packed."

Ash's eyes grew wary. "Take a vacation if you can. Seriously."

"I would if I could. Tuition is ridiculous since I'm not from Massachusetts, but I really wanted to attend Salem State." She shrugged. "So here I am."

"Where are you from?" Ash asked.

Tracey smiled proudly. "Houston, Texas. Born and raised."

"Ah. Hell on Earth," I said.

She looked at me with questions in her eyes. "It's not so bad if you don't mind the humidity... Oh, I get it!" she laughed. "Yeah, it can be hotter than Hell in the summertime. I'll be right back with your drinks." She disappeared through a swinging door.

"Why do you call me Dave?" I perused the restaurant's offerings, not bothering to lift my gaze. I could feel her irritation with me rolling off her skin in waves, and I hadn't yet decided if I should make it worse or relent to her yet again.

"I suggest you don't speak until I have some food in me. Hangry Ember doesn't know how to be nice." She turned her menu over and scanned the backside.

"I didn't realize you ever tried to be." It appeared I'd decided to make it worse. I simply couldn't help myself when it came to her.

She cast a sideways glance at me, her mouth tightening as if she were trying, in this moment, to be nice.

"As far as anyone else needs to know, you and I are fire witches," Chaos said. "I'm from Maine, and apparently you're now from Texas."

"You're lying to your coven?" I turned to Ember, and her nostrils twitched as she silently stewed.

"Just a few lies here and there." Ash glanced at her sister. "We're mostly omitting the important details, which I know..." She held up her hands. "Lying by omission is still lying, but here we are."

Stacey returned with four large glasses of iced tea and took our food orders. Ember asked for a hamburger containing beef and a fried egg. Based on my limited experience with modern food, the combination sounded odd, yet interesting.

"I'll have the same." I handed the menu to Stacey, and Ember side-eyed me, her nostrils flaring again. How my request for the same meal as hers could be upsetting, I couldn't fathom. Perhaps I should back off and let her cool down before resuming our normal banter.

We sat in silence until our food arrived. Ember used a serrated knife to cut her burger in half before taking a bite. While it was massive in size compared to her hands, mine were nearly twice as big as hers. I picked up the whole sandwich and took a bite.

The moment my teeth sank into it, the egg yolk burst and half the contents fell out the back of the bun in a heap. Mayonnaise coated my fingers, and gooey cheese dangled from my chin.

Ember snorted. "Did you think I cut it in half to eat like a dainty lady? Now you'll have to finish it with a fork and knife."

I chewed the surprisingly tasty combination and swallowed before scooping the mess from my plate with my fingers and shoving it into my mouth.

She shrugged. "Or do it the heathen way. It suits you."

I wiped my hands and face with a napkin and sipped my tea, giving her ample time to get food into her stomach. When she finished half the burger, I set down my glass. "My reason to believe the fae are organizing is this…"

"Stop." She wagged a finger at me. "What you did out there, making those men violent… That's not allowed. We protect the humans. We don't hurt them."

"Those men were already violent in nature. I barely sent a suggestion to them before they turned on one another." I used a fork to scoop a bite of egg and beef.

"It doesn't matter." She gestured between herself and Ash.

"We're light witches. You have to at least pretend to care about human life if we're going to get through this."

"But I don't care about it."

She threw her hands in the air and dropped them on the table. "Are you sure we can't break the curse without him?"

"Positive," my brother answered. "I'd have done it already if there were any other way."

"Fine. Just..." She rubbed her temples. "Don't do it again, okay? I'm sure you want to get rid of me as much as I want you gone, so work with us. Please."

That word again. Every time she directed it toward me, it felt like silk running over my skin. "I will try. I swear."

Her shoulders slumped. "Sadly, I know that's the best I'll get from a demon."

Indeed it was. "I believe the fae are organizing because the latest two bodies were hidden. They targeted those who would not be missed, fed out of sight, and removed their leftovers from plain view."

She curled her lip. "They're humans, not leftovers. Try to show a shred of decency."

"I'm the most indecent man you'll ever meet."

Her pheromones flared at my words, the intoxicating scents of campfire and sandalwood making my mouth water. She cleared her throat. "No kidding."

"Their methods are evolving, but I don't believe organizing is the right word." Chaos laid his fork and knife on his empty plate. "If it were the greater fae horde behind the attack, they'd have struck in full force by now."

"I see your point." I drummed my fingers on the table. "It

must be a smaller faction. Someone who has fallen out of favor with the king. Doesn't Argon have a half-brother?"

Chaos nodded. "Ignacus. He was never afforded the training of a true fae prince, and this invasion reeks of inexperience, especially his choice of Salem. The veil may be thinnest here, but the coven is the strongest."

"Indeed it does. And he is unaware that two of the three Princes of Hell currently reside in the town he has chosen to invade." I couldn't fault Ignacus for trying. Though born of royal blood, his mother was a mere servant, so the king had never taken him seriously. Invading another land to claim it as his own was a logical move.

"How do you know so much about the fae?" Ember asked.

"The same way you learned about demons," Chaos said. "With research and experience."

Ash rubbed her forehead. "So there's not going to be a full-scale invasion?"

"It depends on how many followers he was able to amass." I laid my napkin across my plate, putting my exploding lunch to rest.

Ember shoved her plate away. "Are we talking twenty? Two hundred? Two thousand?"

"Could be," I said.

"Which?"

"Any or all."

"Hey, y'all." Stacey stood before our table, clasping her hands. "I'll get these plates out of your way, and I was wondering if you'd mind closing out. My shift is over, and I've got to get to class."

"Yeah. Of course." Ember handed her a card, and she tugged a machine from her belt, tapping the plastic rectangle against it before handing both to Ember.

"Thanks for coming in."

"Thank you." Ember handed the machine to Stacey and slid off the bench. "Let's continue this chat at home. I have even more questions now."

CHAPTER 18

EMBER

Way too many tourists milled about the streets for us to continue our conversation outside, so we walked most of the way home in silence. Ash slowed down as we passed an antique shop, but I kept going full speed ahead. One of her jobs in the coven was perusing the local shops and confiscating any artifacts that contained real magic.

"Ember," she shouted, but I kept walking.

"We don't have time for that now," I said over my shoulder before returning my gaze to the pair of demons in front of me.

"Ember!" she nearly screeched, stopping me mid-stride.

I whirled toward her as she jutted her thumb toward the window and mouthed *there's a gnome.*

"Oh for Hecate's sake." I started to call for the guys, but what good would they do? Gnomes were a breed all their own, not demonic, not fae or vampire either. They were just venomous little pests who lived amongst the elves across the veil, tending to their gardens, but digging up ours every chance they got.

Ash disappeared into the shop, and I followed right behind. The dim lighting inside starkly contrasted the bright afternoon. I blinked, trying to force my eyes to adjust, when a two-foot-tall ball of fur and blubber darted past me and headed down the book aisle.

Ash linked arms with Betty, the shop owner with soft pink hair and more laugh lines than I could count, and led her toward the back corner, far away from me and the annoying little bugger chewing on the corner of a children's book.

He spat out the paper, wiping his tongue with his grubby hands in disgust, and I reached beneath my jacket for my knife. Gripping the handle, I scanned the ceiling and corners, making sure Betty hadn't invested in security cameras since the last time I was here. She hadn't, so I crept toward the gnome, doing my best not to startle him.

The door opened, making a bell chime, and Chaos called, "Ash?"

At the sound of his deep voice, the gnome jumped, startled. His gaze locked on me, and he growled, peeling his lips back to show me his cat-like teeth. He scurried toward me, completely unafraid of the knife-wielding witch who towered over him.

I grabbed him by the scruff of his neck, but the bugger wiggled and kicked and grabbed hold of my sleeve, giving himself enough leverage to rip from my grasp. He hit the ground with a thud, but before I could get another handful of fur, he sank his teeth into my leg, the sharp points penetrating my pants and breaking the skin.

"Goddess dammit!" Searing pain surged through my calf, the venom working its way toward my veins. I brought the knife down into his back, and he yelped, releasing my leg. Yanking the blade out, I pressed my boot onto his torso and shoved the knife into his heart.

"Oh my! Is everything okay out there?" Betty hurried as fast as her arthritis would allow, and I yanked off my jacket, wrapped it around the bloody carcass, and picked it up.

"Oh." She stopped, pressing a hand to her chest. "Ember? What...?"

I looked at Ash and the guys and then at the bundle in my arms. "A rat. Huge. It was gnawing on a book."

"Your leg. You're bleeding." She pointed to my blood-soaked pants.

"It bit me, but I'll be fine. I'll just take this out the back and toss it in the dumpster for you." I limped around her.

"Let me get you a bandage." She patted me on the shoulder.

"I'll take care of her, Betty." Ash wrapped an arm around my shoulders. "You might want to mop up the mess before a customer slips in it."

"You're right dear. Come back when you can. I set aside some things for you." She held the door to the storage room open for us. "Make sure the lock clicks on your way out."

"Will do."

"There's a small rift in the corner." Chaos pointed to our right.

"Ash, can you handle it while I get rid of *this*?" I sneered at the bloody bundle in my arms.

"Sure thing."

I took six steps out the door and dropped the wad of gnome…kicking it for good measure. Fire ignited in the core of my being, and I let it build, allowing it to roll down my arm and gather in my palm until I held a massive fireball.

"I sure hope no one is watching," Ash muttered, pulling the door shut as she stepped outside.

Frankly, with gnome venom climbing up my leg and my favorite jacket about to burn to bits, I really didn't care. I tossed the sphere of flames onto my jacket and gave the bitty beastie a one-fingered salute. "That's for ruining my clothes, you little shit."

The gnome and my jacket turned to ashes in seconds, and I hobbled away, the feeling of icepicks jabbing into my leg making me cringe with each step.

"I can carry you if—" Chaos began.

"Don't touch me." I glanced at Mayhem, expecting a taunting remark, but his blank expression looked scarier than I'd ever seen him.

Okay, maybe scary wasn't the right word because I wasn't afraid of him in the slightest. Even when he'd had me by the throat, he'd squeezed *just* hard enough to make breathing diffi-cult…not impossible. He'd been angry, sure, but he wouldn't have killed me. Something about his energy…the way he looked at me…said it was true.

Or maybe the gnome venom was affecting my brain.

The icepicks in my leg jabbed harder and harder, moving up to my knee and burrowing into the joint. A simple cringe was no longer enough to express my pain. My face contorted, my suppressed groan coming out as a wheeze.

"Do you..." Chaos started again.

"Let her walk." Ash caught up to me and whispered, "Seriously though, do you need help?"

I couldn't bend my knee, my calf swelled until it felt like it would bust out of my pants, and the icepicks now felt like they were hooked to a generator. "I'm fine. Keep an eye on the wild one so he doesn't try to escape while I'm not able to outrun him."

She fell back to join the demons, and I forced myself to hobble the last three yards to our building. The back steps posed a challenge since I couldn't bend my knee. Luckily there were only three and my hip still worked. I leaned to one side and swung my stiff leg up to the next stair, hauling myself up with a tight grip on the handrail.

I limped inside, down the hall, and into the library to peer at the stairs. No way could I make it up to our apartment, so I hopped on one leg to Ash's desk and gingerly rested my butt on the surface. "I'll wait down here while you mix the antivenom."

"Nonsense. You won't be comfortable." Without warning, Mayhem scooped me into a cradle carry, my stiff right leg sticking up as if I were posing for a social media *look how great my life is* post.

I'd like to say shock and pain kept me from protesting, and they did play a role in my temporary submission. But the effortless way he lifted me and held me close to his chest gave me the warm fuzzies in more places than one.

I held onto his neck, bracing myself for the pain when my leg knocked against the wall on our ascent. But he angled me just right, taking the steps sideways and making it all the way to the living room without jostling me in the slightest.

He laid me on the couch, sinking to his knees next to me, his stoic expression still unreadable. Was he angry at me? At the gnome? Or was he indifferent? Perturbed? Who knew?

Brushing my hair off my face, he leaned toward me, and for half a second, I thought he might kiss my forehead. "I will eradicate the entire species for what that one did to you."

Angry at the gnome. Got it. "There's no need to commit genocide. Ash will have me good as new in a few minutes."

"You should have called for me. I would never have let it hurt you." The intensity in his eyes said he meant it. *Yikes.*

I laughed and winced, the movement ramping up the electricity in the icepicks. "First of all, I didn't need help. I've battled way bigger beasties than that. And second—yes, there is a second this time—you had no problem letting the fae soldier knock me around...and you nearly snapped my neck...so I'm not buying what you're selling."

"Hmpf." He rose and tugged my boot off before grabbing the hem of my pants and ripping them open from my ankle to the top of my thigh.

"I guess I won't be salvaging those." I leaned my head back and closed my eyes. With the pressure on my leg gone, the icepicks relented a little, but the swollen, dark purple sausage it had become made my stomach turn.

"You want to keep them as a reminder of the time you were bested by a two-foot ball of fur?"

I lifted one lid to see his teasing smile. There was the Mayhem I knew.

"Here we go." Ash padded into the room, carrying a glass of bright yellow liquid. Chaos followed, a copper bowl in one hand, a rag in the other.

She handed me the glass. "Drink up. This one requires two parts."

I did as instructed and drank the potion. It tasted like lemongrass and relief, cooling my insides and taming the electrical current running through my leg. Chaos set the bowl on the coffee table, and Ash dipped in the rag before rubbing the concoction, which had the consistency of pudding, over the bite and up my leg.

As the magic did its thing, drawing out the venom and easing the pain, I let out a long sigh. Mayhem watched intently from a chair, and Chaos cleaned—yes, cleaned—the mess Ash had made in the kitchen.

"From now on, I'm not leaving the house without sigils. Thicker skin, resistance to venom. Those are easy ones, right?"

Ash dropped the rag into the bowl and rose. "I can do them with my eyes closed."

"That's our next step then." I pushed to sitting, the swelling already subsiding. "Sigils for me, you, Shade, and Miles. We'll only activate them when we need them."

"I can do that." She carried the bowl to the kitchen and washed the dishes before bringing me a beer. "You look like you could use it."

I laughed and accepted the bottle. "We all could."

My leg returned to its normal size and color, and I rotated my ankle, bending my knee to work out the rest of the stiffness before sitting up fully and resting my feet on the floor. "Okay, guys. What else do you know about Ignacus the Ignorant?"

CHAPTER 19

EMBER

"He sees his chance to build a kingdom, and he's taking it." Mayhem shrugged as if invading our realm and slaughtering us all was a completely normal thing to do. "It's not uncommon for those with power to prey on the weaker species."

"Weaker?" I shot to my feet and wobbled on my bare leg. My skin had absorbed all the magical pudding Ash had smeared on it, but it seemed my muscles hadn't fully recovered. I fell backward onto the couch, straightening my spine the moment my butt made contact with the cushion and scooting forward to the edge. "We are not weaker than a bunch of over-grown bugs."

He arched a brow. "Their exoskeletons are nearly impenetrable, their soldiers are invisible, and their saliva is venomous." He leaned toward me, resting his elbows on his knees. "You thought the gnome venom was bad? If a fae bites you, you'll be dead in minutes."

I scooted down the couch, closer to my verbal sparring partner. "Been there, done that, and I'm still around to show off the t-shirt. They're hard to kill, not impossible."

"Hard for you and Ash. For the others?" He gestured toward the door. "A millimeter shy of impossible."

"Don't underestimate the witches of Salem," Chaos said. "When they work as a team, they are a force to be reckoned with."

"And we won't allow the bugs to wipe out humanity." I straightened my spine. "This is *our* realm."

"They won't wipe you out." Mayhem leaned back, steepling his fingers. "The fae lack an enzyme required to exist in this realm...one that your livers produce. They'll keep you as live-stock, breeding you, slaughtering you, taking only your livers, and disposing of you like garbage."

"There's a lovely thought." I crossed my legs and massaged the injured one to spread the antidote through my muscles. I needed to move. My brain worked better when I walked. "And let me guess. The sheep don't produce enough of the enzyme to sustain them. That's why they slaughtered the entire herd."

"Precisely."

"We need to find the rest of the amulet." Ash sat on the arm of Chaos's chair. "With any luck, we can summon Discord and mend the veil before Ignacus and his followers pass through."

"Yes." Mayhem moved forward again, his knee resting against mine.

My stomach tightened, warmth spreading through my core like it did in the restaurant and again when he carried me up.

His gaze drifted down to where we touched, his brow scrunching as if he could feel the way my body reacted to him. I scooted back, breaking the connection, and he blinked twice, giving his head a tiny shake.

He cleared his throat. "The amulet is the answer to everything. We must find it."

I let out a dry laugh. "We were planning to scry for it this morning. We'd already have it if you hadn't snuck out to roam the streets and nearly gotten us shot."

"Scry for it now."

I rubbed my temples. "We can't."

"Why not?"

"Because scrying takes a lot of vim. Vim is part of a witch's life force. Body, mind, and soul have to work together to replenish it, and even if I had enough in me to go into the trance it requires, I wouldn't be able to come out. My body is injured, my mind is reeling, and my soul is so goddess damned tired I feel like curling into a ball to hibernate."

His head jerked back as if I'd slapped him. "I am to blame for this?"

"Well, yeah." I dropped my arms to my sides. "Not entirely, but having you here isn't making it any easier, and speaking of my mind..." I looked at my sister. "What did you do to me out there? That guy wouldn't have pulled the trigger if I'd kicked his ass, but all I wanted to do was keep the peace. I went from Jason Statham to Mother Theresa in half a second. You promised you'd never mess with my mind."

"We didn't do anything." She looked at Chaos for confirmation, and he shook his head before giving Mayhem a pointed look.

"It was me." He waved a hand dismissively. "I intended to wind you up so I could watch you fight without remorse. Had I known it would have the opposite effect, I would have kept my power to myself."

My mouth hung open, so I snapped it shut. "So you could watch me fight without remorse? I'd have killed them."

"They intended to kill you."

I took a deep breath, holding it for a count of five before releasing it. It was pointless to argue with a demon. He didn't even have a moral compass, much less one that pointed in the right direction. Chaos knew how to behave in this world, because Ash had taught him. He learned because he loved her.

This guy...?

Even if I had the patience to teach him right from wrong, you couldn't pay me enough to try. He was unteachable.

"Now do you believe it's fate?" Ash asked. "Chaos's power has the opposite effect on me too. Some things are meant to be."

Mayhem's face blanked again, but my eyebrows shot toward my hairline. "Are you implying that he and I..." I laughed incredulously. "I'll admit the goddess or *someone* nudged us in the right direction to find these guys. Was it all meant to happen exactly the way it happened? Doubtful."

Ash lifted a finger. "But—"

"But..." I mirrored her pose. "To imply that the universe is now a matchmaker is ludicrous. You and Chaos fell in love.

Good for you. But don't you think, if the universe or fate or whatever wanted you to be together, they would have given you a way to *stay* together?"

She straightened, lifting her chin. "Who are we to question fate?"

"Who are we, indeed?" I cast a glance to Mayhem, who looked indifferent AF. He wasn't going to back me up, not that I expected him to.

I stood, testing my weight. When I didn't wobble, I picked up my boot and headed for my room.

"Where are you going?" Ash asked, following me into the hall.

"To shower and change. Miles has an early date with Wendy, and we need to be there to listen." I kicked off my other boot and opened my underwear drawer. The shard of amulet glinted in the overhead light, reminding me how much easier this would be if we didn't have to babysit an unruly demon.

Ash leaned against the dresser, crossing her arms. "Do you seriously not see the way he looks at you?"

"Like he's trying to decide which way he wants to kill me? All the time." I knocked on the drawer her butt was against, and she pushed off, crossing the room to sit on the bed. I yanked it open to find one lonely pair of fireproof pants. "I know it's mean of me to say, but I miss Patrice for the laundry and grocery shopping she did for us. Think we can convince Miles…?"

"Ember, listen to me."

"I will when you speak rationally." I slammed the drawer shut.

"Why is believing in fate so hard for you?"

I tightened my grip on my last pair of pants. "Believing in fate isn't hard. I *truly* believe we were meant to find these guys so we can end the curse. And their magic having the opposite effect on us makes sense. It's karma. They cursed our bloodline, so they can't scramble our brains to bring the curse to fruition themselves."

I grabbed a shirt from the closet. "But Mayhem is not my meant-to-be. I don't believe that person exists for me, but if he does, it is certainly not that arrogant, self-centered brute who doesn't give a flying eff about anyone but himself."

She raised her brows. "He's enamored of you."

I scoffed. "How can you tell? Is it the constant needling, the way he doesn't lift a finger to help me fight, or the fact he lifted me from the ground *by my throat* and threatened to snap my neck?"

She gasped. "He didn't."

"He most certainly did. The only reason he put me down was because I dug a blade two inches into his chest."

"Why didn't you tell me?" She stood and paced toward me. "That's so scary."

"Not really." I shrugged and headed for the bathroom, dropping my clean clothes on the counter before peeling off my socks.

Ash leaned in the doorway. "You don't have to be a badass all the time. It's okay to be scared."

"I wasn't." I unzipped what was left of my pants and fumbled my way out of them.

Ash smiled smugly. "You knew he wouldn't do it."

"No, I didn't."

"Yes, you did."

I took off my shirt and dropped it in the hamper before turning on the tap. "We were at a draw."

She lifted herself onto the counter and swung her legs. "Somewhere, deep inside, you knew he wouldn't kill you. It's not rational because he gave you every indication that he would, but your soul knew he wouldn't."

I rolled my eyes and stepped into the shower, closing the curtain before taking off my bra and undies and tossing them into the hamper. What could I say to that?

"You know I'm right," she sang.

"No, I don't." The hot water felt fabulous beating down on my tired muscles, and the peppermint in my shampoo helped to wake up my mind. Tired and weary didn't begin to describe my level of fatigue.

"And for some goddess only knows reason, even through all the bickering, he's growing on you," Ash said.

"Like a fungus." I stretched my neck beneath the stream, willing the knots in my muscles to release.

"Your body reacts when he touches you."

"Whose wouldn't? He's smoking hot, and you've seen what he's packing." I shut off the water and reached out for a towel.

She handed me one. "You've seen Chaos, too. Does your body react like that when he touches you?"

No. No, it did not. "Chaos is your lover boy, not mine."

"You didn't answer the question."

And I didn't intend to, so I dried off and wrapped the towel around my chest. "Hey, will you text Shade and see how many shadow spells he's bottled? If he's got enough vim, maybe he and Miles can come over and scry for the amulet before the fake date." Because this entire ordeal could not be over quickly enough.

"Done."

As I pulled back the curtain, her phone rang, "Asshole Alert" lighting up the screen.

"Guess I need to change that." She laughed and answered on speaker. "Hey. Em's with me."

"This is Miles." His hushed voice raised the hairs on the back of my neck and made my stomach dip.

"What's wrong? Where's Shade?" I pulled on my undies and shoved my legs into my pants.

"Hold on." A door squeaked on its hinges before clicking shut. I finished getting dressed to the sound of carpet-muffled footsteps.

"He's at my place. He'll be okay, but he didn't get the chance to bottle anything."

I waited a beat. Two. Three. When he didn't continue, I grabbed the phone and brought it to my mouth. "What *happened*?"

"We ran into a soldier. Literally."

Ash gasped, touching her fingertips to her lips, and I jerked my head toward the front of the house.

"Did it bite him?" She followed me to the living room, and I turned up the volume before setting the phone on the coffee table.

"No, thank Hecate," he said. "We caught it off guard, but it was fast. It grabbed me, which let Shade know where it was, even though it was invisible, and he..." Miles drew in a breath, and we all leaned toward the phone. "He sucked the light...the life...out of it. I'd never seen him do it to a sentient being before, but the way it shrieked... It has to be the most painful way to die."

Ash nodded. "It's not pleasant, but getting all the liquid sucked out through your pores might be worse. How's Shade?"

"Sleeping. He said it drains him almost as much as it does his target."

"Because he doesn't practice," Mayhem said. "With the amulet's help, he could be an asset."

"He already is an asset," I said. "He doesn't practice because light witches don't kill people."

Mayhem crossed his arms. "You're Veil Keepers. You kill."

"Vampire ghouls and the occasional gnome or mosquito fae." I matched his posture. "He's never had the need to use that kind of power against a beastie."

"Now he does."

"Anyway..." Miles cleared his throat. "Patrice is coming over to sit with him while I meet with Wendy. From the looks of him, he'll be asleep all night."

"Good. I'm glad she's still willing to help," I said.

"She might not agree with our methods, but she'll do what she can for the good of the coven, just like the rest of us." A faint knocking sounded through the phone. "Oh, she's here."

"What time should we pick you up?" I grabbed my own phone off the counter to check the clock.

"I'll drive myself. I don't want her to be suspicious if she sees me getting out of the coven van. I'm meeting her at six at Pennino's."

"Good plan. We'll be there early and stay out of sight."

"See you then."

Ash ended the call and returned the phone to her pocket. "It would be convenient if Shade could work that kind of magic without completely draining his vim."

"That small piece of the amulet could be enough to help him master it in a short time," Mayhem said. Fabulous. Demon number two never bothered to back me up, but he had no problem agreeing with Ash.

"There's one way to find out." She lifted her hands palms up, and I stared at her with wide eyes. First the coughing when we smudged the room, and now she was willing to experiment on a coven member with magic forged in Hell?

Holy Hecate, we needed to get our butts in gear.

I pointed at Ash. "No." Then at Mayhem. "No. Absolutely no one is messing with the shard. It's broken. It could kill him."

Ash blinked as if finally coming to her senses. "You're right. I don't know why I suggested that."

I looked at Chaos, whose grim expression said we both knew why.

CHAPTER 20
MAYHEM

Had fate finally dealt me a winning hand? I sat in the passenger seat of Ember's van, stealing glances at the enchantress driving us to Boston. Her gaze remained locked on the road, her brow lowered in concentration, and I wondered what thoughts raced inside her mind.

The moment Ash had connected the dots, explaining the reason Ember reacted to my magic the way she did, all the pieces to the puzzle of my existence clicked into place. The tether, which had attempted to connect us previously, solidified, and the flitting of moth wings in my stomach stilled, my chest tightening with resolve.

Ember would be mine.

I had paid my penance. Four centuries in the dark prison in exchange for a warrior princess bride.

It was true fate led me to her. That, I felt in my bones. But the universe knew me too well and presented me with a challenge to overcome. I would tire easily of a damsel falling at my feet, so fate offered me a woman with a fiery heart and a stubborn mind.

She had laughed at the idea that she should belong to me, dismissing any notion that fate had chosen me to be her consort. Winning her heart and mastering her soul would be the greatest challenge I had ever overcome.

Instinct told me to claim what was rightfully mine. When we returned home, I could take the amulet and the woman and return to Hell, where I could spend eternity with her. But she wouldn't come willingly.

She would fight me every step of the way, and while I would enjoy every minute of the fray, I wanted her heart along with her body. No, I would not take her forcefully. I would convince her she and I were meant to be. It was written in the stars four hundred years ago. Perhaps longer.

"We're here." Ember's voice drew me from my thoughts, and she turned toward me. "This is a reconnaissance mission. You are not, under any circumstances, to use your mind magic on anyone. Got it?"

"If your life is threatened…"

"You still don't do it. I can take care of myself." She cocked her head, her pointed look making heat pool in my groin.

She could take care of herself. She had proven that many times since she summoned me, but she also allowed others to care for her when she was in need.

She would learn to need me.

Ember put on a jacket over her shoulder holster. She hid a

dagger and three knives beneath her clothing, and she offered another to Ash, who slipped it into her bag.

"If we're only here to gather information, why do you go in armed?" I unbuckled my seatbelt.

"It's Veil Keeper 101. Always be prepared for a fight." She opened her door, and the overhead light illuminated the hard set of her jaw before she exited the vehicle.

I fought the smile tugging at my lips and slid out of my seat, closing the door behind me. "You and Ash are the ruling bloodline of Salem. Will Wendy not recognize you?"

"She would for sure." Ember flipped up her jacket collar, crossing her arms against the stinging autumn wind. "But she'll never see us."

The strange urge to wrap my arms around her and shield her from the cold overtook me. I wasn't keen on having a knife jabbed into my side, so I didn't dare. But the fact she would do it only added to her appeal.

"How will we hear their conversation if we're out of sight?" I asked.

"With technology. Let's grab a table, and I'll explain." She led us to the restaurant, and a young man wearing black pants with a stark white button-up opened the door to greet us.

We entered the restaurant's foyer and found another young man in the same clothing standing behind a podium., his face a mask of boredom and contempt. "What name is the reservation under?"

"We don't have one," Ember replied. "We'll take a table in the back."

"This establishment is reservation only." His judging gaze

raked over her form. "And we have a dress code. Yoga pants are not allowed."

Her hands curled into fists. "I don't do yoga. Can we sit at the bar?"

"Not unless you have a reservation."

Her jaw ticked. "It's five o'clock. Most people don't go out for dinner before seven, and you've got dozens of empty tables."

He rolled his eyes. "I can't seat you without a reservation."

"Can I *make* a reservation then?"

His mouth tightened, and he blinked at her twice before lowering his gaze to a tablet screen. "We're booked tonight, but I can get you in next Tuesday."

She stiffened, and I smiled, imagining her wishing she could jab her dagger into the man's neck.

Chaos stepped forward, holding Ash's hand. "The table in the back by the kitchen is free. You'll seat us there."

Our indignant host snapped his gaze to my brother, confusion contorting his features for half a second before they smoothed. "No one ever reserves the table in the back by the kitchen. I'll seat you there. This way."

Interesting...

He picked up a stack of menus and strode into the seating area. I followed silently, taking in our surroundings. A massive crystal chandelier hung in the center of the room, and widely spaced tables covered in white linen held etched glass goblets and gold chargers. Savory scents of garlic and thyme filled the air, and a server passed by carrying a plate covered with a silver dome.

The host waited as we took our seats and then placed a white napkin on each of our laps. He opened the menus one by one, handing them first to the women and then to us. "Your server will be with you shortly. *Bon appetite.*"

Ember shook her head, and I could practically see the thoughts racing through her mind. "I want to berate the two of you, but I know that pompous bitch wouldn't have seated us otherwise."

Ash shrugged. "Sometimes a little gray is necessary."

I narrowed my eyes at my brother. "That didn't look like your normal magic. What did you do?"

"Ash's power counters mine. She can send it to me through the mark she bears, giving me the ability to control minds rather than scatter them."

"And they promised not to do it unless it's absolutely necessary." Ember's shoulders slumped. "Which it was in this case."

Interesting indeed. I wondered how Ember's power might counter mine. If it meant I could guide people to peaceful resolutions, I'd rather not try.

Our server arrived to fill our goblets with water, and Ember ordered a bottle of wine. "We're going to be here a while, but don't worry. We tip well."

"It's fine. This table is rarely sat, so I'm happy to serve you." The woman smiled warmly. "The manager thought it would be a good idea to have a secluded spot for any celebrities who might want to dine in peace." She tugged on a curtain, isolating us from the rest of the dining room. "But he put it right by the kitchen. Guests get annoyed with all the foot traffic, so the idea flopped. I'll be right back with your wine."

"It couldn't be more perfect for us." Ember laid her phone on the table as the server walked away. "Miles will be wearing an earpiece. When he gets here, he's going to call. He'll leave his phone face down on the table so we can hear everything they say."

"Impressive." I nodded my appreciation.

She shrugged. "Sometimes I have good ideas."

She didn't give herself enough credit. Ember was a natural leader. She preferred being in the heat of battle, as did I, but she commanded her small army of Veil Keepers with the skill of a general.

She looked at the menu, and her eyes widened as she let out a low whistle. "They're proud of their food, aren't they? I'm surprised Miles decided to bring her here."

"He probably let her choose," Ash said. "He owes it to her for leading her on."

"These prices are nearly triple those of our lunch restaurant," I said. "I assume you have some form of income to afford it?"

"Ember makes bank at Spellbound Axe in tips alone." Ash sipped her water.

"Not anymore." Ember sighed. "I got fired."

"Damn." Ash grimaced at the menu. "I'll just get a small salad."

"You could use your mind trick to convince our server the food is complimentary." I was surprised they didn't do it all the time.

"Absolutely not." Ember glared at me, making my pulse quicken. "Our world could end in a matter of days, and my credit card is paid off. Order whatever you want. I'll worry about the cost if we make it through."

Our server delivered the meal in courses, with baked cheese, a salad, and a small bowl of soup coming before the main meal. I didn't dare order the same entrée as Ember, though her steak *foie gras* sounded delicious. My meal consisted of roasted chicken with rosemary potatoes that melted on my tongue. I could get used to the delicacies of this realm.

Ember's phone buzzed on the table, Miles creating the connection for our investigation. A minute or two passed with nothing but muffled sounds before the *clunk* indicated he had set the phone down to begin the interrogation.

I pulled the curtain back slightly, giving myself a view of the pair. Miles wore a brown sports coat—I'd learned the names of modern attire through the television—and Wendy wore a black dress that sparkled in the chandelier light. She had dull brown hair, pulled back in a clip with a lock hanging loose across her forehead.

"I was wondering if you'd ever make good on your promise," Wendy said. We could hear their words clearly through Ember's phone.

"Yeah, sorry about that. With all the rifts forming, I've been busy. Are they bad in Boston too?" Miles got straight to the point. Good man.

"Obviously. Being this close to Salem, we get the aftershock of everything your coven does. How'd you do with the spells from our library? I hope the money one worked so you can pay for the lobster I'm about to order." She lifted her napkin from her lap and wiped her nose, sticking the corner of the cloth into her nostril.

I cringed. "This is the type of woman Miles finds attractive?"

"Good goddess, no." Ember laughed. "He used her to get into the Boston coven library."

Miles cleared his throat, reminding us of his earpiece. He could hear our conversation as well as we heard his.

"Sorry." Ember pressed the mute button, her finger hesitating over the device before she pressed it again. "Steer her back to the rifts and the fae." She muted the call.

Our server cleared our plates and returned with four dishes of *crème brûlée*. As she set them on the table, we heard Miles and Wendy ordering their meals.

"He's our friend," Ash said quickly. "He knows we're listening."

"We're giving him pointers on his date," Ember added.

The server refilled our water goblets. "That's none of my business. I'll give you some privacy." She smiled and walked away.

"So the rifts…" Miles said. "What do you know about them?"

She narrowed her eyes. "That they're happening more and more, and they're only going to get worse when Halloween rolls around. Why?"

"Just curious." He took a giant gulp of water. "Those fae,

though, right? The lesser ones are annoying, but the big guys... Man, they're hard to kill."

Her brow slammed down. "How big? What do they look like?"

"Like giant, venomous bugs with impenetrable exoskeletons."

Her brows crept toward her hairline as she straightened her spine. "You've fought them?"

"My coven has killed three. We found a massive rift just north of Salem. Four or five more probably got through."

Her complexion paled. "Are your fire witches burning them?"

He shook his head. "They're fireproof."

She laid her hands on the table, leaning forward. "How do you kill them?"

They paused their conversation as their food arrived. When their server left, Miles spoke, "You've got them here too, don't you? The serial killer they're talking about on the news? It's the fae."

She swallowed hard, though she had no food in her mouth. "How do you know?"

"They eat human livers so they can survive in this realm. We've done some research, and we think there's going to be an invasion. You might want to warn your coven since they're killing in your territory too."

She picked up a glass of wine and drained the contents in three gulps before wiping her mouth with the back of her hand. "Can you keep a secret?"

Miles leaned toward her. "I won't tell a soul."

She shifted her gaze from left to right before resting a hand on the table. "They're here because of us. Well, because of Adrian, our High Priest. He called them here."

Ember locked eyes with Ash, her expression one of alarm.

"What do you mean?" Miles asked. "They're coming through the rifts. The lesser fae have come through for years."

"The big guys...?" Her hand trembled as she picked up her spoon and scooped the soup. The liquid fell from the utensil before it reached her mouth. "They can make themselves invisible, right?"

Miles nodded.

"It's the same ones then." She blew out a hard breath. "We have several volumes of a fae encyclopedia in our library, and Adrian has been obsessed with reading them. With the veil as thin as it is now, he got this delusional idea that, if he could convince this half-blooded prince to invade, they could join forces and basically take over the world."

Miles tilted his head. "Your High Priest thinks he can achieve world domination with *the fae*?"

"I told you he was delusional." She dipped a piece of bread into her soup and shoved it into her mouth. "It's why I joined Chrys's coup."

Ember unmuted the phone. "Get her to elaborate."

"Obviously," Miles said, quickly straightening at his faux pas. "I mean, that's the obvious thing to do when your leader wants to upset the balance of the realms."

"Right? I tried to tell people that, but they didn't want to listen." She waved a hand dismissively. "If Chrys hadn't gone nutso and tore our library apart, we might not be in this situation. She killed one of your members too. The woman was certifiably batshit."

"Poor Miles." Ash scrunched her face. "The person she killed was Miles's girlfriend."

Anger sparked in my chest. Miles was a loyal witch who obeyed orders without protest. Any coven would be lucky to have members like him. "You should have let me burn through her to avenge his lover's death."

"Shh." Ember pressed a finger to her lips. "Listen."

"We're still reeling from that," Miles said. "How did she recruit? What was her purpose in staging the coup?"

"She was secretive about it all. She'd hang around Boston, catching us when we were alone and feeding us BS about how powerful she was, and that once she summoned some demon prince, she'd have the power to overthrow both Boston and Salem." Her hands steadied, and she poured herself another glass of wine, leaving Miles's glass empty.

"When we told her about what Adrian had done, she promised to stop it from happening. Then she went nuts and got herself killed. I figured we'd be banished, but Adrian forgave us all."

I leaned back in my chair. "He probably planned to feed them to the fae."

"Indeed," Chaos agreed.

"How did Adrian contact the fae?" Miles added more wine to Wendy's glass. I appreciated his interrogation technique. Loose lips spilled more secrets.

"He attached a letter to a lesser fae and sent it through a rift like a carrier pigeon. They went back and forth for a week or so before the scouts arrived. Now that the soldiers are here, though..." She took another drink.

"They're like mindless killing machines." She scoffed. "There's no alliance. Adrian invited the monsters into our realm, and they've already turned against him. I don't think the fae ever planned to work with us."

She swayed in her chair, her words beginning to slur. "You should talk to your High Priestess. Maybe our covens can form an alliance to kick the fae to the curb."

"That's not a bad idea," Miles said.

"Don't tell her about all this though. I'm not even supposed to know the details. People talk in front of me because no one takes me seriously. But we haven't killed a single one. You have, so Adrian will listen to you."

Miles patted her hand on the table. "I'll see what I can do."

CHAPTER 21

MAYHEM

We waited in the restaurant until Miles and Wendy left before returning home. Now, Ember paced in her usual spot in front of the television.

"An alliance with Boston. I can't decide if that's a good idea or a bad one." She unhooked her shoulder holster and laid it on the counter next to her sword. "What do you think?"

I thought she should continue removing the articles she wore, beginning with her shirt. Sadly she didn't ask me.

"Let's think about the pros and cons." Ash sat on the sofa next to Chaos, drumming her fingers on her knees. "We could use the manpower, for sure. Especially if an entire army gets through."

"True, true." Ember clasped her hands behind her back as she walked. "But keeping our involvement in how this all started a secret has been hard enough with our own coven. And BSM is a dark coven. We can't trust any of them."

I sat in a chair, watching her pace and think. Her mind was as brilliant as her body was beautiful, and though I normally enjoyed discussing battle plans, all I could think about was how to convince her she and I were fated.

"We don't even know if what Wendy said was true." Ash tapped a finger to her lips. "She could have been baiting us."

"Doubtful," Ember said. "Drunk people don't lie."

"I don't get the impression Wendy is of a mind to spin such an elaborate tale," Chaos said. "Or to remember all the details if she were tasked with delivering it."

"No, she's definitely not." Ember stopped and rested her hands on her hips. "What's our next step?"

"What does your gut tell you?" Ash asked.

Ember paused, casting her gaze upward for a moment. "Stay on course. Knowing why the fae are invading doesn't change the fact that they are. It doesn't change anything."

"Right." Ash nodded.

"We chill tonight, scry in the morning, and then we go from there." She gave me a pointed look. "That means *you* have to stay inside and not cause any trouble."

"Perhaps I should sleep in your room so you can keep an eye on me."

"Maybe I should chain you to the bed, so I know you can't move." Her eyes widened as she realized her words conveyed a different meaning. Rather than backtracking on her statement, she crossed her arms and arched a brow.

I couldn't stop the growl from rumbling in my chest.

"Ahem." Ash eyed Ember and tilted her head toward me.

Ember held up a hand. "Don't start."

"I would like to hear what your sister has to say." I rested my elbows on my knees. "We are supposed to be 'chilling' tonight, so let's have a conversation about something other than the direness of our situation."

"Okay." She raised both hands and let them fall at her sides. "Ash insists that just because your mind magic had the opposite effect on me like his does to her, it means you and I are soulmates. Tell her how ridiculous that is."

It wasn't ridiculous in the slightest. I pressed the tips of my fingers together, an idea forming in my mind. "How does Chaos's power affect you?"

She crossed her arms. "He's never tried."

I nodded, the corners of my mouth tugging upward. "I propose a way to lay the ridiculousness—or truth—of Ash's hypothesis to rest."

"I'm listening."

I rose to my feet. "Allow me to hold Ash's mind for a moment. Just long enough for her to feel the effect and act accordingly. Once we have our answer, I'll release her and never use my power on her again."

Ember drummed her fingers against her biceps. "No way. Neither one of you is going to mess with our minds."

Ash's face held a thoughtful expression before she raised her brows at my brother. "I'm game if you trust him. At the very least, it'll put Ember's mind at ease."

"Or it will prove we are, in fact, soul mates."

She rolled her eyes. "It won't prove that, but okay. Fifty

bucks says you can't make Ash violent. Her magic will counter yours."

"I could never take money from someone who just lost her job. How about this instead?" I leaned against the counter, crossing my legs at the ankles. "If Ash's magic counters mine, I will become your obedient servant. If I can make her violent, you agree to share your bed with me...for sleeping purposes only...unless you wish to do more."

She raised her chin, her eyes calculating. "Sleeping only? You won't touch me?"

"Not until you want me to." I offered my hand to shake.

"It doesn't matter. You're going to lose, anyway." She placed her palm in mine.

Ash chuckled. "I never thought I'd see the day when Ember made a deal with a demon."

"Indeed," Chaos said.

"Whatever." She tugged from my grasp. "Let's get this over with."

Ash stood and padded across the room, dragging Chaos behind her. "I'm going to stand over here just in case. I doubt I'm strong enough to hurt a demon if I do get violent, so I'll stay close to him."

"You swear you'll release her the second she feels the magic?" Ember moved next to me.

"You have my word."

She blew out a hard breath, her expression skeptical.

"I'll be fine," Ash said. "I want to know how he'll affect me."

"And if he doesn't release her, I will make him." Chaos flashed a cold, hard stare in my direction, the silent threat imminent, though I had no intention of holding Ash any longer than necessary.

She would turn violent, and while I would enjoy watching her try to beat my brother, my purpose for this experiment was singular.

To convince Ember she should be mine.

I continued leaning, making my posture as casual as possible to keep the women calm. At Chaos's nod, I called on my magic, sending a trickle toward Ash. She looked back at me, either not feeling the effect or calming, like Ember had done. It could not be the latter. I refused to let it be.

I gathered my power, letting it build in my being, growing stronger with each breath I took. On a hard exhale, I pushed the brunt of it out, seizing Ash's mind. Her eyes widened, and she blinked rapidly, but still she did not move.

"See?" Ember said. "No violence."

Ash heaved a breath. She grunted. And then she screamed.

She whirled toward Chaos, her fist striking his stomach. When he didn't flinch, she growled.

"No violence, eh?" I chuckled and drew my magic back, but a thread of it stuck, hung up on some part of her psyche like a fishhook in seaweed. She drew her arm back and punched again.

"Let her go." Ember clutched my shoulder and shook me.

"I'm trying." My pulse raced, my head aching with the exertion. I pulled and pulled, but the thread remained.

Chaos grabbed Ash from behind, pinning her arms to her sides as she kicked and wailed. "Release her!" he boomed.

"I can't." I moved closer, desperately trying to sever the tie between her mind and mine. "Something is wrong. It's stuck. It's..."

The sigil on her arm pulsed bright red. "It's your mark. It's holding my magic."

"Turn it off." Ember snarled. "You're hurting her."

"If I could, I would." I turned toward her, and the anger burning in her eyes morphed into hatred.

Lucifer help me. What had I done?

"I'm trying. I don't want to hurt her." My mind scrambled for a solution, but before my thoughts caught up with what was happening, Ember lunged for her sword. The rest of the events unfolded in slow motion.

Screaming like a scorned Valkyrie, she spun, raising the blade above her head and hurling it downward at an angle, slicing into my neck. My head hit the ground, my eyes wide with shock as Ash heaved a breath, finally free of my hold.

Ember's blade pierced my chest, searing silver penetrating through my heart, the force of her jab sending it out through my back until the hilt met my flesh. Her hand in my hair, lifting me from the floor, was the last thing I felt, Ash's breathy voice the final thing I heard before the dark prison yanked me across the veil...

"Oh my goddess, Ember. What have you done?"

MENDING MAYHEM

FIRE WITCHES OF SALEM
BOOK FIVE

CARRIE PULKINEN

CHAPTER 1
EMBER

What had I done? That was a loaded question. Physically, I had vanquished a demon prince to a dark prison, saved my sister's life, and stopped the family curse from coming to fruition in my living room. Metaphysically, I'd probably caused the veil between our worlds irreparable damage and ushered in Armageddon with a slice and a jab of my sword.

Interpersonally, I'd dissolved any type of trust or bond—or whatever was happening—with Mayhem and set our journey to salvation back so far, we might never recover.

But, hey, at least Ash was back to her normal self. I hoped. "Are you okay?"

She blinked twice. "I'm fine. Are you?" Her gaze drifted down to my left hand, where Chaos's eyes were also locked. No, not my hand. They were focused on the severed head spilling blood onto the hardwood.

My brain finally received the message from my fingers, recognizing the soft tuft of hair clutched in my fist. Mayhem's body had turned to smoke when I pierced his heart, the veil opening and whisking him away to the dark prison we'd freed him from only days ago.

But his head, which I'd lobbed off in one stroke, hung from my grasp, his eyes wide with shock, poisonous blood dripping onto the floor from his neck. *Well, Ember, what now?*

"If we summon him again, he's going to kill me." I lifted my sword, resting the flat side of the blade against my shoulder. "Get a bowl. If we collect his blood, maybe we can use it in a spell to harness enough of his power for Chaos and Discord to break the curse."

Neither of them moved.

"Okay, I'll get it myself." I tried to turn around and make my way to the kitchen, but my feet remained rooted to the floor.

My head spun, the gravity of our situation reaching my nervous system and making my muscles tremble. What had I done, indeed. "I bet there's something in Chrys's dark grimoire. If we just…"

Hellfire erupted in the puddle of blood, the flames licking upward, engulfing Mayhem's severed head. The blood on the tip of my blade incinerated, and the scent of burning hair and flesh made my stomach turn. As the fire consumed him, his skin turned to ash along with the silky locks still clutched in my fist.

His skull tumbled to the floor, the jaw disconnecting from the upper part when it thudded on the hardwood.

Damn. It looked like we wouldn't be collecting demon blood after all.

"I can't believe you did that." Ash sank onto the couch, holding her head in her hands.

I gazed at the skull. The smooth bone almost glistened in the ambient light. "That was hellfire, not witch fire."

"Not that." She jerked her hand, gesturing at me, my sword, the skull...everything in my general direction. "*All* that."

"It wasn't unexpected." Chaos sat next to her, resting a hand on her knee. "She warned him she would do it several times."

Ash tilted her head, looking at him like he'd grown a second set of eyeballs. "She vanquished him. Again."

"He was hurting you." Chaos shrugged. "I would've done the same if Ember hadn't acted so quickly."

She rubbed her temples. "He released me the second you took off his head. You didn't have to vanquish him."

"I didn't know that." Besides, what good would a headless demon do? He'd have to carry it around tucked under his arm, which would freak people the eff out. This was Salem, not Sleepy Hollow...and he didn't have a horse.

My sword suddenly felt like it weighed a hundred pounds, so I set it on the counter, my hands trembling with nothing to hold. "I was protecting you."

"Thank you," Chaos said. "You acted when I didn't. He could have caused permanent damage to her brain."

I picked up Mayhem's skull, trying my best to ignore the magical pinpricks dancing across my skin as I balanced the top part on the jaw and set both pieces on the coffee table. I lowered into a chair, my entire body convulsing as the cushion absorbed my weight. What the *hell* had I just done?

I raked a hand through my hair. "I'm sorry. I screwed up. I..."

Ash sighed. "It's okay. Luckily, he's immortal. We'll summon him again."

I nodded, words escaping me.

"Thank you," she said after a long pause. "It was scary feeling that much rage. If Chaos hadn't held me back, I don't know what I would have done."

"It was stupid." I pressed my thumb between my eyes to counter the pressure building in my head. "I never should have let him do that to you. I wasn't thinking clearly."

"I gave him permission to do it," Ash said. "It wasn't just you."

"As did I." Chaos leaned back on the sofa. "You are the first beings who have ever counteracted our magic with your own. It's new territory for us all. No need to place blame."

"Yeah." My stomach roiled, my dinner threatening to come back for an encore appearance.

"The debt he owed you has been forfeited," Chaos said, his expression grim. "When we bring him back, he'll have to help us break the curse out of the goodness of his heart, and I'm afraid nothing more than a shred exists inside him. If any."

"That makes sense. Sort of." My knee bounced incessantly, so I laid my hand on it to stop the movement. "Of course he doesn't owe me for freeing him last time...but I'm freeing him again. He'll owe me for this time, right?"

"I'm afraid not." He ran a hand down his face. "You are the

one who imprisoned him. His jailer freeing him incurs no debt...merely his wrath."

"Merely." I laughed dryly. "Well, if that's all..."

Ash furrowed her brow. "But we vanquished him before, and he still owed us a debt when we summoned him. Why then, but not now?"

He nodded, looking thoughtful. "A technicality. He had no corporeal form the first time, and you and Miles vanquished him, not Ember."

"So if I summoned him..." Ash said.

"You were here, a part of the vanquishing, no matter how indirectly," he said.

"I didn't have a clue what was happening the first time." I drummed my fingers on my knee, my thoughts racing. "Once we got him out of Chrys, my focus went to her. That's why he owed me this time. I wasn't a part of the initial vanquishing."

We sat silently, contemplating the ramifications of what I'd done. At least, I assumed Chaos and Ash were contemplating too. They weren't making goo-goo eyes at each other for once, anyway.

I stood and paced in front of the TV. "We'll get Miles to draw the sigil this time. He's even-tempered enough to work with a demon, right? Because Shade is out of the question."

Ash shook her head. "It has to be you."

I parked my hands on my hips. "I cannot deal with soul-mate talk right now, so stop."

"She's correct," Chaos said. "Whether or not you are soul-mates doesn't matter. Fate brought all of us together to fix this. Bringing in an outsider could be detrimental to our cause."

"It's a family affair," Ash said.

I threw my arms into the air and dropped them at my sides. My sister, ever the logical one, was right again. Bringing Miles any deeper into the mix would be irresponsible. This *was* a family affair, and it was up to me to protect the rest of the coven from our curse.

"He's going to kill me."

She pursed her lips, giving her head a tiny shake. "No, he's not, Em."

"You don't know that." I continued pacing.

"I do, and so do you." She rose and stretched her arms above her head. "But just to be sure, you're going to bear his mark."

"The hell I am." I whirled to face her. Was she cuckoo? "Did you forget you almost *died* when you summoned Chaos that way? That Chrys *did* die?"

"Chrys and I had no idea what we were doing, and I didn't have Chaos's skull." She padded toward the hall, pausing at the threshold. "We have Mayhem's. We'll summon him into you and then exorcize him from your body to let him reform in a containment circle."

"Ash, no..." My hands curled into fists. I couldn't do it. I wouldn't.

"He'll be incapable of causing you harm." Chaos joined Ash by the hall, taking her hand.

I crossed my arms. "Yeah, right. He's probably so pissed, he'll burn through me the second I'm possessed."

"We won't give him the chance," Chaos said. "Ash will exorcize him immediately. Then, when he reforms, you won't have to worry about him killing you because you'll be connected through his mark. He'll be vanquished again if you die."

Ash chuckled. "She isn't worried about him killing her. Are you, Em?"

I narrowed my eyes, refusing to acknowledge her ridiculous statement.

"Sleep on it." She rested a hand on her demon's chest. "We have to re-summon him tomorrow morning, and you know this is the best way to do it."

"I don't *know* anything." I shifted my weight to my right leg, jutting out my hip in protest. "If we get the amulet first, we can get it over with all at once. We don't need to summon him until we find it."

"Yes, we do." She flashed a knowing smile, though what she thought she knew was ludicrous. "I'll see you in the morning, bright and early."

"Good night, Ember." Chaos followed Ash down the hall, leaving me alone with Mayhem's skull.

I eyed the hunk of bone, debating whether or not to pulverize it and be done with the insufferable demon. If my sister's life...and the lives of every witch in the coven...weren't at stake, I wouldn't have thought twice.

Much to my chagrin, however, we needed him. Dammit.

Even more chagriny...chagrinish...*annoying*... I owed him an apology. As usual, I had acted before my brain could warn me of the consequences. Hell, sometimes I wondered if I had a brain at all.

I closed my eyes, taking two deep breaths to center myself.

This whole ordeal had to be one long-ass dream, right? When I opened my eyes, there would be no skull sitting on the counter, no demon in my sister's bed. Cinder and my parents would be sleeping down the hall, and I could sit on the couch and binge the last season of *Why Women Kill* like a normal person.

"As I will it, so mote it be." I lifted one lid, then the other. Mayhem's eyeless gaze stared back at me. "Oh, for Hecate's sake."

This was my life now. Might as well get used to it. I locked the door and turned off the lights before scooping up the skull in one hand, my sword in the other, and padding to my bedroom.

"You really gave me no choice." I set Mayhem on my night-stand and hung my sword on the wall before sinking onto the mattress. "I won't say I was starting to like you, but I was toler-ating you better. You were growing on me."

And my body enjoyed the way touching him made me feel, despite my protesting brain.

I reached for the skull but stopped, fisting my hand and jerking it back to my lap. "What is it about you that burrows into my psyche and makes me feel things no mortal should feel for a Prince of Hell?"

My sigh came out more like a growl as I stood and headed to the shower. When I finished and put on my PJs, I opened the door and steam wafted into my bedroom, dissipating before it reached the ceiling.

Settling into bed, I turned off my lamp and brushed my fingers over the skull. It still gave me the same not-unpleasant pin pricking sensation that spiraled up my arm and warmed my chest.

"What *is it* about you?" I shook my head, attempting to chase away the intruding thoughts taking up residence in my mind, and lay back on my pillow. "If I had a type, you would be the exact opposite."

Well, personality-wise, anyway. Looks-wise... Let's just say my body wanted him to bang me like a screen door in a hurricane. "What the hell is wrong with me?"

I rolled over and put my back to him, closing my eyes and begging Morpheus to grant me a dream-free slumber. Sadly, my prayers went unanswered.

His purple eyes glittered with mischief as he trailed strong hands down my arms, turning my skin to gooseflesh. Lacing his fingers through mine, he lifted my arms before taking the hem of my shirt and tugging it over my head.

His pupils dilated, blackness spreading outward until only a thin ring of purple remained, and he inhaled deeply, his lips curling upward in approval. His tongue slipped out to moisten them, and warm shivers ran through my body in anticipation of him moistening mine.

He glided his fingertips up my stomach, cupping my breasts and brushing his thumbs over my nipples, hardening them instantly. My breathing grew shallow, every nerve in my body firing on overdrive, making my ears ring.

He moved closer, his cheek scant centimeters from mine, and he took another deep breath. A contented growl rumbled in his chest, but I barely heard it over the incessant ringing in my ears.

The culpable sound grew louder as he turned his head toward me, his nose brushing my skin.

Louder yet, the annoying sound yanked me away from him, my lids flying open, the ceiling coming into view. My breath came out in a huff, though I wasn't sure if it was irritation or relief that the dream didn't go any further.

I swiped my hand down my face and lightly slapped my cheek to wake myself up fully. Rolling to the nightstand, I grabbed my phone and answered the call. "Hello?" My voice sounded like I'd swallowed gravel.

"There's a ghost in the library," Higgins said. "Take care of it."

"What? What time is it?" I sat up and rubbed my eyes. "A ghost?"

"It's tearing the place apart. Security footage looks like it's reading some of the books too." Rustling sounded on his end. "We've never had a problem with ghosts before. Invisible bastards."

I held in my groan. "I don't think it's a ghost."

EMBER

The needle of Ash's tattoo gun raked across my skin, the resistance to venom sigil taking shape on my arm. I winced as the ink approached the bend in my elbow, sucking a breath through my teeth.

Ash laughed and finished the final line. "All done. You should be used to this by now."

"My nervous system is fried from yesterday. From the past few months." I set the tip of my finger ablaze and lit the thicker skin, protection, and venom resistance designs, activating the magical ink. The sigil trio glowed bright red before fading to a cool blue.

"I'd ask for speed and strength too, but I don't think I can handle any more ink."

"Offensive sigils tax my vim too much. *I* couldn't handle doing five on each of us." She wiggled her tattoo machine at Chaos. "You're up."

"I'm not sure your sigils will protect me. I'm not of this realm." He sat at her station and laid his arm on the table.

"It's worth a shot." She changed the needle and dipped it into a fresh well of ink. "The fae venom got to you last time, so we have to try."

While she applied sigils to her demon and herself, I checked my phone. I'd messaged both Miles and Shade twice, but they hadn't responded, so I dialed Shade's number, the phone ringing five times before sending me to voicemail.

"Fae are destroying the library," I said. "Meet us there ASAP."

I hit End and tried Miles. He picked up on the third ring, his voice thick from sleep. "Hello?"

"Higgins called. There's a fae soldier in the library." I assumed it was a soldier, at least. What other beastie would be invisible to the cameras? I sure as hell didn't want to know.

"What time is it?" Sheets rustled through the phone before he sighed. "It's five in the morning."

My phone pinged, and I checked the screen. Higgins's text read, *Where the hell are you? The reference section is being shredded.*

"I don't think the fae care about the time. Neither does Higgins, so wake up Shade and meet us there."

"On it," he said through a yawn. He hung up the phone, and I hoped to Hecate he didn't go back to sleep.

"They should come here first so I can give them ink." Ash lit her finger ablaze and activated the sigils on herself and Chaos. "Defensive sigil magic doesn't tax my vim as much as healing does."

"I'll let Patrice know to be ready." I sent her a text and grabbed my sword from the table. "He's tearing apart the reference section."

"Oof. We better hurry then."

I knew that would get her in gear.

She slung her bag over her shoulder and cast a forlorn glance at the tattoo mess we were about to leave behind. "We have to save the books."

With my sword sheathed in my back scabbard and four knives strapped to my legs, I led the way out the back door. If we lived in any other town, the number of weapons I wore on the daily would set off alarms. Thankfully, Salem was a booming tourist attraction, so most people assumed I was in costume.

Not that it mattered this morning. Sea fog had rolled in overnight, desaturating the dark city and making it look almost like we were walking through one of Shade's shadows. The crisp morning air raised goosebumps on my arms, and I rubbed them to chase away the chill.

"We should have worn jackets." Ash matched my determined strides, her teeth chattering as the library came into view.

"Nah. Things are about to heat up."

My phone pinged with a response from Patrice: *Let me know if you need me. Oh, I spoke to Chrys's mom. Someone messed with the ward on her building and broke into her and a human's apartment. Could be Boston again.*

I replied: *It was us. I'll explain next time I see you. At the library now.*

It pinged again when I shoved it into my pocket, but I ignored the message and crossed the street.

Higgins stood on the front steps, his meaty arms crossed, a toothpick hanging out of his mouth. "It's about damn time you got here. You stop for breakfast along the way?"

My eye twitched. How could a man in his position hold so much contempt for the people who saved his ass on the regular? "Maybe next time you should take care of it yourself. Or are you too scared?"

"I ain't afraid of no ghosts." He ascended the stairs and unlocked the door before curling his lip at me. "But I left my proton pack at the station."

"Scrub the footage when we're done." I unsheathed my sword and stepped through the door before I could lob off his head too.

A few lights glowed softly overhead, which was all I needed to see the mess the soldier had made of the fiction section. Paperbacks and hardcovers lay haphazardly about the floor, no doubt thrown aside when the overgrown fly-man couldn't find whatever he was looking for. Loose pages littered the tables and chairs, and claw marks marred the dark wood shelves.

Ash gasped behind me. "How dare he?"

"There's a rift." Chaos marched ahead, pointing to an area on the right where a shelving unit lay on its side, the books it once contained strewn around it. "We should seal it."

A thud and a scrape sounded from above, like furniture dragging across the floor.

Ash ground her teeth. "We have to save the books first."

"Is the reference section still on the second floor?" I headed for the staircase.

"Yes," she said, and they followed me up.

As I reached the landing, I slowed, my gaze cutting left and right, searching for the *Predator* shimmer in the air, listening for the grotesque rustle of giant insect wings. The sound of footsteps echoed from below before Shade and Miles pounded up the stairs, alerting the enemy of our arrival. I held in a groan.

"You couldn't have waited five minutes?" Shade drew two knives from his harness.

"You couldn't have gotten here any faster?" I held my sword in both hands, gathering fire in the core of my being and sending the flames up the blade to illuminate the dark hallway.

"Where's Mayhem?" Miles asked.

"I vanquished him." I crept forward, my arms tensing, ready to swing at the first snap of the beastie's pincers. "Which way, Ash?"

"Wait. Seriously?" Shade laid a hand on my shoulder.

I shrugged him off. "Which way?"

"We'll explain later," Ash said before taking a deep breath. "To the left. Dammit, he's in the Salem history room. Those volumes are priceless."

My sister marched ahead, her hands fisted at her sides, and I smiled. The only time Ash Holland ever threw caution to the wind was when books were in danger.

I extinguished my sword and walked next to her, matching her determined pace. We flanked either side of the entry, and Chaos joined her, while Miles and Shade stood on my side.

One of the double doors stood ajar, and I peeked inside. Destroyed books littered the floor, their pages ripped out and shredded into hundreds-of-years-old confetti. I was never a bookish gal, but seeing our city's history torn to shreds hurt my heart.

"Someone digitized all these books, right?" I asked.

Ash's brows slammed down. "Not yet…"

Tearing paper sounded from inside, and the thud of a tome dropping to the floor followed. My sister's eyes widened.

I turned to the guys. "We have sigil protection, so we'll go in first. You two follow."

Shade opened his mouth to argue, but Ash threw the doors open and stepped into the room. "Oh, hell no," she said.

I focused my intent on recognizing the fae shimmer and followed her in to find a giant roach-man flipping through a book of historic property deeds. Of course they'd send a scout to gather information, but… "Why doesn't he show up on cameras?"

"Must be something in his DNA." Chaos gathered hellfire in his palms.

"No fire." Ash clutched his arm. "We can't risk any more damage."

Roach-man snapped his butt-ugly head toward us and hissed.

Ash held a hand toward him. "Standing tall or on—"

The fae rushed her, knocking her to the ground and chomping on her shoulder. Her sigils fought back. His teeth barely grazed her thickened skin, and her body expelled the venom in seconds.

Chaos kicked Roachman in the head, exposing his unprotected neck, and I jabbed a dagger into the soft spot beneath his ear hole. He screeched, flapping his papery wings and jetting to the ceiling before yanking out the blade. "How did you do it?"

I made a stabbing motion with my hand. "It's not hard."

He peeled back his thin lips to expose jagged teeth. "The soldier. How did you kill her?"

I laughed dryly. "Which one?"

Ash rose to her feet, the flesh wound on her shoulder already healing. "You won't find the answer in here." She grabbed Chaos's hand and nodded at Roachman.

"You will come down and allow us to kill you." He splayed his fingers, and hellfire licked down to their tips before returning inside him.

"The hell I will." He fluttered his disgusting wings, the sound making my skin crawl. "The world will be ours."

I shook my head. "You giant buggers keep saying that, but we keep taking you out. As long as witches exist, this world will never belong to the fae."

He hurled the dagger at me, the blade barely nicking my arm before it hit the ground. Yay for protection sigils.

Roachman roared and flew at me like a witch-seeking missile, slamming into my chest before pinning me against the wall. He opened his revolting mouth, venomous saliva dripping from pointy teeth, and I pressed my lips together, rolling them inward. No way in hell was I tasting that shit again.

Miles hit him with an energy ball, but it ricocheted off his exoskeleton and hit Shade in the stomach. His body convulsed, and he doubled over, clutching his gut. "Goddess, that hurts."

"Sorry." Miles touched his shoulder.

Roachman reared back, ready to chomp my face, but I pulled the same trick on him as I had on Mayhem. Grabbing a knife from my thigh holster, I shoved it upward, beneath one of his armored plates. Sadly, I missed his heart.

He recoiled, glaring at me like I was the vilest, most insolent creature he'd ever seen. I started to tell him the feeling was mutual, but he shoved Shade aside and darted out the door before I could open my mouth.

I gave chase, barreling down the stairs after him and setting my sword ablaze. When I reached the ground floor, I swung. Fiery enchanted silver sliced into his wing, making him howl. He flapped, bits of char raining onto the floor, but he couldn't take flight.

My team closed in behind us, the guys with their weapons drawn and Ash holding three potion bottles. Roachman screeched and chittered, speaking a language that didn't even sound like words.

Ash recited a perimeter-locating spell and blew powder into the air. It collected around a two-foot rift, revealing four sets of talons trying to rip it open wider. The claws shimmered and disappeared.

"Effing soldiers. Seal it before they get through." I swung my sword at Roachman, but he feinted left and lashed out a clawed hand, cutting into Ash's arm and knocking the second potion bottle out of her hand.

It shattered on the floor, liquid spilling around her feet, sizzling and turning into purple smoke.

"Crappity crap! That's a nerve hex." She tensed, drawing her shoulders toward her ears, her face contorting with pain.

Chaos threw a punch, hitting Roachman in the jaw. The fae careened backward, falling on his ass before hissing and darting through the rift.

An oblong shimmer protruded from the tear, and I brought my blade down, slicing through it. The cloak disintegrated, revealing a soldier's insect-like arm, and Ash wheezed, collapsing against Chaos.

"Is this the sealing spell?" I pried the last bottle from her rigid fist, and she nodded.

I tossed the bottle to Miles and let the guys take care of the rift before turning back to my sister. "Do you have the antidote?"

She nodded, patting her bag. Her knees buckled, her legs swelling, turning purple beneath her fishnets, and Chaos lowered her to the floor. I rummaged through her bag while Chaos removed her boots and tore off her tights.

"Those protection sigils don't last long enough." There must've been thirty bottles in her satchel, some individual ingredients, some premixed spells...none of them labeled. "Which one is it?"

"Red jar," she said through clenched teeth. Sweat poured down her face, and her body seized, every muscle tensing before she passed out from the pain. Nerve hexes were the worst. I knew that from experience.

"Help her," Chaos demanded, not hiding the menace in his voice.

"I am." I twisted off the lid and smeared the semi-gelatinous liquid over her swollen legs. Sparkles gathered on her skin, the purple fading to her normal pale complexion, the swelling receding instantly.

Her eyes flew open, and she sucked in a massive breath before bolting upright. "Where'd the bastard go?"

"Through the rift. He got away." I found a towel in her bag o' magic and wiped my hands.

"It's sealed." Miles handed me the empty bottle.

I returned it and the jar to the satchel. "Since when do you play with nerve hexes?"

"Shade's was so effective on us, I thought it might work on the fae." She put on her boots. "I didn't plan on dropping it."

"You should use capsules like the witches in New Orleans." Chaos helped her to her feet.

"As soon as I have a moment to breathe, I'll figure out how to make them." She rotated her ankles and shook out her legs. "All better."

"Be more careful with those." I sheathed my sword and tucked my hair behind my ears. "If the smoke had spread to all of us, we'd be dead."

She laughed. "But you said being too careful would get us killed. Make up your mind."

"You know what I mean." I jerked my head toward the exit. "Let's get out of here so Higgins can concoct his story and deal with the mess."

The Chief arched a brow as we filed past him, expecting a

detailed report but not using his words like a big boy. When I didn't give him what he wanted, he grabbed my arm. "Well?"

I looked at his hand before glaring into his eyes. "I suggest you let me go before I—"

"Ember…" Ash's voice dripped with warning, and yeah, okay… Threatening to decapitate a police officer wasn't in my best interest, but I was so goddess-damned tired of his disrespect.

"Will you please let me go?" I forced a smile, trying my best not to sneer.

He dropped my arm, and I stepped back out of his reach. "Did you kill the ghost?"

Hecate, please give me the strength to answer him without sounding like a snarky bitch. "Even if it were a ghost in the library, you can't kill something that's already dead." I crossed my arms. "The creature inside was a fae scout looking for information, and no, we did not kill him. He went back to his own realm, and we sealed the rift. Call it whatever floats your boat. The library is empty now."

That sounded okay, right?

He narrowed his eyes. "What kind of information?"

"He wanted to know how we killed his friends. Of course he didn't find what he was looking for. We keep the books about real witchcraft in our coven library."

"You'll have to show me that library."

"Not a chance." I turned on my heel and descended the steps.

The sun peeked over the horizon as we made our way back home, but it wasn't yet high enough to warm the bitter wind.

My hair whipped into my face as we entered the alley behind our building, and I brushed it out of my eyes, stopping short on the back porch.

"Something feels off." I closed my eyes, opening my senses to the magic surrounding the building. Only remnants remained. "Someone broke our ward."

"Hold on." Ash cast her magic-revealing spell, and sure enough, only a few sparkles clung to the door frame. Someone had dissolved the magic meant to keep out those with ill intent.

CHAPTER 3
EMBER

My pulse thrumming, I slowly turned the doorknob. Someone had picked the lock. I held up my hand, telling my team to hold their positions, and stepped to the side as I inched the door open, ready for whatever awaited us inside to attack.

Eerie silence greeted me instead.

Ash cast her spell on the entry hall, but the only magic clinging to the walls was the residue of decades of our own work. I drew my sword, holding it down at my side as I crept inside. The library stood in its normal state of disarray, but Ash's desk, always neat and organized, held a messy stack of books and one half-open drawer. She would never leave it in that state.

"Did one of you use the desk?" I asked.

The guys shook their heads, and Ash frowned, pacing toward it and restacking the books.

"I was the last one to use it." She opened the drawer fully and rummaged through it. "Nothing is missing." She closed it and shrugged. "But I left my studio a mess this morning, so it's possible I did this. I haven't had time to keep things organized lately."

"Or someone was looking for something." I stepped into the studio. Everything seemed as we left it, but the storage cabinet had one door ajar. "Ash? Is anything missing from here?"

She joined me, opening the doors and examining the shelves. "It looks like everything is here." She moved a few items, tidying up the space.

I peeked into the darkened storefront. The layer of dust on the counter said no one had been inside for weeks, yet a sinking sensation formed in my gut. Nothing was missing so far, but something felt wrong. *Very* wrong. "Shade, Miles, check the basement storage and meet us upstairs."

"On it," Miles said.

"Do you sense any beasties in our midst?" I headed for the stairs, pausing on the first step.

Chaos inhaled, stilling as he sent out his demonic feelers. "Nothing of my kind. I don't sense anything from across the veil."

My heart joined my sinking stomach, roiling into a tangled mess of dread. "Boston. Mayhem. They tried to find his skull before." I darted up the stairs.

I'd left the skull on my nightstand for anyone brave enough to break in to steal. With Higgins on my back to hurry up and bust his "ghost," I hadn't bothered with a ward or even a hiding place.

If someone had stolen my demon, we'd be screwed.

I ignored the partially open drawers in the kitchen and barreled through the living room. Stopping in my doorway, I gasped at the sight, my roiling innards twisting and tumbling, taking the blood from my head with them as they threatened to splatter on the floor.

"Mayhem." My voice barely registered in my ears as I dropped to my knees. "I'm so sorry."

His skull lay in pieces on the hardwood. Someone had smashed him to bits and left the fragments for me to find as a big ol' *eff you*.

Pressure built in the back of my eyes, my throat thickening as I cradled the biggest piece in my hands, hoping for the not-unpleasant pinprick sensation to dance across my skin. I felt nothing but cool bone.

"Oh my goddess." Ash grabbed an empty shoe box from my closet and helped me gather the pieces. "What happened?"

"I don't know." I counted twenty-three fragments as we added them to the box.

"Someone does not want my brother to reform." Chaos went to my dresser and rummaged through the open drawers, pushing my clothes aside. "The amulet isn't here. Did you move it?"

I opened the nightstand drawer and held up the container. "It's here."

Chaos pursed his lips, narrowing his eyes in confusion. "Did the fae hit you in the head?"

Ash's expression matched his. "That's your vibrator, Em."

"No, this is my vibrator." I held up the device in question. "*This* is an amulet with a cloaking spell." I returned them both to the drawer and closed it.

My sister nodded her approval. "Smart. Nobody would mess with that."

Chaos raised his brow. "I suppose not."

I picked up the box o' bones and sat on my bed, holding it in my lap. My lower lip started to tremble for some goddess-knew-why reason, so I bit it. My mind reeled. Who could have known the skull was here? The only people I'd told were the ones who'd been with me all morning.

I took a piece of skull from the box, running my finger over the jagged edge. "Can he still reform? We have to bring him back. We can't do this without him."

And I suddenly missed the big beast. Sure, he drove me batty and needled me every chance he got, but I wouldn't wish an eternity in the dark prison on anyone.

If I were honest, I'd admit I kinda liked our banter.

"If all the pieces are there, he can reform." Chaos eyed the floor where his brother had lain. "You'll need the debris as well." He pointed at a few pea-sized shards lying on the wood in a pile of bone granules.

"I'll get the dustpan." Ash turned on her heel and stepped through the door.

"Who would do this? Nobody knew he was here." I kneeled on the floor and picked up the tiny bits, adding them to the box. "And how will we know if all the pieces are here? I won't chance possessing myself if we can't exorcize him."

"Exorcizing him won't be a problem." Ash swept the granules into the dustpan and emptied them into the box. "But if his skull isn't complete, he'll look for another host. He tried to possess you when we exorcized him from Chrys."

"I thought he was in a containment circle." I stood and carried the box to the living room.

"It cracked." Ash followed. "His smoke poured through and circled above you before we vanquished him."

"Why am I just now hearing about this?" I set what was left of Mayhem on the coffee table and plopped into my favorite chair. Normally, news like that would have me reeling. Now...it seemed like par for the course.

Chaos shrugged. "It's not important. Do you have all the pieces?"

Not important that a demon prince tried to possess me, and it never crossed their minds to tell me. In the grand scheme of things, I supposed it wasn't. Not anymore.

The door swung open, and Shade stepped through. "The basement seems fine."

Miles followed. "It's hard to say if anything is missing, but nothing appears out of place. Whoa. Is that...?"

"It's Mayhem. Can you get the superglue?" I sat cross-legged on the floor and grabbed the two biggest pieces, turning them until they fit together. "It's arts and crafts time."

"Here." Miles set the glue on the table and joined me on the floor. "What happened?"

"That's the million-dollar question." I applied a thin strip of adhesive to one of the pieces and pressed them together, counting to fifteen for it to set before picking up another piece.

"Someone was obviously looking for something." Ash sat across from me and helped rebuild the skull.

"Yeah, but what?" I found another piece that fit. "If they were here to destroy the skull, it was in plain view in my room. They wouldn't have gone through my dresser."

"It has to be the amulet." Ash handed me a triangular piece to add to the cranium. "Maybe one of Chrys's followers knew about it."

"How would they know it was here?" Shade grabbed a protein bar from the pantry and shoved the whole thing into his mouth. "They'd look for it at Chrys's," he mumbled around the food.

"They could have scried for it." Miles tried a tiny shard in the hole on top of the cranium, but it didn't fit. "Maybe they went to her place first. Who knows?"

"Wait." I handed the partially assembled skull to Miles and grabbed my phone. "Patrice said Chrys's mom knew about our break-in. Maybe she..." I swiped open the screen and read the message I'd ignored. *Oof.*

"Someone went in after us." I swallowed the bile from the back of my mouth. "A human was murdered...gutted. A cat too."

"Oh crap." Ash set the piece of skull she was gluing on the table. "Livers?"

"She didn't say. They turned Chrys's apartment upside-down, though." I dialed Patrice's number and put it on speaker. She answered on the fourth ring.

"What else did Ivy tell you?" I asked.

"Hold on." Rustling sounded through the phone, followed

by a door clicking shut. "Just what I told you. Did one of your demons...?"

"No." I shook my head adamantly, though she couldn't see my rejection of the idea. "Mayhem broke down the wrong door, but no one was home. And we unraveled the ward, but we found what we were looking for at Chrys's without tearing the place apart."

"What were you looking for?"

"She had a piece of an amulet that gave her more power." Ash glued another shard of skull. "It's how she got so strong."

"Oh," Patrice said. "That makes sense, I guess. But you have it now?"

"It's in a safe place where no one will find it." I plucked the missing cranial fragment from the box and handed it to Miles. "We have to find the rest of it before we can summon Discord."

"And before whoever else is looking for it finds it," Chaos said. "Did she tell you anything about it?"

"She never mentioned it to me," Patrice said.

"Not even in a villainous monologue when she rooted you to the basement floor?" I held the cranium while Miles glued the rest of the orbital bone into place.

"No, sorry. But the coven has sealed three rifts today, and it's not even noon."

"Thanks, Patrice." I pinched the bridge of my nose. "It's only going to get worse from here. Stay vigilant."

"We will."

I hung up and glued a tooth into a section of jawbone. "What would the fae want with the amulet?"

"If they're even the ones looking for it." Ash handed me the rest of the mandible. "It could be Boston making it look like the fae."

"Shit. You're right." I fastened the two pieces together, completing the jaw.

"The amulet grants immeasurable power to its bearer." Chaos cracked his knuckles. "The half-blooded fae prince and the High Priest of Boston would both benefit from finding it."

"Great. So it's either Ignacus the Imbecile Insect, or it's Adrian the Asshat pretending to be the Imbecile." I arched a brow at Miles. "Can you talk to Wendy and find out which?"

He closed his eyes and let out a slow breath. "For the greater good, yes. But if I have to watch her pick her nose one more time, I might put her out of her misery myself."

"Hey now. That's not what light witches are about." I balanced the top part of the skull on the jaw.

"I'm happy to do the dark work for you," Chaos said, and Ash backhanded him on the shoulder, making him laugh. "I kid."

"Uh-huh. Something's off. It's not fitting right." The skull slipped off the jaw.

"It's missing a piece. Look." Ash turned the left side toward me, and sure enough, a half-inch chunk wasn't where it should have been. "That part probably got pulverized." She ran a finger through the granules in the box.

I held the skull in my hands, staring into the vacant eye sockets. The piece could have been smashed beyond repair, as she said, but something in the core of my being told me that wasn't it. Setting Mayhem on the table, I rested one hand on his skull and put two fingers into the pile of granules, closing my eyes and letting instinct take over.

A faint pricking sensation made my palm tingle, and I focused on what was left of the demon's essence. I pictured his face, the amusement in his eyes when he goaded me, the surprise when I one-upped him with my retort.

My stomach tightened, and the urge to return to my bedroom had me on my feet before I realized I had moved, my mind's eye showing me exactly where the missing piece lay. I strode down the hall and lowered to my knees, peering under the bed. Sure as sugar, there it was, right where I'd seen it in my mind.

Strange. I'd never been able to locate stuff like this before.

I returned to the living room and held it up triumphantly. "Maybe I have a little bit of Dad's magic too."

Ash looked at Chaos, and he nodded, opening his mouth to speak before I cut him off.

"It is not more proof of your soulmate theory, so don't even try." I ignored the looks they all exchanged and glued the final piece into place. "Now he's complete. Has Wendy replied?"

"I haven't texted her." Miles tugged his phone from his pocket and typed on the screen.

I gingerly picked up the skull and laid it in the box with the too-small-to-assemble pieces. "This is all of it. I'm positive."

The moment I let go of Mayhem, the skull trembled. The pieces vibrated against each other, shaking back and forth as if every seam were a fault line. Smoke rose from the glue, spiraling upward and dissipating in the air.

Every fragment we had carefully put together crumbled apart.

"Why is it doing that?" My pulse sprinting, I reached into the box, hoping to save the pieces, but the moment I touched bone, it turned to sand, sifting through my fingers as if it had never been a solid object. "What the hell?"

Chaos leaned forward, scrunching his brow. "It's as if the glue has broken the bonds of the skull...a chemical reaction unlike anything I've seen."

"Oh, crap." Ash grabbed the tube of superglue. "Crappity crap. It's the magic."

"What magic? It's just glue." I took it from her and examined the label. It looked and felt completely mundane, but knowing my sister... "Ash, what did you do?"

She held up her hands. "Not me. It kept getting clogged, so Cinder cast a spell on it so the glue would never dry unless we wanted it to."

"She magically changed the chemical makeup." Shade took the tube from my hand. "That's genius."

"Then why couldn't we feel the magic when we used it?" Miles took a turn holding it.

"Because she focused it only on the contents," Ash said. "She can cast spells through objects."

"And we just turned all we have of Mayhem from bone to sand." I ran my fingers through the grains, and they crumbled even more, turning to a fine powder. Cinder and I would have words if we made it through this ordeal.

"What now?" Miles asked. "We can't summon him without

his skull, can we? I mean, not unless someone wants to sacrifice their life so he can burn through them."

"And that is out of the question." My heart sank. How could I have been such an idiot? I'd screwed us six ways to Sunday when, if I had stopped to check on Ash after I lobbed off Mayhem's head, I would have known I didn't have to vanquish him.

Then I didn't bother setting up a ward on the skull because I let Higgins get to me.

And now, this demon...this man...who'd shown me a shred of humanity, of vulnerability he'd probably never shown anyone else, was rotting in a dark prison because I didn't stop to consider the consequences of my actions. To realize there might be a better way to handle the situation than through violence. My chest tightened, a fist of longing squeezing my heart because, goddess dammit, I missed Mayhem and now I might never see him again.

No. No, I couldn't think that way. I would get him back if I had to go to Hell and bargain with Lucifer myself. *Whoa. Where did that come from?* It didn't matter. We needed him, and we *would* save him.

"It's still his skull." I shot to my feet and paced in front of the television. "Even if it's turned to dust, it's all there. We can still summon him." I squared my gaze on Chaos. "Right?"

"I believe so," he said.

Nausea churned in my stomach. "You *believe* so? If we're going to do it the way you suggested, I need you to be certain."

He ran his fingers through the grains. "It's still bone. It will work."

A flash of red sparked inside the box, and a stream of black smoke rose in a spiral from the center.

"What's happening now?" I dropped to my knees and peered inside. "Holy Hecate. It's turning to ash."

"Super crap." My sister blinked at me, her eyes widening. "Ashes can't be resurrected without a phoenix spell."

"Phoenix spell?" Chaos asked.

"It's the darkest of dark. A form of necromancy." I gripped the table so tightly, my nails made indentions in the wood. "We have to summon him before his skull completely burns away. Go get the grimoire. *Now.*"

CHAPTER 4
EMBER

"Bring the box downstairs." Ash shot to her feet. "All the supplies are in my studio."

I scooped the shoebox into my arms and carried it down, my insides tying into knots with each step I took. The bone powder glowed red as the burning spread from the center outward. By the time I reached the studio, half of it had turned to ashes.

"Here's the containment spell." Shade picked up the grimoire. "Does everyone remember it?"

"We don't have time for that." I poured a ring of salt and set the box on the floor as I kneeled to draw Mayhem's sigil. "And we don't have time to do it your way," I said to Ash.

"This is dangerous." She set candles at the five points of the pentagram and lit them with her magic.

"Do you have a better idea?" I drew his mark from memory,

the familiar pin-pricking sensation dancing up my arm as I completed the final swoop.

"It must be done," Chaos said.

I set the shoebox on top of the sigil and rose, dusting my hands against my pants before scanning the summoning spell. We joined hands around the circle in our usual positions, and the smoke thickened in the box, the bone burning until only a thin ring remained.

"Hit me with all you've got." I squeezed Chaos's hand, and he opened to me, a blast of demon magic surging through my psyche and making my head spin. I gave some of it to Shade, and we recited the incantation in unison.

Still clutching each other's hands, we stared at the box, waiting for Mayhem's purple smoke to consume the bone powder.

Nothing happened.

"Try again." Panic tinged the edges of my voice, and my stomach felt like it was crawling into my chest.

We cast the summoning again. Still, nothing happened.

"It's not working," Ash said.

"No shit." I focused on the sigil, an image of Mayhem's face forming in my mind. "One more time. Don't hold back."

Another tidal wave of magic coursed through my system, the essence of three other witches and a demon spiraling through me, mixing and melding until I thought I might burst. "Hecate, please help us."

We recited the summoning a third time, and I reached as far into the ether as my mind would allow, searching for the low vibration of my demon. I found nothing, and the black smoke in the shoebox faded as the last of the bone powder incinerated, leaving behind a single glowing ember.

Shade loosened his grip on my hand, but I held him tighter, refusing to give up. This had to work. Mayhem had to come back.

"Please," I whispered. "I need you."

The final ember dimmed, taking my hope with it.

My posture deflated, and I dropped my hands to my sides. Pressure built in the back of my eyes, but I blinked back the tears threatening to fall. I would not get emotional in front of my team. Not now. Not ever.

I strode to the table and slammed the grimoire shut. "I'm sorry, Ash. I..."

"Ember..." She grabbed my arm and spun me toward the summoning circle.

A thick stream of purple smoke poured through an invisible rift, billowing inside the ring before swirling around the box. My breath caught at the sight, and I pressed a hand to my chest. My heart sprinted beneath my fingers as I stepped toward him, a mix of relief, wariness, and elation swirling inside me.

"Mayhem?" I reached for the demon.

He recoiled, his face forming in the smoke. "You burned my skull?"

"It was an accident." I held up my hands. "We were trying to bring you back."

"Liar!" He slammed into my chest, and I careened backward, crashing into the wall. An arm formed, pressing against me with nearly enough force to crack a rib, his smoky face two inches from mine as he spoke.

"Now I cannot reform without a host," he growled.

I shook my head, wheezing as I sucked in a breath. "We'll figure something out. Give us some time."

His lip pulled into a sneer. "I cannot exist in this realm without a corporeal form. You, dear witch, just condemned one of your coven members to death."

His smoky form jerked away, billowing toward the door.

"Take me." I stepped toward him. "I'll be your host."

His menacing laugh echoed as if it had formed in the bowels of Hell and traveled across the veil the moment he opened his mouth. "I will deal with you after I reform."

He shot through the door, knocking the books off Ash's desk on his way out the back, and all I could do was watch him leave.

Silence filled the room like someone stuffed it with cotton, no one moving a muscle as what just happened sank in. My mouth hung open, so I snapped it shut and waited for my brain to process it all. The skull was gone...completely ash...before Mayhem crossed the veil.

"How...?" I turned around to find my team with the same perplexed expressions. "There was nothing left. The skull was mostly ash when we started. We shouldn't have been able to bust him out of prison without it."

"*We* didn't." Chaos leaned against the table and crossed his arms. "You did."

"No." I picked up the box of ashes and set it on the table. "We all recited the words. We shared our magic."

"If that was all it took, it would have worked the first time." Ash picked up the candles, extinguishing them one by one. "Any chance of using his skull to summon him died when the last grain went out. Hell, we probably lost our chance when it first started burning. This was all you, sis."

I shook my head. It didn't make sense.

"Did you do something different the third time we tried?" Miles swept the salt ring into a dustpan.

"No." I racked my brain, trying to remember, but the adrenaline from getting slammed against the wall by a smoke demon hadn't dissipated from my system. "I don't think so."

"You connected with him through the veil," Chaos said. "I felt it happen."

"I didn't... How?"

"The same way Ash connected with me. Through your bond." He set the salt canister in the cabinet. "You are two halves of a whole."

"Then why wouldn't he possess her?" Shade asked. "Not that I wish it on her, but wouldn't he want to burn through Ember and bring the two halves together for good?"

"They're soulmates," Miles said. "Of course he wouldn't."

"Do you believe us now?" Ash carried her tattoo machine to the table and pulled up two chairs. "Only you could summon Mayhem without his skull, just like only I could summon Chaos."

Shade laughed, disbelieving. "I supposed that means Cinder..."

"And Discord, yes," Chaos said. "The six of us coming

together was written in the stars long before any of you were born."

I looked at Chaos and then my sister, who raised her brows, giving me her *get over yourself and accept it* look. "You feel it," she said.

"I don't know what you're talking about." Yes, that was a lie. I did feel it, all the way down to the core of my being, swimming in my blood and penetrating my bones.

It didn't mean I had to like it.

"Come on. Sit." Ash poured magical ink into a well and sat at one of the chairs. "You need to catch your demon before he hurts someone else."

"What are you thinking?" I took the chair across from her. "I'd say speed and strength, but I don't think those would help with wrangling a giant puff of smoke."

"No." She dipped the needle into the ink. "You're going to make him possess you."

"You're the only one who can survive it," Chaos said. "He'll hold back as long as he can while you formulate another plan."

Ash swiped open her phone and pulled up Mayhem's mark. "And if we can't reform his skull, we'll exorcise him and send him to prison. We won't let him hurt you."

"I don't need convincing." Because I would not sacrifice a coven member...or anyone else...to bring him back. I laid my arm on the table. "Let's do it."

"Focus on Mayhem while I draw it. Don't think about anything else." She pressed the pulsing needle against my skin. "Picture him in your mind and feel the emotions he stirs inside you, whatever they are."

That was easy-peasy. The infuriating, sexy-as-hell demon hadn't left my thoughts since the moment he arrived. I closed my eyes, imagining the way he looked at me, feeling the adrenaline spiking in my system every time he tried to put me in my place. Even when his smoky form had pinned me against the wall, my fear had bled into...arousal?

Gross. No, that wasn't the right word. Excitement, maybe.

I was so lost in thought, I didn't feel the tattoo until Ash reached the delicate skin on the inside of my wrist. I winced at the burning, stinging sensation and opened my eyes. "Don't forget it goes left."

She chuckled. "I won't."

With the final loop complete, Ash turned off her machine and carried it to the counter. She wiped the excess ink from my skin before admiring her work. "It looks good on you."

I agreed, but I didn't dare say it aloud. "Is there anything special I have to do before I activate it?"

"I don't think so." She emptied the ink well and washed it in the small sink next to her supplies. "I had no clue I was summoning a demon when I did it."

Chaos laughed. "She wanted help organizing her library."

"Which we will do when this is all through." She wrapped her arms around his waist and nodded at the sigil on my arm. "It's time."

I took a deep breath, centering myself. "Let's light this baby up."

CHAPTER 5
MAYHEM

Betrayal didn't begin to describe what Ember had done. I growled as I flowed out of her home, reining in my smoke to blend with the air around me...the one and only benefit of this fluid form. I had only hours to find a host before the dark prison sucked me back across the veil, trapping me in nothingness for eternity.

How could that witch...my soulmate...do this to me?

In the time I'd spent alone, devoid of all my senses, with nothing but my thoughts to occupy myself, I had resolved to forgive her. Ember and her sister had a special bond. Of that I had no doubt.

I also had no doubt that my brother would have torn off my head and clawed out my heart had Ember not acted so quickly. I much preferred her blade to Chaos's talons.

Her decision to end my time on Earth had come from a place of love and devotion, and I would have expected nothing less of her. I had hoped that, perhaps one day, she would find in herself the same love and devotion for me.

Instead, she destroyed my skull and then summoned me back to torment me with her betrayal.

How could I have been so stupid?

It was Isabel all over again, yet this time, for some reason, the witch's treachery cut deeper than I ever could have imagined.

My mission now was simple: Find the strongest witch in the coven—after the three involved in Ember's villainous plot—and possess and burn through him, gaining as much power as possible. I would steal the amulet shard to increase my strength and put an end to the Holland bloodline.

Then, I would take out my brother too. Damn him for his involvement.

I poured down the main street, opening my senses and searching for the high vibration of witchcraft. I had met their healer, Patrice, but she was far too weak. I wouldn't waste my time on anyone who only possessed such passive magic.

My first choice would have been their shadow witch, had he not been involved in the destruction of my skull and the resummoning. Miles, with his underdeveloped energy manipulation ability, would have been my second choice, but both men needed to suffer along with the women.

Humans lurked about everywhere, peering into windows and snapping photos with their phones. Even with the threat of a serial killer in their midst, they risked their lives to post their images and measured their self-worth by how many others liked them.

Idiots.

The only reason the species had survived so long was because their damned souls provided the most potent fuel in the Underworld. Lucifer knew I'd take pleasure in eradicating them otherwise. He'd threatened to end my existence multiple times because of it.

I traveled out of the downtown area and headed toward a residential section of Salem. Surely, I would find powerful witches living amongst the mundane here. A tickle of energy pulled me to a white building with blue shutters on the windows. I stilled, absorbing the essence of the being inside, sifting it through my metaphorical fingers to gauge his power. He was nothing more than a kitchen witch.

I moved on, searching and feeling until a sharp spike of magic gripped my psyche. I fought it, certain the dark prison was already calling me home, but the power was too great, the pull too strong.

This wasn't the prison. No, the vibration was too high to have come from Hell. Before I could contemplate it more, the energy ripped me through the fabric of reality and slammed me into the mind of the one who had summoned me.

Darkness engulfed me. Then piercing white light blinded me. Raw elemental magic, stronger than any I had felt before, surged through my soul, enrapturing me. I reveled in it, rolling in the power like a hellcat in a field of catnip, feeling as though, at last, all the missing pieces of my existence had snapped into place.

My host blinked, her vision still blurred, and she clutched her head. "Whoa. My skull feels like it's going to crack open."

Her warm honey voice soothed me, tempering my rage as I opened myself to all her senses.

"Hold on. I have a spell for that," a familiar voice said. "Shade, slide that trash can over to her. She'll need it."

My host's stomach retched. She dropped to her knees, clutching the rim of the bin, and vomited. Her last meal mixed with bitter acid, burning her throat, and bringing me to my senses. Of course it would be her. No one else would be strong enough to force a demon of my level to possess them.

"Ember..."

"You don't have to shout. You're literally in my head." She accepted the napkin and water Miles offered, taking a sip and swishing before spitting into the bin and wiping her mouth.

"Here." Ash set a grimoire on the floor beside her. "Cast this one. It doesn't require a potion."

Her vision swam, tears blurring her eyes. She blinked them away, bringing the page into focus. "May the light of the goddess lift my pain. My headache will ease like a cleansing rain."

She sat back on her heels and rolled her neck as the pressure eased into a dull ache. "I seriously thought my skull was going to split."

The fury, which her essence had eased in me, returned with a vengeance at her words. *"You dare mock me with talk of your skull after you destroyed mine? I should burn through you right now and take Salem as my own."*

She rose to her feet, gulping down the rest of the water as Miles whisked the trash can out of the room. "You need to calm your hysterics, buddy. If you make my headache come back, there will be hell to pay."

"*How dare you tell me to be calm? I demand you release me immediately.*"

She sucked in a breath through her teeth. "First of all, I'll release you when I'm damn well ready and not a moment before. And second... It doesn't feel good to have your emotions dismissed, does it?"

"The witches have a plan to help you reform without killing a host," Chaos said. "But you must remain inside Ember until it is complete."

"*Treacherous witch. You destroyed my skull.*"

"I told you that was an accident. Now, hush so I can think." She paced the length of the room.

"*You speak with a forked tongue. It was no accident.*"

She sighed heavily. "Chaos, will you tell your brother we didn't do it on purpose? The vanquishing, yes. I meant to do that, but I planned to bring you right back."

"It's true." My brother looked into her eyes, squinting as if trying to see me in her irises. "We were called away to battle a fae. When we returned, your skull had been pulverized."

"*And burned to ash. Only magic could have destroyed it by fire, and you are the only fire witches in Salem.*"

"He's saying only we could have burned it." She pressed her fingers to her temples. "We don't have time for this."

"We did burn it," Ash said, "but I promise it was an accident."

"We were trying to glue it back together," Miles said as he

returned to the room. "We didn't know Cinder had enchanted the glue."

"Come on. We've got research to do." Ember strode out of the studio, stopping in the library by Ash's desk.

"What kind of enchantment?"

"It dissolved the bonds holding the bone together. After your skull turned to powder, it started smoking. We rushed to summon you before it burned out, but we were too late."

I remained silent, contemplating her story as the others joined her in the library. A large part of me desperately wanted to believe her, but hope belonged to the inexperienced youth. History had proven, time and again, that witches could never be trusted.

"A phoenix spell." She stood facing the desk, drumming her fingers on the surface. "Do we have one?"

Ash screwed her mouth to one side and sank into the chair. "There could have been one in the dark grimoire Mom and Dad gave to the demon."

"A lot of good that does us now." Ember strode to a bookcase and ran her finger through the dust on a shelf. "What about in the ones we took from Chrys or the teens who summoned the shedim?"

"It's worth a shot. Let me grab them." Ash rose and strode to the back of the library.

"Tell me about this phoenix spell. What is your plan?"

"It's dark magic, a type of necromancy...and it's forbidden."

"We know that," Shade said.

"I'm talking to Mayhem." Ember tapped her temple. "If we

can find one, we can use it to resurrect your skull and bring you back to the land of the living."

"And face the wrath of the Higher Power if they find out." Shade picked up a book from a stack on the floor and flipped through the pages before tossing it onto a shelf. "I'm not a fan of this idea."

"You don't have to help." Ember dropped into the chair and crossed her ankles on top of the desk. "But there's no other way to do it. I refuse to sacrifice a living being."

"What is the punishment if your Higher Power catches you?"

She shrugged. "A few years in prison at best. At worst, we could be killed...or stripped of our magic and banished to Arkansas." Her body shuddered.

"You would take that risk to save another witch's life?"

"And to save yours. As long as you behave yourself, that will be the last time you go to the dark prison. You're starting to grow on me." Her breath caught as if she didn't mean to say the last words aloud. "Like a fungus, I mean."

She peered at her arm, where my mark glowed a soft red, and ran her finger over the sigil. The sensation felt like warm silk running through my psyche and caressing every inch of my nonexistent body.

"Mmm... I like that."

She jerked down her sleeve.

"I'm not sensing a phoenix spell in either of these." Ash returned with two grimoires clutched to her chest. "I'll double-check to be sure."

Ember stood, giving her sister access to the desk. "If you don't sense it, it's not there."

"I still need to look. It's a forbidden spell, so it could be cloaked." She opened one book and pushed the other toward Ember. "Check this one."

Ember flipped through the pages, running her fingers over each entry. I felt her psyche open to the energy around her before she focused it into the grimoire. Her magic called to me, my demonic form begging me to take it as my own.

But the man in me didn't simply want her power. I wanted everything. Her body, her heart, her soul. My raging fury cooled to a slow simmer, but I had to be certain of her intentions before I extinguished it completely.

"I believe I can remain inside you for two weeks without burning through your form. If you focus on finding the amulet, you can summon Discord and we can lift the curse without risking your life and your magic."

She sighed. "Not a chance, Your Royal Pissiness. I did this to you. I'm going to make it right."

Hope sprung alive inside me once more as she perused the pages, ready to risk everything to save me from the dark prison. Perhaps her words were true. Maybe my skull's destruction really was an accident.

"I don't sense any cloaking magic in this one. Trade?" She closed the book and turned it toward her sister.

"Nothing in here either but check again." Ash handed her the grimoire. "Better safe than sorry."

"What about you? Do you feel anything that could be masking or cloaking a sinister spell?" Ember turned the page.

"I'll give it a shot," Shade said.

"Mayhem?" Ember turned another page. "Do you feel anything through me?"

I focused on the coarseness of the parchment beneath her fingertips, searching for energy in the ink. *"I do not."*

She stepped away from the book, and Shade flipped through the pages. "I highly doubt we'll find one on the witchy web."

"It's worth a shot." Ash typed on the keyboard. "I'll use a double-encrypted browser to search."

Her fingers flew across the keys as she chewed her bottom lip. A few minutes later, she slumped in her seat. "Nothing. No one would advertise it if they had one."

"I'd bet my left boob someone in Boston does. We can't risk breaking into their library again, but do you think you could sense the spell if we walked the streets? Maybe we could borrow one from a dark witch."

"You're overestimating your sister's ability. Take me to their High Priest and allow me to burn through him. It will solve two of our problems."

"Zip it, dude." She tapped her temple.

Ash inhaled deeply, a look of uncertainty furrowing her brow before she wiped it away and nodded. "If there's a phoenix spell in Boston, I'll find it."

"Fabulous. Another side quest." Ember rubbed her forehead. "I hope we can at least battle a beastie along the way."

CHAPTER 6
EMBER

After a morning fae fight, a demon summoning, and then my possession, I was famished, so we stopped for burgers on our way to Boston. Miles paid the tab this time and thank the goddess for that. Hecate knew I wasn't the best at saving, and my credit card would be maxed out soon.

With all the paranormal shit going on in our lives, it was easy to forget the normal. Thank the goddess for that too, because getting caught up in my head, thinking about finding another job and paying the bills right now, was the last thing I needed to worry about.

We had much bigger insects to fry at the moment.

Shade took the wheel, with Ash riding shotgun, and I sat in the middle seat with Chaos on my right and Mayhem in my head. They didn't trust me to drive with a violent demon chattering in my psyche. Imagine that.

The deep oranges and reds of the trees preparing to shed their leaves whizzed past as Shade drove faster than necessary, but who was I to complain. If anyone had a sense of urgency on our current quest, it was me. Ash lasted as long as she did with Chaos in her head because he held back.

After everything I'd done to Mayhem, I doubted he'd show me the same courtesy.

"Park over there. It's better if I walk." Ash pointed to her right, and Shade turned, rolling to a stop at the curb.

I climbed out and opened the hatch in the floorboard before handing an extra set of knives to the guys. "Better safe than sorry." I grabbed my sword.

Miles arched a skeptical brow. "I hope you have a cloaking spell for that. I don't think you can get away with carrying a weapon in plain view in Boston."

I pursed my lips and eyed my beautiful blade. Shade could put it in a shadow, but if something happened to him, his magic would dissipate and it would be in plain view. "Do you have any cloaking spells in your bag o' tricks, Ash?"

"They're too volatile to carry premixed." She slid out of the passenger seat and closed the door.

"You'll have to sit this one out." I laid my sword in the hidey hole and latched it shut.

"You don't need it. Between your fire and your fighting skills, you are unstoppable."

I laughed. "Should I take that as an actual compliment?"

"It's the truth. Take it however you need to."

"It was a compliment." My mouth threatened me with a

smile, but I fought it. Mayhem's opinion of me shouldn't have mattered. It *didn't* matter.

Ash grinned, and I rolled my eyes.

The guys put on jackets over their knife holsters, and I did the same. Ash stood on the sidewalk and closed her eyes, doing her magical thing, and I couldn't help but smile this time.

Pride swelled in my chest. My little sister had turned into the most amazing witch in a matter of weeks. At least one good thing had come out of this ridiculously terminal ordeal.

"What do you feel?" I asked.

She shuddered. "Icky, sticky dark magic."

"Obviously." I hadn't even opened my senses to it yet, but I could feel it dampening the air and clinging to my skin like a wet sock. Yuck. "What about the spell?"

She shook her head. "Let's walk."

"Boston is almost 90 square miles." Shade strode beside me as we followed Ash and Chaos. "It'll take forever to walk it all."

"We won't have to," I said. "Ash directed you to park in this end of town for a reason."

"It's just a hunch," she said.

"We both know it's more than that." I rolled my shoulders, missing the feel of my sword on my back.

"What is this emotion you're feeling?"

"What does it feel like?" I asked.

"Nothing yet." Ash turned down a side street, and I followed.

"Sorry. I'm talking to the demon in my head."

She laughed. "Now I know how you felt."

A low growl rumbled between my ears. *"If I knew how to name it, I wouldn't have asked."*

"Physically, I mean." I tapped my temple when Shade cut his gaze to me. "Mortals are complicated creatures. Lots of emotions."

"It's pleasant. Your chest feels full. Your lips curve upward, but you're not quite smiling anymore. It seems to be directed toward your sister."

"I'm proud of her. If you'd met her before everything started, you'd see how much she's grown." The full feeling in my chest and my smile were also the result of having him back, but I didn't dare say that out loud.

Yeah, okay, fate had brought us together. I believed it now, no matter how badly I wanted to deny it. After summoning him without his skull...all by my lonesome, apparently...fate was the only explanation. It wasn't logical in the slightest, but logic was Ash's jam.

Action was mine.

Chaos stopped abruptly and grabbed Ash's hand. "I sense a rift."

"As do I."

"Mayhem does too. Where?" I reached into my jacket, wrapping my fingers around a dagger.

"To our right."

"This way." Chaos turned down the street, and we strode toward a massive red brick church with a white steeple.

A four-by-three-foot gash in...the veil?...hung to the left of the building, its edges rimmed in glowing orangish-red.

"Whoa." I stopped and rubbed my eyes, expecting it to vanish from sight, but it stayed there, suspended in midair.

A ripple darted from right to left, and a six-foot-tall beastie with goat horns and the face of a hyena barreled toward it. Four witches gave chase, one of them hurling a blue ball of energy toward the ripple. He missed—fae soldiers were fast AF—and hit the metal fence surrounding the churchyard, electrifying it. It sizzled and popped, raining sparks to the ground before going out.

Thank the goddess nothing caught fire.

"Why are they doing this in broad daylight?" I picked up my pace. "Do they not have a shadow witch?"

"Doing what?" Miles asked, matching my strides. "I don't see anything."

"You don't see the giant rift right there?" I swung my arm toward it. "And the witches trying to fight a fae soldier and a hyena man?"

"I can see through shadows," Chaos said. "She must be channeling Mayhem's power to see through them as well."

"That is precisely what is happening."

"We have to help them." I jogged toward the fray.

"How? We can't see them." Miles ran to catch up.

"I can," Shade said, matching our pace.

I cut him a sideways glance. "Since when?"

"It's an active power. I have to focus to use it, but now that I know there's a shadow here, I can see through it."

"And you never bothered to share that bit of information?" I made a mental note to take inventory of everyone's hidden talents if I ever had the time.

"I'm the only shadow witch in Salem. I never have to use it."

The battle rounded the corner, and I stopped, holding up a hand. "We'll tell them Chaos and I have that power too. They can't know about the demons."

"You need to find the phoenix spell. Let the Boston witches take care of Boston. It's not your job."

"These rifts are happening because of us. That makes it our job." I strode toward a witch who rummaged through a bag, no doubt looking for a freezing spell. "It looks like you guys could use some help."

She snapped her head up, her eyes widening before she shot another woman a chastising glare. "Gray! Our cloak."

"What? It's still in place." Gray looked me up and down. "How can you see through it?"

"It's an active power," I mimicked Shade's words. "I have to focus to use it."

Shade gave me the stink eye. "I have it too."

"As do I," Chaos said. "If you will bring the other two into your shadow, we will assist you."

The soldier rippled toward us, and I threw a fireball, slamming it into his chest. He screeched, his cloak slipping just long enough for me to see the paralyzing venom dripping from his pincers.

"Holy Hecate," Gray said. "Olga, she's a Holland."

"No shit," Olga said. "Hey, Adrian. We've got company."

The High Priest whirled toward me, his brow slamming down over his deep-set eyes. "What are you doing here? We don't need your help."

"Ah!" The fourth witch flew backward, his shoulder slamming into a wall before a massive gash formed in his neck. The hyena man lashed out a taloned hand, slicing into the invisible fae's soft spot.

Bug-man screeched again, dropping the witch and turning on the beastie.

"Are you sure?" I scrunched my nose. "It kinda looks like you do."

His chest puffed as he straightened his spine. "I'm sure."

I nodded toward his fallen witch. "Do you have an antidote for that? We do."

"I haven't found anything that works," Olga said.

"My sister can help him if you'll bring her into the shadow."

Gray rolled her fog outward, enveloping Ash and Miles. They darted toward the fallen witch and administered the antidote while the hyena man railed on the fae. Adrian shot me a steely glare before swirling his hand in the air, creating a little tornado and sending it toward the beasties. It caught the hyena and whirled him around before throwing him three yards away.

"Adrian is an imbecile. If he were wise, he would allow the alastor to kill the fae."

"Alastor?" I asked.

Olga flashed a puzzled look. "That's Adrian, our High Priest."

"An alastor is an upper-mid-level demon. They are skilled fighters and despise the fae almost as much as I do."

"The hyena man. It's an alastor demon," I said, quickly recovering from my faux pas. "You should let it kill the fae."

"How do you know what it is, *light witch*?" Adrian's words dripped with more venom than the fae's pincers. "Why don't you go plant a flower or make some tea? This is our battle. Leave the fighting to the real witches."

I narrowed my eyes. Leave the fighting to the "real" witches? Oh, no he didn't.

I gathered fire in my palms, bringing them together so the flames danced between them, growing bigger and hotter with my anger. I could show him a real witch. "How many fae have you killed, *dark witch*?"

Mayhem's growl rumbled between my ears. *"Now this is an emotion I'm familiar with. You should rip him open and burn him from the inside out."*

Mayhem's magic bled into my veins, and if I'd been anyone else, I would have done exactly that. But I was me. His soulmate. The only being in existence who countered his magic, and, much to my chagrin, the desire to roast Adrian's chestnuts on an open fire dissolved, taking my anger with it.

"As much as I hate to admit it, we're on the same side." I hurled my flames at the fae, but his exoskeleton shielded him, as usual. "And those suckers are fireproof."

"Which must mean you haven't killed any either," Adrian said. "At least I took out the demon."

"Don't let him speak to you that way. Tear off his head and piss down his throat."

"We're on the same side," I said again. "If we work together, we can share information. I'm sure you know things about the fae that we don't, and vice versa."

Mayhem growled in my head. *"It's me. My magic is seeping out of my psyche and making you docile. This isn't you, Ember."*

Holy crap. He was right. I mean, I wouldn't urinate on a foe—no matter how big his ego—but never would I ever let a man talk to me like I was a dainty, useless little girl. Flowers and tea, my ass.

Mayhem pulled back, the oddly calming energy he'd forced into me dissipating, and I gasped.

"Light witches couldn't possibly know more about this than we do," Adrian said.

Olga raised her hand. "Don't demons disappear when they die?"

"I'm no demon." Bugman charged her, and she screamed, ducking behind her High Priest. Chaos blocked the fae's path, landing a punch to the side of his face and breaking off a pincer. He squealed and hissed, stumbling back to where the alastor lay motionless after Adrian's tornado.

I highly doubted a little wind knocked a demon unconscious. Most likely, Chaos was keeping it in check, but I'd let Adrian have this one. If he knew we were in cahoots with the Princes of Hell, we'd have to fight off BSM too.

And we didn't have time for more side quests.

Seriously. No. More.

Ash joined hands with Miles and Shade and hit the fae with a killer freezing spell. Well, not *actually* killer, but the bugaboo's body seized, the blood from its mouth stopping mid-drip as it toppled to the ground.

"Whoa," Gray said. "How...?"

Adrian scoffed and crossed his arms. "It won't hold."

I could feel Mayhem's desire to rip his heart out growing in my mind, so I clenched my teeth and grabbed a dagger from my scabbard. "Let me do this," I whispered as I marched toward it. "You're killing my instinct to fight."

"Sorry." He reeled it in again, and my own anger surged through my veins.

I hurled the dagger at the frozen fae, the blade penetrating the soft spot below his ear hole.

"Gray and I will seal the rift," Olga shouted.

I whirled around, my expression livid. "Don't."

"Okay." She raised her hands, dropping a potion bottle and shattering it on the pavement.

"We don't take orders from light witches," Adrian said. "Seal it."

"That was my last spell. I'll have to mix another one." Olga dropped to her knees and rummaged through her bag.

I mouthed the words *let the alastor go* to Chaos, and he nodded, releasing his hold on the demon. The beast charged toward me.

CHAPTER 7
MAYHEM

"*His heart is lower than a human's, on the right side of his stomach.*"

"Roger that." Ember dropped and spun, kicking her right leg out and knocking the alastor off his feet. He hit the pavement face-first and howled, rolling to his back and clutching his bloody snout.

"*Impressive move. You'll have to teach it to me when I reform.*"

"Gladly." She yanked the dagger from the fae's neck as the alastor rose to his feet. Poisonous blood dripped from his nostrils, and he shook his head, splattering it around him.

"*Don't touch his blood.*"

"I didn't plan to." She marched toward the alastor, the dagger at her side, ready to thrust it into the fiend's heart, and for a moment, I felt remorse.

The alastor would easily slip through the rift and return to the Underworld at my command, but I understood the need for anonymity. Even dark witches despised demons they couldn't control.

Ember's grip tightened, her muscles coiling for the strike, but the imbecile High Priest created another tornado and sucked the alastor away before she could thrust her blade.

"Are you effing kidding me?" Anger surged through her veins, and I reveled in it.

Any doubt that the universe created this witch for me dissolved as she tossed her dagger, handle over blade, and caught it, adjusting her grip and striding toward the High Priest.

"We can take care of the fae," Miles said.

"Don't," she nearly growled. "I'll handle it."

"Kill the High Priest. Take the Boston Society of Magic as your own."

"I don't want Boston." She slowed her pace. "I don't want to fight."

Lucifer have mercy. I'd bled into her consciousness again. I couldn't help myself. Being inside this warrior goddess while she battled her enemies created a feeling of elation I'd never experienced before. Tensing as much as a disembodied entity could, I pulled my magic back, gathering it into a ball of menace and tucking it into the recesses of my consciousness.

She gave her head a hard shake, regaining her senses and continuing her march toward the foolish High Priest. "What are you going to do? Wind him to death?"

Olga cowered on the ground with her spell kit while Gray strained, her face pinching with the exertion. "I can't hold the shadow much longer."

"I'll help you." Shade offered his hand.

She eyed it with skepticism before nodding and accepting the offer.

The High Priest raised his hands toward the alastor, chanting in an ancient tongue. I recognized the incantation immediately.

"He is trying to gain control of the demon. You must stop him before the spell takes hold."

"With pleasure." Ember's fingers tightened around the dagger, and the ball of menace I tucked away in my psyche threatened to explode. She could pierce his heart, gut him and take his liver and a prize, making the coven believe a fae had killed him.

I forced my malice into its place, allowing Ember full control. She hurled the dagger, but instead of piercing Adrian's chest, the handle hit his head, making him stumble.

"You missed."

"No, I didn't." She planted her boot into his stomach, and he doubled over. Her uppercut to his chin knocked him off his feet.

The magical tornado ceased its spin, and the alastor dropped to the ground, landing on his feet and rushing her. My goddess spun, jabbing her dagger into the demon's abdomen right where I told her to and twisting the blade with an upward motion.

The alastor wheezed, his eyes bulging a moment before he turned to mist. The rift sucked his essence into the Under-world, and Ember stomped toward the fae. Ash arched a brow as she approached, but she held her tongue, saving her berating words for another time.

My witch straddled the fae, lifting an armored plate and thrusting her blade beneath it, piercing her enemy's heart and draining his life force.

She straightened and turned to the High Priest. "That's Salem five, Boston zero. Who's the real witch now?"

Adrian rose, clutching his stomach with one hand, his chin with the other. "Brute force doesn't make you a witch."

She shrugged one shoulder dismissively. "Maybe not, but it does vanquish demons and kill fae. Do you want our help or not?"

His expression tightened, his gaze dropping to the ground before he met her eyes. "I suppose we can share information, but then you'll return to Salem and let us protect *our* city."

Ember spread her arms. "That's all we want to do. Now, let's shove the dead Bugman through the rift and seal it before any more beasties get loose."

My brother could have easily lifted the fae himself, but he kept up the pretense and merely assisted Ember and the others. Miles took one leg, Ember the other, and Adrian helped Chaos with our enemy's shoulders.

They shoved the body through, and Ash assisted Olga with the mending spell. The veil closed, and Shade and Gray dropped the shadow, bringing the rest of the world into full color. Ember sheathed her weapon, and we walked four blocks to the coven headquarters.

"I'm going to head home and rest if that's okay," the witch to whom Ash had delivered the antidote said.

"Sleep it off and get ready to fight," Adrian said. "We need all hands on deck."

The injured witch turned down a side street as a three-story, brick building with Boston Society of Magic engraved in the marble above the door came into view.

"I will never get used to witches making their presence known on purpose."

"Times have changed," Ember said before clamping her mouth shut.

"They certainly have, or I would not be inviting you into our coven house." Adrian pushed the door open, and we stepped into a small gift shop filled with trinkets, crystals, and bundles of sage.

The High Priest rested his hand against the jamb of another door and whispered a spell, deactivating whatever ward he'd placed on the threshold. "Our meeting room is this way."

We entered the room, and Ember's mouth tightened as she cut her gaze toward Ash and Chaos. Ash pressed her lips into a thin line, and my brother nodded. They had been here before, and judging by their expressions, no one in this dark coven knew.

"Nice digs." Ember rested her hands on the back of a chair.

A long, rectangular table with at least fifteen chairs crowded around it took up most of the space. At the head of the table sat an ornate throne with dark magic carvings and gilded edges. Olga pulled out the throne, and Adrian sank into it.

"Take a seat." He gestured to the plain wooden chairs. "Tell me what you know about the fae."

Ember mouthed the word *library* to Ash before settling into a chair. Miles and Shade flanked her, and Olga and Gray sat across from them.

Ash remained standing, drumming her fingers on the back of her chair. "I'm the coven librarian, and our library is in shambles. Would it be possible for me to take a look at yours to get some organization ideas?"

"I can take you down." Olga rose to her feet. "We haven't finished cleaning up since the break-in, but I'm happy to show you around."

Adrian cut her a steely gaze, and she shrank in on herself. "If that's okay with you, Priest."

"She did save Hector, sir." Gray's shoulders inched toward her ears, her body drifting slightly away from their Priest.

He straightened his spine. "Give Olga the recipe for your venom antidote, and you may look at the library. But do not open any books."

"Got it." Ash turned to Chaos. "Want to come with?"

"Of course." They followed Olga down the stairs.

"He commands them through fear, but he has not earned their respect." I contemplated this as Ember folded her hands on the table. It was no wonder so many had defected when Chrys offered to overthrow their leadership. The witches in Salem respected the Holland women and did their bidding out of loyalty to the coven rather than fear of punishment.

Interesting...

"We've encountered three types of fae," Ember said. "The blood-sucking mosquitoes, which I'm sure you've been familiar with for years."

Adrian steepled his fingers. "Yes, they always become bothersome this time of year."

Ember leaned back, crossing her legs beneath the table. "The other two are scouts and soldiers. Their exoskeletons are the strongest armor we've ever encountered. They're impervious to fire, but it still hurts like hell when you burn them. Or I assume it does because they screech like banshees when we try."

"They deflect our air witch electricity as well," he said.

"The only way to kill them is to pierce their hearts or behead them."

Adrian blew a hard breath through his nose. "And how, pray tell, do you do that?"

"They have soft spots here." Ember touched the delicate skin beneath her ear. "And their armor is like scales. Get close enough, and you can get beneath them to stab the heart." She sat up straighter. "That's what we know. Your turn."

Adrian studied her, his eyes calculating.

"You might have to force the information out of him. Shall I turn Gray against him?"

Ember cleared her throat, a subtle reminder that she couldn't speak to me. I acquiesced, allowing her to continue the conversation in her own manner.

"I showed you mine. Now, show me yours. What else do you know?" She arched a brow.

He nodded, his expression one of resolve. "Their leader has contacted me. He is a prince whose name is Ignacus, and he is planning a coup to overthrow his brother and take the crown."

"That's not the story Miles's friend told."

Ember blinked, silently urging him to continue.

"Since I recently experienced and extinguished a coup—led by one of your witches, I might add—I agreed to help him." His lips screwed to the side, his gaze cutting left before he continued. "In return, he promised me incomparable power. I would be the strongest witch ever to walk the earth. I'm sure you can understand the appeal..."

Ember shrugged. "Not really. I'm happy with what I've got."

He chuckled, his disbelief evident in his condescending expression. "But the fae being the fae, he betrayed me. His soldiers have been picking off my team one by one, absorbing their power as they consume their hearts."

"Hearts?" Shade's brow furrowed. "I've only heard about them eating livers."

"The livers provide the enzyme they need to survive in this realm. They eat the hearts of witches to gain their abilities while the scouts search the earth for an amulet that gives its bearer immeasurable strength."

Ember stiffened inwardly, though she maintained her composure. "Do you know where the amulet is? Can we stop them from getting their hands on it?"

"If I knew where it was, don't you think I'd be using it? I'd have sent the overgrown bugs home and strengthened the veil a long time ago."

She leaned back in her chair, her posture relaxing. "Is your team searching for it?"

"Every second of every day since Ignacus told me about it.

Your witch Chrys had a piece of it. She wouldn't have had the strength to make so many of my witches turn without it."

Ember tapped her index finger on the table. "So you ransacked her apartment looking for it."

He pursed his lips, shaking his head. "My team searched for it there, but the damage and the murder were courtesy of the fae who followed them."

"Ask him—"

"What's your plan now?" Ember asked, as if reading my mind.

If I had a heart in this form, it would have warmed. Not only was she a skilled warrior, but she was a master interrogator. Her withdrawing this much information without violence astonished and captivated me. I could not wait to have my own body so I could ravish hers.

Adrian steepled his fingers once more. "Find the amulet, murder Ignacus, strengthen the veil, and rule the world."

Ember laughed dryly. "I figured as much."

Footsteps sounded on the stairs, and Ash entered the room, followed by Chaos and Olga. Ash nodded, her eyes conveying conspiracy.

Ember rose to her feet, the wooden chair scraping across the floor with a screech. "Well, thanks for the info swap. We'll get out of your hair."

Adrian rose too, but Olga pulled out his chair, lifting it so it didn't make a sound. "You didn't tell me your plan."

"It's the same as yours, minus the murder and world domination." Ember jerked her head toward the exit, and her team followed.

"It's a race then." Adrian remained in place, not offering the courtesy of walking his guests to the door. "Whoever finds the amulet first wins. I'd wish you luck, but I don't dare put that energy into the ether."

Ember laughed dryly. "Later, loser." She waved and walked out the door.

No one spoke until we reached the end of the fourth block, where Ember paused at the crosswalk and turned to Ash. "Tell me you found the spell."

She patted her pocket containing her phone. "Easy peasy. And Chaos scrambled Olga's mind just enough that she doesn't remember us doing it."

Relief flooded Ember's system. "I love my team."

Ash crossed her arms. "It sure didn't seem that way earlier."

CHAPTER 8

EMBER

"You can berate me later. Let me see the spell." I held out my hand, and Ash's jaw ticked. "You can text it to me if you want, but I'd rather you not send a spell punishable by death through the cloud."

She slammed the phone into my hand.

"Your sister is angry with you."

"No shit." I tossed Shade the keys and climbed into the passenger seat. My team loaded up, and I studied the pictures Ash had taken of the phoenix spell. "Wolfsbane, hyssop... ground bone. Tell me we don't have to sacrifice an animal to pull this off."

"A life for a life. It sounds reasonable."

"Look at the second photo," Ash said. "We need demon bones."

I swiped to the next picture. "'Bones must be of the same or adjacent species you wish to resurrect.' Fabulous. How are we supposed to harvest bones when demons go poof the second we vanquish them?"

"We'll have to keep one alive." Shade started the van and pulled onto the road. "Put it in a containment circle and harvest a limb before we send it back to Hell."

I cringed. "That sounds barbaric."

"You could exorcize me. I'll possess Adrian and burn through him, solving two problems at once."

"Absolutely not. I already told you that's not an option. You've got enough ego on your own; you don't need to absorb his too."

"Let me guess," Chaos said. "He's suggesting he take the High Priest as a host."

"Bingo. But it's not going to happen."

"It's not the worst idea," Ash said. "If we could take over BSM, we could exile the dark witches and stop looking over our shoulders every time we leave the house."

Surely my sweet little sister didn't mean that. I twisted in my seat to see her face, but she looked as serious as could be.

"That's a hard no." I flashed her a WTF look. "We only kill in self-defense, and even then...only if it's absolutely necessary."

"I can arrange for your self-defense to be necessary. Let's return to Boston, and I'll—"

"Stop it. Both of you. We'll do it like Shade suggested, unless..." I drummed my fingers on my knee. "Chaos, can you regenerate limbs? Maybe if we cut off your finger..."

"Only when I return to Hell." He rested his hand on Ash's thigh. "But I will do whatever it takes to save her."

"Notice his only concern is her. He'd allow me to rot in prison for eternity if her life wasn't on the line."

I rolled my eyes. "It's one finger. I'm sure he'd do it just for you."

"He would not."

"Chaos, would you give up your left pinkie to keep Mayhem out of the dark prison, even if Ash wasn't in danger?"

He missed a beat...two...three. "I believe I would. He has suffered long enough."

"There. See? Your brother loves you." I handed the phone to Ash. "Next steps... How much time do I have with you in my mind? Can we sleep tonight and get started tomorrow without you taking over?"

"Yes, I believe so."

"Good. We all go home and rest. In the morning, Chaos will cut off a finger, and Ash and I will perform the phoenix and exorcism spells. I want you guys to scry for the rest of the amulet while we do our thing, but don't try to retrieve it without us. Understood?"

"Got it," Miles said.

Shade shifted in his seat. "We can help you with the spells. The more power we put into them, the better."

"Not a chance," I said. "I don't want you anywhere near the phoenix. If the Higher Power somehow finds out we performed it, we could be executed. I won't put you in that position."

He blew a hard breath through his nose. "We'll be putting ourselves in that position. It's our choice to help our friends."

"And it's my choice as your High Priestess to say hell no. You're scrying. We're breaking the laws of witchcraft. Got it?"

His mouth pinched, and he gave me the side eye before focusing on the road. "Yeah."

We parked behind the building, and Shade went with Miles to his place. I kicked off my boots the moment we stepped through the upstairs door and set them against the wall before grabbing a can of sparkling water from the fridge and gulping it down.

"We need to talk." Ash sank onto a stool at the counter.

Chaos rested a hand on her shoulder. "I'm going to shower." He kissed the top of her head and strode out of the kitchen, leaving me alone to face my sister's wrath.

"What did I do wrong this time?" I tossed the empty can into the recycle bin.

"Absolutely nothing."

Okay, not completely alone. "I think so too, but Ash disagrees." I leaned against the counter and crossed my arms.

She folded her hands in front of her. "Your ego put everyone in danger today."

I raised my brows. "*My* ego? Adrian's the one who tried to stop me from vanquishing the alastor demon just so he could prove a point."

"And you weren't trying to prove one?" She tilted her head in the same condescending way Mom would whenever I acted out.

My nails dug into my biceps. "He insulted me. He said I wasn't a real witch, so yeah, I had to prove him wrong. You'd have done the same."

"No, Em. You didn't *have* to prove anything." She straightened, crossing her arms. "But you insisted on killing them both by yourself just so you could outshine a dark witch whose opinion doesn't matter."

"But he…" I ground my teeth. "He challenged my authority…my abilities. I had to… And Mayhem was—"

"No." She leaned her forearms on the counter. "Don't even try to blame him. I've seen how his magic affects you, and you acted the opposite. Your behavior today was all you, and it was not okay."

"Don't listen to her. Adrian challenged you, and you had to prove you weren't a coward."

"We are a team," she said, "and you alienated us when you told Shade not to kill the fae. How do you expect the witches of this coven to respect you when you act like that? You stooped to Adrian's level, and it was ugly, Em. So ugly."

"I…" The defensive tension drawing my shoulders toward my ears relaxed, and I let out a slow breath. She was right. I'd gotten so caught up trying to put the asshole in his place that I'd cast my team aside. And for what? To prove myself to a narcissist? I knew better.

I nodded, closing my eyes against the pressure building behind them. "I'm sorry."

"For what? You did nothing wrong."

"Yeah, I did. I put myself…my ego…first. I did the one thing that annoys me the most in other people. I acted alone when I should have depended on my team."

"You lost track of the mission."

"I did, and I'm sorry. It won't happen again." I laughed. "I'm not used to getting called out on my bullshit by anyone other than Mom. Why haven't you done it more often?"

Ash shrugged and traced her finger on the counter. "With my defective magic, I always felt like the outsider. I idolized you for your bravery and fighting skills, but I never thought we had much in common. I guess we never sat down and had a real conversation."

My throat thickened, my fight-or-flight instinct begging me to walk away before I showed vulnerability, but I fought it. This could be a moment for us if I could get out of my own way and let it happen.

"I guess I don't have real conversations with anyone. Showing emotion in battle can get you killed, and... I don't know what's wrong with me." The pressure in my eyes threatened to come out in liquid form.

"There's nothing wrong with you. Everyone's brains are wired differently."

"Absolutely nothing is wrong with you. You are a goddess."

I laughed, and a tear slid down my cheek. "I've always been envious of your relationship with Cinder. I've secretly wanted to be your confidant since you learned how to talk. But I was the one who needed to learn. I just... Goddess, I don't know. What good are words when I can't even string them together in the right order?"

Her brow furrowed, her eyes holding sympathy. "Cinder has always been easy to talk to, so I confided in her out of habit. I'm sorry I didn't try very hard to talk to you."

"You shouldn't have had to." Another tear fell, and I wiped it away. "I'm so sorry, Ash. I'm sorry for never being there for you. For never truly listening."

She rose and wrapped her arms around me. "You're here now. That's what counts."

I sniffled and held her tight. "Yeah. I'm here, and I'm not going anywhere. I love you, Ash."

She pulled away, her eyes glistening with unshed tears. "I love you too."

"We're going to get through this. Whatever it takes, I am... *we* are...going to end this curse and set everything right again."

"Or die trying." She smiled sadly and inhaled a shaky breath. "See you in the morning?"

I nodded and wiped the moisture from my cheeks.

"Good night, Em."

"Night." I stayed in the kitchen and watched her walk away. When she disappeared into her bedroom, I double-checked the wards and turned off the lights before heading to mine.

I showered and put on my pajamas in silence. My chest was still tight, my throat thick from our conversation, but the rest of me felt lighter, like a weight had been lifted from my soul. I snuggled into bed, lying on my side and pulling the blankets up to my chin.

"You've been awfully quiet," I said.

"*What would you like me to say?*"

"Anything. You just witnessed the deepest conversation I've had in my entire life. Don't you have a snide remark about me showing weakness?"

He remained silent for so long, I almost fell asleep. "*Your discussion moved me. Your emotions were familiar yet foreign at the same time, and I don't believe you showed any weakness at all. I found your confession brave and inspiring.*"

A smile tugged at my lips. "You think?"

"The more I get to know you, the more convinced I am that we are destined for each other. You make me feel...whole."

"Well, you make me feel like a crazy person talking to herself." I clamped my mouth shut. I'd had a sister bonding moment with Ash, and that was enough feelings talk for one day. Because I honestly had no idea how I felt about Mayhem.

Okay, that was a lie. I did know how I felt...or how I was beginning to feel...and I wasn't anywhere near ready to unpack all that. Hecate, have mercy.

"Goodnight, Your Royal Pain In My Assness."

His chuckle reverberated in my soul. *"Good night, sweet witch."*

I slept blissfully dream-free, letting my subconscious process the day so my conscious mind didn't have to. I might not have woken until the afternoon if the sound of shattering glass hadn't yanked me into the land of the living.

I sat up and peered out the window at the back alley, where an imp was using my van as a trampoline. "Oh, for Satan's sake. Chaos!"

I marched out of my bedroom to find Ash and her demon having breakfast. "Come outside and get your minion under control so I can vanquish him. The effing little bugger shattered my windshield."

I grabbed a butcher knife from the block and rushed down the stairs, not bothering with a jacket or shoes. Chaos and Ash followed, and when we exited the building, the imp yanked off a windshield wiper, gnawing on it like it was a chew toy.

Tiny pebbles in the pavement cut into my bare feet as I paced toward the van, and my arm hairs stood on end as if they could shield me from the cold.

"Stop," Chaos said, and the bastard dropped the wiper to stand at attention for his master.

"Where's the rift?" I adjusted my grip on the knife.

"*I don't sense one close by. He must have come through in another area and found his way here, attracted to our auras.*"

"Good. That means I can vanquish the destructive dickwad." I lifted the knife like Norman Bates, ready to go *Psycho* on the slimy sucker when Ash stumbled.

"Ow! Crap. I stepped on glass."

Chaos, ever the protective boyfriend, diverted his full attention to my sister's bloody foot, losing control of his minion.

The imp took a flying leap at my face.

CHAPTER 9

EMBER

"Son of a basilisk!" I shouted, but I immediately regretted it. Imp slime oozed into my mouth as the bugger clung to my hair, its abdomen sliding across my face and coating my skin in goo.

It tasted like sour milk and disgust.

A tiny worm-like appendage flopped against my lips, and I tried my best to purge my mind of the fact that a gremlin's wee-wee had just touched my mouth. So gross.

I pried the bastard from my face, but it wiggled and slipped from my grip, landing on the pavement with a splat. It was either dazed from the impact or Chaos had regained control, because it lay there in a puddle of slime, its eyes circling as if it were watching something spin.

I hurled the knife at it, but my makeshift weapon wasn't weighted properly. I missed the bugger's heart, slicing into its shoulder instead. The imp wailed and writhed, the blade pinning it to the pavement as it thrashed.

"Are you okay, Ash?" I called over my shoulder as I marched toward the bastard, scanning the ground for more shards of glass on my way.

"I'm fine."

"Good. Chaos, will you hold this monkey still so I can vanquish it?" I yanked the knife from its shoulder and adjusted my grip, ready to stab it in the heart, but the blade had severed its arm. An idea began to form in my mind.

Under Chaos's control, the imp couldn't wail, but it let out a pitiful, muffled moan through its closed lips.

"Put it out of its misery." Ash hobbled toward me, putting her weight on the heel of her injured foot.

"Wait." I lowered the knife. "We can use it."

"Use it for what?" Ash clung to her demon's arm for balance.

"For its bones," Mayhem said, as if he'd read my mind.

"Exactly." I used two fingers to pick up the severed arm, and the hand contracted into a fist. "The phoenix spell said the bone dust has to be from the same *or adjacent* species."

Ash gasped. "An imp is a type of demon."

I turned toward her, holding up the arm. "And we already have a piece of it."

"You are as brilliant as you are brave."

The imp moaned, saving me from the flutter threatening to form in my stomach.

"If I vanquish it, will its arm go too?"

"Hold it tightly with the intent to keep it...like you did my head... and it will become your trophy."

"If you—" Chaos started, but I clutched the whole arm in my fist, spun to the imp, and plunged the knife into its chest.

With one final screech, the imp turned into a puff of smoke, and a tiny rift opened, sucking it through before slamming shut. As I opened my palm, hellfire erupted on the severed arm, burning the flesh and goo and leaving only bone behind.

"Looks like we just saved your finger. You're welcome." I tiptoed back to the house and wiped the grime from my feet onto the doormat before grabbing the box o' burnt skull and heading upstairs.

Chaos scooped Ash into a cradle carry and followed me, setting her on a stool while I dumped the dirty knife in the sink.

"Let me wash the slime off, and then we'll commit what I hope is the biggest magical crime we will ever have to pull off." I headed for the hall.

"Don't forget about the time spell if we make it long enough to mend the veil." Ash winced as Chaos picked a piece of glass from her foot.

"One step at a time." I lifted the box, reminding her we had other things to worry about right now.

"And don't forget..." She pressed her lips into a line and cut her gaze toward her demon. "Never mind."

I strode to my room and set the box and the bones on my dresser before gathering a set of clothes and padding to the bathroom.

"You aren't curious what else she wanted to remind you of?"

"Nope." I stripped out of my jammies and turned on the shower. "One thing at a time."

I turned toward the mirror and grimaced at my reflection. Purple hair coated in slime stuck to my forehead, and some strands stood straight up, while the rest was matted into a knot.

"I'm a mess."

"A hot one."

"Haha." I stepped under the stream and closed the curtain before scrubbing every inch of my body and face and rinsing with water as hot as it would go. Mayhem stayed silent while I dried off and got dressed, and I ran a brush through my hair, studying my reddened skin to make sure I'd gotten all the goo off.

"You're awfully quiet up there." I tapped my temple.

"I'm simply going along for the ride."

"Well, fasten your seatbelt and keep your arms and legs inside at all times."

"I don't understand the reference."

"I'm about to commit a magical felony. Don't make me any more nervous than I already am." My stomach soured as I paced down the hall, and when I got to the kitchen, I found Ash gathering the ingredients for the phoenix spell.

The spell I refused to let her take part in.

"Chaos offered to grind the bone so it won't ruin our food processor." She gestured to a stone mortar and pestle.

"Imps are surprisingly sturdy for their size." Chaos sat at the counter and held his hand toward me.

I laid the arm bones in his palm and held his gaze. "I'm casting this spell alone."

"We'll have to source more wolfsbane after this. I never dreamed we'd use this much in... Alone? Why? We can share our vim to—"

"And share a cell when the Higher Power puts us on trial?" I grabbed the mixing bowl from the cabinet and picked up Ash's phone. "No."

"We're not going to get caught, and even if we did...it's for the greater good. We can't save Salem without casting this spell." She started to measure the hyssop, but I took the jar from her hands.

"Try explaining that to the Higher Power. You wouldn't make it past the 'I accidentally possessed myself with a demon' part." I added two tablespoons to the bowl.

Ash crossed her arms. "I'm the reason we're in this situation. I'm helping."

I scraped the last of the wolfsbane into the bowl, hoping to Hecate it would be enough. "Actually, this guy and this guy..." I jutted a thumb at Chaos and then tapped my temple. "And the one gallivanting through the Underworld with Cinder are the reason we're in this situation, and you..."

"And I what?" She rinsed the empty container and returned it to the cupboard.

I squinted at the screen. "Rose of Jericho? Do we have that?"

"And I what?" Ash took a cedar box from the shelf and handed me a ball of what looked like dried fern.

I broke off a few pieces and crumbled them into the bowl while Chaos finished crunching the bones. Ash's mouth tightened when I tried to hand the herb ball back to her, a vein in her forehead beginning to bulge.

I huffed. "You're already showing signs of the curse. The last thing we need is for dark magic to push you harder into bringing it to life."

Her mouth dropped open, and she took the ball, returning it to the box. "I am not."

I added mustard seed and poured garlic oil on top of the herbs. "You said yourself that your thoughts aren't very light-witch-like lately."

"Well, I—"

"And you nearly choked on the sage when we tried to contact Hecate."

"It was a fresh smudge stick." She put the box down and crossed her arms. "The smell was strong."

"Ember is right." Chaos slid the mortar toward me. "If she does get caught, she will need you to rescue her before the execution. If you are both detained, your chances of breaking the curse and saving Salem are nil."

She fisted her hands on her hips, her gaze cutting between Chaos and me. "The curse is *not* affecting me yet, but I do see your other point. I don't like it, but I see it."

She tapped a finger to her lips. "I'll cast a magic-containment spell over the room, you cast the phoenix, and I'll conduct the exorcism."

"See? We're still a team." I shoved Ash's phone into my pocket, added the crushed bone to the bowl, and carried everything to my bedroom.

"Why are you doing it in here?" Ash asked from the doorway.

"To keep you out of trouble. If I get caught, you had no idea what I was up to." I grabbed a dagger from my nightstand and settled cross-legged on the floor, setting the items in front of me. "Do your thing so I can do mine."

"Let me go mix the potion." She hurried back to the kitchen.

"You are being *really* quiet. Everything okay?"

"For centuries I have believed witches to be the vilest creatures to walk the earth, but you... You have so many layers. I have to rethink everything I've ever believed."

I laughed. "That's me. Layers for days, just like an onion. Careful or I'll make you cry."

Ash returned with a blue plastic spray bottle filled with an amber liquid. "Are you ready?"

"Absolutely." My stomach clenched and my heart attempted to leap out through my mouth, but yeah. I was ready to get on with the shit show.

Ash sprayed the potion over the walls, floor, and ceiling, giving the doorway a few extra squirts on her way out before reciting the magic-containment spell.

The energy in the room thickened, a blanket of magic wrapping around the space. I took a deep breath...two...three...trying to center myself, but my nerves made my hands tremble.

"You can do this."

"I know." My heart pounded against my ribs. Nausea churned in my gut, and when I leaned toward the door to close it, my knee hit the rim of the bowl, tipping it sideways and nearly spilling the contents all over the floor. Sitting upright again, I took another deep breath and lined up the dagger, the box of Mayhem's ashes, the potion, and the phone.

I can do this. I swallowed hard and swiped open the screen, flipping through the photos to find the incantation. "Oil of garlic, eye of newt, hyssop flower, wolfsbane root? Why do I feel like I'm reciting *Macbeth*?"

"Shakespeare offered his soul in exchange for his works surviving the centuries."

"Oh, wow. So now he's what? Simmering in a tar pit for eternity?"

"Worse. He's eternally putting on plays for the denizens of the Underworld."

"Focus, Ember," Ash called from outside the door.

"Okay." Easy for her to say. She wasn't the one about to commit a magical felony.

I shook out my hands and recited the incantation for real. "Oil of garlic, eye of newt, hyssop flower, wolfsbane root. Like the phoenix, ashes rise. Come back to life before my eyes."

Heat built in the core of my being, mixing and churning with the nausea already permeating my innards. I picked up the dagger and pressed the tip of the blade to my finger. Three drops of blood trickled into the bowl, and the mixture sizzled, turning into a blackened goop before popping and going up in smoke.

"Oh crap." I fanned the fumes into the box of ashes. "I guess this isn't one you can premix and carry with you."

"Everything okay?" Ash asked from the hallway.

"We're good." The smoke sank onto Mayhem's cremated remains, clinging to them like an early morning fog on the dew. The heat in my belly intensified, spreading through my body like a surge of lava from an erupting volcano, and I pushed the magic outward, focusing on the skull.

"Whoa." A rush of adrenaline set my nerves ablaze, and every hair on my body stood on end. My breath came out in a huff before I raked in another one, the sensation of dark, primal power raising goosebumps on my flesh.

The energy kept building and building, and it was all I could do not to shout, "More power. Absolute power!" like Jafar when he's turning into a genie in *Aladdin*.

Holy Hecate.

"Mmm... It feels good, doesn't it?"

So. Effing. Good.

With a final push, I released the magic from my being, allowing every bit of it to encompass Mayhem's remains. The smoke thickened and swirled, and green fire erupted in the box, burning through the cardboard as if it were kindling.

Sparks flashed. Flames crackled. Bone reassembled.

A bang that nearly burst my eardrums rattled the windows. Searing white light blinded me. My head smacked the floor.

"Ember!" Ash raced into the room and cradled me in her lap. "Are you okay?"

I blinked, my vision returning, and I swallowed the thickness from my throat. "I'm peachy," I rasped. "Did it work?"

"Indeed." Chaos lifted Mayhem's skull. "It is whole once again."

"I knew you could do it. You are a goddess."

"Do the exorcism," I strained to speak.

"First, we need to cleanse you of the darkness. Come on." Ash helped me to my feet and guided me to the kitchen. I stumbled, my knees...hell, my everything...weak from the power of the spell.

"Rub this on your hands." She passed me a canister of powdered charcoal, and I did as she instructed. "With the energy of a cleansing rain, darkness fades and light remains."

I wiped two charcoal-coated fingers across both my cheeks and inhaled deeply as the icky, sticky dark magic sensation dissipated from my system, taking most of my vim with it. Pressing a hand to my chest, I heaved three more breaths. "That was intense."

"You were phenomenal. With practice, you could—"

"I'm going to stop you right there. There will be no practice of the dark arts in this coven. I hope to never cast that spell again." I chugged the glass of water Ash offered.

"Wash your hands. You're getting charcoal everywhere." She wiped the empty glass with a paper towel before carrying a grimoire to the living room. Chaos set the skull on the coffee table, and I dried my hands before sinking into my favorite chair.

"I'm assuming we don't need a containment circle, right?" She opened the book and flipped to the right page. "If you think we do, we'll need to go to my studio for the supplies."

"We're good." I rolled the stiffness from my neck.

"How do you know I won't kill you all the moment I reform?"

"Well, for one...I have your mark. Kill me, and you'll be

vanquished." I scooted to the edge of my seat. "No more hunting fae for you."

His chuckle vibrated in my chest. *"And two?"*

I shrugged one shoulder dismissively. "I just know you won't."

My stomach tightened the moment the words left my lips. Did I just know, or were Ash's words skewing my perception of the demon? We were about to find out.

Ash sank onto the corner of the sofa and rested the grimoire in her lap before taking both my hands. We read the incantation in unison three times before I felt the first tingle. My lungs seized mid-breath, and a *boom* from the deepest part of my being shook the entire room, knocking a picture frame from the wall.

I gasped, my entire body feeling as if I'd swallowed a box of staples, the tiny shards of metal raking through my veins and filleting my insides. I coughed so hard, I nearly lost a lung. Purple smoke poured from my mouth, burning my throat and threatening to turn me inside out.

As the final bits of Mayhem left my system, I rose, backing away from the skull. He circled around it, forming a funnel cloud and lifting it into the air. Ash and Chaos stood across the room, watching Mayhem reform.

"Are you okay?" Ash asked for the umpteenth time.

"I'm good." Anticipation tightened my stomach, making my heart race.

Electricity crackled, filling the room with light. The smoke swirled and spun, wrapping around the skull and turning into flesh and bone. The storm dissipated, and Mayhem in demon form stood before me, menace and desire dancing in his eyes.

"Ember." He reached me in two strides and grabbed my shoulders, lifting me from the ground. My pulse thrummed, a strange mix of fear and want flooding my veins and making heat pool below my navel.

"Mayhem..." Chaos's voice dripped with warning.

"You deal with your witch. I'll take care of mine." As if I weighed nothing, he carried me down the hall and into my room, slamming the door behind us. Setting me down, he held my shoulder with one hand and locked the door with the other.

Returning his attention to me, he let go and morphed into his human form. His *naked* human form. *Woof.*

"Are you okay?" He tucked a lock of hair behind my ear, concern etching lines on his forehead.

"I wish everyone would stop asking me that. My vim is taxed, but I'm fine." My gaze slid down his body, over his defined pecs and chiseled abs and locking on his package... unwrapped and standing at attention. My mouth watered. I pressed my lips together so I wouldn't drool.

"Ember!" Ash pounded on the door. "Are you okay?"

"I'm fine. Everything is fine. We're umm...talking." I blinked, looking into his lavender eyes. "Everything is fine, right?"

"You're sure you're okay?" His gaze dipped to my lips.

"Yes." My head spun a little, but I was certain the naked man standing before me was the reason and *not* the events that had just transpired. In fact, all I could think about in that moment was how badly I wanted to climb him.

"You are coherent enough to make good decisions? To speak up if you don't approve?" He arched a brow.

I furrowed mine. "Yes…"

"Good. Then tell me to stop." He clutched my shoulders and crushed his mouth to mine.

CHAPTER 10
MAYHEM

Her lips felt like velvet, plush and soft as they yielded to the pressure of mine. I expected her to pull away. I half-hoped she would, because I knew with every fiber of my being that, if we saw this through to the end, there would be no going back. Not for me.

Not for her, if I could help it.

She lifted her hands, tentatively brushing her fingertips against my chest. The sensation nearly crumbled me. Her lips parted, welcoming my tongue into the moist heat of her mouth, and if I wasn't immortal, I could have drowned in her essence, died in that moment a happy man.

I broke the kiss, and she gasped. "Tell me to stop. Say you don't want this, and I'll walk away."

She touched her swollen bottom lip, tugging it down slightly as her gaze wandered over my body before meeting my eyes. "That's the thing." She looked at my cock and swallowed hard. "I don't want you to stop."

Her expression held both disbelief and desire as she returned her touch to my chest and traced her fingers over the contours of my muscles. "I could blame it on stress or fatigue or a million other things, but right now, all I want to do is *you*."

My dick throbbed, another rush of blood hardening it even more. "If you're not of a mind to think this through..."

"I don't want to think. It's not my thing. I listen to my body, and I act...leap first, look later...and I am ready to jump into the deep end." Her tongue slipped out to wet her lips, and she trailed her fingers down my stomach, making it tighten.

"You're certain?" I asked.

She inched her fingers closer to my cock. "Do you want me to change my mind?"

"Gods no." I clutched her hands before they went any lower. "But I do plan to take my time, I haven't been with a woman in over four centuries."

"Lucky me for being your first."

First, last, and only for the rest of my existence, but I didn't dare make that proclamation out loud. Whether she believed it or not, she had a brilliant mind. I saw no need to cloud it with declarations of my devotion.

Not yet.

I tugged her shirt over her head, tossing it aside and taking in her beauty. She wore a black satin bra, and I traced my fingers along the edges, caressing the delicate skin of her breasts and recalling the way it had felt when she washed in the shower.

Having been inside her mind, having felt with her skin, I knew which parts were more sensitive than others. She had experienced no sexual yearning at the time, but I had reveled in the sensations fueling my desire.

She reached behind her back to unclasp her bra and dropped it by her discarded shirt. Taking my hands in hers, she placed them on her breasts and then cupped my face, bringing me forward to meet her mouth.

I kissed her, drinking her in as I massaged her breasts, running my thumbs over her nipples and hardening them like pearls. She unbuttoned her pants, sliding the zipper down before working them over her hips, her mouth never straying from mine.

Kicking them off, she leaned into me, the feel of her bare skin against mine weakening my knees. A growl rumbled from deep within my soul, and I wrapped my arms around her, tangling my tongue with hers.

She clutched the back of my neck, sliding one leg up to my hip before lifting herself from the ground and wrapping them both around my waist, the thin satin of her panties the only thing stopping my cock from plunging inside her.

I clutched her ass, digging my fingers into her flesh and deepening the kiss. She moaned into my mouth and moved against me, the motion making promises of events to come and rendering me incapable of speech.

Ember preferred action to words. I didn't have to tell her how this moment made me feel. I would show her. Again and again, until she begged for mercy.

I clutched her waist and shoved her onto the bed. She

gasped with the sudden impact, but as she moved to the center of the mattress, a wicked grin lifted her lips. She shimmied out of her underwear, and mischief danced in her deep brown eyes.

I had seen her body through her eyes, but now, seeing her with my own… I could have stood there soaking in her beauty all day long. Instead, I climbed onto the bed with her, moving on my hands and knees until my mouth met hers once more.

"Mmm…" She wrapped her hand around my cock and stroked it, circling her finger over the sensitive head, and I nearly collapsed on top of her.

I hadn't felt a woman's touch in so long…and yet…

Being there in that moment with my soulmate, it felt as if it really were my first time. It eclipsed every shred of desire or intimacy I had ever experienced, rendering all other moments meaningless.

I grabbed her wrists and pinned her arms above her head, lest she bring our moment to a premature ending. She would come before I did, even if it took all day.

I nuzzled into her neck, breathing in her sweet citrus scent before gliding my tongue from her shoulder to her ear. She inhaled deeply, and as my teeth caught her lobe, her breath came out in a contented hiss.

Releasing my grip, I slid my hands down her arms and cupped her breasts. Her nipples, still hard from my touch, begged me to taste them. I sucked one into my mouth while pinching the other, and she let out the most erotic moan I had ever witnessed.

I wanted…I *needed*… to pleasure her. To make her forget everyone and everything, if only for a few hours. I kissed my way down her body, every intake of breath, every sound she made pleasing me more than my own release ever could.

Emotion swelled in my heart as I realized the purpose of my entire existence. I was made for this woman. Meant to worship her for eternity. Never had I felt this way about anyone. Nor would I ever again.

Ember was my beginning, my end, and everything in between.

I moved down, caressing her legs, kissing, licking, nipping her inner thighs, down one and up the other before blowing a breath across her sensitive nub.

She let out a breathy, "Mayhem, please," that nearly did me in.

My name on her lips turned my skin to gooseflesh, and I slipped out my tongue, swiping it from her slit to her clit. I couldn't have stopped my moan if I'd tried. "You taste so good."

"More," she whispered. "I need more."

I was happy to oblige. I gently sucked her nub between my lips, teasing it with my tongue as she writhed in pleasure beneath me. A bead of wetness rolled down my cock, and I swiped it with two fingers, moistening them before sliding them inside her. She gasped, her core tightening around them as I licked and sucked her most sensitive spot.

She reached for me, tangling her fingers in my hair as I continued my pursuit. Her scent, her taste, the sounds she made...everything about her called to me...to my soul. The tether that had been trying to form between us since the moment I met her tightened its hold.

I belonged to this witch. I would do anything to make her mine.

I slowed, doing my best to draw out her pleasure, but she arched her back and moved her hips against me.

"Don't stop," she whispered.

"I wouldn't dream of it." I twisted my hand, making a come here motion with my fingers inside her. She moaned, her body tensing as I brought her closer and closer to climax.

"Oh, gods, yes." Her grip on my hair tightened, pulling it at the roots, a pleasurable pain searing my scalp as she called out my name. Her hips bucked, and she released my hair to fist the sheets as she rode wave after wave of her orgasm.

"Mayhem," she panted. "I need you. Right now."

"I will give you everything you need. Always." I rose to my knees. "Do you..."

"Birth control. I'm on it." She clutched my dick and guided it to her folds. "Now."

I rubbed my swollen head against her, sliding it two inches in before pulling out and circling her clit with the tip. She closed her passion-drunk eyes, letting out a slow exhale before pinning me with her fiery gaze.

"Don't make me beg again." She lifted her hips, taking me in farther, and I could no longer hold back.

I plunged inside her, sinking into her velvet vise and pumping my hips three times before I stilled. "Tell me what you want."

Her nails dug into my back. "I want you. I want to make you come."

"You first." I moved, circling and thrusting, her expressions telling me exactly where she wanted me. Focusing on the spot that brought her the most pleasure, I pumped my hips faster, harder. Her core tightened around me, her nails digging deeper into my back until she cried out, release taking her under once more.

"Gods, Mayhem, you're delicious." She clutched my face and kissed me. "I want to feel you come inside me."

I growled and bit her lower lip. "Ask and you shall receive."

My orgasm coiled in my core and released like a monsoon washing over me, drowning me in everything Ember. Talons erupted from my fingers, and my horns began to protrude from my scalp as the beast inside me rode the wave.

Panting, I lowered myself on top of her, burying my face in the pillow to block my semi-transformation from her view. "I'm sorry."

"Don't be." She slipped her hand into my hair, caressing my horns with her fingers. "I know what you are. I'm not afraid."

A half-sob, half-laugh rolled up from my chest. She *did* know. In the short time we had been together, she'd learned more about me than anyone ever had. I lifted my head to look at her and flexed my fingers, drawing my talons back inside.

"I could snap your neck with a flick of my wrist."

She held my face in her hands. "And I could send you back to prison with a swing of my sword."

"Yet here we are, the most unlikely pair, closer than we ever dreamed."

"I'm not ashamed to admit it was the best sex of my life." She pressed a kiss to my lips and tensed, a shadow crossing her features. "But it can never happen again."

CHAPTER 11
EMBER

The second the words left my lips, my stomach tightened and turned, my very being protesting the hypocrisy of the statement. Yes, it was the best sex of my life, and I did want it to happen again. And again and again.

But it couldn't.

Mayhem rolled off me, taking his warmth and compassion with him. His face fell, a curtain slamming down on the vulnerability he'd shown. "I agree. This was a mistake."

"I didn't say it was a mistake." I pushed to sitting, holding the sheet against my chest.

"I did." He slid out of bed and stood, and my stomach tightened even more as I took in the glorious view. My throat thickened, and a tiny voice from somewhere deep inside screamed at me to fix this. To tell him I didn't mean it and that I wanted him in my bed and my life for the rest of my existence.

Down, girl. Don't get attached.

"I spent time inside your mind, and now my mark on your arm is fabricating false emotions. There is no such thing as soulmates, and I was a fool for entertaining the idea. Where can I find clothing? We have work to do."

"Ash's dresser. Bottom right drawer."

He turned on his heel and strode out of my room, leaving me in bed with my mouth hanging open. I don't know what I expected him to do when I said it couldn't happen again, but I definitely did not anticipate he'd plunge a metaphorical knife into my chest.

"Ouch," I whispered, rubbing the phantom pain.

No, not phantom. That pain was real and raw, and I did not enjoy it in the slightest.

I sat still, listening for his voice, but the house stood silent. Sliding out of bed, I padded to my dresser and gathered a set of clothes before heading to the shower for the second time today. His dark, masculine scent lingered on my skin, and I could almost feel his talons against my back as he'd lost control. I had to wash it all away.

After the shower, I scrubbed my teeth and tongue, trying to vanquish the taste of his lips, but it was no use. My mind had grabbed hold of his essence, not just committing it to memory, but etching it in stone.

"Good goddess, Ember. What have you done?" I asked my reflection before I quietly padded into the living room.

Mayhem sat in my favorite chair, his spine straight, his face stoic. Ash flashed me a curious look, and I gave my head a tiny shake, telling her not to ask. I could see the question in her expression: *Are you okay?*

I'll let you know when I figure that out myself.

She nodded. "The guys scried, and they're on their way."

"They're bringing sandwiches," Chaos said, and my stomach growled on cue.

"Do they know where it is?" I sank into the chair opposite Mayhem and tried to make eye contact. He wouldn't look at me.

"You know Shade." Ash folded one leg beneath her. "If they do, he's going to make damn sure we don't go after it without him."

"That tracks." I drummed my fingers on my knees. "The good news is it sounds like the fae aren't planning to take over our realm. If we want to buy what Adrian was selling."

My phone buzzed on the kitchen counter, and I retrieved it, pressing it to my ear. "Another one?"

Higgins huffed. "Washed up at Cat Cove. No liver."

"What about the heart?" I asked as a knock sounded on our door. I opened it and stepped aside for Shade and Miles to come inside.

"You never told me about an issue with hearts." The crunching of potato chips sounded through the phone. "Is there anything else you've failed to mention?"

My teeth clicked. "I pass on information as I receive it. We only found out about the hearts yesterday."

"Hmm. I'll check with the ME. What else do I need to know?"

"If the heart was missing, the victim was a witch. Liver only means they were human."

"Get this shit under control." The line went dead before I

could muster a snappy comeback, which was just as well. My brain was processing way too much information to maintain my sharp tongue.

By the time I finished the call, Miles had set us up with wrapped hoagies and full glasses of water at the table. I sat at one end, and Mayhem took the other...as far from me as possible...while the others filled in the rest of the space.

After firing off a text to Patrice, asking her to wrangle a team to check out Cat Cove, I unwrapped a cranberry chicken salad sandwich and leveled my gaze on Shade. "Well?"

"It's good to have you back," he said to Mayhem, who gave a curt nod, his expression blank.

"Did you find the rest of the amulet?" I took a giant bite of my sandwich and tried not to moan. Savory chicken and sweet, tart cranberries melded together in a flavor explosion. Yum.

"We think so," Miles said. "It's shrouded, but the spell isn't very strong, and..." He cut his gaze to Shade.

"It's strong enough that BSM hasn't found it yet." Shade inclined his chin. "Only a naturally powerful witch could have sensed it like I did."

Miles cleared his throat.

Shade lifted his hands. "Like *we* did. We shared vim."

"*Where* is it?" I couldn't have hidden the annoyance in my voice if I'd tried, but hey. At least I had something else to think about instead of the demon sitting across from me.

Dammit. He was still on my mind. The sigil on my forearm tingled, and I rubbed it to chase away the sensation.

Mayhem inhaled sharply, his gaze snapping to mine. "Don't do that."

Without a word, I picked up my glass and took a long drink. I wanted to spout off a *my body, my choice speech*, but it seemed the tattoo affected his body too. Instead, I squared my gaze on Shade and arched an irritated brow.

"We sense it at Patrice's house," he said.

"That's why we aren't positive," Miles said. "Why would Patrice have it?"

"And why wouldn't she say something if she did?" Ash asked. "You told her we were looking for it."

"I don't know." A sinking sensation formed in my stomach. "You don't think she and Chrys...?"

Shade laughed. "Patrice? She won't even kill a spider. There's no way she participated in a coup with a crazy person."

"Did she ever hang out with you guys while Chrys was manipulating you?" I swallowed the sour taste from the back of my mouth. "We didn't think Chrys was capable of this either."

Miles cast his gaze to the ceiling, looking thoughtful for a moment. "I don't recall her being around during that time. She's always been solitary."

Ash nodded. "And she's healed us more times than I can count. If she wanted to get rid of us, she'd have let us die."

I took another bite of sandwich, chewed, and swallowed as my brain processed the idea. "You're right. It's ludicrous. You probably sensed the amulet's magic there because Chrys used it to trap her in the basement. We need to scry again."

"Or we could go to her house and ask her." Ash rose and carried her sandwich wrapper to the trash. "No sense in wasting vim if we don't have to."

"Great idea." I stood and tossed my trash in the bin. "Everyone, load up."

Mayhem stayed at the table and crossed his arms. "I will remain here."

My jaw tensed, my grip on my water glass tightening. "Fine."

Ash looked from me to him, and back to me. "We don't need the whole crew. How about you and I go, and the boys can stay here and recharge."

"Recharge?" Shade shot to his feet. "It's barely noon. I'm not taking a nap like a child."

"She means our vim." Miles gathered his and Shade's wrappers and wadded them into a ball. "We had to break through the shroud to figure out where it was. I know that taxed you as much as it did me."

"And someone needs to make sure these two don't misbehave." I looked at Mayhem, expecting a sarcastic quip or at least an eye roll. He gave me nothing.

Shade glanced at Miles and sank into his chair. "Yeah. We can do that."

I started to say a silent thank you to Hecate, but with all the trouble we were having finding the damn amulet, it seemed like she'd abandoned us.

"Come on." Ash took a plastic bag from the pantry, grabbed my jacket, and handed it to me. "I just texted and told her we're stopping by."

I checked the inner lining to be sure my knives were there and slipped it on before grabbing the keys and following her downstairs. When we stepped out the back door, I hit the key fob, unlocking the van.

She stopped and put her hand on mine. "I thought we might walk."

"It's twenty minutes on foot. Five if we drive."

She took the keys from my hand and locked the doors. "It'll give us time to talk."

My slow exhale heated the back of my throat. Talking wasn't my thing. Feelings weren't my thing either, and that was exactly what she wanted me to talk about. I chewed the inside of my cheek and gave her the most insolent side eye I could.

She put the keys in her pocket. "It has to come out or it'll fester and make you crazy."

Something inside my chest pinched, and pressure rolled upward, shrinking my throat and threatening to come out as a sob. *What the actual eff, Em?* I closed my eyes and took a deep breath, willing all my insides back to their normal state. It didn't work.

"We had sex." My voice was a whisper over the lump in my throat.

"That much I knew." She laced her arm through mine and guided me to the sidewalk. "I had to cast a silencing spell on your room to give you privacy." I caught her grin from the corner of my eye.

"Thanks for that." I stared straight ahead as we strolled down the street, arm in arm. "It won't happen again."

She waited a beat for me to elaborate. When I didn't, she asked, "Did he hurt you?"

"No." My answer came quickly. He had done the opposite of hurt me.

"Did he force you?"

"Goddess no. I wanted it as bad as he did." A gust of wind blew my hair in my face, and I tucked it behind my ear. "It was good."

"And that's a problem?" she asked.

I blew out a hard breath, trying to find the words to express how I felt. "Yeah."

"Why?"

"Because." I tugged from her grasp to cross my arms. "I'm running a coven and trying to break a curse so we can mend the veil and stop the fabric of reality from unraveling around us... and I am screwing it up every chance I get. I don't have time for romance."

We reached a crosswalk and waited silently for the little red hand to turn into a green walker. When it did, I started to step into the intersection, but Ash stopped me with a hand on my arm.

"You don't have time, or you don't deserve it?" She tilted her head, compassion drawing her brows together, and the pinch inside my chest turned into a vise.

My lower lip trembled as I opened my mouth and closed it again. It still trembled, so I caught it between my teeth and held her gaze, unable to speak.

She clutched my shoulders. "You do deserve it, and he would worship you if you would let him in."

I tried to laugh, but my sob betrayed me. Tears gathered on my lower lids, and when I attempted to blink them back, they spilled down my cheeks. "This is the second time you've made me cry in as many days."

"It feels good to let it out, doesn't it?" She wiped my cheek with her thumb the same way Mom would do when I'd hurt myself.

Another sob-laugh rolled up from my chest. "Have you always been this smart? You see right through me."

The light turned, the red hand flashing before going steady, and Ash pushed the button again. "I don't see through you. I see *you*."

I swallowed, nodding my head and willing the lump in my throat to loosen. "What do you see?" Because I sure as hell didn't know who I was anymore.

"I see a strong, confident, capable woman, who's also filled with self-doubt."

"I'm confident I can kick anyone's ass who crosses me, but that's about it." I wiped my tears and shook my hands, trying to get myself together.

"You're not a people person, and that's okay. You're a full-scale introvert who craves solitude." She shrugged. "We're all wired differently. It doesn't mean you don't deserve love."

The light changed again, and we crossed the street before hanging a right toward Patrice's house.

"Mayhem does love you, you know," Ash said. "He might not express it in a way you understand, but he does. I can feel it."

"It's only been a few days." I tried to scoff, but my heart wasn't in it. I felt it too, and that scared the bejeezus out of me. "He is *so* not my type."

Ash laughed. "He's your perfect match."

"How? You and Chaos complement each other. You're complete opposites. Mayhem and I..."

"Are exactly alike?"

"Not even close. He's hot-tempered and cocky as eff. He's sarcastic and brooding and doesn't play well with others. He's..." I clamped my mouth shut the second I realized who I'd just described. "Well, shit."

"You need to talk to him."

I huffed, shaking my head because I knew she was right. She was always right.

It didn't mean I had to like it. "One thing at a time."

"Some things need to happen simultaneously."

"Not now." I gestured at Patrice's house in front of us. "Let's go see about the amulet."

CHAPTER 12

EMBER

I wiped my face again, running my fingertips over my lashes lest they betray me by holding on to the evidence of yet another emotional outburst. Patrice was crouched near a flower bed, a pair of garden shears in one hand, a bundle of herbs in the other.

I paused on the sidewalk, touching Ash's shoulder and leaning toward her. "Do your thing and see if you can find it while we're talking to her. I want to know if it's here before I bring it up."

Before Ash could respond, Patrice rose and turned toward us. She gasped, dropping the shears and bending to pick them up, her gaze darting around us. "You startled me."

"Sorry about that." Ash strode up the walk, and I followed.

"Is it just you two?" Patrice leaned to look behind us.

"Don't worry." Ash picked up a piece of rosemary she'd

dropped and offered it to her. "We know the guys make you uncomfortable, so we left them at home."

"They don't..." She accepted the fallen herb. "They do, but only because they're demons."

"I get it," I said. "It's hard to trust the royal elite of a species we've been tasked to eradicate."

She let out a breath, her posture relaxing. "They don't belong here."

The sigil on my arm heated, making me thankful for the jacket covering it. "No, they don't." Good goddess, they did not. "But we can't save Salem without them. Can we come in? I'd love an update."

Patrice smiled. "Of course. Tea?"

"I'd love some." Ash took the bundle of herbs from her, and I followed them up the porch steps.

While Patrice busied herself in the kitchen, I gave Ash a questioning look. She shook her head, but I couldn't tell if she meant the amulet wasn't there or if she hadn't tried yet.

"Have a seat." Patrice gestured to the breakfast table before turning on an electric kettle and taking three mugs from a cupboard.

Ash sank onto a wooden chair. "How are things going on your end?"

I took the one next to her. "Is everyone still alive with their hearts intact?"

Patrice froze before slowly turning toward me with a furrowed brow. "We've had a few injuries. Hearts?"

I explained what we'd learned about the fae eating hearts to gain the witches' power. "Has anyone fought one?"

She added tea bags to the mugs and filled them with water. "We've come across a few." She set the cups on the table and sat across from us, clutching hers with both hands. "I'm not supposed to tell you..."

I arched a brow. "Tell me what?"

She sighed, her expression one of shame. "We can't kill them. We've tried, but they're too strong. Now, when we find one, we run away." Her brows drew together as her gaze bounced between Ash and me. "I know we're letting you down, but..."

"It's okay." Ash reached across the table to put her hand on Patrice's. "They're hard for us to kill too. Keeping your distance is the best thing to do, especially now that we know what they're here for."

Patrice pulled from her grasp and dipped the tea bag up and down in her mug. "We can handle the rest. Imps, lesser fae, even a midlevel demon or two."

"I know." I sipped the tea and tried not to cringe. Chamomile was not my favorite. "You're doing great. Spread the word that the new protocol is to contact one of us when you run into a scout or soldier."

I moved my leg beneath the table, hitting my knee against my sister's as a reminder of why we were there.

Ash cleared her throat. "Do you mind if I use your restroom?"

"Not at all." Patrice's smile was warm and genuine, and I was glad we could put her at ease. At least about avoiding the upper fae.

"Did Chrys's mom give you any new information? I don't

think she had gone through her things before we found the shard of amulet at her apartment."

"No." She folded her hands on the table. "She blamed you for the break-in. I didn't tell her about Chaos and Mayhem."

"Good. No one else needs to know who they really are. We'll be sending them on their way soon enough." I tried to ignore the stab of pain in my chest and took another sip of flavorless tea. Coffee was so much better.

Ash returned from the bathroom and gave me a tiny nod before returning to her chair. "So this amulet... We have to find the rest of it before we can summon Discord and put an end to all this terror."

"Do you have any idea where it might be?" Patrice lifted her mug with both hands and took a long sip.

"That's the main reason we're here." I rose and carried my half-full mug to the sink to dump it. "I had Shade and Miles scry for it, and they think it might be in your house."

"Here?" Her face pinched. "Why on earth would it be here?"

"Maybe you have it but don't know what it is?" Ash set her empty mug in the sink. "You've got a lot of stuff in your basement."

"I think I'd know if I had an amulet forged in Hell. I don't practice dark magic. Ever." Patrice padded into the kitchen and rinsed our mugs.

"It could be shrouded. Disguised as something else." But hopefully not as a vibrator like the piece in my bedroom.

She stopped rinsing and turned to me. "If I've had it all along and didn't know, I would feel terrible. But I really don't think it's here. I bet whoever shrouded it put a deflection ward on it too. A spell to make you think it resides somewhere it doesn't."

"Do you mind if we look?" Ash moved toward the pantry door and rested her hand on the knob. "I sense it in the basement."

"Of course." She dried her hands on a dishtowel and stepped into the pantry when Ash opened the door. A shelf hiding the entry stood near the left corner, and she tugged it, swinging it open to reveal a set of stairs. She flipped the light switch and made her way down, pausing at the bottom of the steps.

"I haven't been down here since..." Patrice took a deep breath and kept moving.

To the left lay her work area. Massive bookcases held jars of powders, oils, and who-knew-what else. Bundles of herbs hung from a string stretched across the low ceiling, and the aromas of sage and patchouli greeted my senses, reminding me of a demon I didn't have time to think about.

"What does the amulet look like?" she asked.

"It's a red stone." I made my way to the shelving units and scanned the contents. "Opaque, unassuming."

"My crystals are over here." She opened a cabinet filled with rose quartz, black tourmaline, jade, and every other stone imaginable. Grabbing a translucent crimson one, she offered it to me. "This is red adventurine." She grabbed another one. "And this is garnet."

I accepted the stones, pretending to examine them before handing them back. "The amulet is a different shade."

"In here." Ash turned a corner, disappearing into the unfinished section of the basement.

I followed her inside, but Patrice hung back in the doorway. Who could blame her? She'd nearly died in this room.

Ash rummaged through her bag and pulled out a trowel before lowering to her knees and digging in the back corner. I stood over her, watching as she moved the dirt aside with confident movements.

Six inches below the surface lay the rest of the amulet.

"It's here." I looked over my shoulder at Patrice, and she sucked in a sharp breath, bringing her hands to her mouth.

Ash scooped the amulet shard into the trowel and lifted it, revealing a silver chain attached to the top of the stone. "Chrys must have used it to keep her subdued. The spell on those roots was strong beyond compare." She dropped the necklace into a plastic bag and sealed it before sprinkling a premixed potion on the container.

"Vessel tight, vim bright, hold the magic until the end of our plight," she said. "As I will it, so mote it be."

Patrice sobbed, her knees buckling beneath her as she leaned against the door jamb. "I'm so sorry."

Ash dropped the amulet and the shovel into her bag and rushed to Patrice's side, taking her by the arm and helping her out of the room. "You have no reason to apologize."

"But I remember now," she said as my sister helped her into a chair.

"What do you remember?" I stood in front of her, fighting the urge to cross my arms. Patrice was sensitive, a healer. Demanding answers would only make her...

She dropped her face into her hands and cried.

Ash gave me her infamous *shut the eff up* look and rested a hand on Patrice's shoulder. "Take your time. It was a traumatic experience."

She sniffled and nodded, wiping beneath her nose before lifting her head. "She'd cast a binding spell on me, but not like the one we normally use. It squeezed me like a snake. I thought my bones would be crushed."

Didn't that sound delightful? "I'm so sorry you went through that. I should have known it was Chrys. There were clues."

"Were there?" She sob-laughed. "I didn't notice any."

Ash rubbed her back. "Hindsight is always crystal clear."

Patrice took a deep breath and blew it out hard. "She took me in there, to the dirt floor, and called the roots from the ground to trap me. Then she took off the necklace and used her magic to create a hole where she buried it. As soon as she did, dark magic started seeping into my skin."

"Sounds like Chrys." I paced behind her.

"She told me she'd be back for me and the amulet, and that's the last thing I remember until you got me out." She stood and touched Ash's elbow. "I'm okay. Let's get out of here."

We followed her upstairs to the kitchen. Ash filled a glass with water and offered it to her, and Patrice guzzled half the contents before setting it on the counter.

"What will you do with the amulet?" she asked.

"Put it back together, summon the final demon prince, and break the curse Isabel started four hundred years ago."

She wrung her hands. "Do the demons still plan to take revenge on Isabel's descendants?"

I looked at Ash. Her lips formed a thin line, and her shoulders inched toward her ears. "I think so."

Patrice pressed a hand to her chest. "Goddess help them."

I shrugged. "It's them or our entire coven. Our whole town. Thanks for the tea. We'll let you get back to your gardening." I jerked my head toward the door and strode outside, but Ash didn't follow.

Five minutes passed before she joined me on the sidewalk. "She feels awful."

"I can imagine."

We walked two blocks in glorious silence before the hairs on the back of my neck stood on end. I looked at Ash, and her brow furrowed. We stilled, feeling the energy around us, but I didn't sense any type of threat. The sensation felt earthly. Positive.

"What is that?" I asked.

"I..." She tilted her head. "It's the ether...the veil. It feels different."

I opened my senses, letting the vibration wash over me and through me. "Does it feel...stronger?"

CHAPTER 13
MAYHEM

The women had been gone for over an hour, yet the knife in my heart remained. Chaos had assured us he would know if they ran into trouble, that his connection to Ash spanned any distance. I knew it was true because I felt the same bond with Ember.

The knife twisted at the thought of her name.

We had occupied ourselves with the television, Shade and Miles taking the couch while Chaos and I sat in the chairs. Miles had chosen a program about cooking, where humans created dishes for judges to compare, but I paid it no mind.

I couldn't distract myself, couldn't extract the blade of agony from my heart, for my soulmate had rejected me.

Was I too rough with her? My goal had been to worship her, body and being, but perhaps my perception had been off. She'd seemed to enjoy my affections, and when my beast demanded release, my horns and talons erupting from my skin, she hadn't flinched.

What in Lucifer's name had I done wrong?

I didn't dare seek my brother's counsel in front of the male witches. The business of my heart was none of theirs, and I didn't doubt Chaos would ridicule me for driving the entire meaning of my existence away.

"What's wrong with him?" Shade jabbed a thumb in my direction.

I growled in return before rising and striding out of the room. Ember's bedsheets still lay in a tangle from our lovemaking. The knife twisted harder, and I seethed.

There had to be another vying for her attention. Someone who had entranced her before she met me, confusing her thoughts to the point she could not see that we were meant to be. That there was no other man for her but me.

Hellfire built in my gut, rising up to my chest and melting the blade of betrayal, using the molten metal to fuel my rage. Ember would not betray me. She wasn't capable. The universe had deemed it so.

My palms tingled. Sparks danced across my fingers, gathering into spheres as I curled my hands, my talons erupting from my fingertips. Her interactions with men were few. Their mundane, balding police chief, with his gruff manners and oversized stomach, would never catch her eye. He would need an artifact to entrance her, and he lacked the intelligence to manage one.

My brother belonged to Ash. Of that there was no question.

That left the two males in the living room.

The fire in my palms raged with my fury. I stormed into the room, my expression wild with wrath. Miles saw me first. His knees shot toward his chest before he launched to his feet, springing behind a chair and gathering energy between his hands.

Shade reacted a moment later, joining Miles behind the chair. "Shit, man. Chill."

"Brother…" Chaos stood in front of me, blocking my path, his voice dripping with warning. "These men have done nothing to you."

I moved to the left, attempting to sidestep him, but he moved with me.

"Which one of you has entranced my soulmate?" I growled. "Who has her under his spell? I will rip off your fingers one by one and feed them to you while I skin you alive."

Chaos put heavy hands against my chest, his eyes glowing red in threat. "Neither of them has hurt her."

"Lies. She would not have rejected me otherwise." I shoved him, but he fisted my shirt in his hands and pinned me against the wall.

"Extinguish your fire before you burn this home to the ground. This is *Ember's* home." He released my shirt and used his forearm to hold me down. "Put it out now."

"What in Hecate's name?" The sound of her voice drew the air from my lungs.

I raked in a breath, a fist of anguish clenching my heart. "I will kill them both for what they've done to my soulmate."

Ember's boots thudded on the wood as she stomped into

the room, putting herself between me and the treacherous witches. "No one has done anything to me. What is going on?"

Ash joined her in the middle of the room. "Chaos?"

"Apparently, he blames Shade and Miles for Ember's rejection." He turned his head to me, baring his teeth. "Extinguish and relax."

"Mayhem!" Ember fisted her hands on her hips. "Stop it."

At her command, I drew my hellfire inward, my talons following the flames. Chaos loosened the pressure on my chest, but he did not release me.

Ash touched Miles on the shoulder. "It's okay. He'll listen to her."

The men relaxed their defensive stances, though their bodies remained tense, and Chaos removed his arm to rest a single hand against my chest.

"Take a breath with me." Ember inhaled, her chest expanding before retracting with her exhale. "Do it." She breathed again, and I followed her command. Once. Twice. Three times we breathed together.

The fury in my chest simmered with her presence, her voice soothing me, calming my racing thoughts until I could think clearly. With clarity came the pain of her rejection, and the knife of agony plunged into my chest once more.

She held my gaze as she strode toward me, lifting a hand at Chaos, silently asking him to release me. He backed two steps away, and she rested her palm on my shoulder. Her touch was gentle, but the weight of it nearly crushed me.

"Take a walk with me." She glided her fingers down my arm

to clutch my hand. "Come on," she said when I didn't move, and she tugged, taking a step away.

I could do nothing but follow.

She remained silent as we descended the stairs, not turning to look at me until the late afternoon sun illuminated her purple hair, making it shine like silk. We passed her damaged van and turned right on the sidewalk.

"Where are we going?" I asked, unable to bear her silence any longer.

"Nowhere in particular. Walking helps me gather my thoughts." She released my hand to tuck her hair behind her ear. "What was going on in there? Because it looked like a jealous rage, and that is *no bueno*."

"Your perceptiveness astonishes me." I fought the urge to reach for her hand again and shoved mine into my pockets instead.

"It wasn't hard to figure out." When I didn't respond, she nodded, pressing her lips into a hard line. "So you thought I was involved with Miles and Shade?"

"If I was certain which one had bewitched you, he would be dead already."

"Okay, see?" She stopped and laid her hand on my shoulder, turning me to face her. "That kind of behavior isn't okay. Just because you think someone hurt me or has me under a spell, it doesn't mean you can kill them."

"I would raze the entire world before I would allow anyone to harm you." I grasped her hands, pulling them to my chest. "I would do anything for you."

She swallowed hard, her mouth opening but then closing again.

"Why did you reject me?" I released her hands, returning mine to my pockets so I wouldn't wrap my arms around her and carry her away.

"I didn't reject you. I..." She lowered her gaze.

"You said we could never be together again." I dipped my head, attempting to catch her gaze.

She inhaled deeply and continued walking. "This is hard for me. Words and emotions aren't my thing."

"Nor were they mine until I met you." I walked beside her, matching her strides. "Did something happen in your past?"

"No." She shook her head, drawing her shoulders upward. "It would be so much easier if I could blame it on some traumatic event, but I can't. It's just how I'm wired. I had the same upbringing as my sisters; there's just something different about me. Something wrong."

"There is nothing wrong with you." I grasped her arm, turning her toward me, but she refused to meet my eyes. "Look at me."

It took her a moment, but she finally met my gaze, her deep brown eyes shimmering with unshed tears.

"Words will forever elude me, but the way I feel about you is undeniable. You, Ember Holland, are the reason for my existence."

She laughed and blinked back her tears. "Words don't elude you. The only problem you have is your hot temper. I don't want you killing anyone over me. Understood?"

I frowned. "Not even the fae? Or an attacking demon?"

"That's different. In battle, you have to. In real life...never. Okay? Especially not because you're jealous." She tilted her head, awaiting my answer.

"I will try my best to remember that."

She laughed again. "Your brother has taught me that's the best I can expect from a demon."

"Is that why you rejected me? Because of what I am?"

"Yes and no." She sighed and continued her stroll. "It's hard for a light witch to accept she's fated to a demon."

"Your sister has no problem with it."

"She struggled, believe me. But Ash is better with people than I am, so you have to be patient with me. I'm scared to death of this." She motioned her finger between us.

"And what is 'this' to you?"

"I don't know. I need time to figure things out, and that's the problem, isn't it? We're running out of time."

A crisp breeze rustled the leaves on the ground, and a pink cloud stretched across the sun, dimming the afternoon light as a trail of white smoke extended from the chimney of a nearby home, filling the air with the aroma of burning maple wood. I inhaled deeply, taking in the moment. There would be more like this. There had to be.

"I have waited an eternity to find you. I will wait a thousand more if that's what you need." And I would do everything within my power to make her understand she belonged to me, as I belonged to her. No matter the cost.

She tilted her head, a sad smile playing on her lips. "Yeah, words definitely do not elude you."

I paused beneath an oak tree. "What shall we do now?"

She stopped and faced me. "We need to head back so you can apologize to Miles and Shade. I promise you, they are more interested in each other than they are in me."

My brow furrowed with my confusion. "They are a couple?"

"Not officially...but learn to read the room." She turned around and motioned for us to return. "And put a lid on your pot o' jealousy. It's been ages since a man has caught my eye, and you've given me tunnel vision."

"Tunnel vision?"

She sighed. "You are the only man I am interested in, okay? I like you. Just don't let it go to your head."

The knife once piercing my chest clattered to the ground, warmth and hope replacing the pain. Ember was mine, whether she could admit it or not, and I would never let another man lay a finger on her. I would be her consort, her protector...her everything...just as she was mine.

"This is weird." She huffed out a half-laugh. "You and I are so much alike."

"Why is that weird?"

"Because we're fighters, not lovers. And here we are, taking a walk and talking about our feelings."

I rubbed my chin, my lips pursing. "Very weird indeed. But, according to your television, love can make you do strange things."

She hid her quick intake of air by clearing her throat. "I'm definitely not ready for that word."

It was simple verbiage to express an overwhelming emotion, but I acquiesced. If it made her uncomfortable, I would not use it until she deemed I could. I would do anything for this feisty witch. *Anything.*

We returned to the lot behind her home, and Ember strode toward her van, clicking her tongue as she examined the damage. The imp had shattered the windshield on the passenger side and caused multiple dents in the hood when it jumped.

"It looks like we got hit with a hailstorm." She reached for the hood but stopped, curling her lip at the slime pooling in the dents. "I can't imagine what it'll cost to get this fixed."

"Can you not barter your services?"

"I'm not sure what I could offer a body shop. My talents are throwing sharp objects and killing otherworldly invaders."

"You can offer your protection in exchange for their services. You could make agreements with the entire town."

This time, her laugh resounded from deep in her belly, the musical sound a symphony to my soul. "A: Ninety-five percent of the people in Salem are clueless about real magic. And B: We're not the mafia. Hold on..."

She leaned toward the windshield, squinting. "What the hell?"

With her thumb and forefinger, she grasped a small piece of rolled parchment. Imp slime oozed from the page, and she held it away from her body, shaking it, the offending goo splattering to the pavement. "Is this a normal thing for an imp to carry across the veil?"

"It's not normal at all. Imps can't read or write, and they only consume paper when meat isn't available."

"So this was either his lunch or a message from someone in Hell."

CHAPTER 14

EMBER

"Ash, get downstairs," I shouted as I flung the door open and stepped into the kitchen. "And bring paper towels."

I darted down the steps and met Mayhem in the library, where he held the rolled parchment over a trash can, saving our floors from imp slime. A minute later, Ash and Chaos joined us.

"Is everything okay?" She tore off two towels and handed them to me. "I told the guys to stay upstairs in case..."

"It's fine. We talked." I waved a hand dismissively. "Look at this." I held out the paper towels, and Mayhem laid the parchment on them.

"What is that?" Ash peered at the scroll. "Where did you find it?"

"On the van. I think it might be a message from someone across the veil." I rubbed a towel over the parchment, soaking up the slime.

"And they sent it with an imp?" Her arched brow conveyed her skepticism.

"Remember Miles's friend Wendy saying Adrian sent messages back and forth with the lesser fae? Do you have tweezers?" I sank into the chair at her desk and turned on a lamp.

She opened a drawer and took out a fabric bundle before laying it next to the parchment and unfolding it. A set of silver tools shined in the lamplight, complete with scissors, a scalpel, and three different sizes of tweezers.

I chose the medium pair and a blunt instrument and carefully unrolled the parchment. Ash watched over my shoulder, and Chaos and Mayhem stood across from us, leaning forward to read the elegant script. I recognized the handwriting instantly, and my pulse quickened as I read the letter.

Ash and Ember,

I'm afraid the imp might devour my message before it gets to you, but I have no other way to send it. Halloween will be here before we know it, and the veil has already become too weak to bear its natural thinning. We're doing everything we can to keep it intact, but even the goddess can't hold it forever. There's an amulet somewhere on your side. You have to find it and summon Discord so he can return it to its rightful owner. I can't come home without it.

Blessed be,

Cinder

Ash laid her on my shoulder. "She's alive."

I released the parchment, letting it curl into a loose roll, and placed my hand over hers. "And we can bring her home."

"Did you find the amulet's missing piece?" Mayhem asked.

I smiled up at him. "We sure did. Let's go put that baby back together."

I wrapped the parchment in the paper towel and put it in Ash's desk drawer before leading the way upstairs, with Mayhem behind me and Chaos and Ash following. The moment I opened the door, Miles and Shade shot to their feet, their energy teetering between fight and flight.

"Mayhem has something he'd like to say to you before we put the amulet together." I started for my room, pausing at the hallway to listen.

He stayed in the kitchen, a safe distance away from the guys. "I no longer wish to kill you."

I crossed my arms. "That's not an apology."

"Princes of Hell do not apologize." He relaxed his stance. "However, my behavior was fueled by distress and rage, and I should not have acted before speaking with Ember. Please accept my humble apology." He bowed regally, though I couldn't tell if it was sarcastic or sincere.

Miles stepped toward him. "We would never try to come between you and Ember. Fate is fate, and we won't tamper with it."

Shade stepped to his side. "Fate or not, neither of us is interested in her like that. We never have been."

"I know. She informed me of—"

I cleared my throat, stopping him from finishing the

sentence. Just because I knew the bond between Miles and Shade, it didn't mean they had figured it out yet.

"Apology accepted." Miles offered his hand, and Mayhem shook it.

"Just don't mess with us again." Shade shook his hand as well.

"I will do my best," Mayhem said.

"And that's the best you'll get from him." I started down the hall but paused, turning back to them. "Are we all good?"

"We're good," Shade said. Miles and Mayhem nodded.

"Good." I strode into my room and retrieved the shard of amulet from my nightstand drawer. When I returned, Ash had set the piece from Patrice's house on the counter. I laid mine next to it.

No one said a word, but they all looked at me like I'd grown horns. "What?" I asked.

"Is that a mechanical penis?" Mayhem's face scrunched with confusion. "It's rather small."

"I cloaked it in case anyone tried to find it. Let me remove the spell." I held my hands over it. "What I've done is now undone. As I will it, so mote it be."

Nothing happened.

Ash pressed her lips together, holding in a laugh. "Em, that's your real vibrator."

"No, it's..." I looked at the object in question, and my cheeks heated. "Shit, it is. Hold on." I snatched it off the counter and speed-walked to my room.

My ears burned as I opened the drawer and traded the real deal for the fake one. I couldn't tell you why I was embarrassed.

So what if I used it on the regular? I hadn't had a date in ages, and women had needs too.

But Mayhem had seen it. He'd called it small, which, from his point of view, I supposed it was. But it didn't matter. I had a sexy demon prince ready to worship me if I ever had time to fulfill my womanly needs again.

Oof. Was that a good thing or a bad thing?

"This is it," I said as I returned to the kitchen and laid it on the counter. "What I've done is now undone. As I will it, so mote it be."

The vibrator transformed into the plastic jar with the amulet shard. I opened it, spilling the contents, and Ash did the same with her piece before opening her toolkit and taking out a pair of small wire cutters.

"What did Patrice say about the amulet?" Shade asked. "Where did you find it?"

"It was buried in her basement where Chrys was holding her with the roots." I grasped the tweezers and held the shard still. "She buried it there to keep her spell in place. Patrice had no clue until we jogged her memory."

"Damn," Miles said. "I hope it wasn't there to temper her magic like the ward Chrys put on this building."

"If it was, it's gone now." Ash clipped the cage holding the piece of amulet, bending the wires so I could dump the shard onto the countertop.

"I don't think the chain belongs on this piece either." I gestured to the one we'd retrieved from Patrice, and Ash turned it over. "I guess the original one broke off. It looks like she used glue to attach it."

"Indeed, it does," Mayhem said. "The amulet used to hang from a chain of gold, forged in Hell."

"Do we have to find the missing chain too?" I asked.

Mayhem shook his head. "No, it is the stone that contains the magic. Discord wore it constantly, taunting me with its power."

I snapped my gaze to his. "Don't get any ideas. We're using it to summon your brother so he can return it to the Underworld. Period. Nothing else. Got it?"

"I understand." He held my gaze, and the purple in his irises seemed to undulate in a mesmerizing wave.

A sense of calm washed over me, and for a brief moment, I actually believed everything would be okay. Funny, I know.

I blinked, pulling myself out of the trance and landing firmly in reality. Everything would *not* be okay. The demons had to return to Hell. We had to stay here. Even if we broke the curse, there would be no happily ever afters for us. The thought pained me.

That was why it was best not to get attached. I made a mental note not to forget it, wadded up the emotions, and shoved them into the deepest corner of my mind. With any luck, they'd stay there.

"Ready?" Ash asked.

"As I'll ever be." I used the tweezers to pick up the shard and touched it to the amulet.

We held a collective breath as both pieces of the stone glowed deep red. Heat crept up the metal instrument I held, and while it couldn't burn me, life had taught me heat that intense would melt a mundane's skin. Hell, it would melt a witch's too if fire wasn't her inborn power.

I released the shard and set the tweezers down. The stone pulsed, and the broken piece moved across its surface, melding with the place it had been broken off. A flash of crimson light filled the room, blinding me for a few seconds.

When my vision returned, I blinked the amulet into focus. The glue holding the makeshift chain had dissolved, but the shard fit perfectly, no cracks or lines revealing it had ever been broken. It was rounded and smooth on the left side, creating one half of an oval.

On the right side...

"Jagged edges." My heart sank. "There's another missing piece."

CHAPTER 15
EMBER

"One thing." I paced across the living room, turned on my heel, and paced back. "Why can't *one* thing be easy?"

"To quote our High Priestess, 'Where's the fun in that?'" Ash dropped the two-thirds-complete amulet into the plastic container.

At least, I hoped it was two-thirds complete. If we were missing any more pieces, I might... Ugh. "I've had all the fun I can handle." I resumed pacing.

Shade sank onto a stool at the counter. "We'll find it. It has to be somewhere in Salem or Boston."

"Does it?" My fists clenched, my nails digging into my palms.

"Could it be buried here?" Miles asked. "Since she put up a ward to temper your magic, maybe she left a piece somewhere outside."

"There's nowhere to bury it," Ash said. "And the spell she used on our house wasn't strong enough to require magic like that."

"And we don't even know if she had all the pieces." The heels of my boots thudded on the hardwood. "Was Chrys the one who broke it, or did Isabel do it? Or one of her descendants? We have to scry again. Halloween is next week."

"I'll set it up." Ash padded to the kitchen and filled a bowl with water. "We should all do it together."

I lit two candles and set them on the table. Ash put the bowl of water between them, and everyone took a seat. I laid my hands on the table, and Ash rested her palm in mine. Mayhem hesitated, his questioning gaze dancing across my face, and I nodded.

The moment his skin touched mine, a jolt of...something... shot straight to my heart. My chest tightened, and for a moment, I forgot to breathe. Apparently, this was what holding hands with your soulmate did to you.

The sensation wasn't unpleasant in the slightest. I'd grown used to the pinpricks skittering across my skin, but now they burrowed deep inside me, making my nerves come alive. He must have felt it too, because a hint of a smile lifted the corners of his mouth as he offered Shade his other hand.

Wariness tightened Shade's features, but he recovered. When everyone had joined hands, I inhaled deeply, centering myself and trying my best not to think about the hot-as-sin demon sitting next to me. *Don't get attached, Em. Don't get attached.*

"Everyone ready?" I asked.

"I don't know how to scry." Mayhem squeezed my hand. Definitely not unpleasant at all.

"You just have to share your energy with us," I said. "We'll focus it into locating the amulet."

"Very well." He opened to me before I was ready, a surge of demon magic coursing through my psyche, making me gasp.

Shade's brow furrowed. "How about a little of that over here?"

Amusement sparkled in Mayhem's eyes as he withdrew a fraction of his magic and offered it to Shade. My stomach looped at his playful expression, so I focused on the water bowl instead. If I didn't get myself under control, this would never work.

"Let's begin." I gazed at the water in the bowl, the candle flames filling the periphery of my vision until everything started to blur. I allowed my sight to remain unfocused and thought about the amulet.

Forged in the depths of the Underworld. A joint project between Hecate, our goddess, and Hades, their god. Why would a god and goddess need an artifact that increased a being's power beyond compare? I couldn't fathom it. Then again, I'd never met a deity. Who knew how their brains worked?

Picturing the red stone in my mind, I held on to the image, visualizing the broken piece and how it would fuse with the rest of the gem. Ash's energy vibrated high on my right while Mayhem's low rumble pulsed on my left.

I invited both into my psyche, letting them mix and meld in the core of my being, pulling me deeper and deeper into the trance. Though my eyes remained open, I saw nothing but the darkness of the ether, which I sifted through as if it were sand running through my fingers. All I felt was the void.

"Does anyone sense it yet?" My mouth felt dry, my tongue sticky.

"Nothing yet." Ash's voice was hoarse and thick, a side effect of the scrying trance. "Let's go deeper."

I inhaled and let out a slow, controlled breath before allowing myself to slip in further. The outside world ceased to exist. I couldn't feel the hands I held nor smell the burning wax. With all my senses focused into the ether, I searched for the energy of the amulet.

A tickle formed in my consciousness, the sensation pulling me forward. "*I feel something,*" I said silently.

"*Share it,*" Ash replied in my mind.

I did, allowing it to seep into our shared trance, and a vision began to form. It wavered, sparkling around the edges and fading in and out. My only thought the matter at hand, I focused harder, bringing the amulet into clear focus.

The sparkles dimmed as the image took shape, an unassuming red stone attached to a shimmering gold chain.

"*That's it, right?*" I asked the demons, but they couldn't reply. Even though they shared their magic with us, they weren't part of the collective trance.

"*It has to be,*" Shade said. "*Pull back so we can see where it is.*"

I pictured the area around the stone. It lay nestled on a pillow of black velvet. Pulling back further, I saw the plexiglass container holding it on a shelf. It sat in a massive storage room, with rows and rows of shelving units. Jewelry, hand-drawn maps, and pottery filled the shelves, and antique furniture lined the floors.

"*What the hell?*" I pulled back more and found security guards armed with assault rifles at the entrance to the room. The vision wavered, the sparkles returning to the edges.

"*Stay in the trance. We need to see where the building is.*" I sent out another wave of magic as I pulled back in the vision. A lobby. Three sets of heavy double doors. More armed guards. Finally, I made it out of the building, a brick and glass structure that stood at least ten stories high.

"*I recognize this,*" Miles said. "*I know where it is.*"

"*Let's pull out, then. We've used enough vim.*" I took a deep breath, bringing my senses back into my body. The candles' blurry flames flickered in my peripheral vision, and warmth from Mayhem's and Ash's hands seeped into my palms. I blinked the water bowl into focus and gasped, letting go of Ash to press my hand to my chest.

Mayhem held my other hand tightly. "Are you okay?"

I looked at him, the concern in his gaze making me feel things I didn't know how to name. "I'm good. Everyone good?"

"Yeah," Shade said, and Ash nodded.

Miles's brow furrowed. "I'm okay, but...someone put the rest of the amulet up for auction. It's in New York City."

"A heavily guarded auction house. Fabulous." I rolled my neck from side to side, stretching the tension from my muscles and hoping my spine would crack to relieve some of the pressure threatening to build into a massive headache. Sadly, it didn't help.

"Human guards will be no match for a Prince of Hell and his

fire witch. We will simply go in and take what is rightfully ours."

"Whoa. There are so many things wrong with that sentence." I tugged from his grasp and stood before extinguishing the candles and carrying them to a shelf. A trace tingle of Mayhem's magic still danced across my skin, so I shook my hand, chasing away the sensation.

Mayhem stretched out his legs, clasping his fingers behind his head. "It makes perfect sense to me."

My teeth clicked, the tension in my jaw adding to that in my neck. "Let me dissect it for you. A: We don't know for certain all the guards are human. That's a high-paying job, and witches have to work too. So do shifters for that matter, and New York is home to plenty of them."

He started to respond, so I held up a hand to stop him. Miraculously, he obeyed, though I didn't miss his smirk.

"B: Even if they are all human, I can't stop a bullet, and if I die, you get vanquished. You have to remember that."

He lifted one shoulder dismissively. "I would never let that happen."

"C and D: I'm not *your* fire witch, and however we decide to handle this, we will be working as a team. We *are* a team. No more solo side quests."

Ash nodded her appreciation.

"And F—"

"You're on E," Shade, ever the helpful one, chimed in.

"E is for everyone. F: There won't be anything simple about this. In addition to the armed guards, the building will have cameras and an alarm system to notify the police if anything goes awry. As much as Higgins is a thorn in my side, he protects us from the law here. He can't do that there."

"So we're screwed." Shade lifted his hands and dropped them in his lap.

Ash took the bowl to the sink and dumped the water. "Not necessarily. We could find out when the auction is and go there to bid on it."

"That's a possibility." I paced the length of the living room. "Miles, do you know the name of the auction house? Can you look it up?"

"Yeah." He swallowed hard, sadness tightening his eyes. "Ginger and I spent a weekend in a hotel nearby. We'd hoped to sit in on an auction, but nothing was planned for when we were there."

Shade's brow crumpled. "I'm sorry."

Mile's face twitched before his expression turned neutral. "It's alright. Let me grab my laptop. Can I use your wifi?"

"Of course."

He rose from the table and took his computer to the living room, setting it on the coffee table before sinking onto the sofa. I recited the password, and after he connected, he pulled up the auction house website.

"I'll have to make an account to see the items up for bid." His fingers flew across the keys.

I sat next to him. "Use a fake name. We don't need anything traced back to us if we have to steal it."

He gave me the side eye. "I work in IT."

"Right." I raised my hands in surrender and let him do his thing.

Mayhem sat in the chair adjacent to my spot on the couch. I could feel his gaze on my face as Miles created a fake account for Boyd Anderson from Houston, Texas. He even used "BigOil" as the email address.

I laughed. "Why do I get the feeling you've done this before?"

Miles cleared his throat. "I'm in."

"You claim to be light witches, yet you are firmly grounded in the gray." Mayhem still watched me.

"It's okay when it's for the greater good." I didn't dare look at him, lest he derail my thoughts all over again.

"The auction is scheduled for tomorrow evening. In person only." Miles clicked the event and opened the page of items that would be up for grabs.

"How long is the drive to New York?" I asked.

Ash typed on her phone. "About four and a half hours without traffic."

"We can manage that." I watched as he scrolled through the items, many of them artifacts we'd seen when we scried. He found the amulet in the list between an eighteenth-century vampire-hunting kit and a gem-encrusted swan figurine and clicked the entry.

"'A genuine nineteen-carat Burma ruby attached to a twenty-inch gold chain of twenty-four karats. Circa 100AD.' I wonder where they got that information?" I leaned forward, resting my elbows on my knees.

"The amulet is no earthly gemstone," Mayhem scoffed. "It was created in Hell, not in Burma."

"The humans don't know that." I patted his thigh, and he

sucked in a quick breath. Jerking my hand back to my lap, I glanced at the others. They either hadn't noticed, or they were choosing to ignore the whatever-it-was going on between me and the demon. *Thank you, Hecate.*

"Bidding starts at $400,000," Miles said.

I blinked before squinting at the screen. "Are you sure that's five zeros?"

He zoomed in so I could see it clearly. Yep. Five zeros. "I don't think bidding is an option. Or...is it?" he asked.

I barked out a laugh. "Maybe if we sold the house, all our weapons, and the library."

"Don't you dare touch my books." Ash's phone buzzed, and she swiped open the screen before letting out a dry chuckle. "Patrice wants to know if we've mended the veil...and if the demons are back in the Underworld."

"I wish." I stood and sidestepped Mayhem to resume my pacing. "I mean...not the demons back in Hell part." I made the mistake of looking into Mayhem's eyes and found fierce determination staring back at me. Why did I get the feeling that returning to the Underworld wasn't on his agenda?

Her phone buzzed again. "She said things have been eerily quiet today. They haven't battled a single beastie."

"It must be Hecate's work. Cinder's letter mentioned they were trying to hold it together from that side." My head spun, the vim depletion from the scrying session finally surfacing above my adrenaline.

"She did mention that even a goddess can't hold it forever," Mayhem said. "Discord must have convinced Hecate to help."

"Or Cinder did." I dug my fingers into the muscles at the

base of my skull, massaging the tension. "We have no clue what's happening across the veil right now, but we need to take advantage of the quiet."

Pain ached from my skull, down my neck, and into my shoulders, but I couldn't focus on that right now, because... "We need to plan a heist."

CHAPTER 16

MAYHEM

Ember clutched the back of her neck and paced the length of the living room, back and forth, back and forth, until I would have sworn she'd wear a trench into the wood. The stress of leadership was taking a toll on her body and her mind, and a spark of misplaced anger ignited in my being.

Instinct told me to place blame, take action, and get revenge for the pain my witch endured. But who could I condemn? If her parents had not summoned the trickster that took them to Hell, her sister would not have made a deal with Discord. Ash would not have summoned Chaos, and I would still be rotting in my dark prison, devoid of all my senses, going out of my mind.

Worse than that, I would have never experienced the fierceness of love I felt for my soulmate.

No, I could not blame her family for her pain. The universe

planned the chips to fall exactly as they did to bring us together, and now that my brothers and I had found our missing halves, it was up to all of us to ensure we experienced the elusive happily ever after.

Ember stopped pacing, lifted her hands, and dropped them at her sides. "I've got nothing. If it were a magical heist, I'd already have a plan, but we're dealing with humans, guns, and a possible prison sentence, which is one thing we don't have time for."

"I can make them turn their guns on each other. Then we can slip into the vault and take the amulet while they are transfixed in battle."

"Absolutely not." She put her hands on her hips. "No killing humans."

"Technically, they would be killing each other." I rested my elbows on the arms of the chair and steepled my fingers. "You wouldn't have to harm a soul."

She closed her eyes, her nostrils flaring as she blew out a slow breath. This expression, I had learned, was one of annoyance, and Hades forbid I should become an accessory to her pain.

"No killing humans," I said. "Understood. But you must understand if your life is in peril, I will act accordingly to keep you safe. There may be casualties."

"The same is true of me," Chaos said. "Your lives are worth more than a prison sentence...and no human jail could hold us anyway."

Miles chuckled. "I wish I could find someone who'd protect me with such grit."

"I've got your back," Shade said.

I glanced at Ember, who lifted a brow, her expression conveying what words could not in their presence: *See?*

I gave her a small nod. *Yes, I see.* Hopefully they could find their happily ever after as well.

My brow furrowed. Where had a thought like that come from? As a Prince of Hell, I never cared about...or even considered...the emotions of others, yet the idea that the two men should be happy together rooted firmly in my chest.

How strange.

"Fine." Ember crossed her arms. "But only if it's absolutely necessary to save one of our lives."

"Agreed." I couldn't stop the smile from lifting my lips. Her passion and determination warmed my coal-black heart.

"That sounds reasonable," Chaos said.

"Good." She resumed her pacing. "We'll leave first thing in the morning so we can scope out the place in the daylight. We need to get in, grab the amulet, and get out without causing a scene."

I held in my laugh. She had Chaos and Mayhem on her team...there would always be a scene.

"If you believe the movies," Ash said, "the best time to grab it would be when they're transporting it from the vault to the auction room."

"Yes, that's good." Ember pointed at her sister. "You and Chaos can go in and do your mind control thing. Make the guard hand over the amulet."

Miles had been typing on his laptop, but he stopped abruptly. "There will be at least three guards and an auction official who move it. It's a standard security protocol for high-value items. You'll have to mind control all of them to make it happen."

"Oof. I'm not sure we can do that." Ash rose from the couch to sit on the arm of my brother's chair. "What do you think?"

Chaos rubbed his thumb and finger on his chin. "I can cause chaos to the masses, but your magic is much more focused. I wouldn't chance it without practicing it first."

"You can try it on us," Miles said. "As long as you don't make us do anything embarrassing."

Shade shrugged one shoulder dismissively. "I'm game."

The memory of what happened when I used my power on Ash made my stomach sour. "You will not attempt to control Ember. I will not allow her life to be put at risk."

"Wait. This is deadly?" Shade held up his hands.

"The reason I vanquished him was because he tried his magic on Ash and it got stuck. Her bond with Chaos did something weird to the connection, and Mayhem couldn't let her go." She stretched out her arm, gesturing to my mark on her skin. "And now I'm bonded with him."

Possessiveness tightened my chest. I wanted to take her, to wrap my arms around her and return to Hell, where could spend eternity together. But it would not be our happily ever after. My witch would never leave her family and her duty to her coven behind, and if Ember wasn't happy, I could never be.

"Try it on them. If you can control two, you can manage four." Ember sat on the arm of my chair and massaged her neck, stretching it from side to side as her fingers dug into the muscles.

Her close proximity set my nerves ablaze. She didn't touch me, but she didn't need to. Our bond electrified my soul.

Chaos took Ash's hand, and they both focused on the men. "Miles, you will give your computer to Shade."

Miles's expression blanked, and he nodded. "Yeah. Here you go." He slid the computer into Shade's lap.

"Shade, you will bring it to me so I can destroy it. Miles, stand up and bring me a beer."

Miles did as he was told, padding to the kitchen and taking a beer from the refrigerator.

Shade laughed and closed the laptop. "I don't think so. This thing cost him two grand."

My brother and his witch exhaled, releasing their hold on Miles. Confusion furrowed his brow, and he looked at the beer in his hand.

"I see it worked on me. Do you still want this?"

Chaos shook his head. "We could not control you both."

Miles put the bottle into the refrigerator and returned to his spot on the sofa. "So that plan won't work." He opened the laptop and typed rapidly.

Ember pushed on a spot in her shoulder and groaned.

"Are you okay?" Ash asked.

She kneaded her muscle. "I've got a knot right here, and it's giving me a headache. I can't think straight."

I held my hand toward her. "May I?"

Her hesitation pierced my heart, but after giving me a wary look, she said, "Sure."

Miles continued typing while Shade watched the computer screen. My brother stared at me intently, and for once, I could not read his expression. If it were one of warning, I couldn't fathom what he'd warn me about. This witch belonged to me. It was my duty to keep her happy, healthy, and pain-free.

I rubbed my thumb against my fingers, gathering heat on my skin before placing my hand on her shoulder. I squeezed the muscle she had indicated was ailing her, and it was as taut as a guitar string. With my thumb, I applied pressure, moving it in slow circles over the tightest spot.

Ember groaned, sliding from the arm of the chair to sit on the floor in front of me. "Keep doing that."

Blood rushed to my groin as the memory of our morning encounter played in my mind's eye. I leaned forward, using both hands to massage the tension from her shoulders.

"How are we going to get close to it if it's that heavily guarded?" she asked. "We could use a binding spell but I'm sure they'll have cameras everywhere. We can't go in wearing ski masks."

"I'm on it," Miles said while typing furiously.

Ember leaned back against the chair, nestling between my legs and pitching her head forward, giving me better access to her neck. My entire being ached to be closer to her. To rid ourselves of our clothes and bask in each other's essence. I would massage her from head to toe until every ounce of tension released from her body.

"What are you doing, Miles?" She rubbed her temples.

"He's hacking into the auction house's network," Shade said.

Ember's head snapped up. "You're a hacker?"

A blush spread across Miles's cheeks as he drew his shoulders upward. "It started as a hobby, just to see if I could do it."

"Now companies hire him to hack their systems and find the weak spots and back doors." Shade smiled proudly. "He's good at his job."

"I'm alright." He grimaced at the screen. "They need to verify Boyd's funds. This is going to take me a few hours."

"What's the plan?" Ash asked.

Miles closed his laptop. "I need more power than this. I'll have to go home to finish it, but I will have it done and be ready to go in the morning."

"And you can get us in and out without causing a scene?" Ember asked.

"That's what I'm working on. You have to be registered in their system before they let you through the doors. High-dollar clients can view items up close before they head to the auction floor, which means I have to make Boyd a fake bank account for them to verify. It'll take time."

"M'kay." Ember melted into me, her head tipping back. "Go home and set it all up. Miles, you're taking point on this. Let us know what we need to do."

He rose and put the computer into his bag. "Will do. Oh, and Boyd is from Texas, so one of you will have to learn the accent. I recommend watching *Dazed and Confused* to hear what it really sounds like. Particularly listen to the character David Wooderson. Matthew McConaughey is actually from Texas, so you know it's authentic."

The men left, and Ash spoke into the remote control, "Play

Dazed and Confused." The television responded, bringing up the movie she requested.

"In the past, they would have called this technology witchcraft." I squeezed Ember's shoulders, making her melt even more.

"They called most things they didn't understand witchcraft." She rested her hand on mine, stilling me. "Thank you. It's okay now."

"I can continue if you need more."

She laced her fingers through mine, sending a jolt to my heart. "I'm good. I am starving though. Pizza?"

"I'll order it." Ash used her phone to request the delivery, and the movie began.

Ember didn't move from her spot on the floor. She continued holding my hand, and I fought the urge to pull her into my lap. She had said she needed time to come to terms with our bond, so I would not push her. We remained in the position for half an hour, watching a movie about teenagers acting like imps in Texas.

When the pizza arrived, Ash paused the movie, and she and Chaos went downstairs to retrieve it. Ember inhaled deeply, sliding from my grasp before rising and heading to the kitchen. I immediately missed the sensation of her body nestled against mine.

She gathered plates and napkins and filled four glasses with water, setting them on the coffee table before pausing and looking at me. "I'm going to move to the couch. My butt's getting sore from the hardwood."

She sat down and moved to the middle seat. When she

settled in, she glanced at me and looked at the empty space next to her.

She did not have to ask me twice. I moved from the chair to the couch before she could change her mind, sitting close enough that our knees touched as I turned toward her.

"You are the High Priestess, yet you're allowing Miles to make the decisions about this important quest. Why?"

She shrugged. "I know my limits. My way would be to bust in, knock everyone unconscious, and take it, but I know that's not the best way to do it."

It would have been my first choice as well, though I wasn't sure I could restrain myself enough to simply make the guards unconscious. "It would be efficient."

"Or we could end up in jail...or dead. I trust Miles. If he says he can get us inside without violence, I believe him."

"And that is the sign of a good leader," Ash said as she set the pizza boxes on the counter. "Relying on your team and working with their strengths is the best way to get things done."

Ember laughed. "Yeah, I'm still learning that."

"You're doing great." Ash filled our plates and sat next to Ember before starting the movie again.

We ate the glorious concoction they called pizza as we listened intently to the characters in the movie. The flavors of melted cheese, three different meats, and tomato sauce melded perfectly atop the floppy slices of bread, making my tastebuds rejoice.

When the movie ended, Ash turned off the television.

"Okay, guys. Let's see who can do a better accent. Say 'I'd like to see the ruby amulet y'all have in the vault.'"

Chaos sat up straight. "I would like to see the ruby amulet you...yah...yawl have in the vault."

"Uh-uh. That was terrible." Ember wrinkled her nose. "Let's hear yours, Mayhem."

The sound of my name on her lips sent a warm shiver up my spine. I cleared my throat and leaned back casually, resting my arm on the back of the couch. Texans seemed to speak slowly, in a relaxed manner, and I did my best to emulate the character Miles had specified.

"Ah'd lahke ta see the ruby amulet y'all have in the vault."

Ember blinked, surprise lifting her brow. "That was an almost perfect Matthew McConaughey impression."

Ash nodded her appreciation. "It was fecking fabulous. Say 'alright, alright, alright.'"

I repeated the phrase in the actor's accent, trying my best to imitate his mannerisms.

Ember patted my thigh, my stomach clenching with her touch. "I think we've found our Boyd Anderson. But you'll have to behave yourself. No using your mind-melting magic, okay?"

I leveled my gaze on hers. "I will do anything you want, give you anything you desire. I am here to serve you, my feisty fire witch."

Her lips parted, the lower one trembling before she pressed them together and swallowed hard. "Well, then... I think we should call it a night."

CHAPTER 17

EMBER

I know, I know. I had just told Mayhem I needed time to process all the new emotions flooding my system, but I couldn't lie... Hearing this powerful man, this *Prince of Hell*, say he was here to serve me turned me on to no end.

That was one emotion I didn't need to process.

He had a cocky attitude and anger issues, yet he'd been so gentle massaging my shoulders. I'd been on the receiving end of a back rub from a man a few times, but Mayhem was the only one who paid attention to the task, actually feeling the tightness in my muscles and working out the sore spots. Everyone else just squeezed a few times, hoping it would be enough to get them into my pants.

Mayhem seemed to care about more than my vagina, which made me feel all warm and fuzzy inside, and *that* was an emotion I needed time to process. Warm and fuzzy I was not.

At least, I didn't used to be.

After we cleaned up our dinner mess, Ash and Chaos retired to their room, leaving me alone in the kitchen with Mayhem.

"How is your headache?" he asked like he was genuinely concerned.

"It's better, thanks to you." I drew my lower lip between my teeth, and his gaze slid down to my mouth. "I guess we should head to bed."

"Indeed." His eyes met mine, and we stood there, staring, his gaze penetrating all the way to my soul. "Shall I sleep in Cinder's room again?"

I opened my mouth to say yes, but the word didn't make it past my throat. Instead, I stepped toward him, resting my palms against his chest and rising to my toes to kiss him. His lips were soft against mine, the facial hair around them more like silk than the coarseness I would have expected had I not already kissed him today.

What happened this morning felt like weeks ago. Logically, I should not have been falling this hard, this fast, for anyone, much less a demon prince. Yet, there I was, sliding my arms around his shoulders and leaning into him.

He rested his hands on my hips, opening to me, brushing his tongue to mine before pulling back, his eyes searching mine. "You said you needed time."

"I know. I do." But time for what? To come to terms with the fact that I was fated to him? Really, there weren't any terms I *could* come to. Fate was fate, and fighting it would only lead to trouble. I should listen to my heart. The heart always knew what was right, but my brain wouldn't shut the eff up.

If I allowed myself to go all in, I would get my heart broken.

This budding relationship had a hard and fast expiration date, and I wasn't sure I'd survive the ending.

"Fate is a fickle bitch." Emotion tightened my chest, one fist around my heart, the other squeezing my throat.

"Perhaps. It's possible fate brought us together simply to teach us a lesson before pulling us apart." He cupped my face in his hands. "That isn't what this feels like, though."

"But we will be torn apart. It's the only way to set the world right."

He stroked my cheek with his thumb. "I would gladly destroy this world and mine if it meant I could spend eternity with you."

See? That right there should have been a massive red flag to a light witch, but it wasn't. Not to this light witch, anyway. Never had I ever been desired—loved?—this fiercely. *Hecate have mercy on my soul.*

"I don't want you to destroy anything but my family's curse."

"I know." He tucked my hair behind my ear.

"Can I have your promise that you won't?"

"No." He held my gaze, studying my reaction. "I will not make a promise to you that I can't keep."

Was that another red flag? Or was it a green one? My stomach was doing this weird combination of fluttering, turning, and clenching, and I had no idea how to interpret it.

"You could keep it if you wanted to."

He slid his hands to my shoulders. "If anyone causes you pain, they will pay. I will not be able to stop myself. You are mine to protect."

"I can take care of myself." Good goddess, these emotions needed to chill the eff out.

A smile curved his lips. "I know. It's one of the many things I love about you."

Add flip-flops to my stomach's gymnastics show. "How can you call this love when you've only known me a week?"

"My soul has known yours since the beginning of time. Our energies were created as one, then separated, half into my realm, half into yours. My darkness has been searching for your light since the moment we split, and now that I've found you, we are whole once again."

His words sank deep into my soul, resonating in my being and making themselves at home.

"I call this love because there is no other single word that can convey this connection to you. Even love does not do our bond justice, but there is no other way to describe it."

"You've done a pretty good job." I clutched the back of his neck, pulling him down until his mouth met mine.

An *mmm* vibrated across his lips as he slid his arms around me, pulling me close. Whether or not this was love, I couldn't say, but I was tired of thinking. My mind was exhausted from trying to decipher my emotions, so I gave up.

I wanted Mayhem. He wanted me. Why shouldn't we act on it?

I kissed him harder, reveling in the heat of his mouth and the sensation of his rock-hard dick pressing into my stomach. When I nipped his bottom lip between my teeth, he groaned and lifted me onto the countertop.

I spread my legs so he could fit between them, and he

pulled me closer, pressing his groin against me and kissing me like I was his last breath of air. He slid one hand up my back to fist in my hair while he cupped my breast with the other.

With a tug, he angled my neck, giving himself better access to the sensitive spot beneath my ear. His lips grazed my skin before his tongue slipped out, gliding up to my earlobe and raising goosebumps on my arms.

"You belong to me." His breath whispered across my ear, making me shiver in a good way.

"You've got it backwards." I popped the button on his jeans. "*You* belong to *me*." I reached into his pants and wrapped my hand around his dick.

His breath came out as a hiss. "Yes, I do."

"You'll do anything I want you to." I stroked his length twice, my mouth watering at the contrast of silky-soft skin on his rock-hard girth.

He inhaled deeply, pressing his forehead to mine and closing his eyes. "I will. Anything."

"Take me to bed."

"It will be my pleasure." He lifted me from the counter and carried me to my bedroom, kicking the door shut behind him before lowering my feet to the floor.

I cast a quick silencing spell and pushed him toward the bed, shoving his pants to the floor on the way. He kicked them aside and grabbed the back of his shirt, pulling it forward, over his head, and tossing it onto the pile.

Heat pooled below my navel as I took in the sheer perfection of Mayhem. The dark hair sprinkled across his muscular chest made my fingers twitch to touch him, to follow the trail down his defined abs and take his length into my hand…and then into my mouth. Yes, he was a demon, but he could have been a god.

His deep purple eyes glinted with desire, and when I licked my lips, his pupils dilated.

"Sit down." I pressed my palm to his chest, and he obeyed, sinking onto the edge of the bed and spreading his legs.

Resting a hand on each of his muscular thighs, I lowered to my knees and looked up at him. His lips parted like he wanted to say something, but when I flicked out my tongue, licking him from bottom to top, his words turned into a moan.

I circled my tongue around his tip before grazing it with my teeth. That earned me a groan as he gripped the edge of the bed. I took his first two inches into my mouth and wrapped my hand around his base.

His stomach clenched as I sucked, taking him in deeper, and the tips of his talons began to protrude from his fingers. I rested one hand on top of his, and he curled it into a fist. "I'm sorry."

"Don't be," I whispered against his dick, turning his skin to gooseflesh as I licked him. "I love having this effect on you."

He relaxed his fingers, and as I took him into my mouth as deeply as I could, his talons extended even more. He moaned as I sucked him, and when he rested his clawed hand atop my head, moisture pooled between my legs.

A deep growl rumbled in his chest, and with a sharp intake of air, he tugged my hair, pulling me away from his dick. The purple of his irises bled outward, undulating as it overtook the white, making my pulse sprint.

His nostrils flared, his eyes narrowing, his expression that of a predator about to devour his prey. A trill of fear shimmied up my spine, my body reacting to the imaginary danger of being stared down by a demon.

But this wasn't just any demon. Mayhem was *my* demon, and he was about to make me *his* witch.

I rose to my feet, instinctively taking a step back. Adrenaline coursed through me, heightening my arousal, and as he stood, looming over me, I unbuttoned my jeans, my pulse whooshing in my ears as I shoved them to the floor.

He stepped forward, splaying his fingers. My stomach flipped as I took off my shirt and bra. Another step toward me, and he glided the dull side of a talon across my stomach before hooking the sharp side into my underwear and ripping them off with a flick of his wrist.

My heart pounded so hard, I could see its rhythm in my chest.

With a hand on either side of me, he boxed me in, pinning me against the wall. A hint of tusks protruded from his gums, making me tremble in an oh-so-good way.

I clutched his dick, stroking it as I licked my lips. "I'm not afraid of you."

I fully expected him to tell me I should be, but he didn't. His gaze wandered over my face, pausing on my mouth before returning to my eyes. "Good. I don't want you to be. This is who I am."

"I know." I brushed my lips to his and slipped my tongue between the tips of his tusks. They hadn't fully extended, and they didn't hinder the kiss at all. In fact, they turned me on even more.

He moaned into my mouth, pressing his body to mine, and I wrapped my arms around him, holding him there. "I don't think I can hold back much longer," he said. "I need you."

"Then take me." Because I was about to explode with desire.

He pulled away, grabbing my hips and bending me over the bed before tracing his claws down my back. Goosebumps pricked every inch of my skin, and I spread my legs wider, bracing my arms on the mattress as he rubbed his tip against my wet folds.

I moaned, moving my hips toward him to take him inside. A pleasurable ache expanded in my core as he filled me completely, and he reached a human hand around my waist to stroke my clit.

Electricity pinged through my body, setting my nerves ablaze. He slid out until only his tip remained, and again I leaned into him, taking him deeper. Countering my movement, he pushed into me, circling his fingers on my sensitive nub as he ground his hips against me.

A masculine grunt emanated from his chest. He pumped his hips, a taloned hand clutching my shoulder while he rubbed me with human fingers. An orgasm coiled inside me, the delicious friction of his every move sending me closer and closer to the edge until my entire world exploded.

Ecstasy surged through my body, setting my soul on fire. I cried out in pleasure, shouting his name, and he growled, slamming into me three more times before sinking in so deep he penetrated my very being.

He huffed heavy breaths and placed his elbows on the bed, both his hands in their human form. Resting his front against my back, he nuzzled into my neck before pressing a kiss to the side of my head. "Did I hurt you?"

I laughed and turned, craning my neck to see him. "Quite the opposite."

His eyes and teeth had returned to normal, and with one more heavy breath, he pulled out and collapsed onto the mattress next to me. "You are everything."

I had no idea what to say to that, so I climbed under the covers and lifted the top of the blanket, inviting him in. He lay on his side, and I snuggled against him as the little spoon, clutching the arm he wrapped around me.

Even more emotions built in the core of my being, pinging off each other and swirling in a messy cyclone inside my soul. None of this was going like I'd planned. It felt as if I'd been hijacked by a person who knew how to *feel*. The problem was I didn't know what to do about it.

So I just lay there, staring straight ahead into the darkness and trying not to think about anything.

"I love you, Ember," he whispered against my hair.

I pretended to be asleep.

CHAPTER 18
EMBER

"Do we really think a New York auction house is going to notice if 'Boyd' isn't wearing cowboy boots?" Ash stood in the kitchen, pouring premixed binding spells into a series of small glass bottles. Her hand twitched, and she knocked a bottle over, spilling the contents. "I have got to find out where that New Orleans coven gets their capsules. These bottles make me feel like a boomer."

"With the heavy accent Mayhem will be laying on them, I think they will." I pulled up the map app and entered New York City as the destination before adding 'cowboy boots' to the search. "There are two places to get them between here and there."

"Boots aren't cheap." She corked the bottles and added them to her bag o' spells.

I pocketed my phone. "I'm doing what Miles tells us to. We

can't give them any reason to suspect Mayhem isn't a Texas oil baron who dabbles in occult antiques as his guilty pleasure."

Chaos rinsed the bowl Ash had used and dried it with a dishtowel. "Is a Texan wearing cowboy attire not equivalent to a Salem witch wearing a pointy hat?"

"Not at all," Miles said as he stepped through the door. "Boots are as common in Texas as beanies are here."

Mayhem joined us in the kitchen, fresh from his shower, a lock of damp hair curling onto his forehead. A flitting sensation formed in my stomach, and I brushed the strands into place before they could drip onto his skin.

I'd kept up my charade of not hearing him say he loved me, and thankfully, he hadn't mentioned it since. I did allow myself the luxury of snuggling into his warm embrace for a while when we woke up. But then we had to face reality and prepare for our scariest mission to date.

Battling beasties I could handle, but humans... Sometimes they were the real monsters, and unfortunately, I wasn't allowed to chop off their heads.

That didn't mean I had to leave my sword behind. My back scabbard lay on the counter, the blade sheathed in fireproof leather. Mayhem caressed the rosewood handle and traced the texture of the skull pommel.

"Whoever built this weapon for you had the gift of fore-sight," he said, tapping the skull for emphasis. "Unless you requested this design. If so, perhaps you have a latent gift."

A bark of laughter rolled up from my chest. "I wish." I cleared my throat. "My mom had it forged for me. The creator had free reign in the design."

"You can't take weapons inside," Miles said. "They'll have metal detectors and a body scanner."

"I'll leave her in the van. Is everything set up?"

He nodded. "Shade is outside, watching the equipment. We're ready when you are."

I picked up my sword and a bundle of knives wrapped in thick fabric. "Are you done, Ash? Let's head out."

"Yep." She slung her bag over her shoulder, and we filed outside.

Thick gray clouds blanketed the sky, the air so chilly and damp that I shivered. Mayhem wrapped his arm around me, and though I appreciated his warmth, I stepped out of his embrace. No way in hell was I going to lose myself like Ash had. I could imagine the devastation she would feel when the demons returned to the Underworld, and I refused to expose myself to that kind of turmoil.

At the van, I opened the sliding side door and stowed my weapons in the hidey hole. The guys had removed half of the way back seat to set up a makeshift base of operations. They'd zip-tied a folding table against the wall, and a plastic case with who-knew-what kind of equipment occupied the floor beneath it.

A monitor, also zip-tied into place, sat atop the table, and the power cable running behind it plugged into a battery pack the size of...well, I suppose it was a car battery.

I opened the driver's side door and cringed at the shattered windshield as I climbed into the seat. "At least the imp had the courtesy to only smash the passenger side."

Mayhem took shotgun and ran his finger over the inside of the glass. "The damage is confined to the outer layer."

"Thank the goddess for that." I started the engine.

"If Hecate is holding the veil together," he said, "I doubt she had anything to do with the imp."

"Silly demon. It's just an expression. Load up, guys."

My team climbed into the van, and I pulled onto the road. "It's about two hours to the boot store, and then another two after that. What's the rest of the plan?" I glanced at Miles in the rearview mirror, and he straightened.

"I was able to hack into their security system last night. Everyone will have earpieces so we can communicate." He held up a tiny piece of silicone. "Once the amulet is in your sight, I can loop the security feed so everything looks normal. They'll return it to the vault after you see it, so it'll be up to you and Mayhem to swipe it before they do."

"I will do my best to only render them unconscious," Mayhem said. "Any casualties will be unintentional."

I gave him the side eye. "There won't be any casualties. Why do you think Ash mixed so many binding spells? We freeze them, take the amulet, and get the hell out of New York before anyone realizes what happened."

He raised his brows. "You've thought this through."

"This is the most planning I think I've done in my entire life." I laughed. "Weird, isn't it?"

"Indeed." He studied my profile, a grin lifting one corner of his mouth. "I can't decide if I like this side of you or not."

"Neither can I."

We rode in silence once we got the plan hashed out, which I

normally would have appreciated. With only the radio and the low drone of the wheels on the pavement to occupy my thoughts, my mind decided it was time to mull over my Mayhem predicament. Again.

The problem was...every thought I had about the situation circled back to the inevitable ending. His time in this realm was finite. Sure, we could try to figure out some way to resummon the demons without damaging the veil, but I could never ask him to give up his home and everything he knew just to live a normal, nearly mundane life in our quiet little town.

Honestly, I wasn't sure how *I* could endure normal if we made it through this ordeal. Before our parents summoned the first demon, we didn't get much action in Salem. Not compared to the past few months, anyway. I'd always jumped at the chance to send a beastie back where it belonged, but sometimes we'd go days without any action.

And Mayhem... He was royalty in the Underworld. Hell, he was on a first-name basis with Lucifer *and* Hecate. No way would he want to deal with a humdrum life in the earthly realm.

And I sure as hell wasn't moving to his side of the veil.

"Your destination is on the right," my phone declared, pulling me from my thought spiral. *Hallelujah.*

I parked in the lot and killed the engine. "Time to cowboy up."

Mayhem smiled slowly, his newly learned drawl stretching out his words. "Alright, alright, alright."

"Don't say that, and don't say 'yee-haw.'" Miles pinched

the bridge of his nose. "*That* is the equivalent of a witch wearing a pointy hat in Salem."

"Noted," Mayhem said, his voice returning to normal.

My team waited in the van while Mayhem and I went inside. A bell chimed above the door, signaling our arrival, and the shopkeeper, a squat man with salt-and-pepper hair, rosy cheeks, and a nametag that read George, scurried out from behind the counter. "Hello. How can I help you?"

"I need..." Mayhem started, practicing his accent.

"You need cowboy boots." George's gaze dropped to the combat-style boots he currently wore. "Size twelve? I've got just what you need."

We followed him to the boot section, and he gestured for us to sit in the plush chairs across from the display. "You look like an ostrich man. Do you have a particular color in mind? Black. I'll be right back."

Mayhem frowned as George disappeared into a back room. "He asks questions but does not wait for answers."

"He's good at his job." I patted his thigh, and he inhaled sharply before taking my hand and kissing it.

"Perhaps I wanted brown snakeskin." His warm breath danced across my fingers.

"Did you?" I tugged from his grasp and wiped my sweaty palms on my jeans.

"No, he was correct. I wonder if he's full human or something other."

Before I could explain how retail workers developed a sense for what their customers needed, without using magic, George returned with two boxes. He sat on a stool and reached for

Mayhem's foot. My demon allowed the man to remove his boot and put the new one on, which was weird as all get out at first.

Then I remembered he was a prince. Lesser demons probably did his bidding on the daily back home.

The boot George had chosen had a brown heel, square toe, and a red flame pattern on the upper part. Hmm. Maybe this guy did have a little "something other" running through his veins.

Mayhem walked the length of the carpet and returned to his seat. "These will do."

George smiled triumphantly and rested his hand on the other unopened box. "I knew those were the ones. I'll put these back in a minute, but first, you'll need some bootcut jeans."

He tilted his head, eying Mayhem's belt and t-shirt. "If you're trying to get back to your roots, you'll need a belt and shirt too. Or do you already have clothes at home?"

"I—" Mayhem began.

"You haven't lived in New England long, and your wife has been dressing you. Meet me at the fitting room, and I'll gather what you need." George tucked the box beneath his arm and strode toward the men's clothing.

I wasn't keen on the wife part, but yeah, I had been dressing my demon. "Definitely something other."

We waited outside the dressing room, and George returned with starched black jeans, a black leather belt with a huge silver buckle, and a black button-up. Mayhem put them on, and everything fit perfectly.

I focused on George's aura, trying to sense any type of magic he might possess, but he seemed as mundane as Chief

Higgins. If he was a magical being, the power was either multi-generationally diluted or he'd cast one helluva shrouding spell to hide it.

George gathered Mayhem's old clothes and boots and put them in a bag before ringing up our purchase. "That'll be nine hundred fifty-three dollars and seventy-six cents, please. Cash or card? Card."

I choked on my own spit. A thousand dollars for one outfit? Damn, cowboying was expensive. "Maybe we should see the other pair of boots? Do you have anything less pricey?"

George's brow furrowed, his nostrils flaring slightly as a tiny bit of the something other sparkled in his aura. "This is what he needs. Your choice of clothing for yourself will be fine, but he must wear this."

The magic dissipated as quickly as it had formed, and I dug my credit card out of my wallet. Whatever kind of being George was, he was magically adamant my Prince of Hell had to wear this exact outfit. Who was I to question someone else's ability?

George's smile returned, and he tapped my card against the reader before handing it back to me. The register made a *duh-dun* sound, and he frowned. "I'm afraid your card has been declined. Do you have another payment method? Not with you. In your car, perhaps? Yes. The gentleman will wait with me while you call your friends on the phone. Off you go by the window. We have terrible reception in here." He had the audacity to make a shooing motion with his hand.

My teeth clicked audibly, my hands curling into fists. "What are you?"

He tapped his nametag. "I'm George. This is my shop. If you try to leave, I'll tell you to stop."

My lips pursed, sharp pain shooting from my jaw to my temple, thanks to how hard I ground my teeth. His rhyming cadence made it sound like he'd cast a spell, but the wording was off. *What a weirdo.*

If we weren't pressed for time, I would rip into this guy and make him reveal his identity. But time was the one thing we didn't have, so I turned on my heel and marched toward the window, fuming as I opened a video call with my sister.

"Uh oh." Ash held the phone in front of her so I could see everyone in the van. "What happened?"

"A thousand dollars," I whisper shouted. "A *grand* for one stupid cowboy outfit, and my card was declined. You didn't mention how expensive this costume would be."

Miles held up his hands. "What kind of boots did he pick?"

"Ostrich. Does anyone have a spare grand lying around?"

"Oh, those are expensive. Leather would be cheaper," Miles said. "But 'Boyd' wouldn't wear cheap."

"Even if he would, we can't get leather." I glanced over my shoulder and found George enticing Mayhem with a case of gold watches. "Just the clothes, Boyd. I'll get you a watch for Christmas."

Ash scrunched her face. "Why can't you get leather?"

I lowered my voice. "Because George is *something*, and he insists Mayhem needs ostrich boots and a whole outfit to match. And I would like to throttle him for telling me to shoo."

She opened the van door. "We'll come inside. I might have

room on my credit card, and if not, I say this is a *for the greater good* moment."

"You're right. It is for the greater good. Screw George—if that's really even his name. Come inside and do your mind thing so we can get this shitshow on the road." I ended the call and returned to the counter, taking Mayhem's hand to stop him from trying on a silver bracelet shaped like the ouroboros.

"You didn't tell me your lovely wife's name." George drummed his fingertips together, and I could have sworn faint sparks of magic danced between them.

"You can call me Elenore," I said before Mayhem could tell him my real name.

According to lore, the fae could gain control of a person if they knew their real name. Obviously, that was bogus or the scouts and soldiers would've been demanding our names every chance they got. But the phrase *a named thing is a tamed thing* existed for a reason. Some kind of being had that power, and I didn't care to find out if our shopkeeper was that kind.

"Hmm." George narrowed his eyes at me before opening the bracelet and holding it toward Mayhem. "Try it on. It's yours, free of charge."

"No." I grabbed Mayhem's arm, yanking him away from the counter. "Change into your normal clothes. We'll buy the boots elsewhere."

He reached for the bag, but it disappeared from the counter before he could grab it. George slapped the bracelet on his wrist. The snake writhed, slithering in a circle and chomping on its own tail.

"Ha! I've got you!" George bounced on his toes, clapping like an imbecile. "Two witches for the price of one."

Mayhem blinked and shook his head as if coming out of a daze. He pulled on the bracelet, trying to unlatch it, but the snake bit its tail harder. His eyes widened as he turned to me. "Run."

I bolted for the door.

"Stop," George said, and I froze, unable to move forward.

I strained against the magic, but an invisible force field stopped me from reaching the exit. I could move backward, deeper into the store, but it would take one hell of an unraveling spell to break through this kind of magic.

The bell above the door chimed as Ash and Chaos stepped through. Her brow furrowed, and she looked from left to right, standing on her toes to see over the racks.

I stood right in front of her, but she couldn't see me.

"Ember?" she called, and my heart plopped into my stomach.

"Emberrrr..." My name dripped from George's tongue as a blanket of magic wrapped around me.

A named thing is a tamed thing...

CHAPTER 19

MAYHEM

The ouroboros encircling my wrist was a trap. I could see that now, too little, too late. The being who called himself George had tricked me from the moment I stepped into the store. He had fooled Ember at first, as well, but she'd begun seeing through his charade…also too late.

I gripped the bracelet and pulled with all my might, but the harder I tried to remove it, the tighter it became. "What is this?"

A maniacal laugh emanated from George's throat. "Witch leash. I don't need your real name. You'll come when I call and do what I say. Such is the way for those who can't pay."

He waved his arm, inviting my brother and his witch into our plane. Ash gasped, pressing a hand to her chest.

"Turn around, and walk out the door," I said, but they didn't listen.

Instead, Chaos took Ash's hand and focused on George. "We're in a hurry. You'll allow us to leave with the clothing, free of charge."

George laughed again. "Four witches! Father will be pleased."

Interesting. It seemed our aura shrouds fooled the insolent being. He had no idea we were demons. It also seemed my brother's mind control ability was useless against this being.

Chaos glared at him. "We are leaving and taking the clothing with us."

"No, no. No one is leaving. Because you can't pay, you have to stay."

Ash attempted to step backward, but an invisible wall stopped her retreat. "What are you?"

He tapped his nametag. "I'm George. This is my store."

She crossed her arms. "Not who. What."

"He's George," Ember said, her arms hanging slack at her sides. "We're going to stay here now."

"The hell we are." Ash gathered a fireball in her hand and lifted her arm to throw it at George.

Ember countered her, summoning her own fire and hurling it at her sister. The flames slammed into Ash's chest and billowed around her before dissipating as if they'd never existed.

Ash's mouth dropped open. "Seriously, Em?" She threw her fireball at her sister, the effect identical on her.

"Fire witches! What fun." George bounced and clapped. "Oh, I know. Let's have a girl fight."

Ember glowered at her sister, stalking toward her with her

fists clenched. Ash tried to retreat, but the magical wall stopped her. Ember clutched her shoulders and shoved her to the ground.

"I'm not going to fight you." Ash crab walked backward. "We need to leave."

"We're staying here." Ember lunged, landing atop her sister and punching the side of her face.

"Stop," Chaos boomed. He grabbed Ember's arm and hauled her up, but she turned on him, slamming her fists into his stomach. He lifted her, and she kicked, her arms flailing as her face reddened with anger.

"Get your witch under control," he said.

If I moved to help him restrain her, George would see I was no witch. His witch leash might have tethered me to him, but he could not control me like he did Ember. I needed to keep up my charade long enough to learn his name. Only then could I free my witch from his control.

I crossed my arms to feign obstinance and sent a pulse of my magic into her. I could almost feel my mark heating on her arm as I reached into her psyche. Her magic countered mine instantly, and she stilled, her body relaxing as she scratched her head.

"We don't need to fight," she said. "Violence never solves anything."

Chaos released his hold, and she offered a hand to Ash, helping her to her feet. She ran her fingers over the red spot she'd made on Ash's cheek. "Oof. That's going to leave a mark."

"Ya think?" Ash took a jar of salve from her bag and spread it over the impending bruise.

"What spell is this that defeats my command?" George fisted his hands on his hips. "Not a spell. A connection. A shared magic." He cocked his head at me. "What are you?"

"We asked you first." Ash returned the jar to her bag.

"He's George," Ember said. "This is his store."

Rage billowed in the pit of my stomach. My beast clawed to the surface, my talons and horns growing to their full size as I glared at the being.

"This is his store." Ember put her hands on my chest. "I'm going to live with him."

"No, my witch. You are not." I stepped away from her, and my beast took control.

The new shirt and jeans ripped to shreds as I grew, my muscles building, protruding until all humanness ceased to exist. Teeth turned to tusks, my feet to hooves, yet the bracelet conformed to my size.

I stalked to the being, grabbing him by the throat and yanking him over the counter. "Release her," I growled, "or I will kill you."

"Can't be killed," he squeaked. "Demon!"

"Don't hurt George." Ember clutched my arm and tugged. "Put him down."

I tightened my grip. George wheezed, the shroud he'd placed on himself and the store slipping away, revealing a horror to rival the Sixth Circle of Hell. At least a dozen emaciated bodies lined the wall, their arms shackled above their heads. Their eyes and cheeks had sunken in, their pallor an ashy green, their mouths open in silent screams.

"My sisters," Ember said, her voice filled with fondness as

she circled her arm around Ash's biceps. "This is Ash. We'll be joining you soon."

"Ashhhhhh…" The moment he uttered her name, her eyes glazed.

"Very soon," she said.

Shade and Miles approached from the parking lot, so I slammed George against the door, holding it closed while Chaos turned the lock.

"Release them," I said again.

His face grew purple. He clawed at my talons and kicked, attempting to wiggle free.

"Put him down, brother." Chaos placed a hand on my shoulder. "He can't free them if he's dead."

I lowered him to the ground, releasing my hold.

"Can't be killed." He laughed and tiptoed toward the bodies. "Space for you here." He gestured to an empty spot along the wall. "If you can't pay, you have to stay."

Our witches started toward him, but we put our arms around them. "What are you?" Chaos asked, though I had a feeling he knew the answer, as did I.

"He's George," the witches said in unison.

"I'm George." The being tapped his nametag.

"That's not your name," Chaos said. "You're a Formorian."

Surprise widened his eyes, and he clutched his hands in front of his chest. "Formorians are extinct. Fae vanquished them all." His nose twitched, his true form threatening to break through his disguise.

"I thought so too, but here you are." Chaos crossed his arms. "What is your name, Formorian?"

"He's just George." Ember patted my arm.

"I'm just George. No Formorian here."

"No." I loosened my grip on Ember, though I still held her firmly. "He's no Formorian. I'd call him an imp at best."

"An imp!" His eyes turned yellow, his pupils narrowing into vertical slits as his nose elongated into a snout. "Formorians are better than imps. Better than any demon from Hell."

"So you are a Formorian," Chaos said.

George lifted his head, puffing out his chest. "I am a son of Balor. I...whoops." He disappeared in a puff of smoke.

"I need to join my sisters." Ember struggled against me.

"We must get them out of here." I rushed for the exit and turned the lock, throwing the door open and charging at the threshold.

The bracelet tightened on my wrist, and the sensation of a thousand thorns raking across my skin slowed my escape. I pushed through, as if walking through a tarpit. Ember cried out in agony, clawing at my arms and writhing in my grip. A popping sound echoed around us as we passed through the magical ward, and the pain ceased as quickly as it had begun. Ember sighed with relief, her body going slack in my embrace.

We stood in the center of the Formorian's store.

"No." I ran for the door once more.

Again the bracelet tightened, and thorns scraped across my skin. Ember wailed. We returned to the center of the store.

"What in Lucifer's name?" Chaos stared at me, bewilderment contorting his expression.

"He trapped me." I held up my arm, showing him the ouroboros encircling my wrist.

My brother merely sighed, yet I could feel his disappointment dripping from the breath he exhaled. "You fell for his guise."

"I was…" An idiot. It wasn't his guise that had fooled me. No, it was my own folly that got me…that got us…into this predicament. I'd gotten caught up in my emotions, enjoying this mundane shopping experience with the woman I loved.

My focus had been so pinpointed on the moment, I hadn't noticed there was nothing mundane about it.

"You must get them out." I clutched Ember's shoulders and pushed her toward him. "Take them to safety."

"What about you?" He extended one arm, taking my witch into his embrace.

"I will find a way out." I held his gaze with conviction. Ember's life was worth far more than my own. I would remain in this shop of horrors for eternity if it meant my witch would be free. "Guard her with your life."

"I will." Chaos stepped through the door, and the witches screamed.

In an instant, both women reappeared in the center of the store. Chaos stood just past the threshold, with Miles and Shade flanking him.

"What the hell is going on?" Shade clutched a knife in each hand.

"My sisters." Ember gripped Ash's hand as they sank against the wall adjacent to the bodies.

I spun in a circle, searching with my eyes and my magical senses. George was nowhere to be found. "A Formorian has trapped us."

Miles frowned. "Aren't they extinct? I thought the fae wiped them out eons ago."

"We thought so too," Chaos said. "It was the one thing both demons and the fae agreed upon. Formorians were a blight to all the realms, so we aided them in their battle."

I watched the women intently. No chains magically appeared to bind them. "This one says he's a son of Balor."

"Which means he is a prince," Chaos said. "He's as powerful as us."

"Can you vanquish him?" Miles asked. "Will that dissolve his spell?"

"No. I have dealt with these creatures before." I moved toward the door, keeping Ember and Ash in my sight. "Their magic holds, even if they are vanquished. We must find him and learn his name. Only then can we force him to release the women."

"We're coming in." Shade moved for the door.

Chaos grabbed his arm. "Do not, under any circumstances, use real names."

"That is how he trapped the women," I said. "If he learns your names, you'll be joining the other bodies chained to the wall."

"Bodies?" Miles stepped inside and gulped. "Holy shit."

"Indeed." I peered around the clothing racks. "M, watch the women. If the Formorian reappears, do not allow him to bind them. And feel free to rough him up if you must. I plan to make him beg for vanquishment."

"On it." He pulled out his phone and typed on the screen.

"You said he's a son of Balor, right? I'll see if I can find his name."

"Good." I stalked toward the shoe area. "Show yourself, Formorian."

"He's just George," Ember said. "This is his store."

I growled. How could I, a Prince of Hell, have allowed this to happen? I had no doubt my brothers would have seen through this ruse the moment they set foot inside the store. But not I... Perhaps I deserved their incessant ridicule, after all.

Even Ember saw through the charade before I did. She deserved a mate who could protect her. She deserved better than me.

"It's going to take a minute." Miles held his phone near the window. "The reception in here is terrible."

I eyed the door to the back of the shop. "I will find him."

My fists clenched as tightly as my talons would allow, I kicked the door open, making it bounce off the wall with the impact. George squealed, the sound of his invisible feet scampering across the floor registering to my left.

Chaos and Shade followed me inside the storage room, and we fanned out, searching for the insolent creature. George grunted, and a shelving unit filled with boxes rocked on its base.

"Your race went extinct for a reason." I crept down the aisle. "You cannot defeat us."

"Demons didn't vanquish my kind. Fae did that." His voice sounded from my right, so I turned down the next aisle.

The shelving unit rocked again, and this time, it tipped

over. Boxes scattered across the floor, the shoes inside them tumbling out as it crashed into me.

I caught the brunt of it with my shoulder, and I stumbled before pushing the unit upright. Kicking the boxes out of my way, I rushed for the next aisle. Shade and Chaos stood at the opposite end, trapping the invisible pest between us.

"Son of Balor, show yourself," I said.

"You can't make me!"

Shade grunted, clutching his abdomen and doubling over, bracing himself with the shelf. When he lifted his hand, blood dripped from his palm.

CHAPTER 20
MAYHEM

"**S**on of a bitch," Shade ground out.

"No! Son of Balor." The voice came from deeper in the room.

"Can you freeze him?" I asked as we rushed toward the sound.

Shade stopped, still bent forward and clutching his stomach, and pulled a bottled spell from his pocket. "If we can find him."

Blood soaked his shirt, and he paled. "The bastard got me good."

"Not a bastard." The *slap, slap, slap* of his shoes on the tile moved toward the showroom door. "Dad was king. Mom was queen."

A thud sounded from the aisle littered with boxes. The door swung open and slammed shut. I charged for it, but the handle wouldn't turn.

"Those who can't pay have to stay." George laughed maniacally from the other side. "Time to drain my witches."

"Over my rotting corpse." I slammed my shoulder against the door, but it wouldn't budge.

"Step aside." Chaos braced himself to break down the door. His brow furrowed, and he paused before turning the knob. The door swung open easily.

"It's this damn bracelet." I hooked a talon beneath the offending silver and pulled. The snake writhed and tightened, taking more of its tail into its mouth.

Shade stumbled through the door. I reached a hand out, testing the Formorian's spell, and my arm passed the threshold. I stepped through as if there were no spell at all. His magic was waning. Good.

Miles stood in front of the women, a knife in one hand, his phone in the other. "Sha—?" He closed his mouth before he could finish the name. Concern furrowed his brow, and he cut his gaze between the now visible creature and the shadow witch.

"It's a gut wound. He'll bleed out slowly." George wrinkled his pig-like snout, sniffing the air. "Move, witch. Father needs to eat."

I lunged for the Formorian. He disappeared in a blink and reformed behind Miles, crouching over Ember and pressing his snout to her mouth. Miles spun, swinging his knife. George disintegrated again, reforming in an instant.

Chaos moved for Ash and dragged her away from the wall. She kicked and screamed, begging to return to her place amongst the corpses.

Every swing, lunge, and jab I threw at George, he dodged, returning his snout to my witch's mouth faster than anything I'd seen. Ember's pallor grew pale. Dark circles ringed her eyes as he sucked the life out of her.

Shade threw the binding spell at the creature and recited the incantation. George merely laughed and continued devouring my soulmate.

Fire ignited in my hands, licking up my arms until my entire body was ablaze. I hurled a ball of hellfire at the beast, hitting him in the back of his head.

He squealed like the pig he was and spun to face me. "Hellfire burns. Don't do that."

He waved his arm, and a wall began to grow from the floor. He strained with the effort, the grimace contorting his face making him look like a clone of Balor.

I shot a stream of hellfire from my palms, blasting the growing wall. Fire billowed around it, lighting a rack of shirts ablaze.

"Brother..." Chaos laid a heavy hand on my shoulder. "You'll burn the place down."

"Our witches are immune to fire." The blaze leaped from the shirts to a shelf of folded jeans. "M, take S outside and tend to his wounds. I'm ending this now."

Ash wiggled from his grasp and returned to her spot along the wall.

"If you vanquish him, our witches will be stuck in their trance forever." Chaos tugged my arm, lowering it as the fire consumed the wall and spread throughout the store.

"Call it back," he said. "There is another way." He held up the phone Mile's had handed him. "Angus, son of Balor."

The Formorian froze, turning to my brother. "Angus is an imbecile. He was the first of the royal family to die."

I took the phone. Twenty-three names filled the screen. I called my fire back, the flames rolling into my being, leaving charred bits of leather and fabric in its wake.

"Cormac," I growled the next name on the list.

"No, no. I'll drain them both before you guess it." He turned to Ember and pressed his snout to her mouth again.

She groaned, and my stomach wrenched. "Eachan, Duncan, Cian," I shouted.

My witch's cheeks began to sink in. A vise squeezed my heart. I swiped my thumb on the screen, scrolling to the last name on the list. "Donal, son of Balor, you will release the witches at once."

He jerked his head away from Ember, his body stiffening, a hiss escaping his mouth.

"Donal," I said again, "release the witches now."

"You...can't...make....me," he strained against the magic taking hold.

"Donal," Chaos said, his chest rumbling with his growl as he approached the Formorian. "Release them."

Ember's head lolled to the side, and she slumped to her left, leaning against Ash's shoulder.

"Turn around, Donal," I said, and he groaned, fighting my command as he faced me.

Shade collapsed behind me, and Miles grabbed Ash's bag,

yanking the strap over her head as she sat there in a daze, a maddening smile plastered on her face.

Donal disappeared in a puff of smoke.

"Show yourself," my brother and I said in unison. Donal reappeared and vanished again.

Miles dragged Shade next to Ember and rummaged through the bag, cursing as he looked at bottle after bottle.

"I will not play this game, Donal," I shouted. "Show yourself and do not disappear again."

The Formorian appeared next to Ash, taking her head in his hands.

"For goddess's sake," Miles grumbled and blew a powder on the creature. "Standing tall or on your knees, in the name of the goddess, I force you, Donal, to freeze."

A wheeze escaped his throat, but this time, the magic held. I wrapped my talons around the insolent being's neck and jerked him away from the women. Ember slumped even more, falling into Ash's lap, and the vise gripping my heart nearly burst it.

"Tell me there is something in that bag to help my witch."

"I'm looking, but..." Miles turned it upside down and dumped the contents onto the floor. "I don't know. I don't know what he did to her. I..." He held up a bottle triumphantly, and hope sprung in my heart.

He turned to Shade and lifted his shirt, wincing at the three-inch puncture wound before pouring the yellow liquid onto his skin.

"Ember needs your help. Her state is dire." I kneeled in front of her, dragging the Formorian down with me.

"I know it is, but I know how to help S. I have no idea what to do for her. That's Ash's department." He recited an incantation, and Shade's bleeding slowed. "He'll need stitches."

With Donal's throat firmly in my grasp, I used my other hand to brush the hair from Ember's face. She didn't move, didn't react to my touch. "Take him, brother."

Chaos grabbed Donal's arm and hauled him up before clutching his throat. "Release the witches, Donal."

"He can't while he's frozen," Miles said.

I pulled Ember into my lap and brushed the hair from her forehead. The strands felt dry and brittle, her skin like worn leather. I laid a hand on her breast, searching for the rise and fall of her chest. It moved only slightly, her breathing slow and shallow, but she was still alive.

If she did not make it through this, I would never recover. After I burned the Formorian and shit on his ashes, I would beg Lucifer to end my life. I could not exist without my witch...and this was my fault entirely.

I should have paid attention to the signs. I should have noticed the vibration was off in this store the moment I stepped through the door. A sob rolled up from the core of my being, thickening my throat and making my eyes sting.

"I'm so sorry, my love." I kissed her withered forehead and turned my livid gaze on the motionless Formorian. "Undo your spell so he can release them."

Miles recited an undoing spell, and Donal gasped, clawing at Chaos's hand as he dangled from his grip.

"Release the witches, Donal," I growled.

"Never. I am Donal, Prince of the Formorians. My power is greater than yours."

"Release them, Donal," Chaos said.

The creature continued his struggle.

"Donal, let them go." Miles threaded a needle through Shade's wound.

The shadow witch winced and spoke through clenched teeth. "Do it, Donal. Let them go."

The Formorian groaned.

"Let them go," the four of us repeated again, and Donal let out a breath, his body going slack.

Ash gasped and blinked, confusion clouding her eyes as she took in the scene. "What...? Ember!" She crawled toward us and clutched her sister's hand in hers. "Oh, my goddess."

Ash held her fingers beneath Ember's nose. "She's barely breathing. What did you do to her?"

I gazed at my feisty witch, Chaos's command to answer her barely registering in my senses as my beautiful warrior exhaled a final breath.

MASTERING MAYHEM

FIRE WITCHES OF SALEM
BOOK SIX

CARRIE PULKINEN

CHAPTER 1

MAYHEM

My soul, my life, my reason for *being* lay limp in my arms, her stillness carving a crater in my chest and hollowing my stomach until nothing but blind rage remained inside me.

Rage I could not contain.

"Is she...?" A tear slid down Ash's cheek as I moved Ember from my lap to hers.

"She's alive. Barely." I rose to my feet, my eyes heating, my irises undulating as the fury built. "I wouldn't be here otherwise."

"Mile—" She choked on a sob and rested the back of her fingers on her sister's forehead. "Give me my satchel."

Ember was in expert hands with Ash and the others, which allowed me to focus on the Formorian dangling from my brother's clutches...the reason my beloved barely clung to a frayed thread of existence.

"You will return her life force to her body, *Donal*." I spoke the culpable creature's name with such force, he flinched.

The vile beast kicked, flailing his arms and legs. My brother squeezed his throat harder, yet Donal did not obey. He was a son of Balor, after all. When his race ran rampant, his power matched my own. Even using his name, he was difficult to control.

My fury boiled over, hellfire heating every inch of my skin and threatening to erupt.

"She's not breathing." Ash laid Ember on the floor and blew into her mouth, making her chest rise and fall. "How is she alive if she's not breathing?" Her voice took on an edge of shrillness as she placed her hands over Ember's heart and repeatedly compressed her chest.

"Alive, alive for the time." Donal grasped Chaos's arm with both hands. "Let me go, and I'll send her home."

My brother lowered him to the floor but kept a firm grip on the beast's throat. "You will not disappear, Donal. You will do exactly as we say."

"You want me to send her home, yes?" His voice was thin, his breath barely escaping his compressed throat.

"Yes," Chaos growled.

"Release me, and it's done." Donal patted his hand. "Let go, big guy, and I'll send her on high."

"No! He's a trickster." I grabbed the creature's arm, wrenching it behind his back as my brother released him. "You will not send her *on high*, Donal. You will return her life force to her body."

He strained, the grinding of his teeth audible as he fought

my command. "We should be equals. Tell me your name since I've done the same."

"You didn't tell us anything." I twisted his arm up his back, wrenching it harder. "And we will never be equals, you sniveling, rhyming imp. Now, return my witch's life force."

He hissed through his teeth. "Father needs it."

"Ember needs it." Grabbing the back of his neck, I swung him toward my witch and shoved him to his knees. "Give it back to her, Donal."

"Do it, Donal," Chaos said.

Ash stood, allowing Miles to continue breathing for Ember, sparks gathering on her fingertips as she loomed over the vile beast. "Donal, you better do it right now before I beat you to a pulp and burn you beyond recognition."

He groaned, his body tensing as he ground out, "No."

A fireball formed in Ash's hand, and she hurled it at his chest, setting his shirt ablaze. The Formorian squealed and writhed in my grasp, but I held him firmly, forcing him to feel Ash's wrath.

"If you want her to stop, you will do as we say." I twisted his arm again, and his shoulder dislodged from its socket with a *pop*.

"Enough." Chaos placed a hand on Ash's shoulder.

"Don't you dare try to calm me down." She shrugged him off and grabbed a handful of Donal's hair, angling his head upward and forcing him to look at her. "Do. It. Now."

Smoke rose from her fist, the stench of burning hair joining the reek of charred flesh.

"Okay, okay! Make the burning stop!" Tears streamed down

his face, rolling around his snotty pig snout before dripping onto the floor.

Ash called her fire back and released his hair. The Formorian's shirt had turned to ash, but his burns healed in seconds. He blew out a hard breath, his body slumping into my grasp.

"My arm hurts. Let me go, and I'll do the work."

My eyes narrowed, and I cut my gaze toward Chaos and Ash. They nodded, and Ash moved to my right, the three of us flanking the creature while Miles poured a potion into Ember's mouth.

"Do not disappear, Donal." I loosened my grip, allowing him to lean toward Ember.

"My arm, please."

I let go, and he gripped his dislocated shoulder, forcing it back into place before resting both hands on the floor and crawling toward my witch. He paused and whispered something in the Formorian tongue. Before I could react, he grabbed a handful of ashes, flinging them into our faces and scrambling away.

I blinked against the grit in my eyes and gave chase. Our command that he not disappear remained, but the order to return Ember's life force had never taken hold. He threw clothing racks and toppled display cases as he darted for the storage room door.

I leaped over the obstacles, plowing toward him. My new ostrich boots—the only items of clothing remaining on my demon form—caught on a tangle of western shirts, making me stumble.

I kicked off the offending shoes, and my hooves clomped on

the linoleum as I lunged for the door, catching it before it could close. "Donal, you sorry excuse for a lifeform, return Ember's energy immediately."

"Never will I ever. Father needs it." He darted around a corner as Chaos entered the room.

My brother gripped my shoulder. "Balor is here."

"Whatever gave you that idea?" I stormed forward, stopping short of the corner as a wave of dizziness washed over me. My fingers and nose tingled, purple smoke escaping the undersides of my talons.

Chaos's brow slammed down, his irises rippling. "We're losing her...and you."

"Thank you for pointing out the obvious." I pressed forward, though it felt like I was moving through a tarpit. My muscles screamed, the fabric of my being shredding from the inside out as the Underworld called me home.

"Grab him," Ash shouted from behind me. "I know an extraction spell. We'll force Ember's energy from his body."

One foot in front of the other, I rounded the corner, the force of each step ricocheting through my body, threatening to shatter my bones the moment my hoof hit the floor.

Donal sat on his knees, his hands on the floor, straddling a lump of rotting flesh. "This is a strong one, Father."

He opened his mouth, and glittering gold energy—the essence of Ember's being—crossed his lips, spiraling into the creature beneath him.

The pain in my body ceased, the instinct to save the woman I loved taking complete control and rendering me numb to everything except my purpose. I lunged for Donal, hauling him up by his neck and clutching his throat.

"Balor, Balor, I have valor," he squeaked. "Look what I brought you, Father."

"Give it to me," the lump on the floor wheezed. "Or you're worth less than a sneeze."

"I've had enough of your rhyming, imbecile." I squeezed his neck, my talons digging into his skin and making him bleed. "Last chance. Return Ember's life force."

"Hold him still." Ash dumped a jar of herbs onto the floor.

"Never." He opened his mouth, and Ember's energy shot toward Balor.

My stomach lurched. I tightened my grip, jerking my hand and snapping his neck. The wretched bastard screamed, but my witch's energy continued to flow. Ash lit the herbs ablaze and began reciting an incantation, but I barely heard her words. Purple smoke rose from my skin. My body, once solid, wavered, my corporeal form trying to skate away as Ember's hold on the thread of life slipped.

I could wait no longer.

With the Formorian still dangling from my grasp, I plunged my talons into his chest. His ribs cracked and splintered as I reached for his heart.

"Mayhem, no!" Ash's voice echoed somewhere in the distance.

Twisting and ripping, I dislodged the organ from his veins, yanking it out and tossing Donal's corpse onto the floor.

The heart beat three times in my hand before crumbling to dust along with his body.

Ember's energy rose from the pile, gathering into a ball of light before drifting toward the ceiling. A pricking sensation formed on my skin, and more purple smoke—my essence—seeped from my pores.

I looked at my brother and then at Ash. "I'm fading."

"No shit." Her brown furrowed. "I had an extraction spell ready, but this…" She gestured to the beautiful ball of sparkling light. "I need to mix a containment spell before she crosses over."

A sob rolled up from my chest, but I caught it in my throat and reached a hand into the light. My witch's essence, her energy, her life danced across my waning skin, making my stomach clench. Ember had a kind, pure soul. She would not be damned to my realm.

Which meant I would never see her again.

I squared my gaze on Ash. "You have to save her."

"And you have to quit trying to solve every situation with violence." She swiped a mixture of herbs around the lip of a small container. "Light of life, avoiding strife. Don't go far; enter this jar. As I will it, so mote it be."

The light shimmered. It spread across the ceiling, casting the room in shades of gold and silver as if both the sun and the moon were working together to illuminate the mess I had made.

"No. It's mine." Balor blew out a breath and inhaled deeply. Ember's energy shimmied, drifting toward the king of the Formorians.

"Ash…" My legs weakened. The low vibration of the Underworld called me home, but I fought it. Home was not in the pits of Hell. Not anymore. Home was no longer a place...it was a person.

Home was Ember.

Ash recited the spell again. Still, Ember's light flowed toward Balor.

No. No, this was not happening. I would not return to Hell. I refused to let Ember die.

Dropping to my knees, I shoved my talons into Balor's chest. His bones had not hardened, so my claws passed through easily, even in my weakened state. I fisted my hand where his heart should have been, but his insides were nothing but gelatinous sludge.

How could I vanquish the vile beast if he had no heart?

He let out a pained mewl as I swirled my hand inside his chest, stirring his insides like soup. I hoped it was the most excruciating agony he had ever felt.

Ember's light stilled. Then, it vibrated. It dimmed and pulsed, shimmying between Balor and Ash.

"Balor, I demand you release her." I plunged my talons upward, toward his throat, the tips protruding from the base of his neck. His eyes bulged, and he wheezed.

Ash spoke the incantation a third time. Ember's light flashed twice and soared toward the jar Ash held. It flowed into the container, sparkling like a thousand fireflies danced within the glass.

"Come on. Chaos will watch him." She closed the jar and grasped my arm, tugging me away from the beast. "We need to save Ember."

I followed her into the store. Miles held Ember's head in his lap. When he looked up, a tear slid down his cheek. "I don't know what else to do," he said.

"She's not gone yet." Shade adjusted his position, wincing and pressing a hand to his injured stomach. "But, dude, you're smoking."

I dropped to the floor and pulled my witch into my lap, brushing the matted hair from her forehead. Ash lowered to her knees and opened the jar, holding it toward Ember's face. As her light rose from the container, my smoke swirled around it, creating a protective cocoon.

I could feel her in my soul, lighting the darkness inside me, making me whole.

"Let it go," Ash said. "Her energy can't return while you're holding it hostage."

"I can't." I tried. I tried to call my smoke into my corporeal form, but this body was merely a vessel about to sink. My soul refused to let her go.

Ash grabbed my wrist. "You have to, or she'll die."

More smoke rose from my skin, my body becoming translucent as Ember slipped further and further into the ether. "Take her. Save her."

Ash pulled Ember into her lap, and I crawled away, my legs too weak to carry me. As I moved, my smoke followed, still attached to my semi-solid form. A trail extended to Ember's light, the once-invisible tether holding her tightly in this realm.

Ash looked at me, tilting her head and silently reminding me I had to let her go to save her.

I backed away, dragging myself across the floor and willing the Underworld to let me remain. My soul released her, the agony that followed unbearable. A rift opened above me. My essence flowed toward it.

"Come on, Em. Take it back." Ash fanned the light toward her sister's face.

I could not fight the pull. My arms dissipated into smoke and flowed into the rift. My legs followed, the disintegration inching its way toward my torso until darkness closed in around me.

CHAPTER 2
EMBER

I wanted the pain to stop. My entire body ached and burned. The sensation of a million electrified needles jabbing into my nerves and joints made me both swelter and shiver...convulse...in agony.

My pain tolerance had always been higher than most. My level four could be another person's nine, so I normally considered the discomfort scale from one to ten at the doctor's office useless.

Not this time. No, not now.

On a scale of one to ten, my *discomfort* was a thirty-plus.

I'd felt fine a minute ago. At least, I'd thought I did. Honestly, I couldn't remember much after Mayhem put on the ridiculously expensive clothes and my credit card got rejected.

If you can't pay, you have to stay.

How did I end up on the floor? Did George...?

And why did my nose feel like I'd inhaled a tablespoon of crushed red pepper?

I tried to blow a puff of air through my nostrils, but my body disobeyed the command from my foggy brain and did the opposite instead. I snorted. Then I coughed, wheezing in more and more pepper until my throat burned and my lungs expanded and contracted as if I were hyperventilating.

"Oh, thank the goddess." That was Ash's voice, but either my eyes wouldn't open or I'd gone blind from the pain.

"Come on, Em," she said in a motherly tone. "Breathe it all in."

"Pain..." I rasped.

"I know it hurts, but you have to." A sob choked off her last words. "Mayhem needs you."

Mayhem...

I sucked in another breath. Razorblades sliced into my lungs. My heart did this weird *thud...thud-thud-thud* thing. Mayhem needed me. George... He'd trapped my demon with the ouroboros bracelet.

Nobody trapped *my demon.*

Another breath raked through my lungs, and I licked my chapped lips. Bits of skin clung to my tongue, making my stomach turn. A warm cloth pressed against my eyes, Ash's gentle hand wiping away the crust holding them closed.

One opened halfway, the inner corner still matted with gunk. My vision swam. Miles held the cloth, not my sister. He swiped my right eye again, and it opened fully.

Light pierced my pupil like a white-hot needle, and I fought the urge to squeeze my lid shut and sleep. Mayhem needed me. I couldn't let him down.

"Another breath, Em. You have to take it all." Ash held a jar beneath my nose. What spicy potion had she mixed up to bring me into consciousness? Whatever it was, I hoped to never experience it again.

I might as well have sucked a ghost pepper through each nostril, and oh, man... Hot in was hot out. I was not looking forward to my first trip to the bathroom.

Miles wiped my left eye, and I pried it open.

"There she is." He smiled, but he couldn't mask the concern carving crevasses into his forehead.

I blinked the fogginess from my vision as Ash returned the jar to her bag. "Why does it feel like someone hit me with a Hummer, backed over me, and plowed into me again?"

Ash's eyes glistened. "Because you almost died."

"I can tell." I tried to sit up, but my muscles screamed. The sigil on my arm felt raw...like someone had attempted to rip the magical ink from my skin. "Mayhem?"

Ash gestured with her head, and I followed her gaze to find my demon lying on the floor, unconscious. "What...?"

"He was almost sucked into the Underworld." Shade rose to his feet, wincing and clutching his stomach. "We almost lost you both."

"Is he okay?" I pushed to sitting, and the world turned on its side. My stomach lurched. My head pounded. My breakfast made a reappearance on the floor.

All I'd eaten was a protein bar, thankfully, but the bitter taste of stomach acid made me heave again.

"Here." Ash handed me a bottle of water.

I swished and spit before taking three huge gulps. Big mistake. It felt like forcing avocado pits through a cocktail straw. "What happened? Why do I hurt so much?"

Ash wiped the corner of my mouth with a cloth. "George... His real name is Donal. He sucked out your life force and was trying to feed it to his father."

"Huh?" My lids fluttered, my foggy brain unable to process her words. "His father?"

"Donal is a Formorian. A son of Balor." Shade toed Mayhem with his boot, and my demon rolled onto his back, his chest rising and falling with his slow, steady breaths.

He would be okay. That much I could comprehend, but my face must've been contorted in confusion because Ash patted my knee, her eyes holding so much sympathy, I nearly choked.

"The fae eradicated the species eons ago," she said, "but somehow Donal escaped and brought Balor with him to our realm."

I sighed, closing my eyes and leaning against the wall. "And he opened a store?" Sure, the fog in my brain was jumbling my thoughts, but I couldn't have made sense of her words if I were operating at full capacity. "Why would he open a store?"

"Look. He's been feeding off his customers." She shook my shoulder, so I opened my eyes and followed her gesture to the adjacent wall. At least a dozen mummified bodies lined the space, their emaciated arms chained above their heads.

Holy Hecate. I wanted to feel bad for the people. I really did, but the pain in my muscles and the haze in my brain made it impossible to think about anything else.

Mayhem groaned and rolled to his side, facing us. His demon form, in all its glorious nakedness, didn't stir a single hormone inside me. I didn't even check out his junk.

His lids flew open, his eyes locking on me, his body moving half a second later.

"Ember!" He shot to his feet—erm, hooves—and clomped toward me before dropping to his knees and pulling me into his arms. "Thank Lucifer, you're alive."

My skin felt like road rash, his hands like sandpaper against it. "Ow."

"What's wrong?" He held my shoulders, pushing me back so he could look into my eyes. "What hurts?"

"Everything." My laugh turned into a sob. *Every-friggin-thing.*

He snapped his head toward Ash. "Did you return all of her light?"

She took the empty jar from her bag and held it toward him. "All of it."

A growl rumbled in his chest, and his grip tightened on my arms.

"Ow," I said again.

"I'm sorry." He released me, letting me slump against the wall before turning to Ash. "That wasn't all of it. Balor…"

"Crappity crap. You're right." Ash stood and slung her bag over her shoulder. "Donal had already given some of her life force to Balor when you vanquished him. Come on." She grabbed my arm, attempting to haul me to my feet, but my legs were too weak to hold me.

Mayhem scooped me into a cradle carry, my skin, my

muscles, my joints protesting as he rose to his hooves. I didn't dare complain. If this Balor dude had a piece of me, I would wrench it from his clutches and rip his head from his body.

Just as soon as my own body recovered from whatever the hell happened to me.

We followed Ash into the back of the building where Chaos loomed over a rotted mass of *something*. He crossed his arms, keeping a wide stance, a look of disgust curling his lip. "Balor, you will return her life force."

My gaze snapped to the mound of flesh, my brain finally processing the shape. Balor, King of the Formorians, lay partially formed on the floor. His skin held an ashy-green pallor, his face almost skeletal as he reached an arm toward me.

"Sssshe's mine..." he hissed, and a tiny flame ignited on his fingertip.

Witch fire. *My* fire.

"Oh, hell no. That's mine." I wiggled in Mayhem's arms, and he lowered my feet to the floor, keeping a firm grip on my shoulders so I didn't topple over.

Balor inched toward me, his blob of a body moving like a slug. "Give it to me, and I'll set you free."

"I'm already free, you wannabe Jabba the Hutt." If I had my sword—and if my legs would carry me—I'd lob off his head and make his species extinct for good. Sadly, in my current condition, I was about as useful as wet toilet paper. Single ply.

"Ash, I need an extraction spell." I made a grabby motion toward her. No way in hell could I cast it alone.

"On it, but you're not helping." Before I could protest, she lit some herbs on fire and took Miles's hand.

They recited the incantation together, and Balor's semi-gelatinous form bubbled, his thin skin turning transparent as my energy fought his hold. He strained, his expression looking like he was both constipated and trying not to puke at the same time. I knew the feeling.

Well, not the constipation part. But if my stomach didn't stop lurching every time I twitched, it—along with all my innards—might end up on the floor.

"Nooo... Make it stop," Balor wailed.

Mayhem's growl rumbled through my body, setting my nerves off on a tangent. "How did you escape Hell?"

"Donal did. Please stooooop." My light, a shimmering gold, gathered beneath the surface of his skin.

"How long have you been in this realm?" Ash asked. "Answer us and we'll make the pain stop."

"Months. Months! Rifts in the veil. Donal is smart. Lots of heart."

My stomach heaved. A drumline pounded out a sickening rhythm in my head while Balor's agonizing wails jabbed daggers into my ears. Goosebumps pricked my skin, the fever making me shiver and sweat, and I leaned into Mayhem, willing myself to stay upright. "Let's put him out of his misery."

Ash and Miles recited the incantation two more times in succession. Balor's mouth opened, his jaw unhinging like Imhotep from *The Mummy*, as my light poured from his throat. It shot toward me and blasted up my nostrils, burning like a mixture of Carolina Reaper and ghost pepper oils.

Damn, I was a spicy witch.

I heaved in three breaths, four, five, until the burning

stopped and the drumline ceased their incessant song. My eyes and mouth watered, the cracks in my lips healing and plumping as my life force surged through my body. The strength returning to my muscles, I stepped out of Mayhem's arms and leered at the heap of wasted flesh on the floor.

"There's a reason your kind went extinct." I reached back for my sword, but my hand met only air. "Please tell me someone brought my weapons inside."

Ash shook her head. Balor wheezed, attempting to form words, but without my energy, he'd turned into a slimy blob of yuck...yuckier than he was before.

"His heart hasn't fully formed." Mayhem held up a taloned hand. "I tried to wrench it from his chest, but his entrails are gelatinous."

"That's fine. He has a head I can lob off."

"Here." Shade offered me a twelve-inch dagger. "It's the sharpest one I've got."

I accepted the blade, holding the leather-wrapped handle and testing its weight. "Nice."

Our Jabba wannabe inched away like the slug he was, so I grabbed a handful of his sparse hair, angling his head up and exposing the rolls of his fatty neck.

My grip tightened on the handle, and I was about to jab the blade into his throat when a sense of peace washed over me. My brain had the audacity to search for a non-violent solution to allow Balor to remain in existence.

I narrowed my eyes, cutting my gaze toward my demon. "Mayhem!"

"Sorry." He drew his shoulders upward and tilted his

head down like a scolded puppy, which was kind of cute considering he stood there in all his princely demonic gloriousness.

His magic dissipated from my psyche, and I looked at Ash. "Is there any reason I shouldn't vanquish this asshat right now, and does anyone want to help me?"

"Go for it," she said. "He's all yours."

I jabbed the blade into his neck. The razor edges passed through his flesh as if he were made of margarine, severing his head with one clean stroke. My fingers still clutching Balor's hair, I lifted my prize triumphantly.

"Mmm..." Mayhem's growl sounded more like a purr. "You are a warrior goddess."

Did I mention he was naked? My gaze locked on his massive package, which no longer hung freely in the breeze. His soldier stood at attention, and he licked his lips, his irises rippling like they did when he wanted to devour me.

"You might want to find some clothes." I waved the dagger in the direction of his junk and dropped Balor's head. It rolled, stopping face-up and blinking at me. "Holy shit. He's not dead."

"The only way to vanquish a Formorian is to destroy his heart." Mayhem morphed into his human form, and his soldier finally stood at ease...ish. It was getting there, anyway. "And he has no heart to destroy."

I forced my gaze to his eyes. "So, what then? Are we just going to leave him here, headless?"

"That would be cruel," Miles said.

"And dangerous." Ash set her satchel on the floor and

examined the contents. "If humans come in and find him, he could still drain their energy. We can't take that chance."

"No, we can't." I spotted a shelf filled with packs of men's undies, so I grabbed one and tossed it to Mayhem. "Put those on. It's hard to focus with...all that."

He chuckled and opened the pouch, pulling out a pair of dark gray boxer-briefs. With his package wrapped, I turned my attention to my sister.

"We need a spell to solidify his heart." She lined up three herb bottles on the floor. "If we can force it to form, then we can destroy it."

"We could do that." I eyed the disgusting creature. "But why waste our vim?"

My palm tingled, a fireball igniting on my skin. I tipped my hand, dropping the flames onto Balor's severed head. His hair lit up like a bonfire, and a gurgling sound emanated from his neck as his chest expanded and contracted.

"That hurts, doesn't it?" I picked him up by the ear and dropped his head onto his body. "You picked on the wrong witch."

I shot flames from both hands, setting his entire body ablaze. "You guys might want to step outside the room. It's about to get hot in here."

"It already is." Shade squinted, lifting a hand to shield his face from the flames as he and Miles returned to the front of the store.

"I guess your way works." Ash's expression scrunched, and she placed the bottles in her bag before rising to her feet and adding to my flames. "Incinerate his entire body, and the molecules that would make up his heart burn too."

"Exactly. How about a little hellfire, guys?" I shot another flame and watched the bastard burn.

His form began to melt in our witch flames, and when Mayhem and Chaos shot streams of hellfire into the fray, it crumbled. The fire raged, consuming every piece of the Formorian until nothing but a pile of opaque crystals remained.

"Good riddance." I called my fire back and brushed my palms together as if I could dust off this entire ordeal.

"It needs to be hotter." Mayhem grasped my elbow. "Until he turns to ash, he still exists on this plane."

As if to prove his point, the crystals of Balor vibrated, bouncing off each other, sliding this way and that across the floor until several melded together. Another handful stuck into a clump, bubbling and making a sickening, goopy sound as they formed into a glassy eyeball. It rolled, squaring its gaze—if it could even see—on me.

"You have got to be kidding me." I stomped the eye, squishing it beneath my boot heel.

"Again." Mayhem shot a stream of white-hot hellfire at the remains.

"Ash!" Miles shouted from the next room. "Shade's hemorrhaging. I need your help."

"Gods, I miss Patrice. Can you...?" she asked.

"We've got this. Go." I added my flames to Mayhem's.

"Assist your witch," Mayhem said to Chaos. "Ember and I will handle the beast. This is personal."

"Damn right, it is." I sent another wave of heat into the bonfire of Balor as they rushed out to save Shade.

My flames, bright orange with a base of blue, swirled and spun through Mayhem's white ones. He cut his gaze to me, one corner of his mouth lifting in a grin as he took a deep breath and added to the inferno.

His fire morphed from white to blue to indigo, the tips turning a vibrant purple as it flickered and consumed. The combination of colors shifted and blended, pirouetting and swaying together in a mesmerizing dance of magic.

"It's beautiful, isn't it? The way our colors blend." He slid an arm around my waist. "We are good together."

"When we're not trying to kill each other, yeah."

He dropped his hand to his side, stepping away from me and focusing on the flames.

It took a minute. Okay, more like ten, but finally the crystals smoked, smoldered, and turned into ashes. I called back my flames and heaved a breath. That was enough physical exertion for one day. *Whew.*

"Are your boots fireproof?" he asked.

"Everything I wear is. Why?"

"Lift your foot."

"Why?" I raised a knee, and he sighed.

"The other one." He grabbed my pants at the ankle and raised the sole of my boot toward him. "Even this small amount of the Formorian's eye on your shoe is enough for him to reform." He lit the tip of his finger ablaze. "Unless you want to take him to New York?"

"Fire away." If I ever saw one of these revolting creatures again, it would be way too soon.

With my boot cleansed in flames, I curled my lip at what was left of our captors and followed Mayhem to the front of the store. Shade lay on the floor, a washcloth over his eyes, his stomach exposed.

My heart sank. "Is he okay?"

"He'll be fine." Ash swiped a magical salve across the stitches. "This will speed the healing, but you'll have a massive scar."

"That's okay." Shade pulled the cloth from his eyes. "Chicks dig scars."

Miles shot his gaze to the floor before rising to his feet, and I had to wonder if Shade had any clue about his feelings for him. It wasn't my place to ask, so I went shopping in what was left of the store.

Mayhem had torn through his new, ridiculously expensive clothes when he let his demon loose, so I grabbed him another pair of starched jeans and a black button-up. He dressed and put on his new boots while I grabbed myself a slinky little black number from the women's section. Since I couldn't take weapons into the auction house, I might as well dress the part of the trophy wife, right?

"We aren't going to pay, and we don't have to stay." I gave the cash register the middle finger and turned toward the door. "Let's roll."

Chaos helped Miles support Shade, and we all *finally* left the building. Well, all of us except Mayhem. He stood in the doorway, his expression livid.

"Come on," I said.

He held up his arm, showing me the ouroboros on his wrist. "I can't."

I sighed, my posture deflating. "Well, shit."

CHAPTER 3

EMBER

"Hey, Ash. Bring your bag. We've got a problem." I stomped back into the store, silently swearing to the gods before narrowing my eyes at Mayhem. "I told you not to try on the bracelet."

"And I heeded your warning." He crossed his arms. "If you remember, you told me to change into my normal clothes. Donal put the ouroboros on me when I reached for them."

I clutched his forearm and rotated the bracelet on his wrist, making the snake shiver and chomp its tail harder. "I remember."

"Then why are you angry with me?"

Well, let's see. I'd almost died...had the life literally sucked out of me. He'd almost been vanquished because of it. Wasn't I allowed to be a little snippy?

If I wanted to dig in deep—which I didn't—I'd admit I wasn't angry. I'd tell him the truth: that I was scared to death of my feelings for him and that losing him—which was inevitable—would crush me, so I shut down at every mention of our goddess-forsaken *un*happily ever after.

I couldn't think about it, much less talk about it. Thankfully, Ash came in and got right to work, saving me from my thought spiral.

She set her bag on the counter and pulled out a bowl and six herb jars. "Did Donal tell you anything about the bracelet? I can mix the potion I use to neutralize the unsavory magical artifacts I find in the thrift shops, but I don't know if it will work on Formorian magic."

"He believed I was a witch when he put it on me," Mayhem said.

She pursed her lips. "That's not helpful."

I drummed my fingers on the countertop and grinned. "We could save our vim and chop off his wrist instead. Got a knife?"

Mayhem rolled his eyes. "You are always a comedian, aren't you?"

"I try." Anything to deflect the thoughts, because he was right. It was beautiful, the way the colors of our fire blended. And our fire was deeply rooted in our souls, which meant our souls would blend beautifully if I gave them the chance.

Damn it. I was still thinking. I blamed the adrenaline still flooding my veins.

Ash mixed the herbs and poured six drops of lavender oil into the bowl. "The magic in the bracelet is strong enough to hold a demon prince. Neutralizing it won't be easy."

"Which is why we should just chop off his wrist." I clamped my mouth shut. *Really, Em?* The man only wanted to love me, but every time he broke down a layer of my heart wall, I slapped another glob of mortar on it and added more bricks.

I couldn't tell you what the hell was wrong with me, but it needed to stop. He only wanted to love me. My chest tightened and warmed at the thought. My stomach also looped, and a swarm of moths tried to take flight inside me, so there was that. I had hormones pinging off nerve cells and innards rising and sinking. I needed an hour in one of those sensory deprivation tanks to sort it all out.

"Sure," Ash said. "Let's chop off his wrist and have him bleed out before we make it to New York. Great plan." She stirred the potion, and it smoked, the clean scents of lavender and mint adding to the sickly sweet smell in the air.

"I wonder what spell he cast to neutralize the stench of death." I scanned the far wall, where the dozen-plus bodies sat chained. "Do you think they're all witches, or would human energy work to reform the disgusting king?"

"It doesn't matter what they were," Mayhem said. "They're dead now and not our concern."

"I feel bad for their families." I forced my gaze away. "They must be wondering where they are."

"And we must focus on the task at hand." He held up his magically shackled arm.

"He's right, Em." Ash shot a tiny flame into the potion, activating it. "A lot more people are going to die if we don't get the amulet, and I seriously don't want to be the one who kills them. Donal's body count has nothing to do with us."

Chaos stepped into the storefront. "Miles is tending to Shade in the van. He said we must hurry if he's to have enough time to set up his equipment and hack into the auction house's security system."

"Potion's ready." Ash returned the bottles to her bag and poured a pink powder into her palm before holding her free hand toward her demon. "We need all the help we can get. Come share your power with us."

He strode toward her and grasped her hand.

"I will share my power with you, Ember." Mayhem held his hand toward me.

I crossed my arms. "You're the one who's trapped, dummy. If your magic could break the bind, don't you think you'd have removed it by now?"

"Here. Take Chaos's hand." Ash poured half the powder into my palm, and I slipped my hand into his.

Mayhem's eyes narrowed, his nostrils flaring as his gaze locked on his brother. Was that jealousy I detected in his expression? And did the moths just multiply in my stomach?

Chaos gave me no time to ponder it. A surge of dark magic passed through my skin, filling me with demonic power that felt so different from Mayhem's. Chaos's low vibration—and lack of the pinpricking sensation I'd grown accustomed to with Mayhem—made me shudder.

I didn't like it. Not at all.

Ash sprinkled her half of the powdered potion onto the bracelet, and I did the same. Mayhem caught my gaze as I finished, the intensity in his eyes making me want to rip free from Chaos's hold and throw myself into *my* demon's arms.

Hecate have mercy; the emotion was strong.

"Ready?" Ash asked.

"Absolutely." The sooner I could get this *wrong* demon magic out of my system, the better.

I inhaled deeply, focusing my intent on the ouroboros. "Neutralize, dissolve, dismiss. This magic bind no longer exists."

We recited the incantation two times in unison, feeding off Chaos's power and using him as a channel as we opened ourselves to each other. My sister's high vibration mixed with her demon's low, tempering the sickening feeling in my stomach.

The snake writhed on Mayhem's wrist, eating more of its tail and growing tighter.

"It appears your spell is doing the opposite of what you intended," he said.

"We aren't finished." I touched three fingers to the bracelet, and Ash did the same. "Neutralize, dissolve, dismiss. This magic bind no longer exists. As we will it, so mote it be."

My head spun, and my stomach lurched, though I couldn't tell if it was from the wrongness of Chaos's power flowing through me or from the ouroboros fighting back. Another wave of demon magic crashed into me, and I squeezed my eyes shut, sending it down my arm and out my fingers, focusing every-thing I had on removing the damn bracelet.

"You're hurting her, brother," Mayhem said. "Release my witch."

"I'm fine." I strained, grinding my teeth until sharp pain shot from my jaw to my temple. I pushed one more surge of magic—mine, his, and Ash's—into the bracelet.

The snake hissed. Then it screamed. Its mouth opened, and

I yanked the tail from its throat, hurling the offending little bastard across the room. Chaos let me go, and I stumbled forward, catching myself on Mayhem's chest.

My demon wrapped his arms around me, holding me as I sagged against him. I heaved in a breath, willing Chaos's magic to dissipate, and Mayhem stroked my hair, pressing a kiss to my aching temple as he tucked a lock behind my ear.

"I have you," he whispered. "You're safe now."

And goddess-dammit if I didn't *feel* safe wrapped in his embrace. Safe, secure, wanted, loved. I inhaled his warm campfire and cinnamon scent and allowed myself a moment—just a fleeting moment—before I pulled away and tucked another lock of hair behind my other ear. "I'm fine. This was our last side quest."

"Here's hoping." Ash handed me a cloth, and I wiped the remaining potion powder from my palm.

The building rumbled, the structure groaning against the weight of the roof. Ash looked at me wide-eyed before slinging her bag over her shoulder. "We need to go."

"Hold on." I scanned the room. The walls shimmered as if another layer of magic was dissolving around us. "How much glamour did Donal put on this place?"

"I'd rather not find out. Come on." My sister strode to the door, and Chaos followed her outside.

The walls and ceiling wavered as the magic dissipated. What was left of the clothing and accessories remained intact, which was a good thing. I doubted the auction house would allow good ol' Boyd "Big Oil" from Texas into the building if his clothes dissolved.

"We should leave." Mayhem clutched my hand.

"I want to go shopping first." I tugged from his grasp and grabbed a shirt and a pair of stretchy cargo pants from a rack. "Size six. Perfect." I draped them over my arm along with the little black dress, and Mayhem arched a brow.

"He stole my life force. Comping an outfit or two is the least he can do." I jerked my head toward the exit, and he followed me outside.

My eyes watered in the blinding afternoon sun, and I turned my back against it, facing the store. The outside shimmered, shuddering and groaning, the façade wavering like heat coming off a blacktop. Starting from the rooftop, the magic melted away like candle wax, sliding down and revealing a decrepit barn where the store once stood.

"Holy mother of magic." I tilted my head, my brain refusing to accept the image my eyes clearly took in. "That's the most impressive cloak I've ever seen."

"The Formorians were known for their skill in deception." Mayhem rested a hand against the small of my back. "It's one of the reasons my kind worked with the fae to eradicate them. That and their mind-control power, which you witnessed today."

"When we get to New York, we'll make an anonymous call to the police about the bodies. Eff you, Formorian asshat." I gave what was left of "George's" store a one-fingered salute before turning on my heel and marching to the van.

Shade lay across Miles's lap in the middle seat, and Chaos and Ash sat squished into the half-seat in the way back.

"Is he going to be okay, or do we need to find a hospital?" I climbed into the driver's seat. The van was already running, the heater making it warm and toasty inside.

"I'll be fine." Shade struggled to sit up, but Miles rested a hand on his shoulder, gently holding him down.

"Ash used a salve she got from Patrice," Miles said. "It'll take an hour or so to finish, but he's already healing."

"Good. Everyone ready?"

"Yes, ma'am," Mayhem said in his fake Texas accent, and I suppressed a smile.

He gave new meaning to the expression *save a horse, ride a cowboy*. This demon was one cowboy I could ride all day long.

CHAPTER 4
MAYHEM

We arrived in New York, and Ember and I waited in the van while Chaos, Ash, and Miles stalked around the auction house, peering into the windows and taking photos of themselves in front of it to feign the roles of simple tourists.

The time they were away would have been perfect for a discussion about why Ember dismissed, with an ill-timed joke, my every mention of our bond. About why she'd pretended to be asleep when I had confessed my love to her.

Unfortunately, Shade remained in the van with us, recovering from his encounter with the Formorian's blade.

And oh, the noise...

New York City bustled with traffic—both vehicular and pedestrian—the incessant sounds of engines revving, people shouting, and horns blaring grating on my nerves. It was all I could do to keep from sending them all into a fiery rage and letting them battle each other to the death.

"We've got a problem." Ash climbed into the van along with Chaos and Miles.

Ember pinched the bridge of her nose. "In addition to the eight hundred we're already dealing with?"

Miles shut the side door and slid past the others to reach the back of the van. "Ash found a ward on the building. A fresh one."

"Fantastic." Ember dropped her head back on the seat. "Fifty bucks says it's to keep out anyone with ill intent."

"Bingo." Ash rummaged through her bag. "I have the ingredients to get you through, but I'll need more room to work."

"And I need more room to move so I can think this through." Ember started the engine. "Anyway, I'm sure a black van sitting outside an auction house filled with a bajillion dollars' worth of artifacts isn't suspicious at all."

"I believe it's highly suspicious," I said. "Perhaps we should find a hotel room nearby."

She rolled her head toward me, not lifting it from the seat. "That was sarcasm. Did people not use it four hundred years ago?"

Most women did not, but I didn't dare say that aloud. Ember wasn't most women. She was unlike any I'd ever known.

Shade swiped his phone screen. "It's Friday. There's nothing affordable within twenty miles."

Ember shook her head, and I could almost hear the conflicting thoughts sparring in her mind, her morals insisting we pay for a room while her logical mind argued this quest required us to work in the gray.

"I believe this is one of your 'absolutely necessary' situations," I said. "Perhaps a little mind magic would take away the burden of your maxed-out credit card."

"He's right, Em." Ash leaned forward in her seat. "The closer we stay, the better. It would suck to get stuck in traffic and miss the whole thing."

"All right. Fine." She tugged on the gearshift, putting it into drive. "Where's the closest one with immediate availability?"

"Two blocks east," Miles said as he clicked the keys on the computer. "The Royal Dutch Hotel."

"I'd like to say this is the last time you can use this dark power, but I'm not an idiot." She pulled into the moving traffic, and the car behind her skidded, the wheels screeching as the horn blasted and the driver gave us the middle finger.

"When this is all over, though... No more." She ignored the man's gesture and drove into a parking garage, taking a small ticket from a machine before an orange apparatus lifted, granting us access. We spiraled upward, the low ceiling and dimly lit concrete corridor making me claustrophobic. Finally, she pulled into a spot and turned off the engine before sliding out of her seat and slamming the door.

"I don't like leaving all this equipment unattended," Miles said.

"We'll set up a ward." Ash opened the side door and climbed out of the van.

I joined Ember at the back of the vehicle, watching as she paced a short distance. She was tense, her jaw working from side to side as her shoulders tightened and drifted toward her ears. How I longed to rub the tension from her muscles like I had done a few days ago. Or was it yesterday? Time was meaningless to an immortal.

The moment the thought entered my mind, my chest pinched, an agonizing ache spreading through my body. Ember was mortal. Even if I found a way to stay in this realm, I would have to watch her grow old and die. For a moment, I forgot to breathe.

I couldn't bear it. I refused to think about it.

"Are you okay?" She caught my gaze. "You look like you want to punch something. That, or you ate a bad burrito and need to find the closest restroom."

I straightened, regaining my composure. "I'm fine. My bowels are also fine."

"Good," she said as the others joined us outside the van. "Ash, Chaos, head to the front desk and get us one room. Just one, okay? Don't get greedy."

Her sister gave a mock salute.

"The rest of us will wait in the lobby." She looked from me to Miles and Shade. "Be as inconspicuous as possible. Don't do anything stupid."

"Got it," Shade said, and Miles nodded his understanding.

I arched a brow. "Anything for you, my feisty fire witch."

A ghost of a smile crossed her lips before she cleared her throat. "Let's go."

"Hold on. We need to set up a ward on the van so nothing gets stolen." Ash pulled a bottle from her bag and walked around the vehicle, sprinkling a fine dust onto the windows and doors.

"Cast it together?" Ember asked, reaching a hand toward her.

"No." Ash returned the empty bottle to her bag. "We need to save our vim, so we can break the ward on the auction house. Miles? Shade, are you up to it yet?"

"I'm good." Shade clutched Miles's hand, and they recited the spell aloud. The energy around us thickened, dancing across my skin, before they focused it on the van. They were strong witches, but their power wasn't nearly as potent as the Holland sisters'.

The fact didn't seem to bother them in the slightest.

We made our way inside the hotel, and I sat on a small sofa next to my witch while my brother worked his magic with Ash. Resting my arm on the back of the couch, I pinched Ember's neck, massaging the tension from her muscles.

She sighed, sinking farther into the cushion and closing her eyes for a long blink. "When we get to the room, can you research the people in charge of the auction? We need to know if they employed a witch to put the ward on the building or if they're witches themselves."

Miles patted his laptop bag. "I'll see what I can find."

"We've got a few hours before the auction starts, and I want us to be as prepared as possible." She touched my hand and scooted away. "I'm good. Thanks."

Ash smiled triumphantly as she approached, holding up two small pieces of plastic. "That was easy. Big Oil Boyd is staying in the penthouse. Come on."

We followed them to the elevator, and Ash tapped the card against a small box inside before pressing a button engraved with the letter P. It lit up, and the doors slid shut.

The elevator ascended rapidly, making my stomach feel as though it would slam into my pelvis. Pressure in my head built, and as I moved my jaw, my ears popped. A ding echoed through the small space, and the doors opened, revealing a large room with paintings and ornately framed mirrors hanging from alabaster walls.

A scent reminiscent of cloves and ginger filled the air, and glorious silence hung like a warm blanket over us, putting me at ease. Three closed doors indicated multiple rooms in the penthouse, and a large archway opened into the shared living area.

"This way." Ash motioned for us to follow her through the arch. "Can you believe this is considered one room? It's bigger than our apartment. It even has three bedrooms!"

"I can't believe you got the penthouse." Ember stood in the center of the room, turning in a circle. "I told you not to get greedy."

Ash shrugged. "It was Chaos's idea. I mean, we're already stealing from them. Why not go all out?"

"Room service will be delivering six steak dinners in half an hour." My brother wrapped an arm around his witch's waist and kissed the side of her head.

Ash leaned into him, resting a hand on his chest. Why could she accept their bond so easily, yet Ember fought ours? I needed a moment alone with Chaos to find out how he did it.

"Steak?" Ember rested her hands on her hips. "If Hecate

hasn't already abandoned us, she sure as hell will now. How can you say eating steak is for the greater good?"

I sank onto the loveseat and stretched my arms across the back. "You almost died today. A Formorian nearly drained every ounce of life from your body to resurrect a long-extinct species that has no business in this realm or any other...and I will never forgive myself for allowing it to happen."

She crossed her arms, shifting her weight to one leg and jutting out her right hip. "A: You didn't allow anything. George...or Donal, or whatever the hell he called himself, was a tricky little wart of a man. And B: What does steak have to do with that?"

"We all need to replenish our strength if we're to retrieve the amulet and save the realm...you and Shade especially."

She opened her mouth to argue further but closed it instead, blowing a hard breath through her nose before her demeanor shifted. "I suppose I could use some protein. Miles, have you found anything about the auction house on the witchy web?"

I had been so engrossed in watching Ember's fiery protest, I didn't notice Miles setting up his computer at a table behind the sofa. Shade sat next to him, his gaze glued to the screen as Miles's fingers flew across the keys. How he typed so quickly, I couldn't fathom. I'd seen the keyboard on both the computer and a phone, and the letters were arranged in a nonsensical order.

Miles's mouth tightened, his eyes darting back and forth as he read the screen. Shade swiped a hand down his face and leaned back in his chair while Chaos and Ash sank onto yet another sofa adjacent to the empty one.

Ember, my feisty little witch, could not sit still. She shifted her weight from side to side four times before assuming her normal pacing. "What is it? I don't like the way your faces look."

Miles inhaled deeply and raked a hand through his hair. "The auction tonight is for magical artifacts. It'll be swarming with witches."

"Wh...what?" Her expression was incredulous. "The site we looked at yesterday didn't mention anything about magic."

He hit a few more keys. "That was the public-facing website. Most of the time, their auctions are mundane. I had no idea..."

"How, then, did Boyd gain entry?" I leaned forward, my body feeling as antsy as Ember looked.

Miles rubbed his forehead. "When I created his fake online persona, I mentioned he had an interest in the occult. I guess that was enough. Unless..."

He slid his finger across the trackpad and typed something. "It's possible whoever set this up used a spell to make today's auction invisible to the mundane. Everyone there might be magical."

"Why did the site appear to be mundane when you registered?" I asked.

Miles shrugged. "A failsafe? Maybe the person running it didn't trust the spellcaster, so they made it look mundane just in case a human saw it. Who knows?"

"I better get started on the potions." Ash rose and carried

her bag to a countertop on the far wall. Above it, a glass-door cabinet held multiple bottles of liquor, and crystal chalices occupied a shelf to the right.

"It's okay." Ember paced faster. "This is okay. It could be a good thing. Witches, beasties, demons, I can handle. This is a good thing."

"How so?" I tried to keep a neutral expression, but my brows crept upward and my lips pulled into a smile of their own volition. I adored watching the gears turn in her mind.

"It's good because..." Before she could finish, a buzzer sounded from the hall and a man's voice called through an intercom.

"Room service."

CHAPTER 5
EMBER

Ash pressed a button on the wall, unlocking the elevator door, and an attendant pushed in a linen-draped cart with six plates covered in silver domes.

"Can I get you anything else?" He clasped his gloved hands in front of his chest.

"Shit. A tip," I said under my breath. "He wants a tip." And I'd spent every dollar I had *and* maxed out my credit card. If we made it out of this alive, I had no idea how I'd recover. Maybe I could sell feet pictures on one of those fetish apps. I cringed at the thought.

"I've got it." Shade rose and handed the man a folded bill. "Thanks."

"Thank you, sir." The man bowed and returned to the elevator.

Miles closed his laptop and set it on the counter before

joining the rest of us at the table. Ash passed out the plates, and the moment I took the lid off mine, the savory scents of seared beef and black peppercorn wafted to my senses. My stomach growled on cue.

The steak was so tender, it practically melted on my tongue, and the buttery green beans with rosemary roasted potatoes tasted like heaven. I didn't realize how hungry I was until I finished my plate and gorged myself on three dinner rolls.

When we finished, Ash returned our plates to the cart and rolled it out of the room. "What's the new plan?" she asked as she returned. "We can't let another witch get their hands on the amulet. They might know how to use it."

I leaned back in my chair and tapped a finger against my lips. "I'm not sure we need a new one."

"How so?" she returned to her potion station and sprinkled dried oregano into a bowl while Miles opened his laptop.

"The auction protocol will be the same," he said. "The only difference will be the wards. I'm sure they'll be using magic to guard the relics in addition to firepower."

"Less firepower than they would have at a mundane auction, I'll bet." I drummed my fingers on the table. "Not only that, but if any humans are there, they already know magic is real. If it goes south, we can use our powers openly. This is good. Finally, something is going our way."

"Mmm..." Ash pressed her lips into a thin line.

I flattened my hand on the table. "What?"

"They know artifacts can be magical." She poured a potion

into a bottle and corked it. "I doubt they've witnessed someone shoot flames from her fingertips."

"So I'll say I have an artifact that gives me fire power." I rose and rested my hands on my demon's shoulders. "It'll be fine. We've got this, right, Mayhem?"

"Indeed, we do." He clasped my hand, angling his head to look up at me. "Together, we can accomplish any feat."

His words warmed my chest and made my stomach tighten. At least the moths had settled. "We go in as planned. Big Oil Boyd and his plus one will ask to see the amulet ahead of the auction. While I'm charming the guards with my mad people skills, Mayhem will slip the stone into his pocket, and then we'll jet."

"Hecate, help us," Shade said. "You don't have people skills."

"I do when I want to." I crossed my arms. "Do you have a better idea?"

"I do, actually." He stood and joined Miles at the counter, leaning his hip against it. "I'll go with you."

I barked a laugh. "You think you're better with people than me? Please."

"Ember and I can handle it." Mayhem stood next to me. "We don't require assistance."

Shade bristled, squaring his shoulders toward us. "Like you didn't 'require assistance' at the Formorian's shop?" He made air quotes.

My nostrils flared with my hard exhale. "We'd have been fine if Ash hadn't said my name."

"Sure. Blame it on your sister like you always do." He

crossed his arms. "Poor, incompetent Ash. Always the scapegoat. How convenient."

Mayhem tensed beside me. "The *assistance* you provided made you a liability. If it hadn't been for Miles, you'd have bled out on the floor."

"Stop it. All of you." Ash spread her fingers and shot three separate flames.

One hit Mayhem in the mouth as he tried to speak. He pushed it out with his tongue and sent it back to Ash. Another hit me on the cheek, the impact stinging before my skin absorbed the fire.

The third she directed at Shade, the flame singeing him before she called it back.

"Ow!" He clutched his neck where she'd burned him. "What the hell was that for? You know I'm not fireproof."

"Your arguing is giving me a headache. Keep it up, and I'll burn the whole building down." Her eyes narrowed, her brow lower than I'd ever seen. Something about her expression reminded me of a wild animal that had been backed into a corner and was ready to lash out against its foe.

She looked downright feral.

The sigil on her arm glowed a deep red, and the tension in her jaw eased, the vein near her temple no longer protruding. I glanced at Chaos. He kept his gaze trained on my sister, but the worry in his eyes was unmistakable.

She exhaled, her posture returning to normal, her expression softening to neutral before she scrunched her brows. "Why is everyone staring at me?"

Shade laughed dryly. "I wonder."

"I remember seeing a burn salve in Ash's bag." Miles rummaged through the satchel and pulled out a jar of blue goo.

"Who got burned?" She looked perplexed.

I made eye contact with Chaos and then Mayhem. Concern etched lines into their foreheads.

"You don't remember?" Mayhem asked.

"Remember what?" She corked another bottle. "What's going on? You're all acting weird."

"You burned Shade to stop their arguing." Miles spread the salve over Shade's neck and returned the jar to the bag.

Ash shook her head. "No, I didn't."

"You did." I walked toward her cautiously. When she didn't bristle, I pressed my hand to her forehead. What I was looking for, I couldn't say. Did curses cause fevers?

Her skin felt a normal temperature, so I dropped my arm at my side. "You said you'd burn the building down if we didn't stop."

"I..." Her mouth hung open for a beat or two. "Oh, no."

"I was able to calm you through our bond." Chaos moved to her side and wrapped an arm around her waist. "You'll be fine, as long as we're together."

"It can't be the curse." She returned to her herbs, her hands trembling as she mixed another potion. "Mayhem must have..."

"I did nothing." He grasped my hand, and this time, I let him hold me. The familiar pinpricks danced across my skin, sending a warm jolt to my heart.

"We must obtain the rest of the amulet before your hysterics..." He cleared his throat. "Before the curse takes such hold that Chaos cannot control you."

"We'll take care of you." I lifted our entwined hands for emphasis. "Don't worry." Because I was worrying enough for all of us. If we lost my sister to the curse because I couldn't get my act together and lead this coven, I'd...

Well, I'd be dead. We all would.

Ash swallowed hard, her eyes glistening as if she held back tears. "I know you'll do your best."

I would from here on out. No more arguing with Mayhem or Shade or anyone else. No more letting my ego get in the way. I would keep myself in check, give it my best, and hope it would be good enough...which I should have been doing all along.

"Shade, what was your idea?" Chaos asked. "I assume you planned to go in under shadow because Boyd is only registered to bring one guest."

"Exactly." Shade straightened, turning toward Mayhem and me. "I'll follow you in, under shadow, and both of you can distract the guards long enough for me to swipe the amulet."

I shrugged, reminding myself he was just as capable of stealing a heavily guarded, eons-old amulet as I was. More so, thanks to his inborn power. "I suppose that could work too."

Miles, who had been clicking away on the keyboard, stopped typing. "That's the best idea I've heard so far. People will see your faces. You're the High Priestess of Salem, so they might recognize you. It's best if you aren't the one to commit the crime."

"I'm only the acting High Priestess. Most covens don't have a clue about our situation, and once we get my family back, I won't be in charge anymore." And thank the goddess for that.

"You're part of the governing bloodline, Em. Our pictures

are on the witchy web." Ash bottled the last potion and carried her supplies to the wet bar sink. "You'll have to go in as you, married to Boyd, another fire witch."

"Is his aura shroud still strong enough to fool them?" I rested my hand on his biceps.

"A Formorian prince believed he was a witch," Chaos said. "I can't imagine a witch less powerful than you seeing through it."

I caught my bottom lip between my teeth, chewing on it as I tugged from Mayhem's grasp, and resumed pacing. "One: Donal was tricky. Who knows if he saw through it or not? And two: Mayhem just had one foot...or hoof...in the Underworld. Guys, can you see through the shroud?"

Shade narrowed his eyes at my demon. "Yes, but we've known what he was from the get-go. I could always see through it."

"No, you couldn't." Miles turned away from his computer. "You were in awe at how well the spell worked, remember? You mentioned it after..." He flicked his gaze down before returning it to Shade. "You mentioned it."

Shade pressed his lips into a thin line and sighed. "Yeah. You're right, but I can see through it now. Can't you?"

Miles nodded.

"Did you bring all the ingredients for the spell?" I asked as Ash rummaged through her bag again.

She set a jar of lady's mantel next to the marjoram and cinnamon oil. "I have everything but wolfsbane. I'll need to buy some."

"Okay, next steps." I grabbed the bag I'd packed with my

dress and shoes for the event and slung the new one a la Donal's store over my arm. "Ash, you and Chaos find a metaphysical shop and get everything you think we'll need. Shade, did you bring anything to wear besides spandex?"

"No, but I'll be in shadow the whole time."

"Unless something happens and you can't hold it." I strode toward the hallway that led to the bedrooms, pausing at the entrance. "Go with Ash and Chaos and get something dressy enough that you'll look like you belong there...just in case."

He nodded. "I can do that."

"Miles..." I said.

"I'll stay here and get it set up. We'll need to be within a block of the auction house half an hour before the doors open."

"Good. I'm going to shower and get ready to be a trophy wife." I shuddered at the thought. Though not at being Mayhem's wife, surprisingly. That idea sat unnaturally well in my psyche. It was the trophy part that made me want to wretch.

"I'm unfamiliar with the term 'trophy wife,'" Mayhem said, following me through the bedroom into the en suite bathroom, which was bigger than my entire bed and bath combo at home.

"It basically means a wife whose only value is being arm candy." I grabbed a velvet hanger for my new dress and hung it from a hook near the door.

"Arm candy?"

"She looks good on his arm, but he doesn't give a flying flip about who she is on the inside." I gazed into the massive mirror above the sink. The small bit of mascara I'd applied in the morning had run, rimming my eyes in faded black. My hair looked like both a squirrel and a dove had nested on my head, and my shirt was torn and bloodied. I couldn't say whose blood it was. Shade's maybe? Or mine?

"Ew." I curled my lip at my reflection. "I'm definitely not arm candy."

Mayhem picked up a wide-toothed comb and began working the knots out of my hair. "But you are a trophy."

"Excuse me?" I spun and grabbed his wrist. "Care to elaborate?"

He searched my eyes, his gaze traveling to my lips for a moment before he spoke, "I treasure you, Ember. If I could win your heart the way you've won mine, it would be my greatest accomplishment."

I opened my mouth to argue that I was not a prize to be won, but I couldn't force the words from my throat. That silent vow I'd made to stop arguing with him included this too. It was time to stop deflecting and accept the emotions churning inside me. All of them.

"Why do you treasure me?" I asked.

He blinked as if my question surprised him, but he recovered quickly, one side of his mouth pulling into a teasing grin. "Aside from your value as candy on my arm?"

"Aside from that." I turned on the shower, letting the hot water fill the bathroom with steam. It smelled fresh, like lavender and sandalwood, and I kicked off my boots before stuffing my socks inside them.

"Allow me to count the reasons. You are intelligent, fierce, and feisty." He ticked them off on his fingers. "Despite your self-professed lack of people skills, you lead your coven with dignity and grace."

"I..." *No more arguing, Em. Keep your mouth shut and let the man flatter you. It's not that hard.*

I tugged my tattered shirt over my head, clicking my tongue at the rip. At least it was on the seam.

"What else?" I asked without making eye contact as I shoved my pants down my legs and stepped out of them.

He inhaled deeply, and I could imagine the primal look in his eyes, could feel the need forming between us. "You recognize the talents in others, and you encourage their strengths rather than envy them. It's a lesson I am beginning to learn, thanks to you."

I held my hand beneath the water, adjusting the temperature to a nearly searing heat. The biggest showerhead hung from the ceiling, the flow coming down like rain in the center of the massive, tiled stall. Six other jets lined three walls, and I turned them on as well.

"All that's missing is the rotating scrubber brush, and we'd have ourselves a human car wash." I choked off a maniacal giggle.

"You're doing it again," he said, and I turned around to find his shirt and pants folded neatly on the counter. "Every time I bring up our bond, you make jokes. Stop it."

"I, umm..." I swallowed hard, unclasping my bra and letting it fall to the floor. I could do this. I could let myself feel. "Please continue. Why else do you treasure me?"

His pupils dilated until only a thin ring of purple remained. "When you love someone, you love deeply and completely, and if you will have me, I would be honored to love you the same way in return."

My tongue slipped out to lick my lips against my will, and his gaze locked on my mouth, making my stomach flutter.

"I am your soulmate, Ember. It's time you accept it." He slipped off his underwear and stepped past me, into the shower.

CHAPTER 6
MAYHEM

Silky water fell onto my head like rain, and I turned, allowing the side streams to massage my back as I waited for Ember to make her move. She stood there, staring at me, her gaze caressing the length of my body before she met my eyes.

How I longed for her hands to do the same.

"What if I'm not ready to accept it?" She arched a brow, crossing her arms and drawing my attention to her hardened nipples.

Not that I needed a visual cue to her arousal. I could smell the pheromones rising to the surface of her skin, sweet and spiced, like orange blossoms and cinnamon.

With a deep inhale, I stepped out of the stream and rested a hand on the glass divider. "You don't strike me as a woman who enjoys wasting time."

"We both know I don't. What's your point?" She tilted her head, jutting out her chin in a show of stubbornness.

I exhaled sharply. "Do you not grow tired of these games?"

Her lips parted as if she would respond, but she pressed them together, screwing them to one side in an adorable manner.

"My point is we have a limited amount of time to satisfy our urges, so we should take full advantage of this glorious showering room before we must return to our quest." I held out my hand to her.

"That's a good point." She slipped off her panties and placed her hand in mine.

Before she could change her mind, I pulled her into the shower and shoved her back against the glass, pressing my body to hers and pinning her arms above her head. She gasped at my forcefulness, but her hooded eyes and ghost of a smile told me she enjoyed letting go of control.

I trailed my tongue from her collarbone to her ear, nipping the lobe between my teeth. Goosebumps rose on her skin, and a breathy moan escaped her lips.

"If I had my way, I'd keep you here until our skin turned to prunes and our bodies ached from exhaustion." I released her wrists and glided my hands down her arms to hold her face. "Then I would carry you to bed and make love to you again."

"That sounds..." With her gaze on my lips, she inclined her chin, nearly begging me to kiss her as she wrapped her arms around my shoulders. "That sounds like a good time."

"Indeed." I took her mouth with mine, parting her lips with my tongue and tangling it with hers. My arousal grew, and I reached down to adjust it, pressing my length against her stomach. The feel of her soft skin on my shaft made me shudder, and my demon rose to just below the surface, the tips of my horns protruding from my scalp, begging me to release my natural form.

"Our team will return soon," I whispered against her lips. "I need you with such urgency, I don't think I can hold back."

"It's not..." She pressed her lips together and leaned back to look at me, sliding her fingers into my hair to caress my horns. She searched my eyes, the moment agonizingly long before she finally said, "I want *you* to take me. The real you."

I stepped away from her, my brow lowering as I held her gaze, my talons extending from my fingertips as my hands morphed into their natural form. My horns grew, arching upward while my tusks lengthened. "You can't possibly want me like this."

"No." She ran a finger over my sigil on her arm, making me shiver. "Not like this. Not halfway."

My pulse quickened, my heart thudding in my chest, threatening to burst as I transformed. I grew in height and girth. My skin turned its natural shade of purple-gray, and my feet morphed into hooves. "I've never taken a mortal like this."

She stepped toward me, resting her hands against my chest and peering up, into my eyes. "I'll be your first, last, and always."

Her quick intake of air said her words had surprised her as much as they delighted me. She ran a finger down my chest, stopping just above my cock. "But let's get one thing straight. It's *my* team. Not ours."

A growl rumbled in my chest. With my demon free and my senses heightened, I could hold back no more. I grabbed her shoulders and spun her around, pressing her back against the wall.

"You belong to me, witch. Everything you have is mine...is ours to share." I withdrew my talons and reached between her legs, thrusting two fingers inside her.

She gasped and then moaned, her lids fluttering before she locked her gaze on mine. "That's not..."

I moved my fingers out and thrust them deeper inside her. "You belong to me, as I belong to you. Everything I have is yours."

I kissed her as hard as I dared in this form and pulled my fingers out to caress her clit. "We are but two halves of one being. Together, we are whole. Apart, I am nothing."

She sucked in a shaky breath, leaning her head back against the wall and fighting to keep her eyes open. "I think... I think you're right. I think this is right."

She held my face in her hands and pressed her lips to mine, her tongue darting between my tusks and making me lose control.

I wrapped my arms around her, holding her as tightly as her mortal form would allow, but even with her bare skin against me, I couldn't hold her close enough. "I love you, Ember. My soul has loved yours since the beginning of my existence."

"I think..." She pulled back to look into my eyes. "No, I don't think. I know I love you too. My soul loves yours."

My knees nearly buckled beneath me. I never knew how

badly I needed to hear those words until that moment. So many emotions that I couldn't begin to define rose inside me, swirling and pulsing, tightening my throat and causing my chest to ache. Pressure built in my eyes, the overwhelming sensation of loving Ember—and being loved in return—threatening to escape as tears.

I turned her around, lest she witness my display of weakness, and grasped her hands, pressing them against the wall. My dick throbbed, aching to fill her as she leaned her hips toward me.

Pressing my tip against her folds, I rubbed the head up and down her slit, gathering moisture on my shaft before slowly sliding inside her. "I don't want to hurt you."

"You won't. We were made for each other." She reached behind me and grasped my ass. "But I do want to watch."

She leaned toward the far wall, and we turned as one until we could see ourselves in the mirror above the sink. Her fair skin appeared so delicate, her frame minuscule compared to mine.

"You're magnificent," she said, smiling at our reflection.

"You are a work of wonder." I slid out and in, making her sigh and moan in unison.

The wall jets blasted against her, and she angled the top one away so she could lean closer to the wall. I reached around her and aimed the lower one between her legs, the sensation making her cry out in pleasure.

"Oh, gods." She adjusted her stance, giving both me and the water better access to her center. "Do it slow."

I followed her command, sliding in and out in slow, fluid

strokes while she watched my movements in the mirror. As her breathing quickened, I increased my speed, and when she gasped and screamed my name, I slammed into her, holding her against the stream as she writhed in ecstasy.

But I wasn't finished with her yet.

Her orgasm peaked and subsided, and she angled the jet away to lean her forearms against the wall. "Holy Hecate."

I slipped out of her, turning her around to face me. "I love that I can make you invoke your goddess's name with my cock."

She laughed. "You've got an impressive one. Wow."

"We aren't finished." I brushed her wet hair from her forehead. "I want to look into your eyes the next time you come. I can take you to the bed or do it here."

"Here is good." She swallowed hard.

"I didn't hurt you?"

"Not at all, but I might have to climb you." She clutched my dick and stroked it twice before gripping my shoulders. "Help me up?"

"With pleasure." I grabbed her ass and lifted her, settling her onto my shaft as she wrapped her legs around me. The sensation of her tight, velvet sheath enveloping me made me groan.

With my demon strength and her small frame, it felt as if she weighed no more than a feather. But I wasn't sure my knees would hold me when I found my release. Ember, this witch... this goddess...loved me. The real me. I had never experienced such elation in all of my existence.

I stepped out of the shower and carried her to the countertop, never breaking our intimate union as I set her down and leaned my hands against the surface. I had to bend, due to my height in this form, but my hooves gripped the slickened tiles, giving me enough leverage to thrust into her.

Over and over.

I glanced at my reflection as I pleasured her. My pupils had turned to pinpricks, the purple in my irises rippling with gray. She slid her hands upward to caress my horns with her fingertips.

"You're beautiful," she whispered, her expression turning to one of ecstasy.

"As are you." I plunged deeper inside her, my rhythm growing stronger, faster.

She dug her nails into my back, dragging them downward as she came once more. Her sounds, her scent, her everything consumed me, and I lost myself to her.

The orgasm ripped through my body, shredding my cells and reforming them as Ember mastered me. This woman knew me. Every part of my body, every thought in my mind. She anticipated my every move, she knew me...and she loved me.

If heaven existed, I had taken up permanent residence there, right in this moment.

She ran her hands over my skin and gazed at my face, completely unafraid, unappalled at my appearance. What had I done to deserve this woman? Nothing, except to place a curse on her bloodline. What had the Fates been thinking when they wove this tapestry?

Their plan wasn't mine to question, so I would simply enjoy it, revel in it, until the bitter end.

My breathing slowed in time with hers, and I pulled out, still resting my hands on the countertop and leaning toward her. She gazed into my eyes and smiled.

"As much as I love seeing you like this, we better put your demon away and finish our shower." She kissed my cheeks before pressing her lips to mine. "Our team will be back soon."

CHAPTER 7
EMBER

Holy mother of magic. The past hour or so had felt surreal. *Un*real. If not for the pleasant ache between my thighs, I would've assumed I'd dreamed it. Yet, there I was, standing across the counter from the demon I loved, smiling like a fool.

He winked, and my stomach fluttered. How the simple movement of his eyelid could affect my insides like that baffled me, but hey... I'd just let him do me in his demon form. My mind was scrambled at the moment.

The weirdest thing? I hadn't just let him. I'd *wanted* him in his demon form. Me. In love with a full-on demon. Hecate have mercy.

"I'm glad you had a good time while we were gone." Ash bumped her hip to mine, drawing me from my trance. She held the aura-shrouding powder in both hands and offered one fistful to me. "But it's time to get this shit show on the road."

"What makes you think we had a good time?" I held out my hand, and she poured the powder into my palm, laughing.

"Neither of you has stopped smiling since I walked in. Ready?"

"Let's do it." I held her free hand, and we recited the incantation in unison. "Aura strong, magic deep, we hide your essence from all who seek."

We blew the powder onto my demon, and he inhaled deeply, his conspiratorial smirk never slipping as the magic took hold, hiding his demonic nature.

At least, I assumed it was hidden. Thanks to the sigil glowing softly on my arm, I continued to feel his true self. A self I loved.

Crazy, I know.

"Guys, did it work?" Ash asked.

Miles squinted at Mayhem, and Shade sauntered toward him, his eyes calculating as he circled him. "If I didn't already know what he is, I wouldn't have a clue."

"Same." Miles closed his laptop and slid it into his bag. "All three of you look the part. Getting inside won't be an issue, and Shade, you'll blend right in if you have to drop your shadow."

"Here. To fireproof your dress, just in case." Ash handed me a tiny spray bottle filled with sunny yellow liquid. "Who would've thought a group of light witches...Veil Keepers, no less...would team up with demon princes to rob an auction?"

I sprayed my front before handing it to her so she could coat what little fabric there was on the back of my slinky little dress. "At this point—with what we've been through the past few months—nothing surprises me. And anyway..."

I tested the hem of my dress, trying to singe the threads. They refused to burn. Good. "It's not like we don't have experience in theft and breaking and entering. This ain't our first rodeo. Is it, Boyd?" I winked at my demon, and he smiled.

"No, ma'am, it ain't. I only wish I could have joined you on your previous adventures."

"You're here now. That's what matters." I slipped on my kitten heels and sprayed them with the fireproofing potion. "What do you think?" I turned in a circle for Mayhem to see.

"You look stunning, as always." He put on a black sports coat and adjusted his bolo tie. "I, on the other hand, look ridiculous."

"You look like a Texas oil baron," Miles said. "It's perfect, though Ember, you'd look more convincing in higher heels."

I laughed. "You're lucky I'm not wearing combat boots. If things go south, and we have to fight, I can't kick ass in stilettos."

"It's time." Chaos rested a hand on Ash's back.

"Everyone's clear on their duties?" Miles asked.

The energy in the room shifted, a heaviness settling on our shoulders as we nodded our agreement. We were about to attempt a heist.

An effing heist, for Hecate's sake!

Yeah, we had proficiency in theft, but our experience was in coven libraries and apartments of deceased, so-called friends. "A heavily guarded auction house," I muttered, not meaning to say it out loud.

Mayhem moved toward me, brushing a strand of hair from

my forehead. "With you by my side, anything is possible. We can do this."

The conviction in his words made them almost believable.

"Shall we?" He held out his arm like a gentleman, and I laced mine around his biceps.

"Let's go rob an auction."

Asʜ ᴅʀᴏᴠᴇ, miraculously finding parking a block from our target. She left the engine running and turned in her seat to give me an encouraging smile. "You've got this. In and out, and no egos."

She gave each of us a pointed look before shaking her head. "I don't know why I said that. We're sending in our three biggest."

"It's kind of like telling a wolf not to howl, isn't it?" I unbuckled my seat belt and cast a longing gaze at the hidey hole in the floorboard. I felt naked without my weapons. "We'll behave. I promise."

Mayhem rested his hand on my thigh. "We will do our best."

"Put your earpieces in so I can test them." Miles handed us a small box, and we each stuck the tiny pieces of silicon into our ears.

Mayhem and I climbed out of the van, and he slid the door shut behind us. Squinting, I peered through the tinted window. "Why isn't Shade coming?"

"He's standing right beside you." Mayhem gestured to my right.

"There are cameras all over the city," Shade's disembodied voice said. "It might look weird if I disappeared on screen."

"Testing," Miles said into our earpieces. "Can you hear me?"

"Loud and clear." I pressed my fingers to my ear.

"Don't do that," Ash's voice came through. "The whole point of them being small is so no one knows you're wearing them."

"Gotcha." I fisted my hands so I wouldn't do it again. What could I say? All the FBI and CIA and Secret Service people did it in the movies. I'd learned a bad habit by watching a screen. Imagine that.

"Ready, guys?" I started down the sidewalk, toward the auction house. "Our mission, should we choose to accept it, is simple."

"Have we not already accepted the mission?" Mayhem asked, his expression adorably perplexed.

I laughed. "Yes, dear, we have. In, snag the amulet, and out. As tempting as it'll be to check out all the other artifacts they've gathered, we have to stay focused."

"Indeed." He held out his arm, and I clutched his biceps. "The sooner we obtain the amulet, the sooner we can return to our penthouse and utilize the plush mattress in the main suite."

Shade snorted somewhere to my left as we stepped into a crosswalk. A crisp autumn wind whipped down the street, blowing my hair into my face and raising goosebumps on my bare arms. I should've taken a shawl or a shrug from the store of doom, but oh well. Only fifty yards to go, and we'd be at the entrance.

"Have I told you how stunning you are?" Mayhem asked, his voice low.

"Don't get used to this look." I adjusted the top of my dress, fighting the urge to reach inside it to reposition my boobs. Bras had been around for over one hundred years, and no one had come up with a comfortable, strapless version that didn't slide down the first chance it got.

"Ash, when this is through, I've got a job for you and your sewing skills."

She laughed. "I'll get right on it. After I organize the library, figure out how to make spell capsules instead of bottles, and reopen the store so we can pay our bills."

"Add reinventing the strapless bra to your list." Because we *would* get through this. Ash would have plenty of time to whittle away at her to-dos because things would go back to normal. They had to, and I would keep telling myself that until they did.

We stopped in front of the building, a ten-story brick and glass structure with three sets of heavy double doors. No sign announced the name of the owner, but the magical vibration of the wards turned my skin to gooseflesh.

"Go ahead and powder the doors," I said, looking at my demon because I had no idea where Shade stood.

"It's already done. I'm going to grab your hand. Don't react." Warmth and pressure wrapped around my wrist before Shade slid his hand down to clutch mine.

I took Mayhem's hand. "The spell Ash concocted is temporary. It shouldn't set off any alarms, but we have to cross the ward immediately before it resets."

Mayhem opened his power to me, and I fought a gasp as the low vibration and pinpricking sensation traveled up my arm to spread through my body. I shared a little of it with Shade so we could cast this spell without draining our vim too much.

We recited the incantation together. "Ward of light, this is our plight. Peel away your hood so we may enter for the greater good."

The energy on the building wavered, the pressure of the ward lifting, blinking out. I tugged from Shade's grasp and held Mayhem's arm, ushering him toward the middle set of doors and praying to the goddess that this was the only ward on the auction.

"We're inside," I said, still fighting the urge to touch my earpiece and rearrange my boobs.

"Good," Miles replied. "Someone should approach you to check in."

"Oh, no. You clearly didn't read the rules of the auction." A witch in a dark gray suit and red stilettos clicked toward us, shaking her head and gesturing at what I could only imagine was Shade.

"Either drop your shadow or kindly leave the premises." She tapped her finger on a tablet screen and arched a brow.

Shade sighed heavily and appeared next to Mayhem.

The woman clicked her tongue. "No shadow magic, no weapons, no spells intended to affect the outcome of the auction. You received the rules via email after you registered, Mr...?

"I apologize, ma'am." Mayhem laid on a heavy Texas accent. "My name is Boyd Anderson, and this here is my wife, Ember."

She swiped the screen and tapped it three times. "Yes, you and your wife are registered."

"This is my assistant, Shade. His shadow has a mind of its own when he's nervous." He lowered his voice and winked. "He's kinda shy and as awkward as a nun in a whorehouse. Please forgive his transgression."

A blush spread across the woman's cheeks as she gazed into my demon's eyes, and I suddenly felt the urge to gouge out hers. Okay, I wouldn't really do that, and I knew he was charming her so we could complete our mission, but damn.

Jealousy was such an ugly emotion. I suppose I'd never cared about anyone enough to feel it before.

The woman cleared her throat. "He isn't on the list."

"Surely you can add him... I apologize again, ma'am. I missed your name." Mayhem stepped toward her, his gaze slipping to her mouth before returning to her eyes.

I bristled and clenched my teeth.

She swallowed audibly. "It's Hazel."

"Hazel, Shade is also my accountant, and I need him present when I make large purchases. I plan to spend a lot of money today." He winked again, and my stomach tightened along with my jaw.

"Well..." She let out a breathy laugh. "We don't normally make exceptions, Mr. Anderson, but I see you've been verified as a platinum-level bidder. If I can see his ID, I'll add him to your registration."

The tendons in Shade's neck were so tight, you could've plucked them like guitar strings, and a vein on his temple looked like it was about to burst.

"Give it to her, Shade," Miles said through the coms. "It's not ideal, but we don't have a choice."

He dug his wallet from his jacket and offered her his ID. "I won't be bidding. Just assisting."

She scanned the barcode on the back of his license and returned it to him. "Thank you, sir. This way."

Her heels clicked on the tile as we followed her through the foyer. Mine clicked a little too, but the sound was lower, much more practical. Thudding boot heels would have been better.

"Stop fidgeting," Mayhem said under his breath. "You must appear confident in your clothing."

"You try feeling confident when your bra is about to slip down to your waist and take your boobs with it."

"The ladies' room is down that hall and to the right." Hazel gestured at a massive archway. "Men's is to the left."

My cheeks heated, but I kept following her. "Thank you."

The foyer opened into another room with squishy carpet and a ginormous crystal chandelier hanging from the center of the ceiling. Black and white photos of New York during various decades hung from the dark green walls, and a bar and buffet stood at the back of the space.

"Here, you will find refreshments, and you may pick up your auction paddle on your way to the main event." She tapped her screen and closed the cover before batting her eyes at Mayhem. "May I assist you in any other way?"

Oof. I did not like the way she said that. The emphasis she put on "any other" made her intention as clear as pure quartz.

"We're good. Thanks." I gripped Mayhem's arm and rested my hand on his chest.

"Actually…" Mayhem patted my shoulder. "I would like to see the amulet…item 457…ahead of the bidding. Can you make that happen?"

She glanced at me before smiling at him. "Absolutely. Someone will find you as soon as it's ready for viewing. Please, enjoy yourselves."

Shade laughed as she walked away. "Ember Holland finally met her match."

I blew a breath through my nose. "I could kick her ass with both hands cuffed behind my back."

"Oh, I don't doubt that." He laughed again. "But could you be any more jealous?"

I glared at Shade, trying to formulate a snippy comeback, but my mind blanked. Yes, I was jealous of a shadow witch because she flirted with my man. I could admit that.

Hell, she hadn't even flirted. Not really. Honestly, she hadn't done a damn thing wrong, but I could feel her attraction to my demon and I hated it. *Get a grip, Em.*

"You have nothing to worry about." Mayhem hooked a finger beneath my chin, lifting my gaze to meet his. "You are my first, last, and always, remember?"

"I remember." I rose onto my toes and brushed a gentle kiss to his lips before wiping the lipstick away with my thumb.

"Mr. Anderson?" A man in a dark red jacket approached us. "The item is ready to be viewed."

Hazel the shadow witch flanked him, her mouth tight, her eyes narrowed in a perturbed expression. "I'll be accompanying you this evening, unless your assistant would like to leave the premises."

A sense of smugness made me straighten my spine. Did our friend get into trouble for allowing Shade to stay? I started to think that was what she got for fawning over my man, but the direness of our circumstances sank in instead.

She'd be watching Shade's every move, so he was out of play. I should have anticipated something like this. They had guards with automatic rifles. Of course they would have people actively watching for shadows and spells. Honestly, I was surprised the ward on the building wasn't stronger. They hadn't even hired an elemental witch to cast it.

But now we had to go back to plan A: Me distracting the guards while Mayhem swiped the necklace. But Hazel would have one mesmerized eye on my demon too. *Shit.*

My pulse sprinted, and I took a deep breath, trying to look calm, but Miles's voice over the coms made my stomach take a flying leap into my throat. "All right, guys. It's go time."

CHAPTER 8

MAYHEM

I offered my arm to Ember and fought my smile as we followed Hazel and the guard toward the vault. The shadow witch not only couldn't hold a candle to my fire witch, but she could not ignite a single, minuscule spark inside me. No woman ever would for the rest of my existence.

I had to admit, though, watching Ember's subtle display of dominance added fuel to the already raging inferno of love and desire I felt for her.

We exited the refreshment area and turned left, passing through a second massive archway when a *ding-dong* sound echoed through the corridor. Hazel and the guard stopped short, her gaze snapping to his.

A moment later, a woman's voice sounded through the building's intercom. "Attention guests and staff. Please gather in the waiting area until further notice. Code blue thirty-seven."

Hazel tried to hide her gasp by clearing her throat. "I'm sorry. We'll have to go back to the waiting area."

"What's blue thirty-seven?" Ember asked, crossing her arms.

"Go ahead. I'll bring them in." Hazel gestured at the guard, who turned on his heel and jogged toward the vault.

"We need to go back. Follow me." Her heels clicked on the floor, and another bell echoed before the voice repeated the instructions.

Ember widened her stance. "What's blue thirty-seven?"

Hazel turned toward her, wringing her hands, her gaze jumping from Ember to Shade to me before she leaned toward us and whispered, "There's been a security breach. I don't..." She shook her head and looked at Shade.

"Oh. Oh, hey..." Ember touched Hazel's elbow. "They wouldn't lock the place down over Shade. If they didn't want him here, they'd have made him leave."

"Yeah." She blew out a breath. "I just... I really need this job."

"Then let's make sure you keep it." Ember guided her toward the foyer, and Shade and I followed reluctantly.

The final piece of Lucifer's amulet lay a few yards away. Temptation to run for it, to obtain it by any means necessary, had my muscles tensing and my hands clenching into fists.

I could take it so effortlessly. Getting Ember and Shade out safely would not be as easy.

"What's happening?" Ash asked in my earpiece. "Do you see anyone suspicious?"

"Not as of yet," I replied quietly. "Perhaps your spell to pass through the ward set off an alarm after all."

"Not a chance," she said. "An arrogant, mid-level witch cast it, probably thinking no one would have the gall to attempt a heist at a magical auction in the most secure house in the country."

"She's right," Shade said. "The magic barely fought back. We didn't cause this."

We passed through the foyer and gathered with the other attendees in the carpeted room. I scanned the faces of those present, searching for a sign of the culprit. "Hazel, how many shadow witches are working tonight? Could someone else have sneaked in the way Shade did?"

"There are six of us stationed around the building. Two of us manned check-in, but I don't see Misty anywhere now." She tugged her phone from her pocket and tapped the screen. "Her tracker is off."

"There's your security breach," Ember said. "Does she practice dark magic?"

"No." Hazel shook her head adamantly. "We went through an intense screening process to get these jobs. We had aura readings, one-on-one interviews, personality tests, and mundane background checks. Plus we all had to pass through the ward to get into the building."

Ember spun in a circle, her eyes calculating. "Wards can be dissolved."

"Not without setting off an alarm." She pressed her phone to her ear. "Misty, are you okay? Call me."

"Powerful witches can…" I began, but Ember's sharp look made me stop mid-sentence.

Hazel let out a nervous laugh. "Okay, but who here is that strong? It would take an elemental to break it quietly."

I arched a brow at Ember. It seemed our new friend didn't know she stood in the presence of a Holland witch. We would have to keep it that way.

"All guests are accounted for," the voice over the intercom said. "Initiate seven-five-seven."

"Oh, this is bad." Hazel squinted at her phone. "Better get comfortable."

I was about to inquire why when a pair of men with large guns closed the doors to the foyer. The *thunk* of a massive lock engaging echoed in the room, and the crowd's incessant chatter quieted to a murmur.

"What's happening?" both Ember and Ash on the earpiece asked in unison.

Hazel jerked her head toward an empty corner of the room. "Come over here. I'm not supposed to talk about it."

We followed her, and I picked up a pastry from the buffet on our way, shoving the entire thing into my mouth. The cream cheese center meshed perfectly with the tart lemon frosting.

Ember blinked at me and shook her head.

Hazel motioned for us to get closer. "Seven-five-seven is a lock-down protocol. We're stuck here until they verify all the artifacts are safe and they find the culprit. They'll interview each of us separately."

Her gaze darted about the room, her brows drawing inward

until deep wrinkles formed above the bridge of her nose. "I can't stay in here. I have... I have a job to do."

Ember closed her eyes and pressed her fingers to her temples. "We don't have time for this to turn into an Agatha Christie novel." She looked at me. "What should we do?"

I had no answer of which the team would approve.

"At least we have food. It could be a long night, so we might as well settle in." Hazel shoved her phone into her pocket, her nervous expression contrasting the calmness of her words.

"You have to find a way out," Ash said. "Miles is tapping into your phones to track you, and then he'll guide you to the amulet."

"The—" Ember began before making a face at me. We couldn't speak freely while Hazel remained within earshot.

"How's your vim?" Shade asked, sensing the issue. "It must be draining to use your active power of seeing through shadow for so long."

Hazel laughed dryly. "Right? I'll have to sleep for three days to recover."

With Shade distracting the guard dog, Ember and I stepped away and settled at a small table far from the crowd and any other prying ears.

"There are armed guards at all the exits," Ember whispered. "We aren't going anywhere without causing a scene."

"Perhaps a scene is exactly what we need." I drummed my fingers on the table. "If the crowd were to break out in a mass panic, we could slip out the door during their distraction."

"Absolutely not." Ember laid her hand on mine, stopping my drumming.

"That could work," Ash said, at least one sister agreeing with me.

"How many people would we inadvertently kill if Mayhem did his thing in here? For once, violence isn't the answer." Ember squeezed my fingers and let them go. "We can't make these people start fighting each other, especially not with all the assault rifles in the room."

"Are you trying to convince me or yourself?" I asked.

"Both. As much as I'd loved to kick some ass right now, we can't be the cause of anyone else's death. I'm done leaving a trail of bodies in our wake."

A *clunk* sounded from above, and the chandelier rattled, turning lopsided before swinging violently from its base. A shimmering disturbance dropped to the floor, and a man let out a gurgling scream.

I rose to my feet. "It appears we have our distraction."

CHAPTER 9

EMBER

"Please tell me that's not what I think it is," I shouted over the blood-curdling screams as I scanned the room, searching for anything I could use as a weapon.

"It's the fae. They're here for the amulet." Shade said as he rushed toward me.

"No shit, Captain Obvious." I grabbed a handful of fruit kabobs from the buffet, but the wooden skewers were as light as balsa sticks. If steel broke upon impact with giant insect armor, these would turn to splinters. I shoved a melon ball into my mouth and tossed the rest into a yogurt bowl.

"What is happening?" Hazel pressed a hand to her chest and backed up until she smacked the wall. Her gaze bounced around the room, her brow furrowing in concentration as if she were attempting to see through shadows that didn't exist.

"Those are fae." A growl rumbled from Mayhem's chest, and his talons protruded from his fingertips.

I grasped his hands, covering his built-in Freddy Krueger knives, and whispered, "Put those away, Wolverine."

He growled again, but he did as I asked. "We have no weapons."

"Yes, we do." Shade tossed me a butter knife he'd snagged from the buffet. It had a rounded tip and a dull blade, but it was better than the fruit skewer I'd found.

"What the hell?" a man shouted.

"I can't see them," another one said.

A woman slammed against the wall, her throat collapsing before her stomach ripped open. Her insides spilled onto the floor as the invisible fae wrenched out her liver. The crowd silenced, watching in sheer horror, the sounds of bones breaking and flesh tearing echoing through the room as the soldier plunged his claws into her chest and ripped out her heart, *Indiana Jones and the Temple of Doom* style.

The squelching and munching that followed made me gag, but the gasps of terror from the other witches spurred me into action.

"Where's the rift?" I shoved the knife into my bra and finally adjusted my boobs. I was tempted to whip the damn thing off, but it was the only clothing I had on that could hold a weapon.

"Above the chandelier." Mayhem pointed, and another shimmery *Predator* monster dropped onto the fixture. "I count three."

"Three rifts?" I grabbed more butter knives, creating a bouquet of blades in my cleavage.

"Three soldiers." He gathered fire in his palms. "Make that four."

"How?" Hazel's eyes grew to the size of salad plates.

Mass panic ensued, making the spacious buffet room feel like a tiny, overcrowded closet. Grunts, rips, screams, and gurgling last breaths created a cacophony of horror as the fae wreaked their havoc on the unsuspecting witches.

"This was a setup." I clutched two metal shrimp skewers and kicked off my shoes, scanning the room for the telltale shimmer of overgrown flies.

To my left, someone shouted a binding spell. I waited for a fae to freeze—or hell, I'd have been happy if it affected the entire room—but no magic built in the air. Her words were as mundane as a vampire was thirsty.

"We could use your spell kit about now, Ash." I pressed my fingers to the earpiece, not giving a flying flip if anyone knew I was wired. "We've got a rift and four fae that need freezing."

"Magic won't work in here." Hazel eyed Mayhem's fiery hands. "It shouldn't work."

I ignited a fireball, heating the metal skewers until they glowed red. "What do you mean?"

"I guess they didn't count on elementals." She poked at her phone screen, frowning. "Once you pass the foyer, there's a ward to bind magic on every room. No one can cast a spell, but apparently, elementals can use their inborn gifts."

"She's right," Shade said. "Shadows aren't elemental. I can't create one."

"There should be a door in the back left corner, hidden in the wall," Ash said over the coms. "If you can get through it, we can guide you out."

A guard blasted his assault rifle into the chandelier. The bullets lodged in—or passed through—the ceiling, but glass rained onto the throng of witches, making them panic more. The fifth fae, who'd dropped through the rift at just the right time, took a hit in the neck. He screeched, his shroud slipping as he thudded on the floor, revealing his ghastly nature to the crowd.

"Find the door, Em," Ash reminded me.

"We'll get right on that." I stormed toward the injured fae, elbowing people out of my way and shoving a shrimp skewer into his ear hole. The bug goo inside him sizzled with my heat, and I lifted a layer of his armor and jabbed a butter knife into his heart.

Another fae grabbed the guard with the rifle and hurled him upward, into the ceiling. Sheetrock cracked and bones crunched before he fell, smacking the floor. Blood oozed from a gash in his head, and I cringed as the fae tossed him onto his back and ripped out his organs.

Rising to my feet, I spun toward Hazel. "Can you lift the ward? These witches aren't fighters. Without their spell powers, they'll be massacred."

A fae shimmered three feet behind her, and Mayhem hurled hellfire at him. The bastard screeched, losing his glamour for half a second as he backed away to find an easier target.

Hazel squealed and clutched Mayhem's arm. "I can't. I

didn't cast it, and even if I was strong enough to break it, my magic doesn't work in here either."

"Hecate on a hellhound. Your people didn't think this through. You've trapped us in a barrel. We're the fish, and the fae have the guns."

"Get to the door, Em," Ash said in my ear. "I'll see if I can lift the wards from the foyer."

"Don't you dare come into this building." I grabbed Hazel by the arm, dragging her to the door in question. "Open it."

"I can't." She blubbered, tears streaming down her face. "The seven-five-seven protocol means the doors are bolted by the security system. Only an admin can unlock them."

"Miles?" I asked.

"On it." The sound of his fingers clicking keys filled my ear. "Ash is on her way inside. I tried to stop her, but you know how those two are."

Yes, I knew all too well, and I couldn't fault her. Had our roles been reversed, and she'd ordered me to stay outside, I'd have come in anyway. "How long will it take?"

"A few minutes." He continued clicking.

A fae shimmered to my right and slammed a witch in a blue sports coat onto the ground. Shade hurled a butter knife, but, big surprise, they weren't weighted right for throwing. It bounced off the side of the fae's head and landed on the carpet.

Mayhem threw hellfire, charring a wing, and the fae dropped his shroud to reveal his pincers opening and closing half an inch from his prey's face. Poisonous saliva dripped onto the witch's mouth.

"Help me," the man squeaked.

"Any time now, Miles." I clutched a knife, heating it as I marched toward the fae. Mayhem shot a solid stream of fire at his back, and his wings fluttered, raining bits of char onto the witch as he plunged his hand into the man's gut.

Grabbing a tuft of white hair, I yanked the fae's head up and jabbed a knife beneath his chin. It passed through his open mouth and lodged in the front of his brain, hopefully lobotomizing the bastard.

I kicked the side of his head, and he fell onto his back at Shade's feet. "He's all yours."

"I'd like to draw the life out of you slowly, but I'll make do with a knife." Shade lifted an armored plate and put an end to fae number two.

"Doors are opening," Miles said. "Go out the back and make a left down the service hall, take the second right, go through the third door on your left, and take the stairs to the basement. The vault will be on your right about twenty yards down."

"You expect me to remember all that?" I moved toward the door, still scanning the room for our invisible foes.

"What about the three other soldiers?" Shade asked.

"I'm almost done with the wards," Ash replied. "Get the amulet and get out. The other witches will have to handle them on their own."

"I don't like leaving people to die." I whirled toward Hazel, ready to drag her to safety, but she had already darted out the door.

"Imagine how many more will perish if we don't complete our quest." Mayhem gently touched my elbow, guiding me toward the back exit.

Across the room, the massive double doors swung on their hinges, opening to the foyer, and I caught a glimpse of my sister and her demon holding hands. Ash's eyes were closed as she recited an incantation.

"I will keep her safe," Chaos said in my earpiece.

"You sure as hell better." I slipped through the back door with Mayhem and Shade, yanking it closed behind me.

The sweet bliss of silence engulfed us as we made our way down the wide service hall. The speckled white linoleum felt cool on my bare feet, taming the heat of adrenaline rushing through my veins. A bead of sweat from beneath my left boob rolled down my stomach, and my heart hammered so hard in my chest, I thought it might bust through my ribs.

We turned down the second hallway, and I stopped. "Wait. Is this right, or were we supposed to take the third left?"

"You're good," Miles said. "Keep going."

"The wards are down," Ash said. "We're going in to close the rift."

"No." I turned around, ready to run to my sister's aid, but Mayhem caught me by the shoulders.

"They are capable." He pinned me with a pointed gaze. "We'll do our part. Let Ash do hers."

I ground my teeth. "It's not supposed to be her part."

"And battling fae wasn't supposed to be ours." He squeezed my shoulders and let them go. "The circumstances have changed, but the outcome must remain the same."

I wanted to argue. I really did, but once again, the demon was right. Ash was capable. We would all do what we had to do. "Where next, Miles?"

"Third door on your left."

We followed his directions and headed downstairs to the basement, but a sickening sensation formed in my stomach as we approached the vault. A pair of black boots lay just inside the open door, and as we crept closer, I realized they weren't just boots. They were still attached to someone's feet.

"This whole thing was a setup." I swallowed the bile from the back of my throat. "The so-called security breach, locking us in the buffet room... *We* were the buffet for the fae."

I stopped outside the vault and toed the person's boot. They didn't react. With a deep inhale, I steeled myself for whatever we might find—or not find—inside and stepped around the person's legs.

A single bullet hole marred the center of the guard's head. Blood pooled beneath her, and her hands still clutched a rifle, her finger on the trigger. She never got the chance to fight back.

Mayhem strode into the vault, stepping over the dead woman, and examined the shelves. "It isn't here."

"Are you sure?" I joined him inside, though I knew he was right. We weren't simply a smorgasbord for the overgrown bugs. The fae wanted the amulet as badly as we did. They'd feasted on witch hearts and lifted the artifact in one fell swoop.

"Would they have taken it across the veil?" Shade joined us, scanning the shelves in vain.

Hazel's clicking heels preceded her appearance in the doorway, and she glanced at my bare feet. She clutched a pistol in one hand, and the amulet dangled from the golden chain entwined in her fingers. "The fae want this too?"

"As if you didn't know." I took two steps toward her,

cursing myself for falling for her act. I should have trusted my intuition about her from the start.

She retreated two steps back and adjusted her grip on the pistol. "I don't know anything about those creatures. They weren't part of the plan."

Nervous tension rolled off her in waves, her gaze bouncing around the room before it landed on the dead guard. Her breath caught as she gestured at the body. "I didn't want to do that."

"What plan?" I moved toward her again, raising my hands in a show of fake innocence.

She backed out the doorway and lifted the gun, so I stopped my advance. If I'd practiced spell-casting as much as Ash had, I could freeze her without a potion, grab the amulet, and we'd be on our way. Maybe I'd have time to work on that when all this was through. For now, my choices were burning her or hurling the improperly weighted butter knife still nestled in my cleavage. Neither option sounded appealing.

"You didn't steal the amulet for the fae?" Shade moved beside me. I lifted a finger, silently telling him not to advance. Hazel was on the verge of either killing us or tucking tail and running.

Mayhem stood behind me, not saying a word, but I could feel his anger building. Maybe that was why I didn't want to hurt Hazel. Hecate knew she deserved whatever it would take for us to get the damn amulet.

I ran my finger over his mark on my arm, and he inhaled deeply, calming just enough for me to begin feeling rage.

Hazel's expression pinched. "I don't think so. The man who hired me said he was a High Priest. At first, when you asked to see it, I thought it was you. But why would you tell me to meet you in Worcester if you were coming to New York, anyway?"

"Worcester?" My eye twitched. "Did you get his name?"

She laughed. "No, but now that I know how valuable this is, I'm going to renegotiate my price. What's it do?"

"Bad things." My legs tensed, my muscles coiling, ready to spring. There were three of us and only one of her. Sure, she had a gun, but we could take her. We'd subdue her and get the amulet before she handed it over to Boston. I had no doubt Adrian was the High Priest who'd hired her.

"You can't sell it." I lunged toward her, but she slammed a heavy metal gate in my face, the lock engaging with a *thunk* as my forehead struck a bar. *Oof.*

"You have no idea what's going to happen if you do this." I reached through the grate, but she stepped farther back, tucking the gun into her waistband. "Hazel, please. We need that amulet. The fate of the world is dangling from your fingers."

She cocked her head, shrugging one shoulder. "I need the money."

I was done being nice. Mayhem and I gathered fire in our palms, ready to throw it, but before we could, she slammed the massive vault door, six *clunks* sounding as she spun the dial and locked us inside.

CHAPTER 10
EMBER

"Effing Adrian." I grasped the metal gate and shook it, not that I thought I could tear it from its hinges. Mayhem might be able to, but we'd still be stuck behind a two-foot-thick vault door with a complex, massive locking system that Ash's little lock-picking toolkit wouldn't stand a chance against.

"Effing Hazel and mother effing fae." I paced in front of the door, tripping over the dead guard and pressing my hands to my cheeks. "Shit. This poor woman."

"We have worse things to worry about." Mayhem lifted her and carried her body behind a shelving unit, out of sight.

I closed my eyes and pinched the bridge of my nose. Never did I ever dream my life would come to a point where I had worse things to worry about than a woman getting killed for being in the way of what I needed.

"Ash, Miles, are you there?" I pressed my fingers to the earpiece, but all I heard was a bit of static.

"The walls are too thick." Shade examined the gate, shaking it like I had done. "Best we can do is hope they heard us before Hazel locked us in."

"Fabulous." I lifted my hands and dropped them at my sides. "What about phones? Mayhem, hand me mine."

He fished my device from his jacket pocket and gave it to me. The words *No Service* lit up the center of the screen, so I handed it back to him.

I took a deep breath and blew it out hard. "Let's take stock. What do we know?" I made a grabby motion at Shade. "Tell me."

"Hazel has the amulet." He leaned against the gate, crossing his arms. "And she's planning to sell it to Adrian...or so we assume."

"Worcester doesn't have a coven, and it's on the way to Boston. Adrian hired her for sure." I continued pacing, keeping my body occupied so my brain could do the work. "What else?"

"She appeared to be as surprised about the fae dropping in as we were," Mayhem said.

"Right. She didn't know she was setting us up to be slaughtered. That's obvious." I grabbed the sides of my bra and hauled it up, putting my boobs back into place.

"She is a skilled actress, though," Mayhem said. "We all fell for her show of innocence."

"Did Adrian know about the fae?" Shade ignored his admission. "Or was it an unfortunate coincidence?"

"That was no coincidence." I tapped my index finger against my lips. "I think he pretended to make amends with Prince Ignacus and set up the whole thing. *We* were the peace offering."

"Ignacus promised him immeasurable power in return for his fealty. Why would he need to pretend?" Mayhem examined an antique apothecary chest, opening and closing the drawers, finding them empty.

"Ignacus lies. Adrian lies. Neither can trust their right hands to know what the left is doing. Why would Adrian turn over the amulet when he could keep all the power to himself?" I crossed my arms, shifting my weight to one leg. "He wouldn't."

"So Hazel's on her way to Worcester," Shade said. "If she makes it that far, she'll sell the amulet to Adrian. We still have two-thirds of it, so he won't get 'immeasurable' power. Just a little boost."

"A little boost like Chrys? You saw what it did to her. It changed her." I rested my hands on my hips. "Adrian is a thorn in our side now. Once he gets his hands on the amulet, and it affects his brain, he'll be an entire bramble."

"We must intercept it before Hazel initiates the exchange." Mayhem strolled toward the gate and shook it the same way Shade and I had. One corner of his mouth lifted into a smirk as he glanced sideways at me. "Back up, please."

I moved to stand next to Shade as Mayhem tightened his grip on the bars. His muscles tensed, new ones not normally visible protruding beneath his skin as he strained. He inhaled, exhaled hard, inhaled. On his next exhale, he ripped the gate from the wall and tossed it aside as if it were made of foam.

"Impressive." I couldn't fight my smile or ignore the flutter in my belly. I was in love with a strong man. So what? "Can you do that to the vault door too?"

My demon ran his fingers around the seal before bracing his palms against the center and pushing with all his might. No hinges creaked. No walls groaned against the pressure.

He leaned his shoulder against it, pushing for a few seconds before backing away and slamming his weight against the door. Nothing. "I'm afraid even my strength is no match for this."

"What if we all tried together?" Shade braced his arm, angling his shoulder toward the door. "On three."

He counted. We shoved. Twice. Three times. Nothing moved.

I gripped my aching shoulder, rotating it to loosen the tension. "When brawn doesn't work, we have to use our brains. Fabulous."

"We are surrounded by magical artifacts." Mayhem leaned down to kiss the bruise already forming on my shoulder. "Surely you can find something of use."

I spun in a circle, taking in the possibilities. "Except we don't know if these things actually do what the tags say they do. They were wrong about the amulet."

I lifted the information sheet. "'A nineteen-carat Burma ruby, rumored to increase physical strength tenfold.' They had no idea."

"How could they?" Mayhem picked up a gem-encrusted dagger, the blade intricately etched with Celtic designs. "The amulet was never meant to see this side of the veil. Discord should have left it in Hell when Isabel summoned us."

"Our lives would be a helluva lot easier if he had." I tossed the info sheet into the black velvet box where the answer to—and cause of—our problems should have lain. "I wonder who listed it, and why they'd want to sell it."

"If the bearer lacked a strong inborn ability such as fire or another element, the amulet's power would be difficult to ascertain."

"You have to have power to increase power," Shade said.

"Precisely. Which is why your friend Chrys was able to harness it fully. She was a force." He said it matter-of-factly, and I knew deep down he was *my* demon and what experiences he'd had before we got together didn't matter.

But he'd been inside Chrys the same way Chaos had been inside Ash. The way he'd been inside me for a short time. Jealousy reared its ugly head again, but I squelched it. Mayhem was mine. Period. End of story.

He handed me the gem-encrusted dagger. "Perhaps this could be of use."

"It's beautiful." I accepted the weapon, but the moment my skin touched the blue and green stones on the handle, sparks ignited on my fingers. "Son of a bitch." I dropped it, letting it clatter on the floor as I wiped my hand on my dress.

The sparks hadn't just ignited on my hand; it had felt like the dagger was drawing my fire out. "What does the info sheet say?"

"I didn't check." Mayhem handed it to me and picked up the dagger, turning it over in his hands.

"It's a vessel." I read and re-read the description. "It can hold magic and release it later. A spell or an inborn power. Let me see it."

I held out my hand and focused on keeping my magic inside me. This time, it didn't pull my power from my skin. "I wonder..."

Focusing my intent, I let fire build in the core of my being and sent it down my arm, into the dagger. The blade glowed deep red as I filled it, and when I'd given it all it would hold, the metal faded to its normal hue.

"See if you can release the fire." I offered the handle to Shade. "But keep your own magic inside you."

He accepted the weapon and examined the blade before pointing it at the floor. "Is there a trigger or something I need to say?"

I flipped the info sheet over, but the back was blank. "It doesn't say. Maybe it just needs your intent."

He lifted the blade and thrust it toward the floor. Fire—*my* fire—shot from the tip to billow on the tile. I called to it, drawing it back inside as if I'd been the one to shoot the flames.

"That's cool." Shade arched a brow and studied the gems on the handle. "It's not going to open the door, but it could definitely come in handy later."

I took the dagger and returned it to its velvet box. "We need to focus and find something that can help us with an unlocking spell."

We scoured the shelves, reading the info cards and examining the artifacts, my stomach sinking further and further. I could think of sinister uses for nearly every item in the room, especially a dagger that could steal power from an unsuspecting witch.

We could murder, maim, and drive people mad with the stuff in the vault. Sadly, we couldn't find a single item to help us walk through walls or magically pick a lock.

"There's nothing." My sinking stomach twisted, pulling my heart down with it. My insides tightened, my heart hammering so hard, I could see each rapid beat in my chest. I took a deep breath, trying to stave off my anxiety.

Panicking at this disco wouldn't do us any good, but my body ignored my brain's command to chill the eff out. My palms slicked with sweat, and my mouth went dry. "What are we going to do?"

Mayhem took both my hands and kissed the backs of my fingers. "You must cast an unlocking spell without a potion. You are strong enough."

I laughed dryly. "Even if I could, I'd need access to the witchy web to look up an incantation. I don't know one off the top of my head."

"I do." Shade set a wooden box onto a shelf and cast his gaze to the floor before meeting my eyes. "I remember the one I used to break into your house."

I crossed my arms. "Ah, yes. Good times."

Mayhem gave me a questioning look, and I shrugged. "Long story. He's forgiven." I returned my attention to Shade. "Did you cast it without a potion?"

His jaw tightened. "No. It was a complex spell."

"Which you only had to use on a couple of deadbolts." I

gestured to the circular vault door. "Do you really think it'll work on that?"

Shade straightened, his knee-jerk egotistical reaction simmering just below the surface before his shoulders slumped. "Not without a potion, no."

"It must." Grasping my hand, Mayhem led me toward the door. "We have no other options."

Shade sauntered toward us and stood on Mayhem's other side. "It's worth a shot. I have no intention of dying in here."

I ground my teeth. "Spellcasting has never been my strength. Ash…"

"Is not here." Mayhem squeezed my hand. "Spellcasting is not your strength because you prefer to fight. That doesn't mean it's your weakness. You can do this."

"We'll do it together." Shade held his hand toward my demon, and Mayhem accepted it. "The incantation is easy, but your focus has to be intense." He recited the words he'd memorized.

I swallowed the dryness from my mouth. Two sentences. That's all it was. Two simple sentences that we had to infuse with so much power, our vim would dwindle to nothing when we were through.

And even then, the spell might not work.

No, I couldn't think that way. I refused to manifest our demise with negativity. Ash needed me. Cinder needed me. Salem…hell, the world…needed me—us—to break the curse, mend the veil, and set things right again.

"Let's do it." I tightened my grip on Mayhem and rested my free hand against the circular door. Setting my intention, I said a silent prayer to the goddess and gathered my vim into the core of my being. *Hecate, please don't forsake us.*

My power built, growing hotter, stronger inside me, and the energy in the room shifted with my magic. Pressure formed around us, squeezing and filling the room with buzzing electricity. Shade rested his hand against the door, and Mayhem opened to us.

Demonic energy surged through my veins, my entire body electrifying with pinpricks and dark magic. I reveled in it, rolling the sensation over and over in my mind, my soul. It no longer felt foreign inside me. Mayhem's power felt as much a part of me as my own.

"Ready?" I asked.

Shade gasped before clearing his throat. "Yeah."

"Lock engaged, hear my page. Open now; my passing you'll allow," we said in unison., and I swear I heard electricity crackling around us.

We repeated the spell a second time. Then a third. The buzzing increased, Mayhem's low vibration mixing and melding with Shade's and my high. I willed the magic outward through my palm, but the lock didn't budge. I focused, listening for the gears turning in the door. Not even an infinitesimal sound indicated the spell was working.

Because it wasn't working.

Not yet.

"Give us more," I said, and Mayhem released another surge of magic. It crashed into my psyche, making me sway on my feet.

"Too much," Shade ground out, but I couldn't get enough.

"Come over here. I'll filter it." I reached for Shade, and he dropped my demon's hand.

His breath came out in a rush, and he stumbled, catching himself on the door. "I can't."

"You can. Don't give up." I took his hand and tugged him to my side. "Touch the door."

He did as I asked, and I sent a tiny amount of Mayhem into Shade. "You okay?"

"Yeah." He raked in a breath. "I'm ready."

Mayhem gave me more, no longer having to divide it between us, and I let the power trickle into Shade's palm. We recited the incantation again, and the door groaned.

Adrenaline surged through me, spiraling around Mayhem's magic, merging and intensifying the sensations as we spoke the words a second time.

Shade panted before heaving in a breath, his body trembling with the magical exertion. We recited the spell again, and my head spun. Darkness closed in, my vision tunneling, stars swimming in front of me.

I pushed out as much magic as I could, focusing my intent on the massive lock inside the door. Sharp pain sliced from my jaw to my temple. I strained. Shade wheezed. The door groaned.

"One more push," I said as if we were giving birth to a ten-pound magical baby.

The lock clunked once. Twice. Six times.

Shade tugged from my grasp and slumped against the door. Mayhem pulled his magic back, leaving me empty, my vim depleted to nothingness. My tunneling vision went black.

CHAPTER II
EMBER

Sunlight streaming in through the window turned the backs of my eyelids red. I kept them closed, willing myself to slip back under, into the deep sleep the morning had dragged me out of. The pillow, so indulgent it had to be made of down, cradled my head as I snuggled into the softest sheets I'd ever felt.

Mayhem lay beside me, his arm draped across my stomach, the heat of his body adding to my blissful comfort. I opened my eyes, turning my head toward him and smiling at the sight of him sleeping peacefully.

So this was what it felt like to wake up next to your soulmate. My chest warmed, squeezing my heart in a way that felt simultaneously euphoric and painful. I rolled to my side to face him, and he stirred, snorting gently before his eyes opened, his gaze meeting mine.

"Good morning." I caressed his face, running my thumb

across his cheek.

He sucked in a quick breath and rose onto his elbow. "It isn't morning. I didn't mean to fall asleep." He pushed to sit upright. "How are you feeling? Is the headache gone?"

"Headache?" I furrowed my brow. "I feel fine. Actually, I feel great. Lay back down with me."

He rested his palm on my forehead, his posture relaxing with his exhale. "Thank Lucifer. The fever is gone."

"What fever? I'm fine." I rose onto my elbow and took in my surroundings for the first time. Massive windows provided an amazing view of the bustling city below, and plush, beige carpet covered the floor. My bedroom floor was hardwood, and I didn't own anything made of down. We weren't at home, snuggled into my bed like I'd thought. I scrunched my brow, trying to put the pieces of this puzzling scenario together.

"I'm confused." I sat up fully and ran my hand down the little black dress I wore. I'd slept in my clothes? Well, most of them. "Where's my bra?"

"You complained about the garment multiple times, so I removed it when I laid you down. You are fully recovered?"

"Recovered from what? I can't remember how I got here. Are we in the penthouse? What time is it?"

"Indeed, we are. It's just past two in the afternoon." He brushed his fingers to my forehead, smoothing an errant strand of hair into place. "What is the last thing you remember?"

"Two? I slept all day?" I scratched my head, my fingers getting caught on a knot of tangled hair. "I don't... The amulet. We stole the amulet."

He smiled sadly. "We tried. The shadow witch Hazel took it and locked us in the vault. Do you remember that?"

"I don't." I worried my bottom lip between my teeth, racking my brain for the memories. "I remember Hazel. She was so hot for you, I nearly strangled her, but I..."

The memories came flooding back. She'd let Shade in, and then there was the security breach. And the rift. And... "The fae. Ash! Is she okay?"

"Your sister is fine. She and Chaos helped the others fight. She sealed the rift, and Chaos used his magic to make them forget what had happened."

"Thank the goddess. And Shade and Miles? Are they?"

"Miles is attending to Shade as he recovers. Hopefully, he'll wake up soon so we can be on our way."

"Recovers from what? Why can't I remember?"

"You and Shade cast an unlocking spell that drained you both. You passed out as the vault door opened, and we carried you here so you could rest comfortably."

"Oh. Oh!" His description finally jogged the rest of the missing memories into view. "Hazel is selling it to Adrian. We have to stop her."

I untangled myself from the covers and stood on the floor. My head spun, and I sat on the edge of the bed. "That was one helluva spell."

"You also channeled more of my magic than you ever have before. It's no wonder you slept so long." He sat next to me. "The power I gave you would have killed anyone else. You truly are the most amazing woman I have ever met."

I rested my hand on his thigh, my heart warming at his words. "I'm your soulmate. You have to say that."

He grasped my hand, bringing it to his lips and kissing the backs of my fingers. "I love hearing you say that. I love you, Ember."

"I know." My stomach did flip-flops as he held my gaze. "I love you too."

A giggle bubbled up from my chest, and I pressed my lips together, cutting it off short. "I love you too."

He inhaled deeply, the purple in his irises turning fluid before he leaned in and kissed me. The softness of his lips made me shiver, the slow, purposeful movements of his tongue against mine making me forget the rest of the world existed.

I could have stayed in that moment forever, feeling him, drinking him in, relishing his love. But my brain, ever the strategic bitch, wouldn't shut up about our next steps. I broke the kiss, pulling back to gaze into his eyes.

"We have to go to Worcester. Good goddess, she could have already made the exchange. I need to scry for her. For the amulet." I stood, and thankfully the room didn't tip on its side.

"Your sister and Chaos are following her. They borrowed a car from a rental place."

"Borrowed." I laughed dryly, my gaze locking on the jewel-encrusted dagger lying on the nightstand. "I suppose you borrowed that too?"

"Oh, I have no intention of returning it. Consider it an early wedding present."

Wedding. The word on his lips made my insides twist into

knots. None of us would get to experience the elusive happily ever after fate wanted us to believe we would have. There would be no weddings. No settling down, no starting families. Nothing.

So, stop thinking about it, Em. I pushed the thoughts from my mind.

"Thank you." It was all I could think to mutter. Truth be told, I'd considered stealing the dagger too...before I'd blacked out.

Gah! I'd wasted so much time sleeping. We needed to get moving, but... "I'm starving. Do we have any food?"

"I will order room service while you get dressed. When Shade recovers, we will take the van to Worcester to meet Chaos and Ash."

"Sounds like a plan. I'm going to take a quick shower." I licked my lips, remembering the last shower I'd taken. When Mayhem had taken me.

"As much as I would love to join you," he said as if reading my mind, "we are on a schedule. I'm afraid I would keep you here all day if we became intimate now."

I'd be lying if I said I wasn't disappointed, but he was right. He'd keep me there all day, and I would enjoy every second of it. "Will you order me a burger with extra fries? And the biggest Coke they have."

"Of course." He smiled and strode out of the room.

I tossed my dress and underwear onto a chair and padded to the bathroom, cringing at my reflection in the mirror. My mascara had run, giving me raccoon eyes, and my hair looked like a squirrel had nested on my head again. Lovely.

I showered, using the expensive hotel conditioner to work

the tangles out of my hair, and dressed in my normal fire-proof black pants and shirt. After putting on my boots, I strode into the living room to find all three guys sitting at the table.

"How are you?" I asked Shade as I sank into a chair next to my demon.

"Better now. That's the most comfortable bed I've ever slept in."

"I know, right? I forgot where I was and that the rest of the world existed when I woke up this morn...this afternoon."

"Room service," a woman called over the intercom.

"Come in." Miles pressed the button, and she pushed in a cart draped in white linen, with four plates covered in silver domes. He gave her a tip, and she went on her way.

I devoured my burger before moving on to the mountain of thick-cut fries and washing it all down with a quart of Coke. The guys did the same, and we gathered our gear to load the van. Mayhem hit the button for the elevator, and I cast a longing glance at the penthouse.

"One day, we'll stay in a place like this on vacation," I said. "No beasties to fight. No mysteries to solve. No artifacts to steal."

"No veil to mend," Shade added.

I sighed, trying to ignore the way my heart wrenched at his words. That was the one part I was not looking forward to. There had to be a way to mend the veil with the demons on this side. How could I live if there wasn't?

People cast us strange glances as we filed out of the lobby, which was fair. Dressed in all black and carrying duffel bags rather than designer suitcases, we certainly didn't look like their normal clientele.

A sense of calm washed over me as I climbed into the driver's seat and started the engine. This van was one thing I could manage while my life spiraled out of control. I could turn the wheel and press the pedals and take my team to the roadside motel in Worcester, where my sister and her demon had set up to spy on Hazel.

According to Ash's texts, Adrian, or whoever would be his delegate, hadn't arrived to claim the amulet. With any luck, we'd be there before the exchange went down. Hazel would be lucky if we were. I doubted Adrian planned to pay her a penny.

Most likely, she'd pay him with her life.

CHAPTER 12

MAYHEM

It took three and a half earthly hours to reach the town they called Worcester. The sun sank behind the horizon, painting the sky in shades of deep orange and purple before it disappeared, making way for the moon to reflect its light in silver hues.

The motel in which Chaos and Ash had spent the night resembled a dumpster compared to our New York penthouse, but they assured us Hazel resided in the room next door. Ember parked the van on the opposite end of the building, out of sight from the main road...and Hazel's view. Miles and Shade placed a ward on the vehicle, and we gathered weapons before creeping quietly to room one-twenty-seven.

Two beds, each barely large enough to sleep a single demon, took up most of the space, and a minuscule round table with two stained chairs sat near the shaded window. Ash spoke, though she emitted no sound. In fact, even the heated air blowing from the vent created no audible vibrations.

Ash waved her hand, and my ears popped, her voice becoming clear. "I brought you into the silencing spell so you can speak freely. I also put an amplifier on her room so we can hear her better."

"She hasn't left since we arrived," Chaos said. "She had food delivered once, and she talks on the phone to a friend in New York."

"Any idea why Adrian's making her wait?" Ember curled her lip at the untouched bed and took off the thin, brown covering before sinking onto the edge of the mattress.

"We're not even sure he's the one she's meeting," Ash said. "She's spoken to both a man and a woman about it, but we'll find out soon enough. It's going down in half an hour."

"I'm glad we made it in time." I sat next to Ember, and the mattress squeaked as it absorbed my weight. A red ring stained the faux-wood nightstand, and one side of the drawer handle hung loose. "I'm also glad we won't have to stay the night in these sub-par accommodations."

"You spent four centuries in prison, and you're worried about sleeping in a seedy motel?" Ember adjusted her position, curling her lip as the mattress springs groaned. "Can't say I blame you."

"Any minute now." Hazel's voice sounded as if she were in the room with us. "You know how melodramatic High Priests can be. He probably wants to meet there for the aesthetic."

I gave my brother a questioning look. "Adrian isn't coming here?"

"He wishes to meet her in the cemetery across the street," Chaos said.

"That tracks." Shade laughed dryly and sank into a chair. "She's not wrong about the melodrama. Remember his throne?"

"Why are we waiting for Adrian to arrive?" I asked. "Could we not break down her door and take the amulet now, saving all of us the trouble of dealing with the High Priest again?"

"Good question." Ember patted my thigh. "Why are we just sitting here?"

"She doesn't have it on her person," Chaos said.

"She hid it somewhere before she got here." Ash rose and padded to a sink at the back of the room. "Apparently, she wore it on the drive over and it's already affected her. She's been bragging to her friend about how strong the wards she put on the amulet and her room are."

An array of bottles sat on the counter, and Ash arranged them in her bag. "I tried scrying for it, but she hid it well. We'll have to follow her when she leaves and wait for her to uncover it. Shade can cloak us."

"She can see through my shadows." Shade drummed his fingers on the table. "Can't you mind control her and make her hand it over?"

"We tried that too," Ash said. "The wards she set up are stronger than anything I've experienced. If she hadn't checked in under her real name, we'd never have found her."

"Yet you were able to amplify the sounds of her warded room..." I arched a brow.

"The amulet made her stronger, not smarter." Ash

shrugged. "She's not letting anything in, but she didn't bother herself with noise getting out."

"As far as she knows, we're still locked in the vault." Ember rose, turning left and right, but there was no room for her to pace. She sat back down. "She's got dollar signs in her eyes. I doubt she considered someone might try to intercept it."

"What about her?" Hazel's voice drifted through the wall. "Unless she can conjure four times what she offered, she's not a player in this game. The High Priest offered me twenty grand."

Ember's brows crept toward her hairline. "She has multiple prospects?"

"That explains why she's been negotiating with a man and a woman," Ash said. "I didn't make the connection that it could be two different buyers."

"I'm going to demand forty," Hazel said. "Because, Mom, with forty, we can keep the house."

We remained silent, waiting for her to speak again.

"I'd like to see them try," she continued. "It made me so strong. You'll see. I'll be home tonight with *fifty* grand in my pocket and more power than all our ancestors combined. I have to go... Yes, I'll be careful. Blessed be."

Hazel's lock disengaged. The door opened and closed. Miles pulled back the curtain slightly, watching her as she exited the motel. "She's heading to the cemetery on foot. Maybe she hid the amulet there."

Ember rose and stretched the tension from her neck. "Here's the plan. Shade, you'll cloak us. Like you said, seeing through shadow is active magic. She's so distracted with the thought of money, she might not use her power."

"And if she does?" Chaos asked.

"We'll do our best to stay out of sight." She slipped past me and stood at the foot of the bed. "Ash, can you make our bubble of silence mobile?"

"I can do that."

"She is away from her ward of protection." I stood and moved toward the door. "We could grab her now. Put her out of her misery if she refuses to cooperate."

My witch held up a finger. "Everyone is keeping their misery intact. Understood? No more dead bodies."

I spread my hands, conceding. "I understand, though she did attempt to kill us. You would have suffocated slowly had you not mastered the unlocking spell."

"She's in the cemetery." Miles let the curtain fall into place.

Ember clutched our stolen dagger, filling it with fire magic before handing it to Shade. "Just in case."

"I don't..." He started to protest but clamped his mouth shut and accepted the weapon, also accepting his magical limitations. He was the only one of us who could not throw magic at a distance.

"Let's head out. The moment she grabs the amulet, we move in." Ember turned to me. "Subdue her, but do *not* kill her."

If anyone else spoke to me in this manner, I would make a point to kill Hazel the moment I saw her. But Ember wasn't anyone else. She was *my* witch, and I would gladly obey her every command.

Or do my best to obey. I could make no guarantees.

We filed out of our tiny room, and though Shade's cloak

turned the world gray around us, we kept to the shadows. Our team remained silent, the weight of the task at hand settling on our shoulders, the fate of this world a heavy burden on our backs.

How easy it would be to grab Ember and whisk her to the Underworld, ridding ourselves of the encumbrance. A witch of her power would survive the transition. Her sister had proven that. She would technically be dead when she reached Hell, therefore unable to return to this realm.

But she would be mine for eternity.

Though, if I took her against her will, she would be certain to make eternity a *living hell* for us both. I chuckled, wondering how Discord was fairing with Cinder. If she were half as feisty as her sisters, he would no doubt be suffering.

"Something funny?" Ember asked, drawing me from my rumination. We had crossed the street and now gathered behind a mausoleum, out of Hazel's line of vision. She peeked past the wall, pressing her fingertips to the stone.

"Not at all," I said, my thoughts turning to darkness. Their plan to mend the veil involved bringing Cinder back from the dead. They couldn't possibly understand the consequences of such an act. Without Lucifer's blessing, the feat would be nearly impossible, and even with his approval, necromancy was dark magic. They had already cast a phoenix spell to bring me back. What would performing the darkest of dark magic do to their vim...their souls?

"Your sister—" I began.

"Shit. Adrian's here with his posse." Ember ducked behind

the mausoleum, leaning her back against the white stucco wall. I could see her heart pounding against her chest.

"There's something—" I tried again to discuss the issue we'd have with Cinder, but she cut me off, holding up a finger.

"Shh. Listen." She leaned her head against the wall and closed her eyes.

"Where's the amulet?" Adrian asked, his voice grating on my nerves the same way it had when we'd encountered him last.

"Where's my money?" Hazel answered with a question of her own.

I moved in front of Ember, the urge to pull her into my arms, open a rift, and run to Hell so strong, I nearly did just that. Instead, I leaned to my left, peering around the building to witness the attempted exchange.

The same witches we had encountered before fanned out around Adrian as he scoffed. "Gray, who's with her?"

His shadow witch narrowed her eyes, and I stepped back, out of view. "She's alone as far I can see, but..."

I waited a beat or two for Gray to finish—she no doubt had qualms about Hazel's strength since she had the amulet in her possession—but she trailed off, leaving her opinion unspoken.

"We'll wire you the money when you hand over the amulet," Adrian said. "Where is it?"

I peered around the mausoleum again. Hazel had her back to us, and Gray no longer squinted, so I stepped closer to get a better view.

"Mayhem!" Ember whisper shouted, though Ash's silencing spell still held strong.

"I'm not an idiot." Hazel crossed her arms. "Set up the wire. Show me you have fifty K ready to send me, and then I'll get the amulet."

The High Priest laughed, the noise sounding like it belonged to an exaggerated movie villain. "Our agreement was twenty."

She shrugged one shoulder dismissively. "I have another buyer lined up if you don't want it."

"Who?" Adrian asked. "Are they from Salem? I highly doubt they have the funds available to beat my offer."

"The Salem witches tried to steal it." Hazel shifted her weight to one leg, resting her hand on her hip. "I left them in the vault in New York."

Ember tensed beside me, her energy shifting into fight mode. Good. I would love to tear Adrian's head from his neck. Perhaps I could use it as a bowling ball in the Underworld. The Severed Heads League had invited me to join their ranks before Isabel imprisoned me.

"Does she have it yet?" my witch asked through clenched teeth.

"She has not revealed its location," I said.

Chaos moved beside me, his expression grim. "Do you feel it? Focus on the veil."

I shifted my attention from the imbecile witches playing with a force they could never fully comprehend to the energy around us. The low vibration of the Underworld registered immediately, making my arm hairs stand on end.

"A rift is forming." I scanned our surroundings but found no visual clues. Not yet. "Wait. There are two."

"I feel them both as well," Chaos said. "Ready yourselves for company. We aren't the only ones preparing to intercept the amulet."

Ember unsheathed her sword while Miles and Shade clutched daggers in each hand. Ash rubbed her thumbs against her fingertips, making them spark before adjusting the strap of her bag.

"Bring it on," Ember said.

"One rift is there." I pointed to the shimmering line of red forming three feet away. It hadn't yet opened, but the energy from the being wishing to cross over was palpable.

"Let's seal it before anything gets through." Ember gripped her sword in one hand and offered the other Ash. They spoke the incantation, and Ash dusted the tear with her potion. The red line faded, closing before it could fully open.

Adrian laughed again, drawing my attention to the exchange. "Did one of them have purple hair? And one with blue?"

"Purple, yes. A woman with two men. I didn't see anyone with blue."

He laughed harder. "You locked the High Priestess of Salem in a vault. I suppose I can give you a bonus for getting her out of my hair." He snapped his fingers at a male witch. "Hector, pull up the wire transfer and change the amount to thirty thousand."

"I want fifty or I'll take it to the other buyer."

Adrian arched a brow. "You'll take thirty and hand it over... if you value your life."

Hazel shifted her weight from foot to foot, crossing and uncrossing her arms. "Forty-five."

Adrian inclined his chin, tilting his head in warning.

Hazel's posture deflated. "Okay. Thirty. Show it to me."

Adrian jerked his head toward her, and Hector showed her a phone. I was too far away to see the contents of the screen, but Hazel nodded and stepped away.

"It's a deal," she said.

"It's about damn time." Ember stepped around the wall to stand next to me. "You said two rifts were forming. Where's the other one?"

I focused on the vibrations in the air. "Behind Adrian. I believe it's from the fae realm."

"I agree," Chaos said. "The question is, did Adrian invite them?"

"Doesn't matter." Ember clutched her sword with both hands. "We're here for the amulet. Let Boston deal with their own problems."

A blast of power shot through the rift, blinding light enveloping us, the force of the wind so strong, Adrian and his witches stumbled. Three fae soldiers entered our realm, the first latching onto Hector so quickly he didn't have time to gasp before the creature plunged his talons into the witch's chest and ripped out his still-beating heart.

CHAPTER 13
EMBER

"Well, that escalated quickly." I crept toward Hazel, planning to drag her away from the fray and force her to give us the amulet, but another, bigger fae crawled through the massive rift.

This one had glistening wings like a dragonfly and round, faceted, silver eyes protruding from his forehead. An array of stone-like extensions circled his skull, or the top of his exoskeleton head, or...whatever these buggy bastards had...in the shape of a built-in crown, and soldier number one lowered to one knee, holding the heart up like an offering to the big guy.

Adrian dropped to his knee like the follower he was, and his minions cowered behind him while poor Hector lay heartless—and liverless—at the fae's feet.

"Ignacus," Mayhem growled beside me, his lip curling in disgust before he sucked in a sharp breath. "Another rift is forming."

"Adrian said they weren't planning an invasion here." Ash clutched a potion bottle in one hand and held a ball of fire in the other.

"Adrian lies." I crept a little closer. "They all do. Is our silencing spell still intact?"

"For now. Want me to reinforce it?"

I shook my head. "Take Shade and Miles around the mausoleum and get behind them. Seal the rift before any more fae get through."

"My shadow won't reach that far," Shade said. "I won't be able to cloak you."

"Same goes for the silencing," Ash said.

"That's okay. Things are about to get messy, anyway." I jerked my head, urging them to go, and turned my attention back to the display before us.

Adrian, still kneeling in faux deference, held one hand behind his back and twirled his finger, quietly gathering the air toward him and answering our question. No, the cocky High Priest did not call the bug men to this little shindig.

Ignacus, the half-blooded fae prince, accepted the offered heart, opening his wide mouth and revealing a set of dagger-like teeth. Gooey saliva strings stretched from the top row to the bottom, making my stomach sour, and I tilted my head, scrunching my brow.

How could this guy be a prince and look so much like the lesser fae we unaffectionately called overgrown mosquitoes? Wait... Did the fae king get it on with a...?

That would be like a Great Dane going for a Chihuahua. Ew. I shook away the thought.

A squelching, chomping sound drew my attention back to the moment, right in time for me to watch Ignacus devour Hector's heart and move on to his liver.

He made a clicking sound in his throat and wiped the blood from his face with a clawed hand, completely missing the dribble running down his chin. "What happened to our deal?" He straightened his spine and inclined his head, looking both regal and ridiculous at once.

No, not his spine. I kept forgetting these guys wore their skeletons on the outside. *So gross.*

Adrian looked up at Ignacus. "It's still on. I came to get the amulet, and I was planning to give it to you."

"That was not the deal." He wrapped his long, spindly fingers around Adrian's neck and hauled him to his feet. "You were to find the amulet and send word of its location."

Adrian fisted his hand, ending his call on the wind. "I did. The auction," he squeaked. "I gave you all those witches. The amulet was there."

Hazel took a tentative step backward. I clung to the edge of the mausoleum, doing my best not to draw attention. Olga looked at Hazel and gave her head a tiny shake before her gaze locked on me. Her eyes widened, her mouth dropping open with her gasp.

I pressed a finger to my lips, shushing her, and crept forward a little more. So far, the fae were focused on Adrian and his minions. If I could just grab Hazel...

Ignacus growled. "You gave us witches who knew our weak spots. Your blue-haired woman shouted orders to the rest.

They slaughtered my men. Only one got away before she sealed the rift."

"That wasn't my work." Adrian swirled his finger again, finally realizing his lies and excuses weren't going to save him. "The blue-haired one is from Salem. They're your enemies, not us."

"A witch is a witch. Where is the one you sent to take my amulet?"

"Shit." Hazel turned to run, but Olga hit her with a binding spell, stopping her mid-stride.

"Apprehend her," Ignacus shouted at his soldiers, who turned on their glamour, becoming nearly invisible in the dark night.

Adrian raised his hand and slammed a gust of wind against Ignacus's head. The fae stumbled, losing his grip and allowing Adrian to jerk away and dart behind Olga and Gray.

A shimmer appeared in front of Hazel before a soldier grabbed her and dragged her toward his leader. I hurled a fireball at the culpable fae. Mayhem threw one a split second later, and the soldier dropped his camouflage.

His pincers opened and closed, poisonous goo dripping from them as he dropped Hazel and lunged for me. I sidestepped, smacking his back with my sword and letting him plow past me, into my demon. Mayhem caught him by the throat, and Chaos plunged a taloned hand beneath a breastplate, ripping out the creature's heart.

"One down, three to go." I sheathed my sword and clutched Hazel's arm, hauling her upright. Mayhem grabbed her around the waist and carried her behind the mausoleum while Chaos charged into the fray.

"I'm going to unfreeze you." I gripped her shoulders, pressing her against the wall. "And then you're going to tell me where you hid the amulet. If anyone else gets their hands on it, life as you know it will end. I'm talking catastrophic consequences. Do you understand?"

Hazel's eyes, the only part of her body she could move, darted back and forth. Why had I wasted my breath? If Olga's binding spell worked like ours, Hazel wouldn't remember a word I just said.

"The rift is sealed," Ash shouted, "but there's a new one with another beastie trying to get through."

"Go help them," I said to Mayhem.

"But the amulet—"

"I'll take care of it. Go."

He raised his hands, giving me a weird look before shaking his head and joining the others in the battle.

"What was done is now undone. Break this bind and restore her mind." I tightened my grip on Hazel's shoulders, leaning all my weight against her as I repeated my warning. "Tell me where the amulet is so I can save the world."

The witch had the audacity to laugh in my face. "Unless you've got sixty grand in your pocket, you can screw yourself."

"What part of the world ending don't you understand?" Now would be the perfect time for Ash's mind control thing she and Chaos did. Could Mayhem and I do it...? It didn't matter because I had sent him away, dammit.

Hazel laughed again. "I have problems of my own to deal with. The amulet is mine. I'll find another buyer."

"The hell you will." I sent a wave of heat down my arms and out my palms. I didn't burn her shoulders. Not yet, but I would if I had to. It wasn't very light witch-like, I knew. But *it's for the greater good* had become my excuse for doing anything unsavory lately.

"Get your hands off me." She narrowed her eyes.

"Not until you tell me where you hid the amulet." I turned up the temperature to a slow roast.

"That's not happening." She wove her hands upward, between my arms, and grabbed the back of my neck, pulling me forward with otherworldly strength while simultaneously kneeing me in the gut.

I swear my stomach nearly shredded on my spine and came out my back. The ridiculous thought of *how the hell did she get so strong* flashed through my mind, but I knew the answer. She'd worn the amulet for three hours. Of course she was strong.

Hazel shoved me into the wall, my head hitting the stone with a *thwack*, and sprinted toward another tomb. I gave chase and tackled her, but she wiggled free and kicked me in the shoulder, dislocating it with a *pop*.

I ground my teeth, groaning, a slew of cuss words flying from my lips as she dove into a mausoleum. Stumbling to my feet, I clutched my useless left arm, holding it against my body.

Shouts, grunts, and more cuss words sounded to my right. I spun toward my team. Ash kneeled next to Gray, smearing a salve on her injured neck, while Chaos knocked a soldier off his feet. Mayhem charged toward Ignacus, but effing Adrian sent a tornado for my demon, knocking him backward before he could reach the prince.

Miles hurled an energy ball at the second soldier, making him stumble, and Shade raised a hand toward the creature, attempting to suck the life from his body. I glimpsed the back of Olga's head as she high-tailed it out of the cemetery, and a massive beak protruded from a rift, followed by a feathery head with enormous golden eyes.

"Please tell me that's not another chicken-snake." I took two steps toward Hazel's mausoleum when Ignacus let out a screech, the sound so loud, it hit me in the chest, knocking me —and everyone else—to the ground.

Hazel grunted behind me. I pushed myself to sitting and turned toward her. The amulet dangled from her fingers as she clambered to her feet. "Holy shit. Is that a griffin?"

I followed her gaze to the beastie, which was definitely not a chicken-snake. This creature had the head of an eagle and the body of the biggest lion I had ever seen. It shrieked and stomped its murder mittens, making Hazel freeze in her tracks.

My instincts turned to fight, and I shot to my feet, unsheathing my sword with my good arm. The griffin prowled toward us. Hazel whimpered. I sent fire licking up my blade and swung. The griffin took to the sky.

Did I mention the beastie had huge, feathered wings?

I had never seen a griffin in real life, and apparently, neither had my team. We all stood there dumbfounded for a second, and that second was all our foe needed to gain the upper hand.

A soldier grabbed Shade by the throat and Miles by the hair. Ignacus lunged for Chaos, tackling him to the ground while the other soldier knocked Ash onto her back, pinning her to the dirt and dripping poisonous saliva onto her face.

Adrian narrowed his eyes at Hazel and lifted his hands, creating a cyclone of grave dirt around her. She coughed and gasped, scratching at her neck as her supposed buyer sucked the air from her lungs.

Panic made my blood run cold. I used to say I could kick anyone's ass with both hands tied behind my back, but now, with one arm dangling like a limp yogurt slinger, I knew what a crock that was. I couldn't save them all...couldn't save any of them unless I acted, but for possibly the first time in my life, out of the three Fs, my body chose to effing freeze.

I stood there impotent, useless, watching... No, not even watching. My mind all but blanked while everyone around me hung on the precipice of death.

"Ember." Mayhem's voice shattered the ice, and my mind kicked into overdrive.

I lunged at him, grasping his hand. "Use me. Use my energy and make the violence stop."

"I can't stop violence, my love. I cause it."

"Not with me, you don't." I focused on the sigil warming my injured arm and pushed my magic into him.

He sucked in a breath and closed his eyes, but now was not the time for him to bask in my essence.

I squeezed his hand. "Send it out. Stop them before anyone else dies."

"Mmm...yes." He opened his eyes and shared his energy with me, drawing more of mine into him and causing the air around us to thicken. Our magic mixed and melded, and as he sent it outward, I gasped. Every nerve in my body fired at once, electrifying me, heightening my senses, sharpening my vision until I could see the griffin in the sky as clearly as if it were on the ground.

The fighting stopped. The fae soldiers backed away from my team, smacking into each other and looking confused as all get out. Adrian blinked at me, cocking his head, and Ignacus rose, offering Chaos a hand up.

Hazel sucked in a massive breath and dropped to her knees, the amulet falling from her grasp. Both Adrian and Ignacus lunged toward it. I would have done the same if I weren't busy keeping everyone from killing each other, but it wouldn't have mattered if I'd tried.

The griffin swooped from the sky, half-screeching, half-roaring, and snatched the amulet from the dirt before flying off, into the horizon. My mouth hung open as I watched it ascend and head toward the distant mountains.

"Well, what now?" Shade asked, drawing my attention to our current issue, which involved three teams ready to murder each other at the first crack of our magic.

"We will leave peacefully." Ignacus bowed slightly. "My soldiers require enzymes to remain in this realm, but we will not take them from you." He waved an arm, slicing into the fabric of reality and opening a rift to the fae world. "We will obtain the amulet another time. Do not doubt it."

The two fly-men stood at attention as their prince slipped through the veil. When they followed, the rift slammed shut, stitching itself back together. The air around us shimmied. No, not the air.

The veil.

It was as if a wall existed on every plane, like I could reach out in any direction and touch it. It was everywhere and nowhere at the same time, and my brain could not comprehend the ethereal geometry.

Squeezing my eyes shut, I shook my head before blinking them open again. Mayhem's magic still flowed through me. Adrian stood there looking as dumbfounded as I felt, and Hazel made the most of our inaction, doing an about-face and sprinting out of the cemetery.

My muscles trembled with the wavering walls, the pain in my dislocated shoulder screaming with my magical exertion. I tugged from Mayhem's grasp, breaking our magical hold, and everyone around us gasped.

"I had it." Adrian glared at me, his hands curling into fists. "I could have ended him with its power."

"There are six of us and two of you." I rested my hand on my hip, wishing I could cross my arms. "What are you going to do?"

He sniffed, lifting his chin like a spoiled, stubborn child. "Where did your griffin take it?"

"It's not our griffin, and I have no idea." But I hoped to Hecate our demons did because, otherwise, we were screwed.

Adrian moved his chin from side to side like a cow chewing cud. "Let's go, Gray. You've got scrying to do."

She swallowed hard. "What about Hector?"

"Leave him for the vultures," he said, locking his gaze with mine for a moment before he turned and walked away.

"Was he trying to say we're the vultures?" I asked.

"Half of what he says doesn't make sense," Gray whispered, hesitating to follow her leader. "Will you...?"

She moved toward me, lowering her voice even more. "I know you don't owe us anything, but will you cremate him? The thought of him being eaten is..." She visibly shuddered.

I wanted to tell her to go eff herself because she was right. We didn't owe them a damn thing. But if that were one of my friends laying dead on the ground and I didn't have the power to do it myself, I'd probably ask the same thing.

Nobody deserved to get eaten.

"We'll take care of him," I said.

"On one condition," Mayhem added. "You must distract Adrian. Do whatever you can to stall him so that we may reach the amulet first."

"I..." Fear rounded her eyes, and her lower lip trembled.

"Just go." I rolled my eyes. "Bow to your master, kiss his ring or suck his toes, or whatever the hell it is you do. We don't need your help."

She gave me a blubbery nod and scurried away, leaving us to deal with the bodies of an overgrown bug and the unfortunate witch who'd gotten in his way.

CHAPTER 14
EMBER

"Holy Hecate. What day is it?" I leaned on the steering wheel, squinting at the sea of brake lights ahead of us.

"It's the twenty-ninth. Halloween is the day after tomorrow," Ash said, her voice grim. I had never felt such ominous doom coming from my little sister, but she had every reason to embody it.

Halloween was the biggest tourist day of the year in Salem. The day humans packed themselves into our quiet little town like a can of biscuits waiting to burst. The day the normally thinnest part of the veil became its absolute thinnest, and they had no clue it was all about to fall apart.

I'd seen it. When I'd held Mayhem's hand and we'd shared our magic, the veil itself had become visible to me. I'd felt it too. Even in Worcester, seventy miles from Salem, the entire fabric of reality was about to unravel around us.

And an effing griffin had taken the one thing that could've saved us all.

"How is your shoulder?" Mayhem asked from the passenger seat.

"It's fine." I waved off his concern. Yes, it had hurt like a beast while it was dislocated, but once Ash popped it back into place and applied her healing salve, I couldn't even tell I'd been injured.

It had taken a good half hour to cremate the fae, but Hector had turned into ashes in seconds. I felt bad for using my boot to spread his remains in a cemetery so far from home, but I sure as shit wasn't packing him into a box and returning him to Adrian the asshat.

"Come on, people." I laid on the horn, though I knew it would do no good. Traffic inched forward, and my fatigue inched further and further up my spine, threatening to pull me under. If we could just make it two more blocks, I could take a side street and get us home.

In the meantime, we might as well make use of our time. "Tell me what you know about griffins."

"Who are you asking?" Shade said from the way back seat.

"Anyone who knows anything." I tightened my grip on the wheel. "Why would it take the amulet?"

"I'm searching the witchy web," Ash said. "It's hard to distinguish between what's real, what's popular fiction, and what every random Dungeon Master in the D and D world has made up about them."

"The griffin took the amulet for one simple reason," Mayhem said. "They like shiny things."

I barked out a laugh. "Wait. Are you serious?"

"She was probably drawn to its power as well," Chaos said. "And to ours."

Mayhem nodded. "Three beings of royal descent in one place. A High Priestess and Priest from rival covens. Air and fire magic. I'm surprised the griffin and the fae were the only ones who got through."

"I thought the more power a being has, the harder it is to cross over," Miles said.

I leaned my forehead on the steering wheel and closed my eyes. "Hecate's hold is slipping. Remember Cinder's letter? They're doing what they can to keep it intact, but 'even the goddess can't hold it forever.'"

A horn blared behind me, the offending noise like a dagger to my eardrums. I jerked my head up as a blue SUV jutted onto the shoulder and passed me, filling in the single car length I'd let grow between our van and the sedan in front of us.

"Asshole." I straightened, leaning my neck from side to side, stretching the tension in my muscles. Mayhem reached across the console and dug his thumb into the sorest spot as if he could feel exactly what hurt.

He massaged from the base of my skull, down to my shoulder, and back up again before letting go and winking. "I'll get the other side for you when we're home."

I grinned. "You better. Because now I'm lopsided." How odd was it that I could still enjoy the flutter in my belly his flirting caused? If I were a good High Priestess, my thoughts would have been laser-focused on saving my coven. Instead, giddiness bubbled in my gut from simply being near him.

"I found an article on Witchipedia," Ash said. "It has links to sources, so maybe it's true."

"What does it say?" I inched the car forward, nearly kissing the SUV's backside as I turned on my brights.

Mayhem laughed. "You are much more patient than I am. He'd be missing a bumper by now if I were driving."

"Can we not cause a fender bender tonight?" Ash glared at me through the rearview mirror. "We have enough on our plates."

I dimmed my lights. "What does the article say?"

"Griffins reside in the Underworld and rarely cross the veil." Ash slid her finger up her screen, scrolling the page. "Females line their nests with gems and other shiny objects so they can find them from the sky."

"Does the Underworld have a sky?" I asked.

Mayhem chuckled. "You know our realm isn't actually *under* yours, right? We don't live in a cave in the ground. It's another dimension, parallel to yours."

I gave him the side eye. "Of course I know that."

"Then why did you ask?" He arched a teasing brow.

My belly fluttered again. "Because I'm tired and lopsided. So the griffin is making a nest somewhere in this realm. What else?"

"They nest in the mountains." Ash continued to scroll. "When her eggs hatch, she'll nurse her young until their wings are strong enough for them to fly away."

"Nurse?" Shade sounded perplexed. "A mammal who lays eggs. What other anomalies do you have in the Underworld?"

"It's not that unusual," I said. "Platypi are mammals who lay eggs."

"Platypuses is the right way to make it plural," Ash said.

"Thank you, grammar police." I blew out a hard breath. "You know what? Screw this."

I jerked the wheel to the right and plowed up the shoulder to turn down a side street. The main road was normally the fastest route home, but there was nothing normal about... well...about this entire year. I took the back roads, going the long way around Salem so we could enter the town from behind the mess.

"So, we have a momma griffin about to lay eggs, the key to our salvation lays in her nest, and we have no idea where she decided to build it. We can scry for it, but how the hell will we get to it on the top of a mountain? And how will we get her and her eggs back to Hell?"

"Griffins are generally docile creatures. They won't attack unless you agitate them...like trolls." Chaos gave me a look, and yeah, okay, I deserved it.

I had agitated a troll, and we'd had to kill the poor beastie because of me. But I was getting better at not causing trouble. Someone should've acknowledged my progress, right? Baby steps were still steps, and I was a changed woman. I was in the process of becoming one, anyway.

"If she's already laid her eggs, us just getting near her nest will upset her." Ash swiped away the article and laid her phone in her lap. "Moms are vicious protectors of their babies."

I turned left and made my way up the alley, a sense of relief washing over me as I pulled into the driveway behind our house. I allowed myself to feel peace for a moment before opening the door and sliding out of the van.

"Tonight, we sleep." I opened the hidey hole and pulled out my sword. "Tomorrow morning, we scry. After that...I guess we're climbing a mountain."

"You have no idea the mountains we will have to climb." Mayhem slid his arm around my waist and took the duffel bag from my hand.

"That's why we're going to scry." I grabbed another bag of equipment and headed for the door.

"There are things you need to know." He lowered his voice to a whisper and walked beside me. "We'll talk inside."

Well, that didn't sound ominous at all. Honestly though, I was too tired to talk. At the moment, my one priority was snuggling with my demon and falling asleep in his arms. Something I wanted to do every night for the rest of my life. My heart wrenched at the thought.

This could be the last night I ever spent with Mayhem. *Ever.* Halloween was in two days. Once the sun came up, we'd have until midnight to get the amulet, summon Discord, bring back my family, and mend the veil.

Then...he'd be gone forever.

If we failed? The curse would come to fruition, and Ash would kill me...if the veil didn't unravel and kill us all first. Either way, fate would tear us apart. *Fickle, fickle bitch.*

A sob rolled up from deep within my soul, but I caught it in my throat. I tried to swallow it, but the damn thing was the size of a baseball. Tears gathered on my lower lids as I led the way upstairs. I could not let my team see me like this.

"Set your alarms," I said as I dropped the bag onto the counter and tugged Mayhem toward the hall. I caught a glimpse of Ash before I turned into my bedroom, and the expression on her face nearly made me lose it.

She realized what was about to happen too.

I dragged my demon into my room and locked the door before hanging my sword above the bed. A tear slid down my cheek, and I wiped it away, trying to compose myself before I turned to face him.

He rested his hands on my shoulders. "We will figure out a way."

"Will we?" The sob hanging out in my throat finally surfaced, racking my entire body as it flowed past my lips.

He squeezed my left shoulder, massaging it for a second before sliding his arms around me, pulling my back against his front. "Bringing your sister back will be difficult at best, but it can be done."

I laugh/sobbed as another tear rolled down my cheek, and I twisted in his arms to face him. "That's not what I'm thinking about right now."

His lips parted, sadness softening his eyes. "We will figure out a way for us as well."

"Don't." I rested my palms on his chest, pushing him away. "I don't need you to lie to me. We both know how this has to end. I just wish..."

He pulled me to his chest, wrapping his arms around me firmly. "I will do whatever it takes."

I leaned into him, laying my head on his shoulder and letting him hold me. "I just wish I'd accepted all this sooner.

Deep down, I think I knew from the moment we summoned you. I wasted so much time."

"Nothing has been wasted." He tucked my hair behind my ear and kissed the side of my head. "We are together here, now, in this moment. We should cherish it."

He was right. I'd been so busy thinking about next steps, planning, leading... I'd become High Priestess and lost myself. Before everything happened, I lived in the moment. I appreciated little things, experiences. I needed to bring that part of me back. It was the only way I'd survive the aftermath.

I pulled away to look at him, and another tear slid down my cheek. "I love you, Mayhem."

He wiped it with his thumb and smiled softly. "And I love you."

Rising onto my toes, I pressed my lips to his. He held me tighter, neither of us moving, both of us frozen in a combined state of despair, determination, and downright anger. His lips parted, and he kissed me harder, bringing his hand to the back of my head before touching his forehead to mine and closing his eyes.

"We will..." he began.

"Please don't." My throat thickened. "If I keep thinking, it will paralyze me. Just..."

I stepped out of his embrace and traced my finger over his sigil. "I know I'll have to remove this before you go home. Promise you'll never forget about me."

My throat, my heart, my stomach, my soul...every fiber of my being twisted and turned, my nerves and emotions so raw, I could have melted into a puddle on the floor without noticing.

Mayhem's Adam's apple bobbed, his lips parting and closing like he wanted to keep assuring me that we'd be together forever and always. But he knew better too. "For the rest of my existence, not a single moment will ever pass when I don't think about you."

He stepped toward me and cupped my face in his hand, kissing me slowly, purposely, drinking me in like...no, not like... *because* this could be the last chance he would get.

I slipped my hands beneath his shirt, my fingertips memorizing the cuts and dips of his muscles, the silkiness of the trail of hair leading downward from his navel. Firm sinew contrasting with soft skin. The creature from Hell simmering beneath the surface of the most amazing man I had ever met.

"Why?" My voice trembled. "Goddess, why did it have to happen this way?"

"Hecate had nothing to do with this. Fate wove our story long before she was born." He grabbed the back of his shirt and tugged it over his head, dropping it on the floor.

Stop thinking, Ember. Enjoy this moment and forget it's the last. I kicked off my boots and continued memorizing his body with my hands and my eyes.

And my tongue.

I kissed his chest and ran my fingers down his arms to lace with his. His nipples hardened beneath my tongue, and as my teeth grazed one, he sucked in a breath. Releasing his hands, I took off my shirt and bra, tossing them next to his discarded shirt.

His pupils dilated, and he licked his lips, slowly unbuttoning his pants and shoving them to the floor. We continued undressing, our gazes never straying from each other's, until every article of clothing we'd worn lay in a heap next to my bed.

We stood there for a moment, looking at each other, once again frozen in the moment. He caressed every inch of my body with his gaze, and I inhaled deeply, reveling in his low vibration as it washed over me.

Based on past experience, this was the part where his pupils should constrict. He should prowl toward me, he, the predator, I, his prey. Instead, he gently trailed his fingers up my arms to my shoulders.

He stepped closer, a look of adoration in his eyes that nearly made me turn into that puddle after all. I sat on the mattress, moving to the center as he crawled on top of me and covered my body with his. The warmth of his skin and his spiced, fiery scent made my head spin in a good way, the passion-drunk look in his eyes telling me he enjoyed the same things from me.

Never in my life had I needed anyone the way I needed him now. I wanted all of him. I wanted to give him my all in return, so I opened to him, allowing my magic to rise to the surface and flow from me to him. Not just through our joined hands like normal. No, this time I let my magic seep from every inch of skin touching his.

A soft growl rumbled in his chest, and one corner of his mouth lifted into a lopsided, satisfied grin before he kissed me, slipping his tongue into my mouth to tangle with mine.

He glided a hand downward, between us, and teased my folds. He slid one finger inside me, then a second, and I gasped, the sensation stronger than I had ever felt before.

"Your sense of touch is heightened while you share your

magic with me." He pulled them out to circle my clit before sliding them back inside.

"Ya think?" I laughed, not because it was funny, but because this was yet another experience I wished I'd had before tonight.

"I know." He pulled his fingers out and pressed his tip against me. "I can see it in your eyes." With a deep inhale, he opened himself to me, allowing his energy to wash over me, to meld with mine.

It felt like I was coming to life. Like my first twenty-seven years on Earth were just a dress rehearsal, and now, this demon was showing me how to live. My skin turned to gooseflesh as our breaths found the same rhythm and our hearts beat in unison.

He filled me with one swift thrust, and we became one. One heart, one body, one soul. Fate had bound us together, and I knew in that moment I would never love another man. I couldn't if I tried.

He made love to me slowly, his gaze never straying from mine, the adoration in his eyes palpable as we shared our bodies and our magic. His every touch electrified me, the delicious friction as he moved inside me like nothing I had ever felt before.

My core tightened, the orgasm exploding through my body without warning, setting my nerves ablaze. I gasped at the sensation, and he moaned his approval, but his rhythm didn't cease.

He kept going, kissing one side of my neck, and then the other, tangling his fingers in my hair as he pumped his hips faster. Another wave of ecstasy crashed through me, tearing apart my being and weaving it back together, stronger than it was before.

The third time I came, he did too. He groaned, his face contorting with pleasure as he slammed into me three times before burying himself so deeply, we could have actually become one being.

He collapsed on top of me, nuzzling into my neck, our hearts still beating in unison, our breaths slowing as we came down from the climax together.

"This time was different." He drew his magic inward and rose onto his elbows. "You tamed the demon in me."

I smiled and brushed a strand of hair from his forehead. "I would never try to tame you. Whether you're in demon or human form doesn't matter. They're both you, and I love them both equally."

Anguish flashed in his eyes before he rolled to his back and pulled me to his side. "I can't imagine existing without you."

"Then don't imagine it. Hold me like the night will last forever." I rested my head on his chest and draped my leg across his hips. "Feel everything now so you'll never forget."

He kissed the top of my head. "A million years could pass, and this moment would be as fresh in my thoughts as it is now."

"Good." I snuggled closer and tried not to fall asleep. I wanted to cherish the moment, to bask in it for as long as possible, but Morpheus had other plans for me.

I couldn't say how long the god of sleep gave me before he dragged me under, but the morning sunlight slicing across my eyes couldn't be ignored. Never had I ever been so reluctant to wake up and start my day, but I had to.

I blinked open my eyes and found my demon lying on his side, watching me sleep. "Good morning," he said. I didn't miss the sadness in his voice.

"I guess it's time to bring Cinder home." I ran a hand down my face and lightly slapped my cheeks, trying to wake myself up. "After we complete all the other tasks on the list."

His brow furrowed. "Once we obtain the rest of the amulet, summoning Discord should be simple."

"Thank the goddess for that." I pushed to sitting.

"But there is something you need to know about your sister." He sat up, his gaze searching mine. There was something in his eyes. Something...off.

"What do I need to know?"

"She's..." He blew out a hard breath. "Cinder is dead."

I laughed.

He didn't.

"What?" I pressed the sheets to my chest and scooted toward the edge of the bed. "Are you serious?"

"I'm afraid so."

CHAPTER 15
MAYHEM

"How could she be dead?" Ember's brows drew together, her eyes rounding. "She's a Holland. She's powerful enough to survive the transition across the veil. It wouldn't shred her. It couldn't. She sent us a letter. She…"

"No one truly survives the transition to Hell." I reached for her hand, but she pulled away.

"And you're just now telling me this?" Her voice held a shrill edge. "The whole plan all along was to summon both of them. To bring Discord *and* Cinder back to this realm and then bring back our parents. Why…?"

"To be fair, I've tried to have this discussion with you on several occasions. I—"

She shot me a fiery glare that cut the words off in my throat. Perhaps now wasn't the time for my defense.

"So, she's dead. Stuck in Hell for all eternity?" She rose and gathered our discarded clothes, dropping them into a hamper.

Gods, she was beautiful. Sunlight filtering through the blinds illuminated her fair skin, giving her an ethereal glow. Three faint scars marred her stomach, claw marks, no doubt, but they didn't take away from her beauty. They showed her strength.

"Hello? My eyes are up here." She snapped her fingers, drawing me from the trance her exquisiteness had put me into. "Can we bring her back?"

"It's possible." I rose and straightened the bedsheets.

"Care to elaborate?" She crossed her arms.

"It's true a witch of her caliber can retain her corporeal form when she passes through to Hell. I have no doubt your sister's body remained intact. Your mother's too. I don't know your father's lineage, so his survival is questionable."

A pained look flashed across her face. "You really need to work on your delivery."

"I'm sorry. I don't know how else to put it." I strode to the dresser and took out a clean set of clothing. "There is hope."

"What will it take to bring them all back?" She gathered a stack of clothes and strode into the bathroom.

I followed, pausing in the doorway to dress. "Unless you wish to employ a necromancer—and break every law your higher power has created for your kind—their safe passage to this realm will require the most demanding act of magic you have ever cast."

"I can deal with that." She shoved her toothbrush into her mouth and scrubbed.

"It will also require Lucifer's blessing."

She spat into the sink and rinsed her mouth. "Lucky for us, we have a direct line to the King of Hell. You can call him up and ask, right? Easy-peasy."

"If only it were." I joined her in the bathroom to brush my teeth as she finished dressing. "We've been absent from our posts for four centuries because of our involvement with a witch. He is angry with us at best. Convincing him to assist us with yet another witch encounter will not be easy."

She laughed dryly. "Witch encounter? You make us sound like aliens."

I shrugged. "To our realm, you are." I brushed my teeth and returned the toothbrush to the stand.

Ember padded to the bedroom and put on her boots. "And if we went the necromancy route, could we bring them back without his blessing?"

"Yes, but you would face the consequences of your Higher Power if you were caught. You would suffer in this life and then face Lucifer's wrath when your time here is through."

"We'll figure it out. I'll do whatever it takes to save my family." She strode toward the door and stopped, turning to me and resting a hand on her hip. "Don't tell them she's dead. It's possible to bring her back, so she's still alive to us. Got it?"

"I do."

"And don't mention necromancy or requiring Lucifer's blessing. Don't mention anything because we can't accomplish any of it without the amulet. We have to focus on one thing at a time."

"Understood. And I will work on my delivery for future bad news."

She shook her head. "We don't have time for more bad news. Let's go scry for the amulet."

I followed her to the kitchen, where she filled a copper bowl with water before setting it in the center of the table. She gathered candles and herbs and readied the space for scrying while we waited for the others to join us.

Chaos and Ash were the first to arrive, and Ash went straight to the coffee machine, starting the brew before nodding at Ember's setup. "I need some caffeine in me before we do this."

We remained silent, listening to the machine rumble as the water dripped into the carafe.

"Oh, good. Coffee," Miles said as he and Shade entered the room. "I was thinking..."

"Careful..." Ember took six mugs from the cabinet. "Too much of that can get you into trouble."

He chuckled. "Right?"

Shade sat at the table. "Doesn't it seem odd that the griffin showed up exactly when it did? It was too random to actually be random."

"You think someone summoned it?" Ember poured the coffee into mugs and handed one to me.

"It's just a thought." Miles carried two mugs to the table and sat next to Shade. "Chrys summoned the basilisk to slow us down. Maybe Adrian or the fae summoned the griffin."

"I'm still impressed that you fought such a beast." I poured sugar into my coffee and stirred it with a small spoon before taking my seat at the table. "Taking on the griffin will be easy-peasy." I winked at Ember as I used her expression.

She fought a grin and sat next to me. "Assuming the griffin still has the amulet. If Ignacus or Adrian summoned it, they could've already taken it and sent the griffin on her way."

"Well, then..." Ash sat down and gulped her drink before holding out her hands. "Let's find out."

Ember slipped her palm into mine, but Shade hesitated, his gaze flicking from my face to my hand.

"What's wrong?" Miles asked, taking Shade's and Chaos's hands.

"My energy overwhelmed him in the vault," I said.

"It didn't overwhelm me." He laid a tight fist on the table. "I'm just not used to it like she is."

"Let's trade places." Ember tapped me on the shoulder. "I'll filter it for you."

"Perhaps Chaos and I should sit this one out." I rose and pushed my chair beneath the table.

"We can't do it without you." Ember twisted in her seat and grabbed my hand, the desperate look on her face giving me pause, making me want to sit down again and hold her hand. To hold on to her for eternity.

But the only way I knew to make that happen would be whisking her away to the Underworld. I took a breath, imagining the centuries we could spend together. Then I thought of what our passage through...that of a demon prince and an elemental witch...would do to the veil. What it would do to her world and everyone in it.

"Yes, you can." I tugged from her grasp. "You've been scrying without us for years. You don't need our help."

Hurt flashed in her eyes, and I quickly continued, softening my delivery. "I say this for your team's sake. You were built to handle every part of me, my magic included. Think of what it felt like when you channeled Chaos's power and double it... quadruple it. That's what it feels like for them."

She stared at me, not saying a word.

I rested a hand on her shoulder. "Your team needs you to do this without us."

"You've gotten used to the extra power boost," Shade said, "but once they're gone, you'll have to live without it. Might as well get used to it."

Ember's neck stiffened, her shoulders drawing inward slightly. She tried to mask her reaction to Shade's words knifing her heart, but she could not hide her feelings from me. Anger at his callousness simmered in my chest. This was what Ember meant about delivery. Shade had stated a fact about which there was no dispute, but his choice of words and tone of voice had caused my witch unnecessary anguish.

I was tempted to plant my fist on his jaw, but I refrained. Acting on my instincts in such a way would only make our quest harder.

"Shall we, brother?" I motioned toward the door before I lost my ability to abstain.

Chaos stood and rested his hands on Ash's shoulders, bending to kiss her cheek before following me into the kitchen. "We'll be downstairs."

We left the witches to their scrying and descended the

steps, stopping in the library. He picked up a stack of tomes and carried them to a bookcase, but he didn't put them on the shelf. Instead, he set them on the floor and retrieved the feather duster lying haphazardly in the middle of an aisle.

"How did you and Ember stop us all from fighting in the cemetery? Even I felt the urge to make peace when you channeled her magic." He swiped the feathers across the shelf, making dust billow in the air. Frowning, he dropped the duster and opened a cabinet containing cleaning supplies.

"We mimicked you." I shrugged and paced in front of the desk. "She held my hand and focused her magic into my mark. It mixed with mine, and I sent it outward. Same as you and Ash."

My brother sprayed a fine mist onto the shelf and used disposable towels to wipe away the dust. "We can only affect one person at a time. What you did was nothing short of impressive. Good work."

I opened my mouth, ready to retaliate with a quip, but I closed it again, turning on my heel and pacing away from him. I couldn't remember a time when he'd paid me a compliment. I had no idea how to respond.

"We must find a way to return to this realm after we mend the veil," I said. "I cannot exist without Ember. She is as essential as the air I breathe."

Chaos lined the books on the shelf. "I've been considering our options for weeks." He sprayed another shelf with cleaning fluid and wiped the dust. "The outcome will be grim at best."

"There must be something we can do." I continued pacing, clasping my hands behind my back. "The witches belong to us.

With us. Fate would not send the missing pieces to our souls only to rip them away. Perhaps Lucifer…"

Chaos laughed dryly. "We've been away from our posts for too long. We'll be lucky to receive his blessing to bring Cinder back."

My heart sank. "I know."

Silence descended upon us, only the sounds of my brother's cleaning and my footsteps filling the room as the gravity of our predicament pressed harder on our shoulders.

If the fate of our eternal happiness rested on Lucifer's whims, we were…as Ember so eloquently put it…royally screwed.

"I believe he'll allow Cinder to return for the simple fact that he wants the veil to remain intact," Chaos finally said. "I highly doubt he'll allow their parents safe passage. They made a deal with a demon and must face the consequences."

My stomach soured. "Cinder did as well. Ash and Ember too."

Chaos stopped cleaning. I stopped pacing. We stood there, our gazes locked, each of us waiting for the other to spout a brilliant solution. My heart sank deeper and deeper, taking a swim in my stomach until the vise yanked it back to my chest, clenching it until I was certain it would burst.

I peered at the floor, willing an idea…or even an inkling of one…to form in my mind. Aside from dropping to our knees and begging Lucifer for mercy, I had nothing.

"I love her." I forced the words over the lump in my throat.

"I know." He tossed the towels into a trash bin and sank

into the desk chair. "I love Ash too, but the only solution I can think of is taking them to Hell with us."

"Ember would never agree to that."

"Neither would Ash. I already asked her." He opened the drawer and pulled out the small, rolled parchment Cinder had sent across the veil. He used two fingers to unroll it, but he let it go, allowing it to return to its previous state.

"I am sorry for the Cerberus incident," he said, "and for joining Discord in mocking you. You've shown immeasurable restraint in this realm. Your strength is formidable, and I'm proud to call you my brother."

Again with the compliments. My gut reaction was to throw an insult his way, but I had noticed a change in him as well. Being in this realm had changed us both.

No, the realm had nothing to do with it. "Ember makes me a better man."

"As Ash does me." He unrolled the parchment again and scanned the words. "Hopefully Discord has a plan. He's been in touch with Hecate at the very least."

I stood behind him and read the letter over his shoulder, scanning the last three sentences repeatedly:

There's an amulet somewhere on your side. You have to find it and summon Discord so he can return it to its rightful owner. I can't come home without it.

"He's already done it." I leaned forward and tapped the final lines. "The rightful owner is Lucifer. Discord has bargained for Cinder's safe passage home, and the amulet is the price he'll pay."

"Maybe." Chaos returned the scroll to the drawer. "But the amulet belongs to Hecate as much as it does Lucifer. The goddess has been holding the veil together. Perhaps Cinder bargained with her, promising the amulet in return for her assistance while Ash and Ember complete their quests in this realm."

My heart sank yet again. That idea made more sense. Hecate was livid when Lucifer lost the amulet to Discord, and she had held the grudge for centuries.

"Speculating is pointless." I walked the width of the room before turning around and striding back. "At this point, it doesn't matter to whom Discord plans to give the amulet. We don't have all of it, so we should focus on retrieving the final piece."

"Hey, guys," Ember said, descending halfway down the stairs. "We found it. Come on up."

CHAPTER 16
EMBER

"The griffin has it, but she's on the move." I paced in front of the television while the others took seats in the living room, just like old times. Well, all but Mayhem.

"How do you know she's on the move?" He stood between the kitchen and living room, shifting his weight from foot to foot, more restless than I'd ever seen him.

"We felt the amulet in motion when we scried," I said. "When we pulled back, we saw her flying. She hasn't laid her eggs yet, so we assume she's looking for a place to nest."

"Or for a way home," Ash said.

I nodded. "She seems agitated. She knows she needs to nest, but something is stopping her."

"How do you know she hasn't laid her eggs?" Mayhem took a few steps toward me before dropping into his usual chair. "Perhaps she's searching for food."

"Her belly is distended, and her mannerisms say she's about to give birth." I stopped pacing and rested my hands on my hips. "So, the question is, how do we call to her and convince her Salem is the place she needs to be?"

"The veil is thinnest here, even with Hecate's magic holding it together," Ash said. "If she's looking for an easy path to the Underworld, this is where she'll find it."

"But if she's going to nest in this realm," Miles said, "Salem isn't the place. We have over a million tourists coming and going this time of year. Every hotel within twenty miles is completely booked. It's loud."

"You're right. It's way too noisy for nesting here." I sank onto the arm of Mayhem's chair and tapped a finger to my lips as an idea formed in my mind. It was a terrible, horrible, no-good idea, but it was the only one I had.

"The griffin is from the Underworld. I know she's not a demon, but can you call to her? Will she be attracted to your power?"

"All creatures from the Underworld are attracted to our power, especially in this realm," Mayhem said. "But she won't blindly obey us like a demon would. She will need an incentive to come here, even if we connect with her."

"And the noise of the city will scare her away," Chaos said. "Griffins are docile, solitary creatures. She'll choose quiet over whatever we have to offer."

"Maybe not." I stood and resumed pacing. "We'll head to the outskirts of Salem, past the residential area and into the woods where tourists rarely go."

"Where we fought the shedim," Ash said. "It's quiet there,

but the guys said we need some incentive to convince her to come. What are you thinking? A mound of birdseed?"

"Griffins are carnivorous," Mayhem said. "A mound of raw meat would entice her more than seeds, but not enough to draw her here. You have something else in mind, don't you?"

He flashed a conspiratorial grin, making my stomach flutter. "You want to open a rift, an invitation for her to go home."

I smiled in return. "That's exactly what I want to do."

"You're both crazy." Ash shot to her feet. "Are you sure I'm the one who's cursed? Because that maniacal grin you're sharing...? You look like you both need to be hit with a binding spell and a straitjacket."

"Opening rifts is what started all this trouble," Miles said. "I don't think creating another one is going to solve our problems, especially this close to Halloween."

"That's the worst idea I've ever heard," Shade said.

"It's brilliant," Mayhem said. "She'll head straight for the rift. We'll intercept the amulet, usher her through, and seal it behind her."

"It sounds easy enough," Chaos said.

Ash parked her hands on her hips, looking from me to the demons as if we'd grown eyeballs where our ears should be. "Name one thing about this entire ordeal that has happened easily."

I inhaled, ready to spout a string of answers, but not a single one came to mind. Nobody said a word as we looked at each other. Shade's brow furrowed in concentration, and Miles drew his shoulders upward, lifting his hands and looking just like the *I don't know* emoji on my phone.

"Exactly. But..." Ash dropped onto the couch next to Chaos. "I don't have a better idea. Anyone else?"

"No." Miles sank further into his seat, and Shade shook his head.

"Then we're in agreement. Let's—" My phone buzzed, so I dug it out of my pocket. Patrice's name lit up the screen as I swiped it open.

"Hey, you're on speaker." I set the device on the coffee table. "How are things?"

She missed a beat before she replied. "Tomorrow is Halloween."

"We're aware," I said. "How's your team doing? Everyone still accounted for?"

"So far, but activity is picking up. We took out a horde of vampire ghouls last night."

I tapped my foot on the floor. "That's standard stuff. Has anything bigger gotten through? Any trouble with the fae?"

"Not recently, but tomorrow is Halloween," she said again.

I rubbed my forehead, wishing people would stop stating the obvious and offer solutions instead.

Rustling sounded through the phone, followed by a cabinet opening and closing. "I ran out of wolfsbane and stopped by your house yesterday to borrow some, but I couldn't get in. Why the super strong wards? Did you find all the amulet pieces?"

"No, but we'll have them by the end of the day. Stay vigilant. Things will get worse before we make it all better."

She hesitated. "So the demons are..."

"Sitting right here," Ash said.

"Oh, okay... Who has the missing piece?" Patrice asked.

"A griffin. Long story." I grabbed the phone. "Did you have anything else to report?"

"No, that's it."

"Keep us posted. We'll do the same." I hit End and returned it to my pocket.

"Poor Patrice," Ash said. "She's a healer thrust into a fighting position."

"We've all had to step out of our comfort zones." I rose and headed toward the hall to get my sword. "Gather your things. We need to summon a griffin."

AFTER ASH RESTOCKED her spell kit and gave us speed and strength sigils, we loaded our weapons into the van and headed for the woods where we'd encountered our first demon. Of course, now I knew the shedim wasn't Ash's first demon. She'd already summoned Chaos and brought him along for the ride, but that didn't matter now. I might be dead if he hadn't taken up residence in her mind, so who was I to complain?

I parked along the side of the road, and we filed out, gathering our knives and swords and bundles of enchanted rope before creeping deeper into the trees. Clouds blanketed the sky, casting the forest in an eerie shade of washed-out gray, and dry leaves crunched beneath my boots as we made our way to the clearing.

No remnants of the teens' poorly cast circle remained. If I didn't know the story, I'd have no clue a mid-level demon had feasted on a wannabe witch's makeshift coven nearly a month ago.

To be fair, we'd had nothing to do with those kids summoning the shedim. They'd done that all on their own, but I doubt they would have accomplished it if we—my family—hadn't already thinned the veil and started this mess into motion.

I couldn't bring myself to count the number of bodies we'd left in our wake. The sheer amount of death and destruction, caused by the very people who were supposed to keep Salem safe, seemed infinite. I paused, letting my team walk ahead of me.

Mayhem stayed by my side. "What troubles you?"

I laughed dryly. "Take your pick."

He rested a hand on my hip. "This is something new. Tell me what you're thinking."

I shrugged one shoulder and shook my head. "I don't want to believe this is all happening because of us. My family. If our mom would have been honest with us from the start, if Cinder hadn't taken matters into her own hands... We caused this."

"No, Isabel caused this when she cursed your bloodline. The Holland witches are not to blame."

"Do you know why she cursed our bloodline? Did she ever tell you?"

He lowered his gaze. "I never asked."

Something between a sob and a laugh rolled up from my chest. "She cursed us because my great-great-times-however-many-greats grandma stole her man and founded the coven she was planning to build."

I waited for him to respond, but he remained silent.

"So, yeah… The Holland witches are to blame." I stepped toward the others, but he grasped my hand.

"I'm sure your ancestor had no way of knowing the ramifications, and anyway…" He cupped my chin in his hand, bringing my gaze to his. "When fate brings two people together, there is no use fighting it."

"Don't you dare give me the 'everything happens for a reason' spiel."

"Some things do. Some don't. We shouldn't focus on what might have been while ignoring what is. That kind of thinking paralyzes people. Believe me, I know." He dropped his hand to his side.

"Are you ready, brother?" Chaos called from the clearing.

Mayhem looked at me, silently arching a brow. He was right. Guilt was a paralyzing, useless emotion, and we didn't have time for my pity party. He offered his hand, and I took it, allowing him to lead me into the clearing to join our team.

I left my sword sheathed and tugged the rope I carried from my shoulder, adjusting the lasso end until it was balanced properly for throwing. "You're sure she won't try to eat us?"

"Not entirely." Mayhem moved next to Chaos.

I lowered the rope. "Not the answer I was expecting. You said they were docile."

"I said they were docile unless provoked," Chaos answered. "So don't provoke her."

"Because lassoing and hog-tying aren't provocational at all." I clenched my teeth, closing my eyes and reminding myself we were on the same team. "I'll try my best. At least they're not venomous."

I tilted my head and batted my lashes, giving my sister's demon the best demure face I could pull off. "Or are they?"

Mayhem chuckled. "They are not venomous, though their claws are razor-sharp and massive."

"Note to self: Steer clear of the murder mittens. Got it." I readjusted the rope. "She wasn't far from here when we scried. Do your thing, and we'll catch her."

"Hold on! I'm here," Patrice shouted as she scurried through the trees, her ginormous medical bag bouncing against her hip as she ran. "Sorry it took so long. I used the main road like a dummy."

She stopped in her tracks when she reached the edge of the clearing and smoothed her hair back into her ponytail. Her gaze cut between the demons a few times before she focused on Ash. "I've got sutures, salves, and everything in-between."

"Umm...?" I gave Ash a quizzical look.

"She texted and wanted to help." Ash adjusted her rope. "We're about to trap a magical combination of two apex predators, so I figured there might be injuries for her to heal."

"That's fair." I nodded.

"Plus Inga and Luis are driving me bonkers. You'd think they were married with how much they argue." She let out a nervous laugh and took a tiny step away from the demons.

"Also fair," I said. "Mayhem and Chaos are about to work their demon magic to create a mental connection with the griffin. Once they do, they'll open a rift and invite her to go home.

Before she passes through, we'll trap her and get the amulet. Then we'll let her go and seal the rift."

"Sounds better than getting covered in ghoul goo." She lifted the shoulder strap over her head and carried her bag to a nearby tree. "Why rope and not a binding spell?"

"Of the animals in the Underworld, griffins are near the top of the chain," Mayhem said. "A bind strong enough to hold a mother ready to lay eggs would deplete your vim for hours. I'm afraid we have very little time remaining to complete our quest."

She returned the bottle she'd grabbed to her bag and pulled out a set of green crystals instead. "I'll be ready if you need me."

"Everyone else ready?" I asked.

My team nodded, and I gave the demons a thumbs up. They closed their eyes and breathed deeply. Miles kept his gaze glued to the sky, while Shade's bounced between the demons and the treetops. Ash stared at Chaos intently while Patrice dug through her bag, doing her best to ignore the palpable low vibration building in the air.

At least, the vibration was palpable to me. I watched Mayhem work, a sense of peace washing over me as he and his brother called to a beastie that could murder me with a single swipe of her mitten.

Crazy, I know, but the man had that effect on me.

I focused on the sigil glowing softly on my arm, and his vibration grew stronger around me, inside me. I could feel him reaching out into the ether, searching for the griffin's signature, and when he found her, it felt as if I had found her too.

Her vibration was unmistakable, not as low and strong as the demons, but definitely not of this world. Ash inhaled quickly, no doubt feeling the same connection herself.

Our demons raised their arms in unison, swiping their hands from left to right, tearing through the fabric of the universe and creating a rift...an opening to Hell itself.

I gasped and pressed a hand to my chest as if the gesture could keep the air in my lungs...could keep my boots rooted to the ground.

The glowing red edges of the rift drifted farther apart, creating a massive hole in reality, the earthly realm on one side, utter darkness on the other. I couldn't ignore the pull. It drew me toward it, my feet moving of their own volition, the need to cross through it, to go *home*, so strong, I couldn't have fought it if I tried.

My vision tunneled until all I could see was my soulmate standing in front of the sure path to our happily ever after. My strides quickened, breaking into a run as the overwhelming call from the other side refused to be ignored.

"Ember, no." Mayhem caught me around the waist. "The rift is for the griffin, no one else."

"Don't you feel it?" I clutched his arm. "I know you feel it."

He gripped my shoulders, turning so I faced only him, my back to the rift. "Of course I feel it. I've felt the pull with every rift I've encountered, but I fight it."

"Why?" I grasped his shoulders too. "We can be together there. Forever, Mayhem. Isn't that what you want?"

His eyes searched mine, the purple in his irises growing

fluid, pulsing, drawing me even further into the frenzied madness. "Forever in the Underworld," he said. "Is that what *you* want, Ember?"

"I..."

CHAPTER 17

EMBER

Fear flushed through me, turning my veins to ice and battling with the pull of the Underworld. My nails dug into Mayhem's shoulders as I tried to wrench myself free from his grasp.

He held onto me tighter. "That is the griffin's fear, not yours."

"The hell it is." I turned, yanking my shoulder away, but he refused to loosen his grip. "Let me go."

"Ember, stop." He ducked down to catch my gaze. "Breathe for me, my love. Breathe and focus inward. What do *you* feel?"

Icy veins, nausea, full-on flight mode. "Sheer terror."

"Ignore my sigil and look deeper." He released one shoulder to press his palm to my chest. "What do you feel here?"

I swallowed the thickness from my throat and focused on the sensation of his hand against my heart. His irises returned to their normal amethyst hue, and my pulse slowed to a manageable speed. "I..."

"Have you ever been afraid of me?"

I gave my head a tiny shake. "No."

"Mayhem..." Chaos's voice sounded strained.

My demon raised a finger to his brother, his gaze never straying from mine. "Are you afraid of me now?"

"No, I could never. I want to be with you always. We can if..." I tried to move toward the rift, but he held me tightly.

"Release your hold on me. Close the connection before the Underworld drags you through."

"I don't want to. We need to go through."

"You must. This is too much for your body to bear." He covered the sigil on my arm with his hand. "I'm not going anywhere, and neither are you. Please, Ember, shut it off."

I sucked in a shaky breath and focused on our connection, trying to close it, but the moment it grabbed my focus, I wanted nothing more than to run through the rift, taking my demon with me.

"Please, Mayhem. We have to go."

"No." His grip on my arm tightened, his brow slamming down over his eyes. "Close the connection, Ember. I demand it."

"I can't."

"You can, and you will." His eyes softened. "You must if you want to survive."

I gasped as the sensation of a heavy door slamming rocked my system. A moment of clarity brought the world into focus before the door cracked and my desire to drag him to Hell returned.

"Do it, Ember." He pushed the door closed once more.

My stomach churned and pain sliced through my veins like razors as I tried. I imagined the glow of his mark fading, leaving behind only the black ink from which it was created. Panting with the exertion, I mentally erased the ink, leaving my arm unmarred.

With another deep breath, I closed the connection, finally freeing myself from the grips of...*whatever* that was. "I don't. I don't understand."

"I don't have time to explain. I must help Chaos keep the rift in check." He kissed my forehead and released my arm. "Don't try to connect with me again. Not while this rift is open."

"Okay." My voice was barely audible over my pulse whooshing in my ears. "How...?"

He locked the imaginary door between us, severing our connection from his end and nearly ripping the breath from my lungs. I gasped and turned a circle, my lungs burning, my soul aching as if it had been torn in two...shredded. The rest of my team stared at me with concerned expressions. Even Ash.

"Did you not feel that?" I pointed at the demons.

Ash pursed her lips, her gaze flicking to my arm before she met my eyes. "I felt something, but definitely not whatever you felt."

I huffed, my mouth hanging open as I stood there dumb-founded. What the actual eff had just happened? One minute, I was poised and ready to rodeo with a griffin. The next, I wanted to leave everything behind and jump into the rift.

"She is here." Mayhem's voice sounded normal. No straining since he shared the load with his brother, but I didn't dare turn around to look at him. My legs felt numb, my mind mushy, and my insides tangled and twisted.

I squinted into the sky, but without Mayhem's magic flowing through me, I couldn't see the griffin above us. "Where?"

"She will arrive from the east," my demon said. "You must capture her before she makes it through the rift."

"That's the plan." Ash unwound her rope, holding the lasso by the loop. Miles and Shade did the same while Patrice mixed a healing potion.

My mouth still hung open, so I snapped it shut and shielded my eyes against the sun. I caught a glimpse of my forearm in my peripheral vision and sucked in the biggest, sharpest breath I had ever inhaled.

Mayhem's sigil was gone.

I checked my other arm, in case I'd forgotten where my demon's mark lay—as if that could happen—but only the speed and strength sigils Ash had applied remained on my skin. I rubbed my unmarred skin and glanced at Mayhem. The rift was now invisible to me, the urge to plow through it and spend eternity in Hell gone.

My brow crumpled as I caught Mayhem's gaze. "What did you do?"

"Incoming!" Miles said, drawing me back to our current predicament.

The griffin seemed to glow in the late morning sun, her white feathers gleaming, fading into shiny brown fur. She screeched, sending the forest critters scampering, and I widened my stance, my muscles tightening, my thoughts narrowing, pinpointing on my task.

Because if I stopped to think about what just happened with Mayhem, I might crumble into dust.

The beastie circled above us, half-screeching, half-roaring her disapproval. Shade threw his rope, yanking it back to tighten the loop when it hit her paw, but she flapped her wings, ascending before he could get ahold of her.

A growl rumbled from her chest, and she did a little loop-de-loop above us before perching at the top of a tree. Its branches groaned beneath her weight, a few of the smaller ones snapping and falling to the ground.

"Here, kitty, kitty." I crept toward the tree. "Pspspsp."

"Her head is an eagle." Shade rolled his eyes. "I doubt cat noises…"

"Reow," the griffin replied, her eyes darting in their sockets.

"She's scared. Can you calm her down?" I glanced at the demons.

"We will not harm you," Mayhem said. "Give us the amulet, and you are free to return to the Underworld, where you can nest in peace."

She let out a nervous mewl and adjusted her perch.

"Where is the amulet, guys?" Patrice inched toward the tree, pointing at each paw before circling her finger to indicate the griffin's beak. "I don't see it."

"Neither do I." I strode toward the beastie, my stomach souring. "She must've dropped it somewhere."

The griffin let out an ear-splitting screech. Her claws extended from her murder mittens, her giant bean-toes curling around the branches, snapping them as if they were twigs. I stumbled back as she scrambled to grab another branch, but the tree couldn't support her weight anymore.

She tumbled, smacking her head against the ground before sitting up, stunned. I tossed my lasso, using her temporary immobility to loop it around her neck. She scrambled to her feet, and Ash got a loop around one paw.

"Why are we trapping her if she doesn't have the amulet?" Miles asked.

"She has it," Mayhem said. "I can sense it nearby."

"As can I," Chaos said, "but you must act quickly. If this rift gets any larger, we won't be able to stop the horde gathering on the other side."

"Big demons?" I tightened my loop.

"Many big demons," Mayhem said.

"It's okay, sweet girl." I inched closer, wrapping the rope around my hand to take up the slack as I approached. "Do you have a pouch somewhere or did you drop the amulet?"

She let out a nervous chuffing sound as she eyed our demons and the rift, stomping her paws like a bull ready to charge. I held up my hands, widening my stance and feeling an awful lot like the raptor-tamer guy from *Jurassic World*. There I was, trying to calm a ginormous animal that shouldn't even be in this world, when she could take my head off with one snap of her massive beak.

"What do we do, guys?" I took another step forward, and she growled. "Okay, I won't get any closer. Can you talk to her?" I looked over my shoulder at the demons.

"She's an animal," Mayhem said. "She understands as much as a house cat would."

Patrice said something under her breath. I snapped my gaze to her as she tossed a pint of blue liquid on the griffin's side. "She must have it!" Her voice took on a shrill edge, her eyes widening and her nostrils flaring as she recited a binding spell I'd never heard. "Ties that bind and control. With this spell, I have full hold."

The griffin jerked her head toward Patrice, yanking Ash's rope from her grasp. I'd coiled mine around my hand, so I kept my grip. But as the beastie roared and snapped at Patrice, she hauled me with her, knocking my feet out from under me and dragging me across the ground.

So much for the new binding spell.

Patrice screamed and stumbled into a tree. The griffin huffed and stomped, and Shade pulled out the enchanted dagger, pointing it at the beastie's rump and releasing a blast of Miles's energy.

She screeched and snapped at Shade, swiping out a paw. Lucky for Shade, the tip of her claw barely nicked his arm. Sure, she opened a massive gash in his biceps, but if she'd been five inches closer, she'd have sliced him in two.

"What happened to not agitating her?" I dusted off my pants.

The griffin unfurled her wings.

"Oh, shit."

She flapped, taking to the sky and—since I'd so brilliantly coiled the rope around my hand—dragging me along with her. I grabbed it with my free hand as she ascended, and I hung from her neck like a human albatross, swinging in the breeze as she circled just above the trees.

At least I was right-side-up this time.

"Can you see the amulet?" Chaos shouted from below. "Perhaps it's matted in her fur."

I gazed up at the momma-to-be. Her white eagle feathers blended perfectly into sleek, brown fur. Not a mat to be seen. Her belly was even bigger than the day before, and her udders... or were they called nipples on a lion? Whatever the proper term, they looked painfully red and swollen.

Something in her tummy shifted, her eggs, I assumed, and she let out a deep, distraught bellow that nearly broke my heart. This poor creature needed to nest...now.

"I don't think she has it," I shouted as I climbed the rope. What I planned to do when I reached the top, I wasn't sure, but I was too high to let go and fall. My legs would snap on impact from this altitude.

"She does," Mayhem said. "Use your magic to sense it. She has it somewhere on her person."

Oof. Yet another skill I hadn't practiced in a while. Ash was the one who scoured the thrift stores and collected magical artifacts before the humans could get their hands on them.

The griffin bellowed again and swooped toward a tree. Branches slapped across my arms, cutting into my skin, and I buried my face in her feathers as she unsteadily perched in an oak. The blob in her stomach shifted again, moving closer to the exit, and she huffed out a mewling moan.

"Hey, sweet girl. I'm not going to hurt you." I tentatively rested a hand on her shoulder, running it over her silky fur. "I just need to see if you have the amulet. I don't think you do, but the demons down there insist."

I grabbed a handful of fur and hauled myself onto her back. She made an irritated chuffing sound, and I stroked her, running my hands from her feathers to her fur and focusing on sending soothing energy into her.

"My love is wide, my caring deep. I wish you calm so you may sleep." My mom used to say those words to me when I was a kid and was too wound up for bedtime. My palms warmed, my peaceful intent seeping into her as I recited the spell again.

I continued petting the griffin and glanced at the scene below. The demons no longer strained, which meant they had closed the rift they'd opened. Shade sat with his back against a tree trunk while Patrice stitched up his arm, and Ash and Miles worked together on a potion.

The griffin began to relax, the tension in her muscles easing as my calming energy soothed her.

Me, calm and soothing. Crazy, I know.

With the beastie subdued, I shifted my focus to sensing the amulet. I lay on the griffin's back, resting my cheek against her feathered neck and spreading my arms, creating as much contact as I could. Her low, underworldly vibration registered in my psyche, growing stronger and stronger until my entire body hummed.

Wait. I lifted my head and smiled. That wasn't her magical vibration I felt. She was purring.

"That's a good girl." I laid my head on her neck and tried again. "Confess, expose my magic sleuth. I call on you to reveal your truth."

I didn't think the spell would actually work. Not without a potion to amplify my intent. But the moment the last word crossed my lips, I felt it. The griffin's magic was unmistakable, low and gray. She hadn't come to this realm with ill intent.

I felt Patrice's new binding spell too, though it was nothing like the one we normally used. This bind seemed to be more about controlling the receiver. Forcing compliance. It was an interesting choice for a healer witch, but we were all acting outside our comfort zones lately. Lucky for the griffin...and unlucky for us...she was too powerful to be subdued by Patrice's magic.

The amulet's energy was the strongest. The mix of Hecate's high and Lucifer's low vibrations registered in my being, and I scooted down the griffin's back, following the magical pull and searching for a pouch in her skin where she might have hidden it. She was already an eagle and lion combo. Why not kangaroo too?

I kept moving down, running my hands over her fur until...

Oh no.

I moved up to her neck, straddling her back and leaning toward her ear. "I know the guys said you don't understand words any more than a house cat does, but I think they're wrong. I think you understand me, don't you?"

Her purring intensified.

"We want to send you back home so you can raise your babies in peace, but we need your help first." I dug my hands into her feathers, gently gripping them. "I promise no one on the ground will hurt you. Will you please take us down?"

She let out a noise that sounded half-chirp, half-meow, but the communication I received wasn't audible. I couldn't tell you if she put the words into my mind or if I simply felt what she wanted to say, but her message was clear. She just wanted to go home.

"We'll get you home. I promise." I focused on the strange connection we shared. Could all griffins communicate this way, or was it the amulet's doing? At the moment, it didn't matter. "Please take us to the ground so I can tell my team what's happening."

I felt her compliance a moment before she leaped from the branches. I squealed, tightening my grip on her feathers as she flapped her wings. She circled above the trees, and the chilly autumn air whipped my hair back, stinging my cheeks as we soared.

She swooped toward the clearing at a speed that would surely turn into a crash landing, and I forced myself to keep my eyes open. I was riding an effing griffin! Talk about your once-in-a-lifetime experiences.

We didn't crash., thankfully. Instead, she landed softly in the grass and lowered her front end so I could slide off.

"Put your weapons away," I said. "She isn't going to hurt anyone."

Shade and Miles hesitated, their expressions wary, but they sheathed their knives. "How did you tame her?" Miles asked.

"She was already tame. I only comforted her." I glanced at Mayhem. "And she does understand words."

"Amazing." The look of awe in his eyes made my stomach flutter.

"Did you retrieve the amulet?" Chaos asked.

"About that..." I ran my hand down her silky shoulder. "She swallowed it."

CHAPTER 18
MAYHEM

I couldn't tear my gaze away from my witch. Not only had she tamed a creature from Hell, but she had discovered a way to communicate with it that no one had found before. Ember was the strongest, most capable woman I had ever met, and I was in awe of her abilities. Of everything about her.

And she had almost become mine for all eternity.

By opening the rift to Hell, my connection to her had amplified one-hundred-fold. I could no longer tell where my soul ended and hers began. Nor could she, it seemed.

She had tried to cross over, to take me with her. Why had I stopped her? We could have been done with this quest. All the turmoil and strife we had endured could have ended if I'd simply let her step through the rift.

But the feral look in her eyes, the way she'd behaved... I couldn't tell how much of that was Ember versus an amplified version of my own desires. She wasn't completely herself in that moment, and that was why I stopped her.

Had I done the right thing by removing my mark? I wasn't yet sure, but it was the only way I could think to end her hysterics.

I missed the connection the second we severed it. My love for her remained intact. We didn't need a sigil to recognize that we belonged together, but the magical bond we had shared was no more. I was free to do as I pleased, no longer bound to do her bidding. But the emptiness I felt without it made everything clear.

I would choose to serve her for a million eternities before I would endure a single day without her.

"All she wants is to go home. She didn't mean to come here." Ember stood there, resting a hand on the griffin's shoulder as if they were the best of friends. "As soon as the amulet passes through you, the guys will open another rift and send you home."

"Fabulous," Ash said. "The fate of the world lies in the timing of a griffin's bowel movements."

"All we can do is wait for her to pass it." Ember shrugged. "Let's hope she has to poop before she lays her eggs. I'd hate to shove them through a rift not knowing where they'll end up."

"The demons can carry them through when they go home," Patrice said, the tone of her voice indicating the moment couldn't come quickly enough for her liking.

I narrowed my eyes, unable to stop the growl rumbling in my chest. "We are already home."

"That's a sensitive subject." Shade laughed humorlessly. "I've learned not to bring it up."

"I have ipecac syrup." She held up a brown bottle, ignoring the warning. "If you can convince her to drink it, she'll throw up."

"It's already in her intestines." Ember glided her hand down the griffin's side. "The only way it's coming out is through the back door."

The griffin let out a pained groan and lay on her side, the eggs shifting inside her visible beneath her fur. As I stood there in awe of both the creature and my witch, my skin turned to gooseflesh. Vibrations from across the veil registered in my psyche, and I snapped my head toward Chaos, who nodded, confirming my suspicion.

"We must find a safe place to hide her," I said. "The veil is too thin after what we did here. Ember, can you speak to her? Let her know she isn't safe in this location."

My witch kneeled by the beast's head and rested a hand on her feathers. "Can you still move? It's not safe here."

The griffin rolled to her stomach, lying in a sphinx position and watching Ember intently. She let out a quiet squawk and dipped her head as if agreeing.

"She can move." Ember rose to her feet. "She's not in labor yet, but she thinks she will be soon."

"Is she speaking in your mind? Do you hear her voice?" I asked.

"Not really. It's more like I just know." She rolled a length of rope around her arm and handed it to her sister.

"That's an empathic ability," Ash said. "I had no idea you could do that."

"Neither did I." She shrugged. "Go figure, right?"

The goosebumps on my arms turned to pinpricks. "Where can we take her? I can feel the creatures on the other side trying to break through. We must leave this area now."

Ember crossed her arms before tapping a finger to her lips. "We can hide her in the mausoleum where we took out the ghouls. It's big enough for her to lie down, and it's quiet there."

"That's on the other side of Salem," Miles said. "How will we get her there without anyone noticing? She won't fit in the van."

"She'll have to fly," Ember said. "I'll go with her and show her the way. Shade, can you fill the dagger with a shadow so we can stay hidden?"

"I can do that." He held the artifact in his hand and closed his eyes.

"Good. I'll ride her to the mausoleum. The rest of you take the van and meet us there." She tossed the keys to Ash. "Stop by the house and pick up some blankets and whatever we have to feed her. Once we get her settled, Mayhem and I will stay with her until she does the deed."

I smiled as Ember laid out the plan, imagining her commanding a battalion rather than a small coven of witches. She could be a great warrior in the Underworld.

"What will we do after that?" Patrice asked. "I think I should stay with her too. She might need a healer if she gives birth."

"No," Ember said. "I need you to go home and whip up as

many salves and healing potions as you can. Come midnight, all Hell is going to break loose."

"Hopefully not *all* of Hell," Ash said.

Ember continued giving orders. "Miles, see if you can get with Wendy. Find out what Adrian is planning. We haven't seen the last of him. Shade and Ash, scry and see if you can find Ignacus and his minions. They're planning something."

"On it." Shade gave a mock salute and handed her the enchanted dagger.

As the witches gathered their things, I stepped toward Ember and lowered my voice. "I would prefer not to leave your side. Can she carry us both?"

She turned her arm over and gazed at the empty patch of skin where my mark once lay.

"I had no choice." I rested my hand on the small of her back.

She ignored my plea. "Can you carry this big oaf, or is he too heavy?"

She paused, awaiting the griffin's reply. "That makes sense. She said the amulet she accidentally swallowed has made her stronger. She can carry us both."

The others left the clearing, heading for their vehicles, and Ember hoisted herself onto the griffin's back. I joined her, wrapping my arms around her waist, the physical contact filling the void that removing my mark had left behind.

The griffin flapped her wings and rose from the ground to the tops of the trees effortlessly. Ember pointed her in the right direction, and she took off, flying through the late morning sky.

The autumn wind stung my eyes, but I didn't dare close

them. The city below resembled a toy replica, appearing gray, unpainted through the shadow hiding us. In all my millennia of existence, I had never considered riding a griffin. Of course, without my witch's newly found ability, capturing one would have caused the beast unnecessary trauma.

Back then, however, I wouldn't have considered the griffin's feelings. The time I had spent here with Ember had changed me in ways I never could have imagined. I held her tighter, resting my chin on her shoulder.

"It's an amazing feeling, isn't it?" she asked.

"Indeed it is."

We arrived at the cemetery in mere minutes, and though I wanted to ask for a longer ride, now was not the time. Most likely, the time for such leisure would never come, but I couldn't think about that.

The griffin touched down outside the mausoleum, and we dismounted. The trees and gravestones in the cemetery appeared charred, the ground covered in fresh dirt that hadn't yet settled.

"You did more than fight ghouls here," I said.

"Whatever gave you that idea?" She held up her hand. "Stay with her while I make sure it's empty."

I did as she asked, waiting outside the structure and doing my best not to scare away the majestic beast beside me. "I will not hurt you. I swear my intention in calling you was to send you home safely."

I quieted, hoping to hear or feel the griffin's response like Ember could. I received no reply.

"It's clear." Ember strode toward us. "Come inside and rest. Our friends are bringing you some food and blankets."

She gestured with her hand, and the griffin followed her into the chamber. I entered behind the beast and pulled the metal door closed. Ember leaned against a wall as the griffin turned two circles and settled onto her haunches.

"When Ash gets here, we'll set up a ward and cloak her." My witch rubbed her forearm, and my heart wrenched.

I should have felt her touch. My entire body, my soul, should have felt her caress. "Can you reapply my mark?"

She inhaled a shaky breath. "Why did you do it? Why take it away?"

"We both did it. I could not have removed it without your consent."

"I wouldn't have..." She fisted her hands and crossed her arms, pressing her lips into a thin line. "I wasn't myself."

"No, you were not." I tried to hold her gaze, but she wouldn't look at me. The fact that she was not herself was the precise reason I'd convinced her to remove it, but it didn't matter. The deed had been done—by both of us—and now we must face the consequences of my too-quick thinking.

"I wasn't in a state to consent," she said.

"You were an active participant. You severed our connection as I did. It was the only way to stop your hysterics. I couldn't hold open the veil, keep the demons on the other side from crossing over, and call to the griffin while stopping you from dragging me through. Even an immortal prince has his limitations."

She laughed incredulously. "So it's my fault. Is that what you're saying?"

"No, Ember." I strode toward her. "No one is to blame. We did what had to be done."

I took her cheek in my hand, gently guiding her gaze to mine. "It has not changed my feelings for you. We are still soulmates, with or without the mark. Do you not agree?"

She took a deep breath and nuzzled against my palm, her posture finally relaxing. "I agree. I don't like it, but I agree."

She held my hand, pulling it away from her face. "But I wasn't hysterical. I thought we taught you not to use that word in reference to women with emotions."

"You were not yourself." I brushed the hair from her forehead and pressed my lips against it. "Your hysterics came from me."

"How so?" She laced her fingers through mine.

"You were channeling my desires. You could be mine for eternity in the Underworld. I've considered grabbing you and crossing over many times since I came into this realm."

"Why haven't you done it?"

"I could never do anything against your wishes."

"You can now that the sigil is gone." She released my hand to run her finger over the empty spot on her forearm. "You're a free demon."

I gently grasped her shoulders. "The sigil did not bind me to you in that way. Love did. Love does. I don't need a magical connection to tell me what my soul already knows. I belong to you now and for the rest of eternity."

The griffin huffed and laid her head on her paws.

Ember laughed. "She thinks you're too dramatic."

I tilted my head, pinning her with my gaze. "What do you think?"

She held eye contact, letting seconds pass before she spoke. "I belong to you too, and I don't think the desire I felt to drag you through the rift came entirely from you. Checking out of this reality and starting something new sounds amazing right now."

Resting her hands against my chest, rose onto her toes and kissed me. "But thank you for keeping me grounded. I would have regretted it the second the rift closed behind us."

"My only desire is to make you happy."

She ran her fingers along my jaw, stroking my cheek with her thumb. "I know I don't show it, but you're doing a damn good job."

The griffin grunted and closed her eyes, making Ember smile. "I wish we could keep her."

I shook my head. "She would lose herself. Wild beasts aren't meant to be kept."

Ember looked at me, her eyes searching mine, and I prayed to Lucifer she would find everything she was looking for.

Her lips twitched, tugging into a sad smile. "I know you're not."

Chapter 19

EMBER

"I wasn't talking about myself," Mayhem said.

"I know." I pushed from the wall and paced toward the door, tugging my buzzing phone from my pocket on the way. "It's Ash. They're five minutes out."

And thank the goddess for that. I couldn't handle any more sad talk with the demon of my dreams. I sucked at goodbyes, and the finality of ours was ominous. No need to stretch it out from now until the bitter end.

I pulled the door inward and peeked into the cemetery. Everything appeared in full color, meaning the shadow magic I'd borrowed from Shade had fizzled out. We were exposed to the eyes of anyone who might try to venture inside, just as we were exposed to the senses of Ignacus, Adrian, and anyone else who tried to scry for the amulet or the griffin.

Not exactly the safety we'd offered the poor momma.

The minutes inched closer to midnight, to the start of All Hallow's Eve. Normally, my coven would light a bonfire and gather beneath the moon for our annual ritual. We'd give our thanks to the goddess while working in shifts to keep the veil intact until November first was halfway through, when the veil began its return to its normal strength.

We'd managed it well for decades. Hell, probably even centuries. Now, I couldn't begin to fathom what tomorrow would look like. We'd sent way too many powerful beasties back and forth across the veil recently for it to stay intact.

"Are you sure this is a good idea?" A teen girl's voice drew my attention to the left, and I peeked further out the door. She wore a black sweater with a purple witch's hat, which she could have bought anywhere in the city. Everyone sold them, especially this time of year.

"Yeah, it'll be fine." A guy around eighteen walked beside her, a toy store Ouija board tucked under his arm. "I mean it would be better if we waited until dark."

"No!" She tumbled, catching herself on a gravestone before jerking her hand away and wiping her palm on her jeans. "I don't want to be here at night. It's scary enough now."

The back of my throat heated with my annoyed sigh. This cemetery? Seriously? There were plenty of old graveyards where famous...or infamous...Salem residents were buried. This wasn't one of them.

"What's wrong?" Mayhem asked.

"I was hoping not to rack up any more mundane casualties." I rolled my eyes as the guy set the board on a gravestone and rested the plastic planchette in the center.

"Would you like me to get rid of them?" He stood beside me, touching the small of my back.

"I'll handle it." It had been a while since I'd gotten the chance to put the fear of witchcraft into an idiot.

"Put your fingers on the planchette." The guy grabbed the girl's wrist and forced her hand onto the board.

"I don't want to." She tried to pull away, but he held her tightly. "This doesn't feel right, James."

I tugged a dagger from my thigh holster, set the tip ablaze, and strolled toward them. "Oh, James. You really should let the dead rest in peace. You never know what you might stir up."

I touched my index finger to the flat side of my blade, letting the flames lick across my skin.

"It was his idea." The girl scrambled to her feet. "He said we could summon my dog."

James rose and gestured at my dagger. "Where'd you get that? How does it work?"

"It's been in my family for generations." Yes, that was a lie, but I wasn't about to tell him I bought it online. Where was the fun in that?

"Let me see it." He had the audacity to reach toward me, his body language saying he fully expected me to hand it over. If I hadn't been fired, I'd have no doubt I'd see this asshat at Spellbound Axe, getting drunk with his buddies and bouncing blades off the targets.

"Sure." I shot a tiny flame at his hand, singeing his sleeve.

"Ow! What the hell?" He sauntered closer. "Who are you?"

"She'll be your worst nightmare if you take another step forward," Mayhem said from behind me.

James's eyes widened, and he cut his gaze between me, my demon, and the girl. "I don't know what kind of kinky shit you have going on here, but we're gonna walk away and pretend we never saw it."

"That's the first intelligent thing I've heard you say." I extinguished the flames and returned my dagger to its holster.

The girl whimpered, and the guy grabbed her hand. "Come on, Jill. We'll find somewhere else to summon Princess Fancy Pants."

He dragged her away, and I turned around to find Mayhem looming behind me, his horns and talons extended. No wonder the guy changed his tune mid-measure.

I clicked my tongue. "Put those away. You're lucky it's almost Halloween and they can pass as a costume."

"What did you do to them?" Ash laughed as she approached from the direction the kids had run. She carried a bundle of towels in her arms, and her satchel bounced against her hip with her strides.

Chaos carried a stack of blankets, and several grocery bags dangled from his fingers. "He mumbled something about twisted cemetery orgies as they ran for their car."

I waved off their concern. "He was planning to use Princess Fancy Pants to get into *her* pants."

Ash's brow scrunched. "I'm not even going to ask. How's the griffin?"

"She's resting." I took the towels from her and carried them into the mausoleum. "Where are the guys?"

"Scrying. Miles got ahold of Wendy, but she wasn't much help." Ash took her bag off her shoulder and pulled out four railroad spikes. "Adrian has locked himself in his office and isn't communicating with his team, so she has no idea what he's planning. She's waiting outside his door, though, just for Miles."

"Clueless," I said.

"Yep." She rubbed oil on the spikes.

Chaos stepped into the mausoleum with Mayhem behind him. "Where should I put these?"

"Lay them next to her for now. When she gets up, I'll make her a bed." I took the mallet Ash offered and followed her outside.

She handed me a spike, and I hammered it into the ground at the eastern corner. I did the same at the southern before we made our way around the back of the building.

"How does it feel?" She gestured to my sigil-less arm and then pressed her hand to her chest. "Does it hurt?"

"Only when I think about it." I hammered the third spike into the ground, focusing on the vibration shimmying up my arm every time it made impact.

She handed me the final spike. "Do you still…?"

I forced my jaw to unclench. "Love him desperately? Yeah."

Whack, whack, whack. I drove in the last piece and rose to my feet. "Let's get this ward cast before Adrian emerges from his hidey hole."

She took my hand, and we recited the incantations. "Protect this space from malice and harm. If our ward is broken, we will be warned. Hide our auras from all who seek. Our intention is set with the words we speak. As we will it, so mote it be."

My head spun with the amount of vim we put into it, but

we'd recover. We always did, even before we could channel demon magic on the regular. We'd be fine without them… Wouldn't we?

Stop it, Em. Just. Stop.

"That should do it," Ash said. "It would take every witch in Adrian's coven working together to see through that shroud."

"And everyone knows dark witches don't play well with others." I gave her the mallet, and we walked into the building to find Mayhem hand-feeding the griffin raw chicken breasts.

I curled my lip. "You're feeding bird meat to a bird."

"She is not a bird," Mayhem said. "But even if she were, what do you think eagles eat if not other, smaller fowl?"

"I see your point." I sat cross-legged in front of the grocery bags. "Did you bring anything for us? I'm starving."

"Here." Ash opened a bag and pulled out a container of chicken salad and a loaf of bread.

"I guess your credit card isn't maxed out yet?" I used a plastic spoon to scoop out the mixture and spread it on the bread.

"No, it is." She glanced at Chaos. "But we have to eat."

I didn't have the energy to protest, so I handed Mayhem a sandwich before making myself one.

"I also brought this for her." Ash pulled out a jug of water, a plastic bowl, and a white plastic bag with purple lettering.

"Epsom salt?" I poured the water into the bowl.

"It's a natural laxative." She added the salt and stirred it with the plastic spoon. "To help speed things along."

I set the bowl in front of the griffin, and she dipped her beak into it before tilting her head back to swallow.

Ash's phone pinged, and she swiped open the screen. "It's Miles. Still no sign of Ignacus or his soldiers, but the team reported a lesser fae swarm in the Common. He and Shade helped them take care of it."

I chugged a bottle of water. "Tell them to start the All Hallow's Eve ritual now. Every member of the coven is required to participate. No one gets a pass this year. If Hecate is the only person holding the veil together right now, we need to give her all the help we can."

"Only the High Priestess can begin the ceremony," Ash said. "The wood has to be lit by witch fire."

"Which means any Holland can do it, not just the High Priestess. It starts with the founding family and spreads outward. You'll have to light it." I picked up her satchel and shoved it toward her. "Take Chaos and begin the ritual. I'm staying with the griffin until she poops."

Ash gave me her signature look. The one that said everything on her mind, no words required. The ritual always started with the High Priestess. All the ones we had records of anyway. Changing tradition could be risky. I knew that, but I doubted she could name one thing we'd done in the past month that wasn't.

She also didn't like splitting up the team. Neither did I.

"You can call them to do it here if you want, but I'm not leaving her." I took the empty bowl o' laxative and shoved it into a grocery bag.

Ash's jaw ticked, her expression a silent acquiescence. "One fire in this cemetery was more than enough, thanks. I'll get it started in the usual clearing."

"Good. Leave Patrice in charge of the first shift and then go home to set up Discord's summoning circle. With any luck, we'll complete the amulet and join you well before midnight."

The griffin stood and turned a circle, pawing at the blankets and arranging them beneath her before she settled and closed her eyes.

"At this rate, I'll have to poop before she does." Ash swiped open her phone, her brow furrowing as she typed and scrolled.

"What are you looking for?" Chaos asked as he gathered the bags they'd brought.

"When I was little, I swallowed a tiny lion figurine. I remember being in a lot of pain because it wouldn't pass. Dad wanted to take me to the hospital, but Mom tried Joan, our old healer, first. She cast a spell that drew it out. It was... Oh, I think this might be it."

She rummaged through her bag and held up an herb jar triumphantly. "I have everything here." She dropped to her knees and started mixing.

I took her phone and studied the recipe. "This sounds... forceful."

"It is, and it will make a mess. We'll have to take her outside." She sprinkled amaranth into a copper bowl and added a dash of star anise and marjoram. "We'll focus on drawing the amulet out, but pretty much everything in the way will come out too."

"Will your ward protect her outside?" Mayhem asked.

"We only protected the building." Ash scooped a drop of wildflower honey from a small jar but hesitated to drop it into the bowl. "Crappity crap, we should have made the ward bigger. It's not a quick and easy spell."

"So, we'll point her butt out the door." I shrugged and set the phone by the bowl. "Guys, you can stand outside and retrieve the amulet from wherever it lands."

Mayhem clapped Chaos on the shoulder. "Come, brother. We've been banished to the path of the poo."

"You don't have to stand exactly in her line of fire." I rolled my eyes as they exited the building and took up their posts on either side of the door.

"Hey, sweet girl." I stroked the griffin's feathers, rousing her from sleep. "I know you're tired, but we need you to move one more time. This won't be pleasant, but it'll get you home faster."

She grumbled, but she got up and let us arrange the blankets for her by the door. When she plopped down, her tail hung outside. Mayhem lifted it and tucked it inside the building. Ash added two drops of honey to the potion, making it pop and sizzle before she handed the bowl to me.

"Let's get Operation Beastie Bowels underway. We need you to drink this." I set the bowl in front of the griffin, and she sniffed it before turning her head away.

"Please." I laid a hand on her shoulder. "It will help you feel better."

She eyed me for a moment, and my stomach clenched. She'd been compliant so far, but her agitation was growing, even with me. All she wanted to do was sleep. I knew the feeling.

Finally, she huffed and drank the potion. Ash took my hand and rested her other on the griffin's belly. I did the same, and we recited the incantation.

The beastie's abdomen rumbled, her intestines squelching and groaning. When they quieted, we recited the incantation again.

"Focus on the amulet," Ash said. "Use your intent to draw it down."

I felt the stone inside her and moved my hand over it, brushing her fur downward toward her backside. The griffin moaned, her insides cramping. She made sure I knew what it felt like. I had never experienced labor pains, but I imagined it was similar.

Slowly, steadily, the amulet made its way through her intestines. Every time her body stilled, we recited the incantation again, causing the poor beastie more pain, but getting the amulet closer and closer to the exit.

Her stomach bubbled. A puff of noxious gas shot out her backside, the stench so strong it could have melted the eyebrows off anyone in its path. We said the spell one more time. She rumbled and groaned.

"Get ready." Ash massaged her belly.

"Thar she blows!" I covered my mouth and pinched my nose as our spell peaked, showing us its full effect.

And I mean its *full* effect. Capital F-U-L-L.

The griffin's butt cannon did its thing, shooting out everything she'd consumed in goddess knew how long. I expected the forceful blast to travel at least five yards out, taking the amulet with it.

But the prize for the absolute worst timing in the history of showing up at places you weren't supposed to be went to Adrian and his crew.

Three witches stood a few feet outside the door, covered from head to toe in wet, steaming griffin poop.

CHAPTER 20
EMBER

We all stood there in shock, staring at each other, no one moving at first. Miles's friend Wendy flanked Adrian on his left, and Gray, who had dropped her shadow magic when the shit hit the witch, stood to his right. Her lower lip trembled, and she pressed it against her top, not daring to open her mouth and complain.

I couldn't blame her. She had feces dripping down her face and nothing to wipe it off with. *Gross.*

"How did you find us?" I scanned the ground, looking for the amulet. It must have blasted past our adversaries.

Adrian stared at the doorway, narrowing his eyes like he couldn't see where the voice was coming from.

Oh, right. Our ward.

Mayhem stepped away from the building, and Adrian's gaze snapped to him, his expression livid. Chaos tossed a roll of paper towels at Gray's feet, and she picked it up, unrolling several and cleaning herself before passing it to Adrian.

With her face semi-clear, she took a chance and opened her mouth. "Please tell me this isn't..."

"Explosive diarrhea straight from the bowels of Hell?" I crossed my arms. "Yeah, you deserve it for summoning her to do your dirty work." They were lucky the poor beastie hadn't become an egg cannon too.

"We didn't summon her," Gray said, cutting her eyes to her High Priest. "Did we?"

"Hand her over." Adrian cleaned himself up and dropped the rest of the roll onto the ground, not bothering to pass it to Wendy. Typical. She bent to pick it up.

I laughed, still scanning the ground for the amulet. I couldn't see it, so I stepped around the beastie and stood just outside the doorway. "I don't take orders like your minions."

The griffin let out a relieved moan behind me, curling up to rest, and Ash joined me on the front steps. "Do you see it?" she whispered.

I gave my head a tiny shake. "Did Ignacus tell you where we were? I know you aren't strong enough to see through our ward on your own."

"We have our ways of finding information." Adrian jerked the roll of towels from Wendy's hand and wiped his face again before dragging the cloth down his neck. "Your van is parked outside, idiot. Turn over the griffin. The amulet belongs to me."

Wendy blew her nose and gagged. "This is not what I signed up for." She covered her mouth and dry heaved. "Where's Miles?"

I cocked my head. Did she seriously volunteer to be Adrian's henchwoman just so she could see a guy who'd used her... multiple times? Goddess, bless her heart.

Ash crept away from the mausoleum, giving our foul-smelling foes a wide berth as she scanned the ground. It had to be out here somewhere, but the clouds covering the moon made it nearly impossible to decipher the shapes on the ground. Shadows, clumps of earth, and dead leaves littered the cemetery, and even if we had enough moonlight to make the stone glint, it was covered in dirt-colored poo.

"You can't have the amulet or the griffin." I crept away from the door, trusting the ward to keep the bad guys out. "It's four elementals against you and..." I gestured at Gray and Wendy. "You didn't call in much of a calvary."

Ash lit a fireball in her hand, and Chaos and Mayhem followed her lead, illuminating the cemetery. I unsheathed my trusty sword and sent flames licking up the enchanted silver blade, adding to the brightness, but honestly? I preferred the dark over what I saw.

Twenty-something witches, dressed in black from head to toe, emerged from the shadows. They stepped around gravestones and came out from the cover of trees as if appearing from nothing.

They surrounded us, some of their faces familiar, some I'd never seen before. Many had the Boston Society of Magic emblem embroidered in silver thread on their sleeves. Others had nothing showing affiliation to the dark coven, and of those, a few wore ski masks, hiding their identities.

"Did you hire mercenaries?" I adjusted my grip on the

sword, scanning the ground again before meeting his gaze. "Seriously?"

"I'll do whatever it takes to obtain the amulet." He circled his finger, creating the beginnings of a tornado at my feet. "Did you know it was forged in Hell? Anything created in Hell belongs with a dark witch."

He raised his hand, palm toward me, and I had no doubt he was about to give his team the signal to attack.

I cut my gaze to Ash and closed my eyes for a long blink, hoping to Hecate she would understand the message. We weren't going to find the amulet with our eyes. Not in these conditions.

She nodded and inhaled, and we both whispered the same spell, "Confess, expose my magic sleuth. I call on you to reveal your truth."

I shouldn't have been able to tap into her magic from this distance. Normally, we had to hold hands to cast spells together, but golden sparkles appeared in my peripheral vision anyway. I slowly turned my head to the place they gathered on the ground, two yards from Wendy's feet.

Adrian clenched his raised hand into a fist. The witches attacked.

Mayhem turned his arm into a blow torch and blasted hellfire at our adversaries. I dove toward Wendy, extinguishing my blade and swinging the flat side into her stomach like a baseball bat. She doubled over. Then she fell to her knees. Her hands hit the ground, and she gasped.

"Adrian? Is this it?" She lifted the amulet caked in butt dumplings and turned on her knees toward him.

"Nope." I kicked her hand, and the stone flew across the cemetery before whacking into an ancient gravestone with such force, the monument cracked. Good thing the amulet didn't.

"Ash!" I shouted, and she scrambled toward it.

A blade pierced my shoulder, and I spun, lighting my sword. Instinct nearly made me cut the culpable witch in two. I was used to fighting beasties, not people. Lucky for the guy who'd stabbed me, I remembered what he was and only nicked his arm, setting his embroidered sleeve ablaze.

His shirt must've been one hundred percent cotton, because the fire spread like...well, like wildfire...engulfing his entire abdomen. He screamed, frantically turning this way and that, fanning the flames.

"Did no one teach you to stop, drop, and roll when you were a kid?" I called my fire back, leaving him shirtless and burned, as I yanked his knife from my shoulder. That would require stitches. Where was Patrice when we needed her?

Oh, right. I'd sent her home.

The man gritted his teeth and pulled two more blades from their sheaths. He lunged for me.

I stepped out of his way. "Do you want me to make you pantsless too? I'd rather not singe your naughty bits."

His eye twitched, but he backed away. Smart move.

All around me, shouted spells, clashing weapons, and crackling fire created a cacophony of *we don't have time for this shit.*

Ash reached for the amulet, but someone hit her with an

asphyxiation spell. She clutched her throat and fell to her knees, unable to drag in a breath.

I scanned the crowd, searching for the witch responsible. "Chaos, red ponytail."

The witch stood still, her hands raised toward my suffocating sister. This one, I would have gladly sliced in half, but Chaos beat me to it. He snapped her neck as if her bones were made of toothpicks. Her body smacked the earth, and Ash gasped.

Another of Adrian's minions grabbed the amulet. Based on the person's size and curves, she had to be a woman, but the ski mask hid all but her eyes and mouth. She smiled and wiped the poo off the pendant before moving to drop it into her pocket.

"That's mine. You will give it to me," Chaos said, holding Ash's hand and channeling their mind-control magic. If only they could control everyone here and send them on their way.

The woman froze, her hand fisting around the chain. "I think this is yours."

"No!" Adrian sent his tornado toward her, whisking it from her hand and sending it spiraling upward.

"A rift is forming," Mayhem said as he lit a ring of hellfire around us, blocking at least fifteen witches. "Ignacus."

I threw a hand in the air. "For goddess's sake, Adrian. Do you ever fight your own fights?"

"I didn't call him." He reached upward, and his tornado obeyed, spiraling above us. When he fisted his hand, it dissipated, the amulet dropping from the sky. He caught it and cradled it in his hands, closing his eyes and absorbing its power.

When he opened them, a blast of wind shot out around him, knocking me off my feet and extinguishing our ring of fire. The rift opened fully, and five fae soldiers darted through.

The biggest bug man lunged straight for a mercenary, ripping out his liver with one hand, his heart with the other. He kneeled in front of the rift, lowering his head and holding the organs up in offering.

Ignacus stepped through, one spindly leg at a time, and the other fae bowed at his entrance. His mandibles made a clicking sound, his dinner squelching with each bite as he consumed first the liver, and then the heart.

His soldiers joined the fray, no doubt ready to eat every liver and heart still beating in the cemetery. The good thing about his arrival? Adrian's witches were now busy fighting for their lives instead of trying to take ours.

The bad? Ash and I were the strongest, most potent witches they could consume. It was best they didn't find that out.

Still clutching the amulet, Adrian sent a blast of wind toward Ignacus, his newly multiplied magic allowing him to scoop up the fae prince and toss him against the mausoleum wall as if he were a ragdoll.

Our ward on the building sent a shockwave through his exoskeleton, his body convulsing as he landed face-first in the dirt. He jerked his head up and flapped his wings, sending dirt flying everywhere as he shook himself off.

Ignacus made a high-pitched chittering sound, and his soldiers dropped the witches they were tearing apart to descend upon us.

Ash shot a stream of flames at one. Chaos hurled a ball of

hellfire at another. It bounced off the soldier's chest and set an already-scorched tree ablaze.

"Let the record state I am not responsible for the cemetery fire this time." Ash called her flames back and shot out an even hotter stream.

Adrian's idiotic team followed the fae, breaking blades against their armor and wasting their vim on spells that could be fanned away with a flap of their wings.

I grabbed Mayhem's hand. "Make the violence stop."

"You no longer bear my mark. The connection is…"

"It's still there." I squeezed his hand tighter. "Tell me you don't feel it."

"I do, but the magic is not as strong." He threw a fireball at Adrian, who retaliated with a gust of wind, averting the hell-fire's path.

"Then make it stronger." I focused, not on the tattoo once occupying my forearm, but on the real connection I had with my demon. Magical ink hadn't forged our bond. Fate had, and I didn't need a sigil to link to my soulmate.

I opened and sent my magic into him, picturing my light filling the darkness inside him. He inhaled deeply and opened to me, allowing our vim to pass freely back and forth, to mix and meld and become one force. Two parts of a whole coming together, complete at last.

My pulse raced as he sent it outward. Pinpricks danced across my skin, my blood seeming to fizz as he calmed the entire calamity, making everyone freeze and scratch their heads, wondering what they were fighting for.

"Go home," Chaos said to Gray. He held Ash's hand, their

intention apparently to make each witch leave, one by one, as long as we held them in peace.

"Leave this place," he said to Wendy.

She held up her hands in surrender and backed away. "I just wanted to see Miles. Is he still alive? He hasn't sounded like himself in his texts."

"He's fine," Ash said.

"Please hand over the amulet." Ignacus held a gangly hand toward Adrian. "I do not wish to fight."

Sweat beaded on my forehead even though it was only fifty degrees out. I could admit the tattoo had made it a helluva lot easier to pull this off, but here we were, pulling it off anyway.

Adrian scoffed. Then he laughed. "Did you think your mind magic would work on me? I'm unstoppable now." He created a wind funnel around a soldier, lifting the beastie from the ground and cracking the exoskeleton as he drew the air from the fae's lungs.

I slipped a dagger from my thigh holster. As much as I would have loved to watch him implode every fae here, we needed that amulet. Now.

I lifted my arm, ready to throw the blade, when the griffin's pained bellow registered in my psyche. "She's about to lay her eggs. You have to open a rift and send her home."

"I am a bit busy, as are you."

I strained, goosebumps rising on my skin as I flushed first hot and then cold. "I can't do this much longer anyway. Go help her."

"If I release them, you will have to fight."

"Fighting is what I do best."

He looked at me, his eyes searching mine before he nodded once and tugged from my grasp. I sucked in a breath as he turned and strode into the mausoleum. I hurled my dagger at Adrian. The blade sank into his shoulder.

He yanked it out, losing his grip on the semi-crushed fae. The fly man thudded on the ground, and a witch in a ski mask jabbed a knife beneath an armored plate, piercing his heart. She shot to her feet, brushing her hands on her pants before scurrying behind the mausoleum. If she was smart, she'd keep going and not come back.

"It's done." Chaos dropped Ash's hand and stepped away from her. "He has opened the rift."

Good. At least the poor griffin, who'd wanted no part in any of this, could go home and raise her babies in peace.

"I feel another forming," Chaos said. "We must end this before more creatures descend upon us. They're attracted to our power."

"Let them come." Adrian draped the amulet around his neck. "No one can stop me."

The four remaining soldiers encircled Adrian, but he created a wind tunnel around himself, blocking them. What was left of his witch posse charged us, but Ash and I created another fire circle, encompassing us and the fae.

The soldiers took to the air, divebombing Adrian, but he pushed them away with gusts of wind, his power growing stronger by the minute, his laugh more maniacal, his eyes more crazed. His funnel tightened, lifting him from the ground before spreading outward, the spiral creating a suction that pulled in leaves, dirt, and broken branches, creating a bramble around him.

We had to stop him before he sucked the entire cemetery—and everyone in it—into his storm.

"How is he so strong so fast?" I shielded my eyes and inched toward him while Chaos kept the fire circle blazing.

"It's the biggest piece of the amulet." Ash's hair whipped back as she leaned into the wind, pushing toward Adrian. His funnel shifted, the wind changing direction in an instant. Ash's hair flew into her face, her already forward momentum adding to the drag and making her stumble to her hands and knees.

"He's also an elemental," Chaos said. "The more powerful the being, the more efficiently the amulet amplifies their power."

"And the crazier it makes them." I leaned back, digging my boots into the dirt as Adrian's funnel tried to pull me into it.

My chest squeezed, the griffin's goodbye echoing in my soul. I tried to send her a peaceful sentiment in return, but my foot snagged on an exposed root. I careened forward, landing on my stomach a yard from the bottom of the tornado.

Chaos hauled Ash up by the arm. A fae soldier dive-bombed them. I army-crawled toward the wind funnel, scrambling to my feet beneath it and latching onto Adrian's ankle.

Holy Hecate on a unicycle.

Even through his clothes, the power from the amulet surged through my body, setting my nerves ablaze. He kicked, smacking the side of my head before I grabbed his other leg and hauled myself up. I clutched one hip, then the other, and tried not to think about the fact that my face pressed into his crotch.

And that his clothes were still coated in beastie biscuits and gravy.

My stomach lurched. Thankfully, my innards ignored the command to spew chicken salad all over the place, and I reached higher, clutching his shoulder with one hand, the amulet with the other.

Talk about your power surges. Damn.

My muscles seized, my hands tightening into unbreakable fists, my inborn fire rising to the surface, setting my skin ablaze. I pried my hand from Adrian's shoulder and let myself fall, the chain snapping off his neck with a jerk of my arm.

We weren't that high. A straight fall to the ground might've bruised me a little, but of course, I hadn't thought my escape through.

I did not fall straight to the ground. In fact, I got caught in the spiraling tornado, and it slung me around like a rotating catapult, flinging me against the trunk of a massive birch. Every ounce of air left my lungs in a whoosh, and my vision tunneled and wavered.

The impact nearly bent me in two. My vertebrae cracked like a glowstick, and if I had hit it at an angle a few degrees different, I had no doubt I'd have been paralyzed.

Instead, I pushed to sitting, my head still swimming, and tried to make my eyes focus. My sister dragged Adrian to the ground. Chaos ripped a pincher from a soldier's mandible. Mayhem stood on the mausoleum steps, his taloned fingers wrapped around another soldier's neck. Witch fire mixed with hellfire blazed all around us.

Something made impact with the side of my head.

My face smacked the earth, filling my mouth with charred dirt. I spit and sat upright, the amulet giving me strength to endure what should have rendered me unconscious.

Ignacus loomed over me, poisonous saliva dripping from his pinchers as he slammed a barbed insect foot into my wrist, pinning me to the ground. He pressed one wiry hand against my stomach and snatched the amulet from my grasp with another.

I tried to pull my wrist free, but the barbs protruding from his foot dug into my flesh. I'd have to take off my entire hand to free myself...*if* he didn't rip out my liver first.

I slid my free hand down my thigh in search of a blade. I could live with only one hand.

Ignacus raised the amulet triumphantly. I could feel the power surging through him, burning my wrist where he'd penetrated it.

He snapped his gaze to me, his expression livid. "Where is the rest of it?"

"I have no idea what you mean." My fingers brushed the pommel of my dagger.

He grunted. Then he growled. He opened his mouth, and the most freakish chittering sound I'd ever heard emanated from his throat. Barbs extended from the tips of his fingers, cutting through my shirt and into my skin.

With the amulet amplifying everything, I felt his energy coil in his shoulder half a nanosecond before he plunged his claws into my stomach.

CHAPTER 21
EMBER

A screech sounded from inside the mausoleum. Ignacus paused, his claws an inch inside my flesh, and jerked his head toward the sound. The griffin barreled toward us.

The piercing pain in my abdomen made everything that happened next foggy, but one second, I was laid out on the ground, a feast for the fae prince, and the next, I lay there alone, the gouges in my abs and wrist bleeding profusely.

I pressed my injured arm to the puncture in my stomach and applied pressure with my free hand.

The griffin took to the sky, the fae prince's head in her beak, his body flailing as it dangled from her grip. She flapped her massive wings, turning herself vertically and clutching Ignacus with all four of her murder mittens.

Then, she jerked his head clean off.

She spit, and the head hit the ground, bouncing once before

rolling into the ring of fire. With another ear-piercing screech, she shot to the earth, slamming him down and literally ripping him limb from limb and throwing all the pieces into the fire too.

Only his torso remained, but I wasn't taking any chances. I grabbed the dagger I'd been trying to reach, marched toward our fractured foe, and slammed it beneath a breastplate, piercing his heart.

"Em, the amulet is in the fire," Ash shouted. "Call yours back."

I did as she asked and stroked the griffin's feathers. "Thank you."

She nodded *you're welcome* and turned toward Mayhem.

"She refused to leave until you were safe." He dropped a lifeless soldier onto the ground. "My cousin Havoc is keeping the demons at bay across the rift, but he can't hold them forever."

"Go now." I threw my arms around her neck and hugged her tightly. "Lay your eggs in peace."

I walked with her to the mausoleum and stood outside the doorway, careful not to get too close to the rift, lest I try to pull Mayhem through again. As she lifted a paw to step through, she turned to me, thanking me again.

"Thank *you*." I pressed my palms together, my chest squeezing as she disappeared into the Underworld. "She said we can call her if we ever need her again."

"A noble beast, indeed." Mayhem waved a hand, sealing the rift he'd created.

I turned toward the cemetery and took in the aftermath. The remaining fae scurried through the rift their prince had created, but without his power, they couldn't seal it. Or maybe they could have, but they preferred to hightail it home and beg the king for forgiveness. Either way, it left the job to Ash and me.

Adrian's coven had long since retreated, leaving him alone with us. Ash picked up the amulet, and he lunged, his eyes still wild with affliction.

Chaos caught him by the throat. "Are you sure I can't kill him?"

Ash blinked, looking at him briefly before returning her attention to the amulet lying in her palm. "Yeah, that's fine. Do whatever."

"Chaos, don't," I shouted as Adrian summoned his witch wind, creating a funnel around himself. "Let him go."

Chaos scoffed. "Ash told me I—"

"Ash isn't herself." Mayhem crept toward her. "Perhaps I should hold onto that."

She clenched her fist around the pendant. "The hell you should."

Chaos released his hold, and Adrian's tornado whisked him away. Ten minutes in contact with the amulet, and he could already fly. What would it do to my sister?

"Ash, give it to Mayhem." I cautiously walked toward her. "Remember what that one small piece did to Chrys? I won't let that happen to you."

Her nostrils flared, her jaw clenching. "He's been trying to get his hands on this since we summoned him. No. No way."

Her sigil glowed, Chaos sending his calming energy into her. "Allow me to hold it, little witch. I'll keep you, and it, safe."

She tilted her head at her demon. "My powers have been bound my entire life. I deserve a little boost."

"Indeed you do, my love. But not with a fractured piece. It will damage your mind." He held his hand toward her.

"You need to get it," I whispered to Mayhem. "You're the only one I trust."

He moved so quickly, I nearly missed it. I would have if I'd blinked. He shot out an arm, gripping her wrist and yanking the amulet from her grasp before she realized what was happening.

She gasped and stiffened, her lower lip trembling for a moment before her posture slumped. "That was…"

"*Lord of the* Rings intense?" I asked.

"Yeah." She heaved in another breath. "Thanks for taking it."

Mayhem held the chain between two fingers, letting the pendant dangle in front of him. "We should take this home before anyone else tries to intercept it."

"Yeah." She rubbed her palms on her pants. "What about the mess?"

Leave it to my sister to worry about a mess when we had a world to save. Then again, leaving a fae rift open and bodies of overgrown insects littering the ground wasn't a good idea either.

"Guys, gather the fae parts and shove them through the rift. Ash and I will cremate the witches and pick up the griffin's blankets."

Ash applied a salve and bandages to my wounds before we worked together, cleaning up the evidence. My sister and I sealed the rift, and we carried everything to the van. Chaos drove, giving me a chance to recharge in the back seat with Mayhem.

"How are your injuries?" he asked, stroking my hair as I lay in his lap.

"I'll survive. I got a little boost through Adrian and then Ignacus when they had the amulet. Looks like it speeds up healing too."

"It is capable of a great many things." He ran his fingers over my injured wrist. "No pain?"

"Not anymore." I sat upright and rested my chin on his shoulder. "Why haven't you used it?"

He blew a breath through his nose and laughed softly. "Why would I? I have everything I've ever wanted, all I'll ever need, right here with you."

"Me too. Almost." I snuggled against him and closed my eyes. I had everything I never knew I wanted in him too.

My stomach sank as we pulled into the drive behind our building. This was it. Everything we'd been working toward was about to come to fruition, with a few hours to spare. We remained silent as we entered through the back door, a heaviness settling over us as we trudged upstairs to get the rest of the amulet.

Mayhem set the newest piece on the counter, and I lay a massive blue vibrator next to it.

He chuckled. "I see I've changed your opinion on what's needed for a good time."

"You have no idea." I waved my hand over it, disintegrating the shroud and revealing the rest of the stone.

Using Ash's biggest tweezers, I picked it up and touched it to the shard we'd just obtained. It glowed brightly, blindingly. I shielded my eyes against the flashes and sparks, and when it was through, the most powerful magical artifact I had ever encountered...maybe that even existed...lay on our kitchen counter.

I glanced at the clock. "Next steps. We have to start the All Hallow's Eve ritual. Ash, take Chaos and gather the coven in the clearing. Start the fire, and then meet us in your studio. I'll prepare the circle and have everything ready for the summoning when you get back."

She eyed the amulet and rested her hand next to it. "It really should be you who starts it. I can stay and set everything up."

"Not a chance." I grabbed the chain and handed it to Mayhem.

She blinked three times rapidly. "Yeah. You're right. They should already be gathering, so give me half an hour."

"Perfect," I said.

We all headed downstairs, Chaos and Ash hanging a left to go outside, Mayhem and I going right to set up what would be our final summoning circle.

He watched as I poured the salt and used chalk to sketch his eldest brother's sigil in the center of the ring. "You drew it perfectly, yet I felt ill watching it happen."

I stood and dusted off my knees. "That's because you're my

demon. It felt gross to draw it, honestly. I hope I never have to do it again."

I opened the grimoire we'd used to summon Mayhem. We'd bookmarked both the summoning and the containment spells, but I already had them memorized. "Miles and Shade are good to stay at the ritual, right? Since we have the amulet, Discord should be easy to summon."

"Relatively." He grasped my waist and tugged me toward him. "When our siblings return, things will happen quickly."

"I know." I swallowed the thickness from my throat. "But it has to be done."

He searched my eyes, a sheen forming over his as he held my gaze. "I love you, Ember Holland."

I clasped my hands behind his neck. "And I love you, Mayhem, Prince of Hell."

He kissed my forehead before resting his against it. "I promise to love you every second of every day, with every fiber of my being, for all of eternity."

A sob threatened to roll up from my chest, but I cleared my throat, chasing it away. "Me too."

The insistent sob tried again, and this time, I let it pass my lips. He cupped my face in his hands, the intensity of his gaze rooting me to the spot. I half-expected him to make promises he could never keep. To lie and say he would find a way to return. That everything would be okay.

Part of me wanted him to tell me lies.

But he didn't say a word.

My phone buzzed in my pocket with a call trying to interrupt our moment. I ignored it and leaned against my demon, holding him tightly and resting my head on his shoulder. Three seconds after the call silenced, it started again.

I sighed heavily and looked at the screen. "It's Ash. I better answer."

He held me tighter as I pressed the device to my ear and said, "Hello."

"You must perform the summoning without us." It was Chaos, not Ash, and I did not like his alarming tone.

My heart slammed against my chest as I straightened. "Why? What happened?"

He missed a beat...two...three, making my stomach sink. "It's Ash," he finally said. "She set Shade on fire."

ALSO BY CARRIE PULKINEN

Fire Witches of Salem Series

Chaos and Ash

Commanding Chaos

Claiming Chaos

Mayhem and Ember

Mending Mayhem

Mastering Mayhem

Collection One: Books 1-3

Collection Two: Books 4-6

Crescent City Wolf Pack Series

Werewolves Only

Beneath a Blue Moon

Bound by Blood

A Deal with Death

A Song to Remember

Shifting Fate

Collection One: Books 1-3

Collection Two: Books 4-6

New Orleans Nocturnes Series

License to Bite

Shift Happens

Life's a Witch

Santa Got Run Over by a Vampire

Finders Reapers

Swipe Right to Bite

Batshift Crazy

Collection One: Books 1-3

Collection Two: Books 4-7

Haunted Ever After Series

Love at First Haunt

Second Chance Spirit

Third Time's a Ghost

Love and Ghosts

Love and Omens

Love and Curses

Collection One: Books 1 - 3

Collection Two: Books 4 - 6

Stand Alone Books

Flipping the Bird

Sign Steal Deliver

Azrael

Lilith

The Rest of Forever

Soul Catchers

Bewitching the Vampire

About the Author

Carrie Pulkinen is a paranormal romance author who has always been fascinated with things that go bump in the night. Of course, when you grow up next door to a cemetery, the dead (and the undead) are hard to ignore. Pair that with her passion for writing and her love of a good happily-ever-after, and becoming a paranormal romance author seems like the only logical career choice.

Before she decided to turn her love of the written word into a career, Carrie spent the first part of her professional life as a high school journalism and yearbook teacher. She loves good chocolate and bad puns, and in her free time, she likes to read, drink wine, and travel with her family.

Connect with Carrie online:
CarriePulkinen.com